I0835916

SAM GAO

BOOK 2

Cover design by MiblArt.

Edited by Alley Rehfeldt, Gennifer Ulman, and Aimee Blowey

NOTE: This series contains sensitive content, including but not limited to: Abuse; Cultural Appropriation; Eugenics; Graphic Gore and Violence; Murder; Racial Slurs; Racism and Colorism; Slut-Shaming; Torture; Underage Drinking; Victim-Blaming.

E-book ISBN: 978-1-962099-13-4
Paperback ISBN: 978-1-962099-24-0

IMMORTAL RULES

1. **Avoid Demonic Cultivation**: You must strictly avoid any practices associated with demonic cultivation. This path often involves using negative or harmful energies and manipulating others for personal gain, which goes against the principles of righteous cultivation. Only qi must be used for cultivation.
2. **Live in Harmony with Nature**: You should strive to maintain a profound harmony with the natural world. Remember, your powers and existence are deeply connected to the balance of nature and the cosmos.
3. **Show Compassion to All Beings**: It is essential for you to practice compassion and empathy towards all living beings. Avoid causing harm and seek to aid others in need whenever possible.
4. **Seek Balance and Moderation**: You are encouraged to emphasize balance in all aspects of your life, including your cultivation practices. Avoid extremes and pursue a path of moderation and equilibrium.
5. **Stand for Justice and Integrity**: You have a duty to uphold justice and maintain personal integrity. Stand against corruption and injustice, act as a protector of the weak, and defend the path of righteousness.

PROLOGUE

NORA KEMP DIDN'T CRY when they lowered the empty coffin into the ground.

It wasn't lack of love that caused her to act so coldly, nor was she holding back tears. Rather, she simply couldn't cry for a cheap wooden box being buried in an overpriced cemetery plot. Body or not, she had to pay full price for the funeral and burial, squandering the meager life savings her father had put away. And for what? A semblance of closure? A goodbye that felt like a lie?

They never found the body. Then again, the school didn't look that hard. Why bother? They had bigger things to worry about than recovering corpses from the Veil. Still, Nora had no doubt her father was dead. Not based on evidence, but rather on a strong feeling. She trusted her gut.

At the time of the horde attack, Nora was visiting her mother in New Hampshire. She had asked her father to join them, but she'd known he wouldn't accept. He wouldn't step foot in the house her mother shared with her new husband.

The divorce had shredded her father's pride, but he clung to what remained with his last breath.

Nora knew him as a quiet man, often keeping to himself, so she wasn't surprised when only a handful of people came to the funeral. Everyone in the shadowborn community seemed more preoccupied with the hundreds still missing from Northeastern College. Many had yet to lose hope, despite the very likely scenario that their loved ones were not only dead but had died brutally at the hands (or paws) of a feral beastblood.

That was the difference between them and Nora. She knew when to hold on to hope and when to let go. It was a painful thing, for a loved one to disappear without a trace. There was no closure in it, only a vast emptiness tinged with disappointment.

But Nora was used to disappointment, just like she was used to being alone. Her had father worked so many late shifts in order to provide for her. In the end, what came of that? Nothing. She barely had enough money left to scrape together her tuition costs, and her mother hadn't offered to help out. She was too busy with her new baby and her homewrecking husband.

Nora shouldn't have visited, but a morbid curiosity compelled her. Part of her hoped to see her mother drowning in misery, but that wasn't the case. Nora wished she'd just stayed at the school and died. At least she would have been with her father. Now, she had nothing.

But people who had nothing to lose were dangerous. Nora didn't care about heaven or hell, good or bad. All she wanted was the person responsible for her father's death to pay: that bitch, Kitty Swan.

ONE

KITTY SWAN WAS INDEED A BITCH, but she wasn't a bloodhound. The fact that she was physically capable of sniffing out zombies didn't mean she was *willing*, especially when a scumbag like Blake Blackwood asked.

At the beginning of August, upon returning to Northeastern College, she'd told him in no uncertain terms what would happen if he came within a three-foot radius of her. It involved sticking a sword where the sun didn't shine. But Blake was not deterred in the least. If anything, mentioning his asshole had made things worse. She should have expected that from the perv.

Kitty was not a young woman with an overabundance of positive traits, which was to say, she had exactly three things she liked about herself:

1. Her strength
2. Her shiny hair
3. Her loyalty

And part of being a loyal friend involved shunning her best friend's ex, especially after a nasty breakup. So the fact that she was in the Veil, on a hunt for ferals with Veronica's ex-boyfriend? A sure sign that Kitty had spent too many hours sunbathing this week. The heat must have melted her brain.

To make up for not evading Blake as she should, she tried her darndest to make their time together as miserable for him as possible. It was counter-intuitive, as she was trying *not* to be a bitch anymore—a new year's resolution, of sorts. But did being mean to her friend's ex really count? She was being rude, yes, but it was for the greater good. Or so she told herself.

"I don't smell anything, except your rancid breath," Kitty said, crossing her arms.

"Ouch. That hurts," Blake said with a wide grin. "If you keep talking to me that way, I'm going to start thinking that you're not actually flirting with me."

"I'm not."

"Aw, come on. How can you deny our sizzling chemi—ow! You're violent!"

She breezed past him, trudging on through the jungle. The faster they found the nest, the faster they could get the hell out of there.

You'd think a realm filled with magic would be more... well, magical. But the Veil was a total shithole, filled with monsters, giant insects, and a miasma of pollution filling the sky. No wonder native truebloods flocked to the mortal realm. And Kitty wasn't even going to *start* on the WiFi situation!

She hadn't been to the jungle before, but it was just as unpleasant as she imagined. And the weather certainly didn't help. Insects aside—with eyes as big as her head, mind you—it was hotter than Satan's asshole. The humidity hadn't affected her hair, thank God. It remained silky and straight, a curtain of black down her back. But her arms and legs felt sticky, and the air was heavy, making it difficult to breathe properly.

Blake's assholery aside, Kitty wasn't supposed to be hunting ferals. She had come back to Northeastern College of Magic in early August, a month ahead of the start of the semester, because she'd wanted to help Bàba prepare the apartment. Kitty's mother and younger siblings, Noelle and Jax, were still in South Carolina. They would arrive on campus next week, a few days before classes would begin.

Bàba's official start date was at the end of August, but he was already being pulled into the lab, leaving Kitty unsupervised for the majority of the time. They no longer ate any meals together, barely seeing each other due to the urgency of his project. So she spent her time valuably: lounging by the pool, working on her tan, and writing in her affirmation journal. Because, apparently, she was the type of skank to have one of those.

Well, she was the type of *girl* to have an affirmation journal. She was trying not to use 'skank', 'slut', 'whore', or any other variation of that anymore. It was going very poorly.

Anyway, that's how Blake found her: struggling to write her daily prompt.

DAILY PROMPT: DESCRIBE AN ACCOMPLISHMENT YOU'RE PROUD OF AND WHY.

~~I'm proud of being so strong I could squeeze someone's head and crush their skull, having it splinter into their brain and kill them.~~

That wasn't a very nice affirmation, so she crossed it out. But let's face it: the only other accomplishments she could think of had to do with either violence or how pretty she was. What did that say about her? Nothing good.

In her mentally vulnerable state, Blake found her and told her he needed help, stroking her ego. When that didn't work, he lied and said Cyrus would be joining them. She should have known better. Now, it was just the two of them, tracking a group of ferals for the extra credit Blake so desperately needed to graduate on time.

The tall, dreamy blonde had a face made for magazines and a personality that belonged in the garbage disposal. "Hey, do you see that?"

"Your dignity? Nope, haven't seen that anywhere."

"Very funny. I meant *that.*" He pointed ahead, toward the mouth of a cave that looked both promising and terrifying. It was so dark, Kitty couldn't see how far it went inside, but it seemed to be just the type of place a zombified colony of monsters would be.

The smell hit her as they approached, the unmistakable scent of rot and decay. Kitty recoiled, but Blake didn't notice it.

"Okay, there's definitely a feral in there." She tried not to gag, turning away and plugging her nose. "Put a magitech tracker down and let's head back."

"I think we should gather more data," Blake said. "Come on. Let's investigate further."

"Are you an idiot?"

"Hey! Words hurt, you know."

"So will my fist in your throat," Kitty told him. "We need to report this to Professor Everleigh. He can decide to send a team out here if he wants to. We have no clue how many ferals are in that cave—could be one, could be hundreds. We don't even know the type of beastblood they are."

"Used to be," Blake corrected. "And if this is the nest we're looking for, you know they're wasps. Not the kind you'd find at a country club, either."

Any beastblood could turn feral, from hydras, to chimera, to even dragons. The disease affected the Veil-dwelling monsters, turning them into mindless beasts. It usually killed shadowborn outright—and, with no cure, bites were typically fatal.

She just learned over the summer that insect-type beastbloods could also become feral. A zombie snake? Fine, whatever. A zombie centipede the size of a human? Fuck that. Kitty *still* had nightmares about the feral bugs she'd encountered, though they had been dead and brought back to the mortal realm for dissection. Feral bodies rapidly decomposed, so bringing them back before they turned to sludge was imperative.

When Kitty discovered magic—the Western kind, anyway—existed, she thought it was going to be like Harry Potter. Going to a magic college should have been a dream come true. But instead of posh accents, cute uniforms, and a classic battle of good versus evil, she got smelly zombies, a contaminated magical realm, and New Yorkers. She didn't know which of the three was worse.

"Don't be such a wimp," Blake said, like the true hypocrite he was. "Do you want me to hold your hand?"

"I'd rather jump into a pool of needles, salt, and lemon juice than have you touch me."

"Has anyone ever told you that you're a disturbing chick?"

"Has anyone ever told *you* to shut up?"

"Yes," he said, "but usually it's because they want to kiss

me. I'm a very good kisser, you know. If you don't believe me, I'd be more than happy to show you."

"Go ahead. You can show me that, and I'll show you what it feels like to get kicked in the kidney."

"Fine, fine," Blake grumbled. "You're so violent. I don't know what Cyrus sees in you."

"The feeling is mutual. Can we go back now?"

"Nope. Come on. Let's go on an adventure!" He wiggled his fingers. "We'll be quick as cats, which is funny, since your name is—"

"You go first," Kitty said flatly.

He put a hand to his chest. "Aw, you have that much faith in me?"

"I need to be able to use you as a human shield."

"Hey!" Blake exclaimed. "I'm a shadowborn *werewolf*, so I'd prefer if you said 'wolf shield'."

"You're not a wolf, but you sure are a dog."

"Says the bitch."

Kitty seriously contemplated shoving him into the cave and making a run for it, but she needed him. He was her only way back to the mortal realm.

As a cultivator, Kitty couldn't open rifts. She had a host of other abilities—enhanced senses, super strength and speed, high endurance and stamina, minor healing, to name a few—but all her powers were weaker in the Veil.

There were two realms: the Veil and the mortal realm. Shadowborn were children of mortals and truebloods, humanoid creatures originating from the Veil. Think vampires, werewolves, angels, and demons. Because shadowborn possessed blood from both worlds, they could open and close rifts from the mortal realm and the Veil. While they didn't have as much magic as their trueblood relatives—

Blake's father was a werewolf, but he himself couldn't shift—they had enhanced physical abilities, healed faster than humans, and could use magic.

Kitty and her family practiced cultivation, which was taking qi—energy emitted from all living things—and using it to strengthen their bodies. Eventually, they would pass through nine stages of cultivation, becoming immortal. It sounded more sophisticated than it actually was.

In the end, cultivation bolstered her strength well above her shadowborn classmates. At least, in the mortal realm. Here in the Veil? Her powers were weakened by the lack of qi.

Even without qi around her, Kitty was at the third stage of cultivation—the core formation stage. Her golden core, a ball of qi inside her abdomen, should have been able to store more than enough energy for emergencies. Unfortunately, it had been damaged last semester, rendering her vulnerable. Her powers flickered on and off like a dying lightbulb, not that she could ever admit that. Only her parents knew, and they'd told her to take it easy. Going into the Veil and encountering ferals could damage her golden core further. She needed to give it time to heal; if it was destroyed, she would never be able to cultivate again.

So why was she in the Veil, again?

Oh yeah. Cyrus.

"Let's go," Blake said, exaggeratedly marching toward the cave like a soldier.

"This is a dumb idea! I know that's pretty on point for you, but I, at least, have a lot going for me!" Kitty said, following after him.

"What? Your future as a Pilates instructor?"

"I didn't choose a major yet." She didn't have to decide until next year, though she had entertained the idea of going into physical therapy or computer science. She wasn't sure what the future held, only that hers was long, and her friends' futures...weren't.

The further they ventured into the cave, the worse Kitty felt. The smell only grew stronger, and it was pitch black. She kept a hand on one of the rough stone walls. She didn't hear buzzing, which was a good sign, right? No buzzing, no wasps. She'd prefer to avoid getting impaled by a giant stinger.

"Okay, this is far enough," she said, her voice taking on an unusually high pitch.

"Fine, if you want to be a party pooper." Blake sighed, passing her as they headed back the way they came.

Kitty's shoulders sagged in relief when they saw the mouth of the cave.

They were close to the exit, and yet...

The smell was following them.

She grabbed Blake's arm and practically jumped outside the cave, onto the jungle floor. A creature dove at them, but Kitty shoved Blake away and rolled to the side. Springing to her feet, it occurred to her that she was unarmed. She didn't mind fighting hand-to-hand, but feral bites and scratches were dangerous.

The creature unfolded as it exited the cave, doubling in size as it stood. Its body was nearly skeletal, with paper white skin stretched over a broad frame. Its arms, of which there were six, were rotting, with flesh sloughed off in chunks. Meanwhile, on one thin leg, the skin peeled from the muscle in a grotesque flap, leaking dark sludge. Eight eyes, all milky, took up most of its face. Its mouth had pincers covered in a thin layer of short hairs, its breath steaming in a plume of putrid gas.

It wasn't a spider, yet it was certainly not humanoid,

either. It had a torso, its spine hunched and protruding like a handle from its back. Its legs, too, resembled a human's, while its pale fingertips were long enough to reach the creature's knobby knees.

"Huh. Well, it's not a nest," Blake said, slowly getting up.

Kitty was on the left, careful not to make any sudden movements as she straightened. "Looks like some sort of chimera."

"Should we run?"

"Hell yes."

They sprinted toward the beach, Blake leading while Kitty followed close on his heels. The feral gave chase, its bare feet and many hands beating loudly against the ground. Oh fuck, it was moving on all its limbs, its back arched and bare butt in the air. Reaching out, it grabbed Kitty by the hair, its putrefied hand tangling in her long locks.

She fell back with a cry, landing on her back as the creature drooled on her face.

She was *so* going to need a shower after this.

Kitty's body moved without thought. She grabbed whatever she could find—two fistfuls of rocks and dirt—and slammed both hands into the creature's many eyes. Oh God, they were bursting! The eyeballs were popping and bile rose to the back of her throat! But she couldn't throw up now.

The creature howled and Kitty scrambled out from beneath it, scraping her elbows and ass as she crawled away.

"Kitty!" Blake called, grabbing her roughly by the arm. She was shocked he hadn't left her behind.

The creature was too fast. They wouldn't be able to escape. Ferals felt pain, but it didn't keep them down for long. She had seconds before it would be upon them again. Kitty hesitated, unsure of what to do.

Her parents believed that, somehow, ferals were cultivating with demonic energy. The opposite of qi, demonic energy came from death. It was unstable and against the immortal rules to use it to attain immortality. Generally, demonic cultivators failed to become immortal, experiencing deadly qi deviation and either going insane or dying. Usually both.

Kitty, apparently, had some sort of affinity for demonic energy. If she used it, she would destroy her golden core and never become immortal. But, at the same time, she felt a draw to it. Almost as if she could reach out and pull the corruption from the feral before her, restoring it to its original state and undoing the horrible disease.

The last time she'd cured someone, her golden core had cracked. She knew she couldn't risk it. And yet, the indecision froze her.

Would she really kill someone to become immortal?

She couldn't fix *all* the ferals, so would it really matter if she saved this one? Would it be *fair*? Yes, it looked...terrifying. But it was still a living creature, probably going about its business until it was infected. (Then again, its "business" could very well have been eating children and kicking puppies.)

Being a righteous cultivator involved being a good person and upholding Taoist morals, but it was easier said than done. What if she saved this spider chimera, at the expense of her own immortality, and it turned out to be carnivorous? Would it just get re-infected if exposed to the feral illness again? She had no idea its level of intelligence, or if that really mattered. Her parents would say that animals are integral to the natural world and have their own role to play in the harmony of the universe. Even if they looked like boogeymen who lived under children's beds. Hey, maybe she looked like a total freakoid to this spider thing. Maybe, to it, *she* was the monster.

But now was not the time for introspection. Now was the time to kick some spider ass.

Blake readied his sword. "On the count of three, we run."

"No. It will catch us." Kitty took his sword from him. Though she didn't currently train with a dual-ended sword—she usually used a saber, which of course, was sitting comfortably in her dorm room—she was familiar enough with the weapon.

Making a quick decision, Kitty moved in front of Blake. As the creature recovered, she noticed that half its eyes on the right side of its face had, er, exploded. Yuck. As such, it wobbled as it moved, slightly slower than before. She didn't want to torture it, nor did she want to draw the fight out. Throwing the sword might be viable, but she couldn't risk missing and losing their only weapon.

Kitty lowered the blade, positioning it at her side. As the spider moved toward them, Blake tugged at her arm.

"Uh, Kitty? Now's when we run."

"Get out of the way," she warned, staying rooted to her spot. The spider reared back in front of her, hissing as it lifted its body up before bringing itself down on top of her with such force, it would have crushed her had she been a regular mortal.

Kitty plunged the sword up, aiming for the spot where its neck met its head. She hadn't been sure if Blake's blade was sharp enough to cut through bone, otherwise she would have decapitated it. Instead, the sword went directly through its brain, its own downward momentum driving it directly through its skull.

Blake cursed as a shower of black goo, brains, and blood

rained down upon them. Kitty jerked the blade to the side, spinning the feral corpse on its back and yanking the dirtied sword from its head.

"Well, this shirt is officially stained," Blake said, looking down at his white tee. "Thanks a lot."

"Don't even talk to me about stains." Kitty gestured down to her white beach cover up, now completely ruined. "I didn't have time to change before coming here. You? You've been assigned this mission since this morning! You could have prepared better."

"Well, we got it, didn't we?"

"*We?*"

"You used my sword."

"You wouldn't let me run and get my saber. You told me we would just be *finding* a nest, and that it was an emergency. That we wouldn't see action. Now look what you've done!" She pointed to her clothes. "I have spider eyeball on me!"

"Maybe it's moisturizing—"

"Shut up! I don't want to hear another peep." She shoved the sword at him. "Just open a rift and get us back home."

Blake, for once, listened to her. Taking his sword, he slashed through the open air. The rift—a portal to the mortal realm, which looked like a tear in fabric—opened. He pulled at the edges, making the opening bigger so they could pass through. The surface was like a mirror, rippling as water would when touched. But it didn't feel wet. They both stepped in, their hair blown back by a concentrated breeze as they entered the mortal realm.

Blake closed the rift behind them, so nothing else could sneak in—a special ability of the shadowborn. While true-bloods and beastbloods could open and close a rift from the Veil, they could not do the same from the mortal realm. Shadowborn could, as they had the lineage of truebloods and humans. That was the main reason truebloods begrudgingly valued their half-breed children. Truebloods were more powerful than shadowborn in every other way, but this particular power was very necessary if they were to keep their existence a secret from humans.

When they returned to the other side, they were in the middle of a forest. Fantastic. Generally, rifts were finicky. One could open a rift in the mortal realm in the same spot every day and end up at a different spot in the Veil. Each place in the mortal realm had an anchor point in the Veil, and rifts opened within about a five-mile radius from that point.

Kitty looked up. Above the forest were the school gates. The college was built on a steep hill, and you had to take a bridge to get to it. There were no roads or walkways, so she and Blake would have to traverse the woods to make their way back to civilization, which could take an hour.

Great.

"Come on," she muttered, peeling off her dirty cover-up. It felt gross, sticking to her skin. "Let's go back."

Blake grinned, his eyes raking over her body. "Hey, maybe after this, we should get some dinner. Just the two of us."

"Bite me."

"Don't tempt me. Seriously, that bikini is about as big as a postage stamp."

She ignored him for the rest of the journey back, reciting her positive affirmations in her head as they trudged up the hill. At least he had sneakers. She was wearing flip flops and probably getting bitten up by mosquitoes. But, by twilight, they made it back to school.

Passing through the gates, Kitty was ready to shower and pass out. She wasn't as alert as she should have been, so when a car honked at her from behind, it startled her. She tripped, falling flat on her face on the hot cobblestone.

"Shit." The car stopped and the door opened. Kitty rolled to her knees, dazed from exhaustion. It wasn't like her to be so clumsy, but then again, she hadn't been herself these days. The sleep deprivation hit her hard.

A warm hand pressed against her back as someone knelt beside her. She knew who it was before seeing them. Cyrus always smelled so good. It was the lavender soap he used, her favorite scent. His had a hint of vanilla sugar, too, a sweetness that contrasted his personality.

Meanwhile, she probably smelled like rot.

"Hey, are you okay?" Cyrus asked.

She glanced at him, hating the fact that she looked a mess and he was, as ever, Mr. Perfect.

Cyrus wasn't OCD, but he liked things a certain way and was particular about personal grooming. All his clothes were clean and wrinkle-free, she'd never seen a hint of stubble on him, and even his nails were always trimmed and clean.

"I'm fine," she lied, rising to her feet without his help.

They had an unspoken agreement to avoid each other ever since last semester had ended. They'd done a pretty good job, when she was in South Carolina and he was in New York. They didn't text or call, and it was out of sight...*mostly* out of mind.

And then Kitty came back to campus. Cyrus had never left, volunteering to kill ferals over the summer. Ever since the horde had appeared and destroyed half of Northeastern, ferals began to pop up much more often. For extra credit, some of the upperclassmen were offered the opportunity to stay and hunt.

Cyrus truly earned his extra credit, being on hunts for

most of the summer. She barely saw him, but regardless, being in the same state caused her brain to go into overdrive. She thought about him a disproportionate amount, which was concerning on many levels. She never chased men, as a matter of pride; they always chased her.

Not that she was *chasing* Cyrus. They had agreed to be friends, and it was perfectly normal to want to hang out with your friends. Right?

"Did you just come back from a hunt?" He looked down at her, then very quickly back to her face. "What on earth are you wearing?"

"Something amazing that she should never change out of," Blake replied, reminding them both that he was also present. Unfortunate. "Do you walk around the pool like that every day? Because if you do, I'm going to have to visit you more often. Maybe you can give me CPR lessons."

"No, but I'll give you STFU lessons."

"And how do you plan on—oh, shit!"

TWO

DAILY PROMPT: WHAT PUTS YOU IN A GOOD MOOD?

When snitches (or, in Blake's case, asswads) get stitches.

"What happened to your eye, Mr. Blackwood?"

"A gorilla hit me," Blake answered, glaring at Kitty beside him. She wasn't perturbed, meeting his gaze unfazed.

"A gorilla?" Professor Everleigh repeated. He stood behind his desk. There was no place for him to sit, his office a mess of papers and boxes. Only Kitty and Blake were seated, in folding chairs with peeling pleather cushions. Cyrus's back pressed against the door, his hands balanced on two stacks of boxes threatening to slip if one of the four in the room breathed in the wrong direction.

Spaces like this made Cyrus's skin crawl. He hated messes. It didn't matter that there was little dust, and that the binders and boxes were probably clean—judging by the empty aerosol cans of disinfectant scattered near the garbage bin. The office was not tidy and there was no space to move, making him feel as though the corners of the room were closing in. With the piles of boxes, it wasn't unrealistic to expect an avalanche of papers to sweep down and kill them all.

That was exactly what he needed. He'd been fighting ferals all summer and hadn't gotten infected, thankfully. Of course he'd die in a messy office, bleeding out due to excessive paper cuts.

"I *think* it was a gorilla," Blake said. "All I know is, whatever creature did this to me was a violent, small-brained animal who can't take a joke."

"Gorillas are actually really smart," said Cyrus.

"This one wasn't."

Kitty flipped her hair over her shoulder, sending a wave of vanilla his way. She just showered and her shampoo was potent. The box against Cyrus's left hand shifted, and suddenly, he thought that if he were to die right now, it would not be so bad.

"I have a feeling that whoever hit you would be eager to take another shot," she said sweetly. "You wouldn't want *two* black eyes, would you, Blake?"

"...Back to the matter at hand," Professor Everleigh said, side-stepping the tension between the two students. "If what you say is true, then we have a problem on our hands."

"I know. Blake should really keep his mouth shut."

"No, Katherine. If you only found the spider chimera, then the colony is still out there, probably causing a wave of infections."

"It's Kitty," she corrected. "It's not short for Katherine. It's actually—"

"We'll call another search team," Blake promised. "They

couldn't have gotten far. I thought Charity and her group were tracking the nest, too."

"They killed twelve drones. But as you know, the Blood Wasps live in colonies of hundreds. This could be a deadly outbreak. Our only saving grace is that the feral illness strips the insect-type beastbloods of their flight abilities."

The wings were fragile and decayed faster. Generally, in the early days of the outbreak, insect beastbloods weren't much of a concern. Cyrus had hunted one or two, but they were always oversized and isolated. Even if they lived in groups, often the feral would turn and kill any other beastblood around them.

A corpse could not turn feral; once it was dead, it stayed dead. The fact that an entire nest had turned suggested that either the ferals were intentionally spreading the disease—perhaps they were not as mindless as previously thought—or that the turn was happening much faster, and the disease was mutating. Either way, not a good sign.

"I'll go out again," Cyrus volunteered.

"That won't be necessary, Mr. Ward. You've already been on two hunts today. Protocol states that you must wait at least eight hours before returning to the Veil for a feral hunt, lest your exhaustion lead to a mistake, or worse, infection. I believe we will send another team in, tonight."

He wanted to protest, but he knew the professor was right. Cyrus had been running around all day, chasing a pack of swamp monsters. He hadn't even known they *ran* in packs, until he killed one and another ten attacked him.

"Thank you for bringing this matter to my attention. If the colony is still rampant in the morning, I will send for you," Professor Everleigh said, speaking directly to Cyrus. Blake was too busy poking the Newton's Cradle to care. While he did well in combat classes, he wasn't known for being the best hunter. Before this summer, Cyrus had had a similar reputation. They called him the best swordsman on campus, something he took pride in. But simulated combat and hunts were not the same, a lesson he learned very quickly. "It's almost seven. The cafeteria will be crowded, if you don't hurry. Oh, but I'd like to have a word with Katherine, if you could stay behind."

Blake nodded. "See you bright and early tomorrow, Professor."

"Yes, Mr. Blackwood. I have no doubt that I'll, er, see you tomorrow."

Cyrus and Blake took their leave, closing the door behind them. The sun wouldn't be down for another hour or so, but all Cy wanted to do was eat and go to bed. He hated the long summer days now, rising before dawn and hunting until dusk. But he supposed winter would be worse.

He hoped that, by then, the ferals wouldn't be so plentiful. But ever since the horde attack, it was as if they had exploded in number, appearing all over the United States. He'd heard that Europe had had a few attacks, but it wasn't nearly as bad over there. Though, to be fair, each European country had its own center for shadowborn. There were only five schools in the US, each covering multiple states.

It didn't look like the ferals were slowing down. If anything, they were becoming more of a threat than before. Cyrus didn't understand it, and he'd had a lot of time to think over the events that transpired last spring.

Kitty and their friends had attempted to make lures, a mix of shadowborn and cultivation spellcraft, to calm a feral while simultaneously drawing them into a specified safe zone. She'd thought that if this could be achieved, they could study a live feral and come closer to discovering the disease. But the magic hadn't worked—or so they thought. Days later, a horde had attacked the school.

The lures had been discovered in Sabine Everleigh's possession. Apparently she modified them somehow, possibly making them work. However, they hadn't calmed the ferals at all. They attacked the school en masse.

What Cyrus didn't understand was *why*. And how. Alright, he didn't understand the situation at all. Try as he might, he couldn't think of a motive. Sabine was a researcher, alongside her husband, and she worked tirelessly to cure the disease. Her own son had been killed during the attack.

The school board was investigating. Sabine was in custody and would remain so until further notice. The entire shadowborn community heard of it. But months had passed and nothing new had come to light. Everyone stopped talking about it—and Sabine, in particular, as if they were afraid of even speaking her name. Cyrus asked his father about it, but learned nothing, except that truebloods were completely incompetent when it came to criminal justice.

"In their eyes, once an accusation has been made, you're guilty," Malcolm Ward had explained over the phone. "Sabine should have been sentenced already. It isn't fair, but it is the way things are done. However, it seems something unusual is going on. Perhaps she has protection from a higher ranked individual."

That made Cyrus even more confused, but it wasn't as though he was in a position to pry further.

"Are you really going to wait until tomorrow?" Blake asked in the hall. "You know as well as I do, if Wyatt finds the nest before you, he's going to be an ass about it."

"Wyatt's not bad. You're just pissed because Sarah Delaney said she liked him better than you."

"He's not even single! He's dating Summer Lennox!" He shook his head. "Whatever, man. Let's just get some dinner and sleep. I'm beat from all that walking around."

Cyrus hesitated. "You go ahead without me. I'm going to hang back for a few minutes."

Blake looked at the closed office door, then back at his friend. "That doesn't sound like a good idea."

Cyrus shrugged.

Blake sighed and headed down the hall, shoving his hands in his pockets and muttering about Kitty's nasty right hook and the personality to match.

Cy leaned against the window, glancing over his shoulder. The campus green stretched behind him, trees lining the main walkway. A handful of students walked in a group toward the cafeteria, each member slouching and dragging their feet. It seemed he wasn't the only tired shadowborn this evening.

The door to the office opened a few minutes later and Kitty exited. He couldn't read her expression, couldn't tell whether she'd received good or bad news.

"You waited for me." It was a statement, a test, to see how he'd respond.

"Yeah. What did Everleigh want?"

"He just said some lady wants to interview me. Dr. Callista Woods? Apparently she's coming to do feral research at Northeastern this semester."

"Are you going to do it?"

"I told him I'd think about it."

"Oh." He felt stupid, but what else was there to say?

Kitty didn't seem to know, either. She shrugged and

walked toward the stairs, expecting him to follow. He matched her pace.

He'd barely seen her at all since she returned to campus, not just because he was avoiding her like the plague. He'd been busy on hunts, and she was... Well, from what Blake reported, relaxing by the pool in bikinis that could break obscenity laws. Cyrus thought his friend was being dramatic... until today.

"You're going to get a hamburger. No cheese, fries with gravy. I'll get the carbonara. You give me half your fries, we'll split my side salad, and you'll pick out the ham in my pasta," she instructed, raising her chin. "I'll eat the top half of your burger bun if the bread-to-meat ratio is off again."

"Only if you get the Caesar dressing on the side," Cyrus said.

"Please. If I don't get the Caesar dressing, feel free to assume I've been lobotomized and put me out of my misery."

The pair passed through the sliding glass doors to the cafeteria. Multiple cooking stations lined the walls, but only a few were open for the summer. They scanned their student IDs—Cyrus's was on his phone, and Kitty had a physical ID card, oddly enough—and entered the cafeteria. He picked up a tray for her, which she accepted, and they went ahead to order. Ten minutes later, they were settled at a table in the corner.

"I can't believe you don't like carbonara with ham," Cyrus admonished, putting all the pink pieces of meat on a separate plate. They sat side-by-side, rather than across from each other. It was better for both of them—the food was easier to share, and he didn't have to look directly at her.

Kitty wrinkled her nose, dipping a fry into the pasta. "Um, how can anyone like ham with *cheese sauce*? Gross."

"When's the rest of your family coming? Classes start next week."

"Tomorrow. I spoke to Nell this morning, and she's all packed up."

"You spoke with her? On the phone?" he asked. "Doesn't that go against your whole 'no tech' policy?"

"It's not a 'no tech' policy," she corrected, shoving a fry in her mouth. "I'm just limiting my screen time."

"Because some self-help guru told you?"

"Because I'm trying to be a nicer person."

"Since when?"

"Since last winter, you jackass."

Cyrus wasn't going to say he liked her the way she was, or some crap like that. He doubted that was what she wanted to hear—if anything, she'd roast him for it until he was burned to a crisp. So instead, like an idiot, he said, "The trick to New Year's resolutions is doing things that are small and manageable. You are neither of those things."

And it was true. She was tall and toned, being only a few inches shorter than him at 5'9". Her muscles were lean but clearly defined and certainly not for show. If anyone tried to 'manage' her, Cyrus figured they'd be on the receiving end of her saber.

"Excuse you. Are you trying to say I'm high maintenance?" Kitty challenged.

"You're not low maintenance."

"Oh, and you are? You dumped a girl because she wore a sunhat, and when she took it off, her hair frizzed up!"

Damn, Blake had run his mouth. "That's not true. One, she wore the sunhat indoors in the winter to hide the fact that she had lice. And it did not work out well for anyone involved. Two, we weren't dating, therefore I did not dump her."

"You weren't dating? You were just sleeping together?"

"No! It was two double dates set up by my sister, a mistake

I won't repeat!" Cyrus exclaimed. "I don't even remember her name. Why do you care anyway?"

"I don't," she lied, badly. "I'm just trying to prove a point."

"That I'm high maintenance?"

"Well, yeah."

Cyrus had hunted for six days straight. He was drained and hadn't been getting enough sleep. What made him think he could handle talking to Kitty? This was the first time they'd spoken—*really* spoken—in months. He should have picked a better time, when he was in the right state of mind.

But he hadn't, so he said, "Two high maintenance people can't be in a relationship."

Kitty's eyes nearly bugged out of her head. Shit. Now, if she closed her eyes, that meant she was counting to ten. It also meant that Cyrus was a dead man.

She closed her eyes.

He saw his life flash before him.

She opened them. Despite his fear, for a moment, he was stunned. He shouldn't have been; he'd seen her eyes plenty of times. But that dark gunmetal grey color stuck out in his mind.

"Well," Kitty said placidly, "it's a good thing we're not in a relationship."

"Yeah," he echoed. "Good thing."

He thought the conversation would be over, as well as any chance he had with her. But, after a long pause, Kitty said, "You know, for a Pre-Med student, you're pretty dumb."

"No. I'm just stupid when it comes to you," he admitted.

"Is that supposed to be sweet?"

"It's supposed to be the truth."

She finally cracked a smile, and damn if that wasn't worse

than when she was angry, moments earlier. "When are you going to give me the opportunity to kick your ass again?"

"I've been hunting all summer," he said. "You think you can take me? You might be surprised."

She laughed. "No matter what the circumstances might be, Cy, I'll always be able to take you."

"How about tomorrow? Bright and early—if the colony has been caught, that is."

"You, me, and the mats." She nodded. "But beware. My dad taught me a new move. It's called the Nut Nudge."

"And this is different from the already-established Ball Breaker?"

"It's like the Ball Breaker and the Nutcracker, with an added burning sensation."

"So it's not just a nudge, I take it."

"You'll have to experience it to find out."

"I really, *really* don't want to. As much as I like you touching my—"

"Melody!" Kitty said loudly, cutting him off. Sure enough, Cyrus's little sister stood behind him with a strange look on her face.

The siblings didn't look similar. They shared the same father but, biologically, had different mothers. Cyrus's mom was a Vietnamese woman who had died shortly after his birth. His trueblood father remarried shortly after, and Mel was born.

Her hair was a mousy brown, with chunky hot pink highlights she'd just got touched up. She wore glasses; it was rare for a shadowborn to even need them. Kitty once said she looked like a punk-rock librarian, and now that was all Cy could think about when he saw his sister.

"What are you two doing?" Mel asked.

Cyrus shifted away from Kitty. "Nothing."

"Really? That doesn't look like 'nothing' to me."

"Well, Mel—"

"We're just very mindful of food waste," Kitty replied, gesturing to their half-empty plates. "The kitchen pre-makes a lot of the dishes, so it's not easy to customize. And the portion sizes are either too big or too small. It's way better to share."

"Right. The food." Of course she was asking about the food.

Melody slid across from them. Her hair was wet from the shower, probably having just come from a hunt herself. She was going out to the Veil just as often as Cyrus this summer, but since she used a crossbow and not a blade, she usually accompanied much larger hunting parties. Cy often went with one or two other shadowborn and maybe a magician.

"I ran into Blake on the way out. He said you didn't catch the colony, but you got some big spider?" she said.

Kitty nodded, describing the creature with wild hand gestures. She lit up the entire room with the story, and other students looked over as they walked by. Cyrus glared at a passing male student whose stare lingered a few seconds too long. The student, startled, looked away and hurried out of their vicinity. Kitty didn't seem to notice, and even if she had, she'd probably put her hands on her hips and say, "Of course he was staring. I'm, like, *so* pretty. Men just can't resist me, and who would blame them?"

And while Cyrus would roll his eyes and call her vain, secretly he'd find it funny.

"It was sick. In a gross way," Kitty added, finishing the story. A hunt she wasn't even supposed to be on in the first place. Cyrus wasn't sure how Blake convinced her to go, and he wouldn't say. When Cy asked, his friend just smiled and laughed. Asshole. "My beach cover-up is totally ruined. Looks like I'm going to have to stop by the mall and get a new one."

"I'll drive you." Mel was eager to drive the new car that their father bought her: a silver Audi SUV with air-conditioned *and* heated seats. "I need to get some supplies before class starts. Maybe, when Veronica comes to campus, we can all go this weekend?"

Kitty nodded. "When exactly *is* Queen Vee coming?"

"She always likes to make an entrance. I think she could be an actress, if she wanted to."

"Because she's so dramatic?"

"Well, that. And she never misses her cue." Melody nodded toward the door.

The group turned.

In walked Veronica Halliwell. Cyrus almost didn't recognize her. The former blonde had gone back to her natural color, a deep garnet red, with curls spilling down her back. Her shirt matched her hair color perfectly, paired with shorts that would make Daisy Duke blush.

"Were you talking about me?" she asked, her Jersey accent coming out as she said "tawkin."

She always had a slight accent, not that Cyrus paid very much attention to her. She was in his dorm often when she and Blake were together. He was hesitant to call what they did 'dating'. More like, Blake was fucking around with her—both mentally and physically. Cyrus, to his credit, hadn't known the full extent of it until recently. He wasn't involved in their drama, but he felt a twinge of guilt toward her. They hadn't been friends, or even acquaintances, but she was still a person deserving of respect. And Blake crushed her dignity like a child would an ant; he did it for fun.

Kitty flung herself at her friend with a squeal. Veronica twirled her around, hugging her tight.

"Your hair looks amazing!" Mel praised.

"Thanks! While I can't say the same about yours, I appreciate the compliment."

"Hey!"

"-is for horses," Kitty finished with a grin. "We have *so* much to catch up on. My God. Do I start with your style, your hair, your kick-ass tan?"

"It's spray-on. I didn't get much of a natural tan in the French countryside. Grandmere's chateau is pretty far removed from civilization—and sunlight, apparently. There was *no* good place to lay my towel out. But she had, like, a bunch of grimoires in her attic, so that's something!" Veronica sat down between Cyrus and Kitty. "How about you? What trouble are you getting into these days?"

"Nothing too wild, which desperately needs to change."

"I know. Listen, why don't we go to the mall tomorrow? We can pick out cute clubbing outfits and this weekend we can go out and see how many guys' numbers we can get?"

"Kitty and I already have plans," Cyrus blurted, without thinking. "And she's cutting down on her screen time, so she's not really using her phone a lot."

The three women stared at him.

"You have plans for the whole day?" Veronica questioned dubiously.

"Hey, it's getting late. I hunted today, and Cyrus has been on two trips to the Veil. I think we're going to skip dessert and head back to the dorm," Kitty said. "Veronica, Mel, I'll see you both tomorrow, okay? We'll catch up over lunch at the mall, and we can paint our toes in my room."

The two seemed to be satisfied by the promise of pedicures. Kitty took her empty tray and discarded it at the station by the door. Cyrus could only follow her, like a dog. They walked side by side toward the dorms in silence. The buildings were beside each other, but neither were co-ed. When they reached the fork in the walkway, Kitty paused.

"I'll see you tomorrow, right?" she asked. "For training?"

Cyrus nodded. "Yeah. I'll reserve the usual room."

"Great. And, uh, Cy?"

"What is it?"

"We're..." She hesitated. "We're still friends, right?"

"Friends." He choked on the word. "Yeah. We're still friends."

THREE

RYDER KINSEY DID NOT HAVE any friends. He was never popular, though he convinced himself—and everyone else, for that matter—that he was a loner, not a loser. Thus, it was perfectly acceptable to be friendless. In fact, it was *cool.*

He didn't even consider his regular hookups as 'friends with benefits'. Aside from the sex, he wouldn't associate with any of those people on a regular basis. And dates? Barf! He knew what he wanted and went for it. As long as all parties were consenting adults, and he was upfront about his desires, there were no issues. Actually, his partners preferred his honesty. He didn't play games, a policy that extended to board, card, and video varieties.

His hobbies were mainly solo activities. Riding his motorcycle, reading Kafka like a pretentious prick, and enjoying the occasional charcuterie board. Which, by the way, was definitely an activity he preferred to do alone. He did not share his food, especially cheese.

He didn't share anything, actually. He was an only child,

thank God. His parents never married—Mom was a trueblood angel and rarely showed an interest in human affairs. And Dad was a jackass who only had a child because it was expected of him, and perhaps, because he needed a lackey.

Ryder was no one's lackey, or so he liked to think. But his father funded his debauchery, so when he made a request, Ryder couldn't refuse. And they both knew it.

Which was why, after two years of dodging his classes, he returned to Northeastern College of Magic in New York. (New York *State*, mind you, which was ninety-percent less cool than the city.) His first stop was his father's office, at the top of the castle serving as the main building. It suited the chancellor, who fancied himself something of a king.

Ryder didn't have an appointment, nor did he tell his father when he would be arriving, so he was stuck in the waiting room. The secretaries, financial aid office, and registrar were all in one room, separated by thin partitions. The center waiting room was the same for all functions, so he witnessed quite a few students come in and out. One, in particular, had a grating voice that carried over the partitions.

He saw her when she came in, though he pretended he didn't notice. She wasn't his type at all, which ordinarily would have completely made him lose interest. But there was something about her, something so genuinely disturbing he had to do a double-take. She was too tall for one, which didn't match her delicate features. Her hair was a bit long and flat for his taste, and her skirt was far too short. He couldn't put his finger on it, but something was *off* about her.

She walked into the room annoyed and left yelling about her student ID having the wrong name.

"Is it really that big a deal?" Ryder made the mistake of muttering.

She whirled on him so fast she must have gotten whiplash. "What?"

"It's just an ID. It works." He shrugged.

"My entire student record has the wrong name. Which shouldn't be possible considering I sent in all my legal documents," she scathed. "I've come into this office twice now to get it corrected, and so far, nothing has happened."

"By all means, throw a tantrum. See how well it works."

"Do you know what the New York State bird is?"

"Uh, no."

She showed him with a succinct one-finger gesture.

Yeah, definitely not his type. She stormed off, though, which was a relief. By the time the door slammed shut, he was called into his father's office.

It had just been renovated and modernized, with a theme of monochrome and glass. Ryder's father sat behind a large marble desk, two monitors in the corner. Behind him were wide paneled windows that didn't open, revealing the campus green below. Sunlight poured through, illuminating the room and hitting the overhead chandelier at the perfect angle, its crystals scattering rainbows all over the office.

Ryder had barely spoken to his father in the past year, save for asking for money. "You rang?"

"Have a seat." The chancellor poured him a glass of scotch, though he knew very well that Ryder was a cocktail man. If it didn't have a tiny umbrella in it, why bother? But the chancellor also knew his son couldn't admit that aloud. Wouldn't do well for his cool persona. So Ryder downed the glass.

"What do you want?"

"I have a problem, Ethan."

Ryder hated when his father called him that. "They have

meds for erectile dysfunction. You should talk to your doctor about it, not me."

"Are you finished joking around? This is serious."

"ED isn't a joke, and the fact that you'd accuse me of making light of it says more about your character than mine."

The chancellor slid a folder toward his son. "There's a student here who just enrolled. I want her gone."

"Get rid of her then. You're the chancellor, aren't you? The head honcho?"

He glared. "It isn't that simple. These are modern times we're living in. You can't touch these people without them claiming discrimination. No, this is a delicate situation. She needs to leave of her own volition. If she's gone, the rest of her family will follow."

Ryder opened the folder and scanned the files inside, along with the photo. "Are you sure the name is right?"

"I know. They chose an English surname when they immigrated."

"No, I mean her first name. I think I just saw this chick outside. She was going on about how her name isn't Katherine."

"It doesn't matter. She'll be gone soon enough, if you do your job right," the chancellor said.

"And why do you want her gone again?"

"That's none of your concern."

"Tell me it's not because she's Asian." He needed to hear the words, even if they were a lie.

"Of course not. But that's what everyone would think if I denied her application. She's simply not up to par with our standards here at Northeastern. She's *mortal*," he said. "She doesn't belong here. It's in everyone's best interest if she leaves.

But thanks to affirmative action, and I suppose some push-back from the higher ups, I'm not allowed to do that."

Ryder didn't think there *were* higher ups.

"We already have diversity at the school. One of the combat instructors is Black. That should be enough, but apparently, it's not," the chancellor continued.

"Please tell me you don't say this shit to anyone else."

"Relax. Everyone is in agreement. The board, the provost, the department heads. They want the girl gone just as much as I do. And rather than face backlash, I think you can get her to quit on her own. You're very good at manipulating women, son. Do what you need to in order to force her to drop out. I don't care what."

"Alright, I know you said this isn't about race, but you're really, *really* making it sound like it is," Ryder said. "I don't have a problem with that per se, but you know how people are nowadays. You can't talk like this with anyone else. Okay?"

"Are you going to get rid of the Swan girl?"

Ryder looked at the photo, remembering the angry bitch who flipped him off in the waiting room. He actually didn't care about that or her. And he didn't care that she was mortal, Asian, or whatever. But if his father asked for something, it was better to comply. Besides, if he didn't do it, someone else would. At least Ryder could just rip the bandage off and get it over with.

He wouldn't seduce her. That would be disgusting—not on a moral level, but on a physical one. He wasn't attracted to her, so forcing himself to be with her, to even *kiss* her, was just...yuck. But there were many other ways he could think of to break her.

"How far can I go with this?" he asked his father.

The chancellor leaned back in his leather chair. The father-son duo looked alike, both with caramel hair and piercing dark eyes. Ryder wore his hair longer than his father, usually in disheveled waves curling around his ears. But they had the same square jaw and strong nose. Both were of average height, though they carried it well. Being lanky and long-limbed, particularly in the arms, made them appear taller.

"Do what you want, short of killing her. I don't want anything traced back to me. If you torment her, make sure you have a good reason."

"Such as?"

"Many parents blame her for the horde attack. I haven't done anything to dissuade them."

"You planted the seed, though," Ryder guessed.

"No, actually."

He believed the chancellor. "Fine. But I wasn't here when the horde attacked, and it's not like I was friends with anyone who died. I'll think of something else. Do you really think anyone cares enough to investigate this?"

Ryder doubted it. Truebloods and shadowborn weren't known for their investigative skills. It had something to do with the different clans of truebloods each having their own justice systems and moral codes. In the Veil, it was easy—truebloods lived in separate territories. If you committed a crime in, say, elf territory, you'd be subject to their laws. It didn't matter if the crime was against an elf or not; what mattered was where the crime took place.

In the mortal realm, truebloods didn't have territories. It was a big mixing pot, so the jurisdictions were confusing. On top of that, each group of truebloods and shadowborn believed they were superior to the other. Angels thought they were better than demons, fae thought they were more powerful than elves, and vampires thought they were more civilized than werewolves. The list went on. *Everybody* thought they were better than magicians and psychics, who were deemed weak liabilities. Power was paramount.

With the political climate being so delicate, usually smaller crimes like theft weren't worth the fight. If it couldn't be handled by the human police, then vigilante justice served its purpose.

Shadowborn were more organized than truebloods in the mortal realm, but still, their investigations were lacking. Detectives were overworked and spread thin across the country, and most prioritized the ferals and possible discovery risks by humans. Hell, there was an issue this past summer at Southeastern, when their summer-at-sea program had been infiltrated by cultists! Had they figured out what happened? Nope, not yet—and probably not ever.

Suffice to say, Ryder had very little faith in the shadowborn justice system. If these Swan people were mortal, as his father claimed, no one would care what happened to them. None of the truebloods had allegiances with them, and neither did the shadowborn.

"There is a lot going on right now, and we cannot afford to have anyone look too closely," the chancellor said. "Once the wallpaper begins to peel, I'll be finished. And so will you, by extension. You'll get the Swan girl out of this school, or it's both our necks."

"Fine," Ryder agreed. What did he care about some creepy bitch, anyway?

"When you meet her, you'll see," the chancellor said. "There's something wrong with Katherine Swan."

NOELLE SWAN HAD NEVER BEEN MUGGED BEFORE. When the man took his gun out and aimed the barrel at her nose, she was thrilled. This was the most exciting thing to happen all summer.

After the disaster at Northeastern, her parents had really loosened the reins. She liked to think they trusted her to take care of herself. It wasn't as if her siblings had suddenly became more capable of defending her. If anything, Kitty completely had withdrawn over the summer. When they returned to their hometown, she picked up shifts at a local restaurant and spent most waking hours working. Even when she returned home after a double, she kept to herself and either read outside in the backyard or slept on the couch.

To be fair, there wasn't much else to do. Their parents quit their jobs and took ESL classes at the local rec center, along with Driver's Ed to get their licenses. They did surprisingly well in both and had normal schedules for the first time in Noelle's life. It was all so...ordinary.

Noelle wasn't a fan.

She spent her summer cultivating and was now on the cusp of forming a golden core like her sister. She could *feel* it. But no matter how much time she spent meditating in the forest, it seemed the next level was just out of reach.

She also trained her body, spending hours with her younger brother working out. It paid off. Under her fluttery ruffled blouse and long skirt, she was jacked. She assumed the robber couldn't tell, because she doubted he would have approached her if he'd seen her muscle definition.

Admittedly, she didn't *look* intimidating. She took after Māma in terms of appearance, with big round eyes, long lashes, and a round face. Her petite stature and effeminate style of dress had probably caused the thief to mistake her for an easy target.

Noelle glanced at the rest stop: a dingy little building on the side of the highway. She was driving up from Parker Ridge to Northeastern with Māma and Jax, but those two played it fast and loose with their Big Gulps, resulting in multiple bathroom breaks along the I-95. Currently, it seemed they were both still occupied.

"I said, give me your purse."

Noelle did not have anything in her purse but tampons, loose change, and her seven-year-old cracked cell phone. Still, she didn't want to give them up. It was a matter of pride—and the fact that she was still on day one of her period. She needed the tampons.

She wished there was some cool one-liner or catchphrase she could spit out, but she couldn't think of any. After a few seconds pondering this, she simply decided to save that thought train for later and proceed to kick ass.

Kitty didn't believe in fair fights—you either win or you lose. Noelle liked to think she was nobler than that, but as she grabbed the barrel of the gun and twisted it away from her face, she realized that there truly wasn't anything honorable about what she was doing. And she didn't really care.

Her grip tightened on the man's hand as she crushed it in her own, kicking hard at one of his knees. His legs buckled and she wretched the gun away, tossing it in a garbage dump a few feet away. The man attempted to crawl away, which was a huge mistake. He really shouldn't have robbed anyone, if he was going to look so pathetic when he lost.

Noelle didn't let the man go, stomping hard on his calf. She didn't break his bones or anything drastic. She didn't want to *hurt* him; she wasn't a sadist. She simply knew it was her duty—as a Good Samaritan—to mentally scar the man so badly that he wouldn't commit a similar crime in the future. Wasn't that what being a righteous cultivator was all about? Doing good, defeating evil?

Noelle dragged the man behind a trash bin and straddled his waist. It was broad daylight, but from here, no one could see what they were up to.

The man shivered as her fingertips caressed his skin, white as a sheet with fear. He had nothing to be scared of. She wouldn't kill him. She'd had nearly three months to practice her control, and she was getting very good at siphoning qi away from living things.

It was expected to cultivate with nature via meditation, gathering qi from plant life and animals and circulating it through one's body. The qi returned to the creature or plant from which it was taken, and it was such a small amount anyway, no harm was done. The Swans were Taoist cultivators, valuing harmony with nature as one of the Immortal Rules, a set of rules which all righteous cultivators must follow.

Noelle never tried to take more than she was supposed to. Fear had triggered her the first time, allowing her to drain a person so completely she hadn't even left a corpse behind. But, with trial and error, she had managed to teach herself control. It was as if every living thing had a ball of loose threads, and if you could grab a fistful of them, you could unravel it.

She closed her eyes and felt the pulse of life beneath her, envisioning fraying gold threads from him. With her mind, she pulled on the threads, carefully extracting just a few. The qi absorbed into her body, flowing through her meridians toward her center, where her golden core would soon form. When

Noelle opened her eyes, the man beneath her was unconscious.

He would wake up in a few hours. Noelle rose to her feet, dusted herself off, and returned to the car.

Her younger brother leaned against the black SUV, arms crossed. The little squirt hit his growth spurt shortly after his birthday, shooting up in height. Finally, all those pull-ups and weight-lifting came in handy. He'd grown into his body and no longer resembled a bobble head.

"Mā's buying some pork rinds. She'll be out in a minute."

Noelle nodded. When it was only her and her brother, the siblings didn't have much to say. Neither shared interests, nor were they particularly talkative. Kitty, blessed with the gift of gab, usually filled the silence with her chatter. Now that she was gone, her absence was evident.

Māma came out of the store with three bags of pork rinds, her short legs carrying her quickly as she crossed the parking lot. She dumped the bags in the car, hustled the children in, and started the engine.

"Lemon tea is no good," she muttered, peeling out of the lot and onto the highway. "No more. Only Sprite from now on."

"I don't think it was the tea, rather, the *volume* of tea—" Noelle began.

"It was the tea. I don't like it."

"Alright, Mā." Noelle looked out the window. She sat in the back. Jax, now a giant, needed to stretch his legs. It saved her the trouble of navigating.

Her body hummed with energy, refreshed by the man's qi; almost like she'd had the best night's sleep of her life, drunk two energy drinks, and showered the inside of her body, all at once. The feeling could easily be addicting, but Noelle was smart enough not to seek it out. This case was necessary: self-defense, if you will. And all those other times, she had tried it on animals. She didn't hurt them, and it was no different from the testing drug and cosmetic companies did with their products. It was for science, not for personal gain, therefore it wasn't against the Immortal Rules.

Alright, so she'd killed a guy. That had kept her up at night, in the beginning. But it was self-defense. He had been *waterboarding* her, and she hadn't meant to do it. At least she wasn't like her sister, who enjoyed fighting, or her brother, who thought he was some sort of hero. Noelle was more realistic than those two, more level-headed, being the middle child.

That was the main reason why she wasn't concerned about starting school this fall. She'd always been homeschooled, and she did work that was usually above Kitty's grade level. Noelle knew she was smart, so getting good grades would be easy. And friends? She had a few people she knew, but she was looking forward to getting her own friends—outside of her sister's influence.

It wasn't that she didn't love Kitty. Of course she did—they were sisters, after all. But hearing about her school life made Noelle think it was time to have adventures of her own. It was healthy to have separate lives, especially since they'd be dorming together.

These past weeks without Kitty had actually been great. Noelle stayed in the room by herself at home; without the constant complaints and drama, it was peaceful.

The car came to an abrupt stop, jerking Noelle awake. She hadn't realized she'd fallen asleep. Sitting up, she looked out the window. They were on the bridge leading to the school gates, and below was a forest of thick greenery. She tried not to look down, seeing as they were stopped and the bridge was narrow.

"What's going on?" she asked, finding her voice.

"Traffic," Jax muttered, rolling down the window to poke his head out.

Māma honked. "This is ridiculous!"

"It's moving again." Jax tucked himself back inside. The cars crawled forward, but at least they were moving. Noelle sighed. She just wanted to go to the dorm and shower.

Something hit the front windshield, landing with a splat. Noelle first thought a storm rolled in, but it was far too heavy to be a raindrop. Glancing up, she saw that it was...an egg?

Māma frowned. "What is that?"

Jax went pale and closed the window. "Just keep going. Don't stop."

"What does that sign say?"

"Mā, just go."

Noelle leaned to the side and looked out the front windshield. By the gates, a crowd gathered—the cause of the traffic. They held large signs on neon poster board, the words written in thick black marker.

Most of them used very poor grammar. No surprise there. They all carried the same general message.

"Go Home, Chinks!"

FOUR

GHOSTS WEREN'T SUPPOSED to leave shadows. They were dead, incorporeal. Nothing but memories and fragmented feelings in the shape of a human. And yet, Tessa Churchill cast a dark shadow over her younger sister in both life and death.

It was cold, too. No one told you just how cold it was, growing up in the darkness of a brilliant older sibling. Perhaps that was why Charity did not live up to her namesake. Those who grew up loved found it easy to be generous; those who survived off crumbs of affection—or none at all, in her case—were guilty of coveting what little they had.

Charity struggled to care whether or not she was a charitable person, or even a good person. She was a train rolling on a track her father laid down, only thinking about getting from point A to point B. Right now, point B was graduating college.

The shadowborn fairy stood above a cliff overlooking the jungle below, her eyes tracking every rustle of leaves and faint buzz of wings. She was close to the colony—she knew it.

"What do you see?" asked the source of her most recent grief: Blake Blackwood. She'd known him all her life, and when she looked at him now, she recognized the man he'd become. He was his father's son.

But Charity would never be her father's daughter. He made it very clear that she was his least favorite, and until he got a son, he'd keep trying. More wives would cycle through, and more sisters would be born, each disappointing in their own way.

There was nothing overwhelmingly disappointing about Charity. Even the ways in which she failed her father were mediocre—story of her life. She wasn't rebellious like Anne and Prudence, nor was she addicted to substances like Mary and Elisabeth. She didn't flunk out of school like Kate, or have a disability like Calista. No, Charity was disappointing because she was not Tessa.

She did well in school, but not as good as her older sister. She was on the swim team, but not the captain, like her older sister. In popularity, appearance, extracurriculars, and charm, Charity did not measure up to her father's favorite child. And her fatal flaw: she didn't take the beatings well. Mentally or physically.

Crying was a sign of weakness. And a child of Gwyn Churchill could never be weak.

"I don't see anything," Charity answered. "But I hear them. They're down there."

"How many, do you think?"

"Your guess is as good as mine." Her voice had a hard edge to it that was grating, even to her own ears. She couldn't help it when it came to Blake. She knew that being civil and calm was the best course of action. If she showed that he hurt her, he would only mock her for it.

Charity would not be like Veronica. She would not give Blake the satisfaction of hurting her over and over again.

"Let's go. We can't lose them," Cyrus cut in.

Charity was glad for his presence. He was always a skilled fighter, but over the summer, he had proved to be an excellent hunter. She actually enjoyed going on these extra-credit assignments with him. It was almost like old times, when they were friends.

Blake and Cyrus were the only real friends Charity had. Not like her schoolmates, who would smile to her face and laugh behind her back. She never needed to explain herself to them, and a comfortable silence often settled between the trio while they dug up worms or studied on the picnic bench in the Ward's backyard. Tessa ruined that, of course, just like she ruined everything else.

Charity picked her axe up. The weight of her weapon comforted her, the sturdy metal handle warm and heavy. It was an extension of herself, and through it, she channeled all the feelings she was not allowed to show, out of fear she would appear weak. But sometimes, she wondered if fear of weakness was, in itself, a weakness.

"It's this way," she said.

The team trailed behind her. Since they were hunting a colony, they left in a group of five: Charity, Blake, Cyrus, Melody, and Wyatt Ainsworth.

Wyatt was the only one not included in their friend group, though Charity liked him well enough. Son of a professor, he was an accomplished swordsman and another buffer between her and Blake. Wyatt, at least, knew how to treat a woman with respect, hence why he was one of the most popular guys on campus.

"I'm allergic to bees," Wyatt mused.

"Why are you even here, then?" Blake muttered.

"If I get stung, I'll die. You're not allergic, but if you get stung, you'll die, too. Either from the feral illness, or from a big-ass stinger."

"Can you really die from a sting?" Melody asked, eyes wide. She hadn't hunted insect-type beastbloods before, and Charity could tell the girl was nervous. She didn't like regular-sized bugs in the mortal realm, screaming and crying for her older brother if one so much as landed near her. Charity thought Cyrus coddled her too much.

"Yes. It's a large, hard, sharp object with venom that can pierce through flesh easily," said Charity.

"And that's a problem? I thought you liked large, hard things, Char," Blake said, wagging his brows.

Cyrus rolled his eyes. "That was a terrible joke, even for you, man."

"She didn't set me up for a 'that's what she said'. I can only work with what I'm given."

"Or you could shut up," Melody suggested. "Just throwing that out there."

Charity ignored them and pushed forward. She hated the jungle areas of the Veil. Everything here felt exaggerated in the worst way, and the sticky, heavy heat clung to her skin and clothes hours after returning to the mortal realm. But even this was better than the alternative: sitting alone in her single-room dorm, lush but isolated, thinking about her father's phone call a week prior. She might have even been tempted to visit him. The trip home would only take her an hour, give or take traffic.

She'd grown up in rural New York, in a community of shadowborn and truebloods. The entire town had some sort of magic inclination, separated by vast stretches of empty fields and thick, towering forests. Her family home was there: a sprawling manor staffed with trueblood servants who still followed her father, despite their strong distaste for shadowborn.

Her father had been a prince, once. He claimed to be, anyway, and Charity believed him. She saw the reverence in the eyes of the house staff when her father stepped into a room: like he was a sun and everyone revolved around him. As a royal, he was not to be questioned, nor was he truly understood. She didn't know why he had so many shadowborn children, instead of settling with a trueblood fae of royal lineage—like himself.

Truebloods looked down on their half-breeds. The shadowborn were named because the truebloods thought them shadows—no more than a simple imitation of a trueblood. It was the cruel nature of sentient beings, a weakness of intelligent lifeforms: social stratification. In the case of truebloods, each group felt the need to be better than the other. Even among the shadowborn, ancestry was a source of pride and ridicule.

Charity's father mocked his shadowborn children, and yet he continued to have them, searching for a specific quality within each of them and being disappointed when he couldn't find it. She lost track of how many wives he'd had. And now, to impregnate another woman?

At least he called to tell her this time. He was moving his whore from a place in the city—he had multiple apartments there, where he kept his human lovers—to their family home, where she would give birth to yet another sibling.

She bet this one was Irish. He liked the Irish because they had many legends about the fae. He liked red hair, too. Charity's mother had red hair, but it was a deeper shade than her daughter's coppery mess of curls.

Charity swept her hair back into a tight bun as they walked further, keeping it off her neck. Sweat stained her tank top, pooling under her breasts, but thankfully she had enough sense to bring a scent-masking pouch and wear it around her wrist. She crossed an arm over her chest and glanced at Blake, but he was behind her, talking to Cyrus.

"Where'd you get that?"

Cyrus brushed a hand over the bruise blooming on his jaw. "Kitty."

"You're sparring with her again?"

"Just this morning."

"And she punched you in the face?"

Cyrus didn't reply.

"Be quiet," Charity admonished them. "You can gossip later."

"You just like to suck the fun out of everything, don't you?" Blake asked.

"You know I don't like to suck anything." She ducked under a tree branch, following a faint buzzing sound. The wasps had a great sense for smells, using their antennae, as well as vibrations. The scent-masking pouches would hide them, but they also needed to be mindful of their movements.

The colony was close. The question was, how close was their nest?

The feral disease could do a lot of damage to a beastblood, but some things about the species still held true even after the turn. A nest of Blood Wasps relied on a queen. Kill the queen, the rest of the colony dies. Simple. And the queen is always in the nest.

Five drones loomed under a canopy of trees, their exoskeletons dulled from the feral illness. Their eyes oozed black goo, and some were missing a limb. They moved slowly, dragging their barbs across the ground as their rotting wings buzzed, broken like shattered windows in an old warehouse. Their antennae were sluggish as they moved, the entire group most likely scouting for their next victims.

Charity readied her axe. She didn't want to confront the wasps—she just wanted to kill the queen. She didn't know how many more there were around, but Blood Wasps fought well in groups. If they started a fight, the rest of the drones would come to assist, and it would be close to impossible to defeat them all.

She skirted around the edge of the trees, avoiding the bushes and other foliage as not to alert the group. The nest *had* to be close. Further into the jungle, they saw several more groups of drones. The Blood Wasps were already intimidating, without the feral disease infecting them, but with the added decay, Charity's palms grew slick and her heart stuttered in her chest.

When she closed her eyes, she went to her happy place: a beach in the Florida Keys, sipping a pina colada and letting the water lick her freshly pedicured toes. She could even picture the polish: Dior 999 Rouge—a bright red her father would never approve of.

But when she opened her eyes, the Veil greeted her.

The buzzing grew louder as they neared a tree so large, the Empire State Building could fit inside. It was substantially bigger than any other tree in the forest, though curiously, she hadn't seen it from the lookout point. Perhaps it wasn't significantly taller?

Either way, she had no doubt this was the nest.

Charity gestured for the group to come closer. They

needed to get into a formation. Melody would be in the center, protected while she shot arrows; Blake and Cyrus would cover the group; Wyatt would carve a path; Charity would go for the kill. Her axe wasn't small, but it was shorter than a sword. It was also heavier and easier to cut through the exoskeleton. Stabbing a feral was a mixed bag, and typically, unless your aim was good, it wasn't fatal. Decapitation was a surefire way to kill just about anything.

Inside the hollowed tree trunk, a smell like no other hit her. She gagged, covering her nose, tears springing to her eyes. The fumes were noxious; Blake choked behind her. And Melody, breaking formation, ran outside to vomit. Well, that plan fell apart faster than you could say 'wasp'.

The sound drew the attention of several drones. The shadowed space had only a handful of them, clinging to the lowest part of the wall. The queen was in the center, seven feet tall, laying down on her back. Sludge and dark liquid leaked from the bed of leaves she nested on, her eyes concave and her antennae vibrating. It didn't seem like she could move at all, her limbs torn from her, leaving gaping wounds on her sides.

At least it would be easy to get to her neck.

The drones weren't fast, but they waddled toward the group. Charity and Wyatt pushed forward, closing as much distance as they could on foot before being stopped by the drones.

"I really don't like bees." Wyatt grinned.

"These are wasps. They're even worse," Charity replied.

"Hmm. Hey, Char? For the next few minutes, we probably shouldn't talk."

She nodded. The ferals' secretions would be flying the moment he pounced.

Wyatt was truly a glorious fighter. He reminded her of a

knight from a fairytale, moving with elegance and purpose. Charity was more of a hack-and-slasher; it took a lot of strength to control where she hit, and even then, when she was primed and ready, she didn't always get a bullseye. But her anger had been bubbling for some time now. It didn't matter where she hit the drones, just as long as they got the fuck out of her way. She chopped at their barbs, the most dangerous part of them, and followed Wyatt's lead. Limbs, antennae, and guts flew as the two made their way toward the queen. Charity's muscles screamed, but she ignored the pain—as she trained all her life to do—and brought the axe down on its neck.

The head rolled away with a wet thud, and after a few agonizing seconds, the rest of the drones in the nest dropped dead. The queen's body began to shrivel at a disturbing rate—they all did—becoming a pale husk so light, it seemed the wind could blow it away.

Charity wanted to blow chunks.

"Let's get the hell out of here," Blake choked out. For once, Charity agreed with her ex.

Wyatt held out his hand. She took it, stepping carefully off the slippery makeshift cushion of leaves where the queen's husk rested. And, just as she predicted, a wind swept through the nest. Wyatt and Charity dropped down, curling into balls on instinct as the Blood Wasp husks swept up with the wind. Once it settled, she was grateful they hadn't landed on her. She wasn't sure she could have controlled her gag reflex. Actually, she was positive she would have thrown up, just like Linda Blair in The Exorcist.

"Char." Wyatt rose, dark eyes wide. He jerked his chin toward the now-empty nest of the Blood Wasp Queen.

Ah. The smell.

Crushed beneath the queen, a broken corpse lay still on the pile of leaves. Covered in black feral goo, Charity was shocked to see the corpse was intact. It looked human, with short hair and bloated features. Its face and lips were ready to explode, puffing out to the extreme, its eyes swollen shut.

"Is it just me," Wyatt asked slowly, "or is that guy wearing a Northeastern sweatshirt?"

FOR THE SWANS, food was an expression of love. So when Kitty walked in to her parents' apartment and saw all the dishes spread out on the Lazy Susan, she knew Bàba must have really missed everyone.

"This is enough to feed an army," she commented, setting the vase of flowers down on the coffee table. As with their trailer back in South Carolina, the apartment was filled with furniture they'd found on the side of the road. Bà and Kitty had used the wood shop tools to fix up some of the broken chairs. And yes, everything was mismatched. But Kitty thought it had charm. The living room and dining room were one big open space, with a kitchen on the side and a bedroom and bathroom down the hall. It wasn't big, but neither was the trailer.

Bàba poked his head out from around the corner. He wore his favorite "Kiss Me, I'm Irish" apron and his dark hair stuck up in every direction. "Māma and your siblings will be here soon. We'll meet them at the gate. Before that, come here and taste."

Before she could ask what it was, he fed her a piece of kibbeh. Her Bàba was the best cook, despite being raised in a cultivation sect in the mountains. One of the sect rules was against cooking—all they ate were raw vegetables and fruit. Unsurprisingly, Māma was a terrible chef. Bàba, on the other hand, knew his way around the kitchen.

He usually stuck to Chinese recipes. Prior to taking ESL courses this summer, he was more comfortable speaking Mandarin and reading traditional Chinese. Now, he was fluent in English, so the language barrier when it came to recipes no longer posed an issue... Which led to the exploration of all different cuisines. Tonight: Lebanese.

"It's good," Kitty said with her mouth full. "But hot."

"Ah, good, good." He popped the rest of the kibbeh—fried, football-shaped balls of lamb meat, pine nuts, and spices—into a dish. "Put these next to the stuffed grape leaves."

She did as she was asked. "You got wine? I thought you weren't allowed to drink."

"No. Just juice—but I poured it in a wine glass I found. These professors have many near the recycling bin outside."

"Tell me you weren't digging through the garbage."

"No, no. Just passing by." Bàba paused. "One professor in this building has many *Playboy* magazines. I found a large stack in a bag."

"Please promise me you'll stop dumpster diving and, I don't know, be normal?" They had money now—the school paid Bàba and Māma enough, and they were no longer in debt.

"I did not dive. I perused," he corrected.

Because that was *much* better.

He washed his hands and took off his apron, hanging it in the kitchen. "Let's start walking toward the gates. I made signs for us. We'll hold them up, and Māma will know how much I missed her."

Kitty noticed the poster board by the shoe rack for the first time. She held the sign up, squinting. "'Welcome Home, Wife & Children.' Uh, are you sure this really conveys your intentions? It seems a bit blunt."

"That is why there are two signs."

She picked up the second sign. "'Have you eaten?' Well, um, this certainly is...something."

Bàba beamed. "You hold that one. I will hold the other one. We should hurry, before they get here. Your brother messaged me and said they are close. He also asks where your phone is."

"I told you, I'm cutting down on screen time," Kitty lied, because the truth would be too pathetic. "Alright, let's get this show on the road."

The father-daughter pair left the apartment and, at Bàba's insistence, took the stairs down ten flights.

"It is healthy for you," he sang. "How are you feeling?"

"The same."

"You have been cultivating? How is your golden core?"

"The same," she repeated. No matter how much she cultivated, it didn't get better. She could sense the cracks, and while her meridians healed, the golden core's damage could not be as easily undone. Thankfully, it was fickle. Her powers hadn't faded—they just chose to quit at inconvenient times. For the most part, though, she was able to cover up her weaknesses because she wasn't actively engaged in hunting. And it was a stroke of luck that she had managed to hold on for her sparring session with Cyrus earlier that morning.

He'd not only gotten stronger and faster, while she had still beaten him at hand-to-hand, he hit her in the stomach so hard she almost blacked out. Taking the blow was one thing, but pretending like it didn't hurt? Torture. But she supposed she should get used to pain, especially when it came to Cy.

Her parents hadn't forbidden her from seeing him, mostly because they weren't aware of it. Even if they were, they would remind her of what she already knew: he would age and die before her.

They weren't star-crossed, which might have been easier. If there was an obstacle in their way, a law or a person keeping them apart, Kitty felt confident she could crush them and take what she wanted, as per usual. But this wasn't a matter of an external enemy; this was just logic. Why would they date, knowing it was going to end so quickly? It was like betting on a horse she knew would die before reaching the finish line.

"What are you thinking about?" Bàba asked.

"Nothing."

"Boy troubles?" he miraculously guessed.

Kitty cursed in her head. Ever since her father had quit his construction job and now actually got a good night's sleep in a comfortable bed, he was much more aware of the goings-on at home. And he read his children like open books.

"You just remember what I taught you, Kitty."

"Always be myself?"

"No," he said seriously. "Every nut has a cracker."

Ah. Aim for the balls. "Thanks, Bàba. I'll keep that in mind."

"The eyes, too. A jab in the eye is also painful. And, if you need, you know your sister has some Anus Annihilator on hand. She came up with a third version—"

"I know, she tested it on me." That had *not* been a good weekend.

They traveled along the walkway, nearing the gates, when they saw a line of people. Cars honked and traffic backed up on the other side of the entrance.

"Oh," Bàba said, "maybe other parents had the same idea as us! Hold up your sign, Kitty!"

She did as he said, glancing around at the crowd. And then she read one of the signs they were holding. No self-help book or positive affirmation could have prepared her to remain calm. There was a period of time Kitty actually blacked out, and no matter how hard she tried, she couldn't remember. All she knew was Bàba's sign was ripped from her hands, torn in half.

And then, nothing.

FIVE

DAILY PROMPT: WHICH GOALS ARE YOU WORKING ON RIGHT NOW?

Controlling my anger. So far? It's not looking so good.

What better way to start the semester than to land herself in the chancellor's office? The newly renovated office, by the looks of it. Man, he'd got a bigger space *and* a furniture upgrade. Good to know where the student tuition went.

Kitty sat across from Chancellor Kinsey, who was typing away on a sleek desktop as he pulled up her file. She crossed her arms, something the self-help books she read had said was a huge no-no. Closed-off body language did not foster an environment of collaboration, which was good. She didn't want to collaborate, she wanted to yell at someone.

"Where do I even begin?" Kinsey muttered. "You do

realize that attacking another student outside of class and duels is against school policy, correct?"

She understood. She didn't give a fuck, though. Not after reading those signs. God, her father had read them too—and worse, he understood. She wished she could turn back time and stop him from seeing that. The more she thought about it, the angrier she got.

"I didn't attack her," Kitty managed.

"You called her a—" he squinted at the screen "—'skank horse'?"

"No, I called her a 'horse-faced skank'. There's, like, a *massive* difference."

"Regardless, it says here that Miss Papageorge had to be taken to the medical office for examination."

"What's to examine?" Kitty demanded.

"She was emotionally traumatized, Miss Swan. You called her a flurry of names, half of which I cannot repeat. We do not tolerate bullying at this institution."

"So you'll tolerate racism, but bullying is a no-go?"

"Now, hold on. Let's not throw that label around so easily," he admonished.

Oh yeah. If you cracked an egg on Kitty's head, it would have fried. "Why not? Are you afraid to hurt someone's feelings?"

"There's no need for sarcasm, Miss Swan. Miss Papageorge and her parents are quite upset, and your little display has been filmed and posted around social media. The school's accounts were tagged, and it doesn't reflect well on us or you."

"Let me see if I'm understanding you correctly. Some bitch writes a sign that says 'Fuck Off Commie Slut', I call her out on it, and *I'm* the bad guy?" Kitty hadn't even touched the whore! Alright, that wasn't totally true—she'd grabbed the sign and torn it apart with her hands and teeth. Not the best look. But she could have killed the bitch outright, dragged her body to the lake, cut it open, and filled it with rocks. Comparatively, this wasn't so bad.

And 'Commie Slut'? Inaccurate. Kitty wasn't a communist, not that she should even *have* to say it, and she was most certainly not a slut! What, it was a crime to be pretty now?

"Technically, the student protests were far enough away from the school building that they didn't violate any policies," Kinsey explained, flexing his hands. "And students have a right to express their distaste for political regimes they disagree with. It's just a fact that communism has taken away the rights of many people, and to ignore what is happening with the Chinese government—"

"I don't have anything to do with that!" Taking three calming breaths, she said, "It wasn't just that sign. I saw some with racial slurs explicitly written on them. I mean, 'Go Home Chinks' and 'Orientals Not Welcome' are pretty clear messages. That's not expressing an opinion about a political regime, it's being a racist asshole."

"Now, now. The term 'oriental' is very commonly used."

"Rugs are oriental. People are not. Why are you even trying to defend this?"

"I am simply trying to reason with you," he said, as if *she* were the crazy one. "Miss Swan, my goal as the chancellor of this school is to create harmony among the students. And I can't very well do that if students, like yourself, refuse to cooperate. I could have you punished for your tirade, as many parents are calling up and asking me to do. But I won't."

"No, instead, you are arguing with me about what is and what is not a racial slur."

"They are just words, Miss Swan. And we cannot resort to

violence over words. Now, believe me, Northeastern does *not* tolerate racism. We have standards here."

Kitty couldn't believe what she was hearing. Her eyes swept over his bookshelf, where there were several sharp trophies she imagined stabbing through the chancellor's eye socket. She was wired in the worst way, and it probably hadn't been a good idea to come here so quickly after the incident. But seriously? Standards? What standards?

"I wouldn't worry about this. They'll get it out of their systems eventually," he continued, waving his hand. "It's just... well, you made quite an impression last semester. And, as you know, many died during the horde attack. There's a group of students and parents who are upset about that even still."

"You mean when you falsely imprisoned my family and blamed us for something we didn't do? Something that Sabine Everleigh is being questioned for right now?"

"They will tire of this eventually, Miss Swan. In the meantime, I suggest you lay low and let this die down. If you create more problems, how will others think of you? Of your family? It's time to be the bigger person, even if you feel you are being wronged. Do you not call yourself a righteous cultivator? You don't want to do something you will regret later."

Who was he to talk about righteousness or justice?

Kitty stood up. "If anything happens to my family, you're the one who's going to have regrets."

"...Is that a threat, Miss Swan?"

"Oh, no. Of course not," she said. "They're just words. Right?"

"FUCK YEAH, IT WAS A THREAT!"

"Kitty, language!"

"Sorry, Māma," she grumbled, serving Jax another heaping serving of tabbouleh. "But can you believe what he said to me? That...that pickle dick!"

"Calm down. That weird vein in your forehead is popping out, and you look like a psycho," Jax told her.

Noelle slumped in her chair. She already regretted not following Kitty to the chancellor's office that afternoon. She was preoccupied, and frankly, with all those self-help and anger-management books her sister read over the summer, she figured Kitty had the emotional toolbox to handle confrontation better. Apparently not.

Noelle hadn't liked the signs either. Who would? Not only were they poorly made, but the handwriting had been horrible, and so was the grammar—the messaging was just...God, so unoriginal! What was the purpose? Did they really think the Swans would see the signs and actually go home? Her parents were doing important research. *She* was doing important research. Noelle had made more headway into this feral illness stuff in a few months than any of their scientists had in the years they spent studying the monsters!

The Swans didn't need Northeastern. Northeastern, and the shadowborn in general, needed the Swans.

"Why are none of you upset?" Kitty demanded.

Because we're not children, Noelle thought to herself. "Kitty, you really should calm down. All this stress isn't good for your health. Besides, you never cared if people liked you. Why does it matter now?"

"I don't give a... I don't care if they *like* me. It's just not fair, is all!" Ah. So mature. "You can't just go around waving around signs with racial slurs and get away with it!" Kitty turned to her parents. "I bet the chancellor would listen to you. March into his office and say something!"

"Did you try the falafel?" Bàba asked. "It's fala-fabulous!"

It really was. Noelle scooped another on her plate, drizzling tzatziki sauce on it. She could dip anything in tzatziki and it would taste amazing. "You really outdid yourself."

"You did," Māma agreed.

"We've been suffering Mā's cooking for too long," Jax added.

"Um, are you all ignoring me right now?" Kitty screeched.

Noelle hated when her sister made that noise—insufferable. "Kitty, we aren't ignoring you—"

"*I'm* trying to."

"Shut up, you little twerp. No one asked you," Kitty snapped.

"You literally just asked me a question! Mā, she called me a twerp again!"

"Oh, gonna cry to Mommy?"

"Shut up!" He shoved her.

"*You* shut up!"

"Sit down, both of you!" Noelle admonished. She was enjoying dinner far too much to deal with her siblings, and if they fought, the dishes would be put in jeopardy. Otherwise, their arguments were sources of endless amusement. "We can discuss this like adults, can't we? Kitty, you're nineteen. And Jax, you're now seventeen. Stay calm. We're a family, right? We need to have a united front."

"Fine," Kitty hissed. "Fine. Y'all can ignore me all you like, but I will not stop being upset about this. I don't understand why none of you care."

"It's not that we don't care," Noelle said reasonably, which was true. The signs had been uncomfortable to read, and she hated the fact that they were created. But the message wasn't anything new. The Swans hadn't exactly been welcomed last semester; they'd been tolerated. Kitty was coddled by her friend group, who accepted her easily. Noelle worked in the lab, and none of the workers hid their animosity toward the Swans.

Sure, Noelle was pissed when she saw the signs. But after seeing her parents' lack of reaction, she realized that was the correct path. Meanwhile, Kitty looked unhinged. No one would listen to her when she was so high-strung, so angry. It was childish, really.

And Noelle was always the more mature one, after all. Despite being younger, she always managed to keep it together.

"I'm not going to calm down. If anything, y'all should anger up," Kitty said.

Noelle sighed, exasperated. "That doesn't even make sense."

"Kitty, what do we always say?" Bàba asked.

"Don't bite my brother?"

"Well, yes. But I'm talking about the other thing. These shadowborn are not immortal. They will all die," he said calmly. "There is no use fussing over them. In the grand scheme of things, this is merely a small disturbance. A test of how we overcome hurdles. Compared to the Heavenly Tribulations, which is more painful?"

"Getting struck by lightning wasn't pleasant," Kitty admitted, "but this is a different kind of...situation."

Māma shook her head. "Kitty, you must practice patience. I am positive that these shadowborn are merely ignorant. Once they learn more about us, they will see."

"What if they don't, though? Why should I wait and risk you getting harassed?"

"What's the alternative? Kicking all their asses? That'll certainly show them!" Jax said sarcastically, with a mouth full of food. "If you fight back, you're proving them right. Just ignore it. Isn't that how you're supposed to handle bullies?"

Kitty rolled her eyes. "Have I taught you nothing? You handle bullies by publicly humiliating and/or beating them so badly they never cross you again."

"You're really the poster child for a healthy mindset, you know that?"

"We get it, you're an angsty teenager. The sarcasm isn't necessary."

"Māma, did you hear what she just said to me?"

"Both of you, stop it. We are trying to enjoy a nice family meal," Māma said. "You are ruining it. We have much to celebrate. We are reunited, we have a nice apartment, good jobs, good food..."

"I'm not hungry," Kitty said, pushing away from the table. At least she had the manners to clear her plate and put it away before storming off, though it kind of took the edge off it. "If none of you are going to do anything about this, then I will. On my own."

She slammed the door behind her.

Noelle could say a lot of things about her older sister, but the girl knew how to make a dramatic exit. "Should I follow her?"

"Let her calm down first. She needs some sleep," Bàba advised, his brows drawn together. "I will make some congee. You take it to her so she can eat it later. She didn't eat much. She will be hungry."

"Yes, Bà."

"You kids need to look out for each other, okay?" Māma said. She was, of course, speaking more so to Noelle than Jax. Noelle was the smart sibling, the dependable and mature one. Jax had no emotional control, and Kitty? She might as well have been a box of explosives. Hence why she had stormed out. She really needed to practice her impulse control and emotional management for the sake of becoming an adult. Hell, if she wanted to be immortal, she needed to focus more on Taoism than fighting. Cultivation was more than a quest for physical power—the true purpose was enlightenment. And how did Kitty expect to become enlightened when she pulled stuff like this? Walking away from arguments, slamming doors, yelling at chancellors. It was all so juvenile.

Māma and Bàba were correct; the protests weren't a big deal. Who were the shadowborn? Insignificant, short-lived beings whose lives would mean nothing. The Swans, on the other hand? They were important. They would make an impact on the world, for the better—Noelle was certain of it.

Of course, she wasn't completely stupid. She knew that, should the protests get worse, they could pose a problem. Maybe Kitty had a point. If only her execution had more finesse.

Machiavelli wrote that people should either be caressed or crushed. Noelle wasn't interested in caressing *anyone*, especially not these weakling shadowborn. But if their actions crossed the line?

Well, she'd be more than happy to crush them.

IN FRANCE, Veronica had woken up naturally every day, sunlight streaming through the windows. All she'd had to do was text the kitchen when she woke up, and an assistant would bring her breakfast in bed while she watched *Gossip Girl*. The floor tiles were heated, not necessary in the summer, and a big claw-foot bathtub sat pristine in the ensuite bathroom.

Waking up to her phone alarm, in a single-person dorm, was a stark difference.

Veronica groaned, turning over and shutting the damn thing off, letting it clatter to the floor. Without an audience, she let out a long, dramatic sigh and rolled out of bed. She landed on a cream shag rug, blinking awake. While she didn't have class until late morning, she'd agreed to meet with Kitty for breakfast and catch up. It would be a welcome distraction from wallowing in guilt, something Veronica had grown accustomed to. Being alone in her dorm didn't help things.

She got up, scrubbed her face, and brushed her hair. One thing she wholly believed in was looking good to feel good. For the first time since she'd begun college, when she looked in the mirror, she actually saw *herself*. Whether that was good or bad remained to be seen. On one hand, she wasn't blonde. She wasn't a replacement for Tessa Churchill, which Blake had so kindly informed her last semester was the only reason he approached her in the first place. Veronica was a redhead again, glowing from her spray-on tan and various skin treatments she'd got while staying with Grandmere.

On the other hand, she was the same on the inside. The same girl Blake humiliated, the same girl who'd failed Rory...

His name hit her like a ton of bricks when she *thought* about it. God. She brushed her teeth and made a beeline for her closet, throwing the double doors open. She chose a pink mini skirt and a tight tank top. She had a feeling Kitty would be dressed similarly, and she liked the thought of matching her friend.

Picking up her bag—a tiny and impractical purse only big enough to fit her cell phone—she left for the lobby. Kitty was there, already waiting. She always looked effortless, despite the fact she put thought into coordinating her outfits. With her hair down and a skirt so tiny it could have been a belt, she leaned against the window. The way the light hit her eyes, they looked almost metallic, like coins.

"Hey." Kitty grinned. "Ready?"

"Mm. Yeah." Veronica linked arms with her.

"How are you doing?" Her tone was light, but there was an undertone of seriousness. She didn't need to mention Rory—Veronica understood what she meant.

With anyone else, she would have lied. It had become a bad habit, at this point; she lied to her therapist, to her parents, to... Well, those were the only people who asked. She didn't have many other friends.

Perhaps that was why she felt the need to be honest. "I still have nightmares about the attack. And...Rory. It's hard, you know? I can't stop thinking about it. Some days are better than others."

The words spilled out of her, but thankfully they weren't followed by tears.

Kitty nodded. "I'm sorry I've been MIA. The whole phone thing, I just...was not a great friend."

"No, I unplugged, too. And I was abroad." Veronica wouldn't have wanted to talk about it, anyway. It took a long time to process what happened, and even still, she couldn't quite remember how it went down. Rory was gone, and Veronica was powerless to help him during the attack because she was just a magician. Magicians weren't as powerful as shadowborn, and her magic severely limited her. Spells required ingredients, time, and concentration.

Veronica always thought, on some level, she could fight just as well as the shadowborn. They fought with weapons primarily, but magicians could cast protection spells. They could heal to some extent, and they could cause explosions with the right ingredients. But it was hard to concentrate and mix herbs when zombie monsters were attacking you.

The horde attack was a rude awakening on many levels. Losing Rory was the worst, indisputably. But realizing Veronica wasn't as strong as she thought? It terrified her.

"I'm just trying to keep an open mind this semester," Veronica said. "I really want to buckle down and study. I've been practicing spells all summer, and it's time to see what I can do, you know?"

Kitty nodded. "Do you ever think about what we did, and wonder—"

"No. We did nothing wrong. The lures didn't work. Sabine is the one who messed with them; she's the one who caused the horde attack, God knows why."

"Yeah. Yeah, you're right." But she didn't sound convinced.

"What class do you have today?" Veronica asked, changing the subject.

"Magic History I. I've never been a huge history person. Or, like, a school person. But we'll see."

"Hey, I think Mel's in that class. We hung out yesterday and she mentioned she has to retake it."

The girls walked into the cafeteria, already bustling with students. They picked up trays and surveyed the breakfast offerings, though they were more or less the same every day. Veronica picked up a fruit parfait, and Kitty went straight for the eggs and sausage. The platters were laid out in a self-serve table, separate from the stations where the food was cooked fresh right then and there. As she filled her tray, she paused, holding up the line.

Veronica followed her eyes to a small sign, taped right above the sausage tray. Printed on a piece of computer paper was a photo of a pug and a huge x over it. In block letters, it read, "We Don't Serve Dog Meat."

"Ew. Why would they put that up?" Obviously the school didn't serve dog meat. Maybe one of the students stuck it to the wall. Still, to print out a photo, most likely from the computer lab, and bring it here? A bit excessive.

Veronica was prepared to leave and pay, but Kitty stared at the sign like she wanted to set it on fire with her eyes.

"Hey, keep moving," a student said from behind her.

That snapped Kitty out of it. She tore the sign down, crumpling it in her fist. "What the fuck?"

"I know. Weird stuff—" Veronica began.

"First the protesting, and now this," she muttered, obviously upset. About the sign?

"Is everything okay, Kitty?"

"No." She stormed over and threw out the sign. Abandoning her tray on one of the tables, she stomped over to the cork board on the side of the cafeteria. There was another sign, similar to the first. She snatched it down and ripped it into four pieces.

"Hey, you really shouldn't leave your tray unattended like that," Veronica warned. "Someone might take it. These students are ruthless when it comes to food."

"I can't believe someone would put a sign up like that," Kitty bit out.

"Yeah, well, people are freaks. Even at magic school." *Especially* at magic school.

"Do you really not understand?"

"What?"

"The racist connotations," she said, exasperated.

It took a moment for Veronica to connect the dots. "You think this is aimed at you? Because Chinese people eat dogs?"

"For the love of—we do not eat dogs!"

"I wasn't saying you do," Veronica said slowly. "Look, it's just a sign. And I doubt it's aimed at you. Someone probably just put it up as a lame joke. You're one of, like, three thousand students here. And there was no guarantee you'd even see that. It's just a coincidence."

"I don't think it is," Kitty said stubbornly. "My parents weren't concerned about the protesting, and neither was Chancellor Kinsey. But you know what? I *know* I'm right. I was right about that, and I'm right about this. Something has to be done, and if no one else is going to do it, then I will."

SIX

HER HYPOTHESIS HAD BEEN DISPROVEN ONCE and for all: history class was boring, regardless of whether magic was involved. Kitty nearly fell asleep in her first class, which was yet another thing mortal schools and magic schools had in common: the teachers didn't take kindly to bored students. At Northeastern, they seemed personally invested...in making her life a living hell.

And if Kitty thought Professor Whatshisname was bad (she could not read his chicken scratch handwriting on the board!), Professor Ugly Pashmina (Professor Hamilton) was worse. Beastblood Anatomy and Physiology should have been interesting, but the woman could not stop going on tangents. Kitty didn't give a crap whether the mating rituals of mortal wolves and trueblood werewolves were similar. She just wanted to take the syllabus and leave!

By her afternoon combat class, however, she perked up a bit. Finally, a freakin' break!

Professor Ainsworth laid out the rules and safety instructions first. They were in one of the gymnasiums, but it looked more like a padded room you'd find in a mental asylum. Fitting, since this school was driving her insane.

Ainsworth wasn't too bad, though. He was a muscular man, broad-shouldered and tall, with a warm, deep skin tone and big brown eyes. He moved with grace that belied his size, and she could tell from his gait that he could fight.

After the whole safety spiel, they were partnered up. Kitty's partner was a shadowborn who could've given Bella Lugosi a run for his money. She wasn't sure if it was the widow's peak or the paper pale skin, or the fact that his popped collar looked vampiric. The bulging muscles he sported spoke to hours at the gym, and he loomed over her.

The rules of the sparring match were simple: if you pinned your opponent to the count of five, you won. Two groups were assigned to a mat, and those who weren't fighting were refereeing.

Kitty looked around at the other guys assigned to her mat: all bodybuilders, apparently. Normally, she wouldn't have minded being the only girl amongst three beefcakes. She swore she'd had a dream just like this...

Except, of course, it had a very different ending. A happy one, some might have said.

The meaty fist came at her head before the whistle blew. Kitty ducked, rolling to the side with her fists up. Buff Dracula might have been strong, but he wasn't fast. As they circled each other, Kitty picked up a few things: his footwork was sloppy, he spent too much time staring her dead in the eyes, and his muscles restricted his range of motion. He couldn't dodge very well, not even her feigned punches, nor did he truly understand momentum when he attempted to grapple her to the ground. And apparently, he had zero stamina. After just a few minutes, he looked faint.

Yeah, definitely not like her dream.

Kitty had him on the ground in seconds of deciding to end the fight. She didn't care to show off, sending him flat on his back with a punch and pinning him beneath her. Cyrus was much more fun as an opponent—even in the beginning, he'd put up more of a fight than this!

But when she looked to the other two guys, who were supposed to count so the match could end, they merely stared at her and said nothing. Really? So that's how they were going to play it?

"Tell your friends to call it," Kitty told the guy she was seated on.

He turned his head, spitting on the mat. How unsanitary.

"Don't be a sore loser," she admonished. "I'm warning you now, I had the chili dog with beans for lunch. I can sit here all day, pal."

The threat of farts worked like a charm, and he called for his buddies to declare her the winner.

Once he was freed, he scowled and stalked off to the sidelines. Weren't they in college?

"You didn't need to goad him like that," one of the other guys told her. "He was already embarrassed."

The sarcastic quip was on the tip of her tongue, but she remembered that she was trying to be a better person, so she bit her tongue.

"It's your turn to spar, then," she replied, heading off the mat. The rest of class passed quickly, and as she was about to head out, Professor Ainsworth called her over. She stayed back while the remaining students filed out, some giving her dirty looks. For what reason? Because she won a match? It wasn't her fault she was so strong and talented.

"Kitty Swan. I've heard a lot about you," Professor Ainsworth begin, which didn't bode well for her. But, surprisingly, he said, "You were great today. I'm looking forward to seeing more of your skills. I have a feeling you will be an asset to my class, maybe teach my students a thing or two about combat."

"Really?" Kitty asked.

He nodded. "I had the privilege of seeing your mother in action when the horde attacked. I know your parents are skilled warriors. Listen, if you need anything, don't hesitate to come to me. I know things at school might be strange, and there are some who...don't want you here. Don't let them get to you. The shadowborn aren't the most inclusive bunch, but if you're strong, they'll respect that. Eventually."

She grinned. "I will. Thanks, Professor. I guess I'll see you next time!"

"Yes, you will."

He waved her off, and she left. Well, at least she had one professor who liked her.

NOELLE WAS the first to arrive to the classroom, being fifteen minutes early. She settled in a seat by the door, unpacking her things: a sparkly purple notebook, two pens in black and red, an audio recorder, and flashcards. After lining everything up on the small desk attached to a metal chair, she second-guessed her seating choice. She moved to the back, because she didn't want to seem like a try hard. Then, toward the door, because she wanted to leave quickly. But if she got up and left immediately after the lecture, would that leave a poor impression? She ended up right in the center of the room. Not perfectly—there were six rows of seats, the even number making it impossible for her to be dead center. But it was close enough.

She stopped fussing when the first student arrived, turning on the lights. Noelle felt foolish, then—she should have done that. The sunshine pouring in from the windows brightened the room enough already, so she hadn't thought of it.

Noelle flashed the girl a smile, but she wasn't paying attention. She slumped in the back and pulled out her phone, playing some music video with no headphones on. Other students trickled in, but most of the class came a minute or two before the official start time. And, conspicuously, the seats around Noelle were the last to be taken.

She didn't think much of it. Tried not to, anyway. No matter how many stories Kitty told her or how many teen movies she watched, Noelle never experienced any sort of schooling. She kept her mind open; she had to, otherwise she'd over-analyze everything. A little too late for that though.

The thought struck her as rather strange, considering she'd never been the type to worry before. That's not to say she *never* felt concerned, but the churning in her stomach and the quick beat of her heart was markedly different from anything she experienced in the past.

It didn't feel good.

You taught yourself English, she reminded herself. *You know more about history, literature, and the arts than Kitty and Jax combined, and they both attended middle school and high school. You can do this.*

But the affirmation failed to soothe her, for some reason.

Blake Blackwood's entrance interrupted her train of thought. The blonde glanced at her with a grin and winked, but Noelle didn't react at all. She didn't like the guy and felt no need to hide the fact, especially when he clearly didn't like her either. He showed off and flirted with every woman on campus, even the custodians and cafeteria staff. When it came to Noelle? Nothing. Sure, he'd just winked. But they were in a classroom filled with other students. Alone, he would have ignored her, she was certain.

She had a total of two conversations with Blake, and she understood exactly what type of person he was. Hollow, shallow, and selfish. He knew what he was and didn't hide it, didn't have to, because he was blonde, conventionally attractive, and wealthy. He probably got everything he ever wanted, and then some.

Blake reminded Noelle of Kitty's ex-boyfriend, Tyler, whose popularity and charm made him the most desirable guy in high school. According to Kitty. But Noelle always thought he looked like a Ken doll, plastic and manufactured. Blake was notably better looking, but what he had done to Veronica was far worse than anything Tyler had done to Kitty.

Blake plopped down in the last seat available, next to Noelle. "I didn't expect to see you here."

"This is a freshman course."

"No. Most students take it the first year, but it's not a prerequisite to anything," he corrected. "It's just an elective."

"A freshman elective."

He shrugged and looked at her desk. "Don't you have a laptop? What's with the notebook, Tree Killer?"

"I prefer paper notes. They help me remember what I've learned," she said defensively. "And if we're talking about who makes a worse environmental impact, I'm fairly certain your hairspray has killed more wildlife than my single notebook."

"Harsh."

A girl sitting in front of Noelle turned around and glared. "I like your hair, Blake."

"Thanks, babe."

"Are we still on for our date tomorrow night?"

"Yeah. Just text me a reminder."

He's the worst, Noelle thought. *I bet he doesn't even remember her name.*

The girl smiled. "Looking forward to it."

"Alright, class." The professor walked in, saving Noelle from having to listen to Blake flirting. Professor Evans couldn't have been taller than her 5'3", with a ring of matted chestnut brown hair around a bald head and blue eyes. He wore a brown tweed jacket—an utter stereotype—and black slacks, with his shirt not fully tucked in. "Let's get started. Here, you pass around the syllabus. I assume you are all literate—I hope so, anyway. This is 'The History of Shadowborn', a course not for the indolent. I expect your undivided attention when I am speaking. Anything less is unacceptable and will be treated as such.

"Do not mistake this class for your typical, coddling history lesson. Here, we delve into the complex and often grim narrative of the Shadowborn: a saga steeped in darkness, power, and the relentless pursuit of knowledge. Lateness, absenteeism, lackluster participation? These are not just frowned upon; they are *condemned* in my class. You will be prompt, present, and prepared, or you will find yourself out of my course. It's as simple as that. Do I make myself clear, Mr. Blackwood?"

Blake leaned back in his chair. "Sure thing. Pleasure to see you again, Evans."

Professor Evans's eyes narrowed. "I cannot say the same, Mr. Blackwood. I pray to God every night, at my dinner table, that you will finally pass this course and get out of my hair once and for all."

"Let's just hope I do pass this time. By the look of things, you won't be able to use that expression for much longer."

Noelle choked on air. A few other students around her laughed.

"Is something amusing to you, Miss?" Professor Evans asked sharply, turning his attention to Noelle.

"No, not at all. Sir," she stammered, straightening.

"What is your name?"

"Noelle. Noelle Swan."

"Do not lie." He rifled through his folder and found the attendance sheet. "You are Elena Suzuki, aren't you?"

A tall blonde girl in the back shyly raised her hand. "Actually, I'm Elena."

"You're not Asian," he argued.

"My dad is Japanese and my mom is German—"

"Show me your student ID," he demanded, turning back to Noelle. "I don't like liars."

"God, they're not lying," Blake interjected, shockingly annoyed. What, did he want to get into Elena's good graces or something? "Aren't you supposed to be teaching us stuff? What does this even matter? You don't want to waste time going over the syllabus, but you'll accuse students of being dishonest about their *names*?"

"Mr. Blackwood, if this young lady is lying about her name just to get out of trouble, I have the right to know."

"Get in trouble for what? I made a balding joke, and others laughed," Blake challenged.

Noelle, her hands shaking, took out her phone and showed the professor her digital ID. "See? My name is Noelle Swan."

Professor Evans looked at the ID. "Why?"

"What?"

"Why is your surname 'Swan'?" he asked. "One thing I teach, and it's important you all know this, is history. The origins of the shadowborn. We have a rich culture, a long past filled with struggles, oppression, and advancements. I am proud to be shadowborn. Why aren't you proud to be...whatever you are?"

She had no idea how to answer that politely. But he was her teacher, and she needed to pass the course, lest she end up like Blake. "It's not that I'm, uh, not proud of being Chinese. But I didn't choose my last name. My uncle actually helped my parents come to America, and *his* surname is Xuan, which kind of sounds like Swan, so when he was going the immigration paperwork—"

"Stop. I understand. I'll have you know that I value integrity very much," Professor Evans said. "If *you* don't respect your origins, why should I?"

"Integrity?" Blake interrupted. "You were put on a leave of absence last year because you called Professor Ainsworth the n-word. Over email, which makes it objectively worse."

"Get out of my classroom, both of you. I think you need some time to cool down. I don't want to see you back here until you've learned some respect."

Blake scoffed, shoving his laptop into his bag. Noelle was too stunned to move. She'd never been kicked out of a classroom before. She'd never been *to* a class before.

Noticing her lack of movement, Blake put her things in her backpack and nudged her toward the door. Elena Suzuki, despite not getting kicked out, trailed behind them.

The door slammed shut, finally snapping Noelle out of her trance. Shame dyed her cheeks, and she wasn't sure whether she wanted to cry or beg the professor for forgiveness.

She wouldn't make a big deal of this, and unlike Kitty, Noelle could handle a few mean comments. They didn't bother her. But there was another part of her that was angry, so much so that she felt she would explode if she didn't expel it.

So she rounded on Blake. "Why did you do that? You got us expelled!"

"Expelled? Hardly," he scoffed. "I was doing you a favor, Noelle. How about a 'thank you'?"

"Thank you? For what?" she hissed. "I don't need *any* favors, least of all from you! Do you know how humiliating that was for me? Now all anyone in class is going to remember about me is...is..."

"Is that Professor Evans is still working here despite his inappropriate comments about students and faculty?" Blake supplied.

Elena, who had been watching their little spat, finally spoke up. "Um, does the blonde hair really make me not look Japanese? Because my stylist said—"

"No one gives a shit about your hair," Noelle told her. To Blake, she said, "I'm not a damsel in distress, and I don't need you to save me. I don't need your pity, either. So why don't you do us both a favor and leave me alone?"

"Fine," Blake said, his voice clipped. "I was trying to do something nice, but if you want to go back there and kiss his ass, be my guest. Kitty, though? She would have *kicked* his ass before I even had the chance to say anything."

Noelle was already furious. But mentioning her older sister? She couldn't explain it, but picturing Kitty waltzing into the classroom and taking care of things was somehow much worse. Her stomach twisted in knots, and she felt the increasing need to throw up.

"I'm not like my sister," she said firmly. "I'm not a bitch."

"Really?" Blake laughed. "Could've fooled me."

SEVEN

JUDGING by the rotting corpse on the metal slab, this really *wasn't* a date. Kitty hated herself for feeling disappointed, but at least this gave them something to talk about other than their relationship.

"Thanks for giving me a face mask," she said, looping the medical mask over her ears. "He's fresh."

"Good job, Sherlock," Cyrus replied.

"Anytime, Watson."

She moved around the table of the morgue, a mostly defunct wing in the basement of the old science building. Cyrus uncovered the body so it lay naked, with a Y-shaped stitch on its chest and stomach from the autopsy. The young man was around her age, with a blonde buzz-cut that was partially grown out and a nose slightly too small for his face. His skin had a gray quality to it, almost making him look alien.

"He's in the active decay stage of decomposition," Cyrus explained to her, his voice muffled by the medical mask he wore. The medical examiner in the corner nodded along, though she wasn't really listening, instead playing Candy

Crush on her phone. "There are five basic stages: initial decay, bloating, active decay, advanced decay, and dry remains. When we found him, he was in the bloating stage. But he was covered in feral goo, so I think that messed with the decomp process. He's not as bloated anymore, and since we're in the chill room, there aren't any insects or maggots."

"He stinks, though."

"An eloquent way to put it."

Cy was a pre-med student, so she wasn't surprised by the fact that he knew so much about this. She had no idea what he wanted her to say, though. Outside of ferals, she hadn't seen a corpse like this, nor had she studied anything about forensics.

"Has he been identified?" she asked.

"Not yet. We didn't find a wallet or anything on him, but the Northeastern sweatshirt and the fact that he was in the Veil makes me think he was shadowborn."

"Is there no way to tell?"

"No," the medical examiner chimed in, not concealing the boredom in her voice. "We tried to sequence their DNA, but the sample was corrupted by the feral goo the body was covered in. We haven't had any conclusive results."

"The scientific term we're using for the feral goo is, in fact, goo?" Kitty asked.

"Well, we were originally calling it spunk, but it was pointed out to us that there are certain connotations with that word. I haven't been laid since this whole feral business started, so it didn't occur to me."

"Got it." She turned to Cyrus. "Did Everleigh ask you to investigate this?"

"No. He told me not to, actually. The school is going to handle it."

"And you're disobeying orders? *You*?" she mocked,

bringing a hand to her chest. "Don't tell me you're turning into a deviant, Mr. Ward."

"If I am, it's your fault."

"Oh, I can hardly take credit for this. But you know, I don't really go for the bad boy type."

"Is that so?" he asked, and even though a mask obscured the lower half of his face, she could tell he was fighting a smile. "What's your type, then?"

Oh. Dangerous. "Hot. Sweet, with a pinch of saltiness. Crispy on the outside with a gooey center. Lots of chocolate, maybe a touch of spice."

"Are you describing a chocolate-chip cookie?"

"You were asking about my dessert preferences, weren't you?"

"If you two are going to flirt, maybe I should just put the corpse back in the metal storage bin," the medical examiner said dryly.

"We're not flirting," the pair replied simultaneously.

"We're just witty," Cyrus said defensively.

"You can hardly blame us for having good banter," Kitty sniffed.

"Yeah, whatever." The medical examiner wasn't paid enough to intervene between two horny college students.

Kitty's eyes swept over the corpse again. She hadn't meant to get distracted. "So you found this body in the Veil, in a nest of Blood Wasps. The queen was sitting on it, but the cause of death is unable to be determined."

"The insides were pretty rotted, similar to how the feral disease leaves shadowborn. But outwardly, it doesn't show signs of the illness," Cyrus explained. "Usually, when shadowborn contract the illness, they leak the goo and die. They rot pretty rapidly, too, even before they kick the bucket."

"You think this guy infected the wasps?" Kitty asked.

"Logically no. Blood Wasps, even the non-feral ones, drink blood and eat organs out from the mouth. They would have drained this guy dry and left him a husk. But either he entered the nest—which would usually mean a death sentence—or they brought him back."

"Wow. Thanks for giving me yet another reason not to go into the Veil. Okay, so let's say the Blood Wasps *do* try to feed on him. But the kid is infected. The wasps turn feral, and they return to the nest and infect the colony."

"But the disease shouldn't have acted so quickly. Even in the fastest cases, it's taken five hours minimum for a feral to become infectious."

"You said the entire colony was feral. Let's just assume the disease has mutated, and the incubation period is minutes. So the kid is infected. The Blood Wasps find him and pull his organs out of his mouth—disgusting, by the way—and they get infected, too. You wouldn't have known in the autopsy because his insides were already rotted, which could be thanks to the feral illness. They have to get infected within the first bite or so, since ferals aren't infectious after death. They bring the body back to the hive for some reason and infect the rest of the colony. You said the wasps you saw had limbs torn off and stuff?"

"That could have been due to general decay. Most ferals look worse for wear."

"Or it could signify a fight. The disease spreads through the magic spunk."

"I told you, we don't call it spunk anymore," the medical examiner said.

"Well, now that you've told me it was once called spunk, I will not stop calling it that," Kitty said, very maturely. "It sounds like you already figured all this out, Cy. And for what you don't know—how the disease mutated, why the kid was out there in the first place—I can't think of answers."

"I know. I just...can you sense anything from the body?" he asked. "Anything that might be in your wheelhouse?"

"Anything to do with qi, you mean?"

He nodded.

"Only living things emit qi. The dead have demonic energy." Something Kitty wasn't supposed to be messing with. "I don't have to use my powers to know that this corpse is radiating demonic energy."

"Can you draw out a core? Like your mom did for those feral beastbloods?"

"I...I don't know. My mom drew out a beast core from the hydra we killed. It was filled with dark energy, though, not qi. If an autopsy was performed, you would have found one."

"Not if they didn't know where to look."

Kitty shut her eyes. "You know, cutting open a decaying body to find a ball of concentrated demonic energy is not very romantic."

"My apologies. I'll make it up to you later." Cyrus wheeled a metal tray of tools over and slid on a pair of thick black rubber gloves. The medical examiner didn't seem to care that they were going to cut open the body again, though she put her phone away and watched with steely grey eyes as Cy prepared himself.

Kitty had touched a lot of gross things in her life. Her ex-boyfriend's penis, for example, right after football practice. Ew. She'd come in contact with plenty of ferals, too, but those were always beastbloods. They weren't human. As much as she hated to think of herself as weak, her stomach churned as she looked at the boy's face, stiff in death. So young, so... mortal.

It was strange to her, since she would be immortal someday—the idea that you could be alive one moment and dead the next, reduced to an object that took the shape of a human without any of the qualities of one.

Cyrus didn't have the same reservations; as a pre-med student, he'd told her that he elected to watch several autopsies last year as part of his curriculum. Kitty looked away as he opened the body up. The smell permeated the mask, making her eyes water.

"Would it be in the stomach?" Cyrus asked, his voice not betraying his emotions.

"It forms slightly above the belly button," she said. "But if the wasps ate some of the organs, it might have moved..."

She heard squelching. He was digging for it. She gagged.

"I could have been at the pool."

"You could have," Cyrus agreed. "It's hard, right?"

"Yeah. Depending on how far along it's come, it can vary in size."

"You have one too, right? How big is yours?"

"My golden core? It's about the size of a marble. Most human ones aren't that big." That was why getting a crack in it was such a big deal. She couldn't actually see it, couldn't get surgery on it—not when one dealt with magic. The only way she healed it, slowly, was by meditating and not exposing herself to more demonic energy.

Clearly, she wasn't doing a great job with the latter.

"I think I got it," he said. His hand popped out of the body and, between his gloved fingers, was a dark, marble-shaped glass orb of black smoke.

The lights overhead strobed, swinging erratically. Kitty

stumbled back in surprise, eyes wide as a cracking sound echoed through the room. The corpse bolted upright, the sheet falling to the ground. It grabbed the demonic core from Cyrus's hands, who was so shocked he stayed stock still.

A few things ran through Kitty's mind at that point:

1. Holy shit, that's a moving corpse!
2. Seriously, when did my life turn into a horror movie?
3. I should probably do something about this.

What could she do, one might ask?

Punch it. Punch it until it stopped moving. That seemed to be the solution for a lot of problems, whether one wanted to admit it or not.

Kitty grabbed its shoulder, noting how squishy the flesh felt beneath her bare fingers. Yeah, she was going to need a bleach bath later. Ugh. When her fist sank into its face, it literally sank, the skull collapsing in like jelly. The next moment, she was against the cooler doors, held by the throat. The lights began to strobe faster, her head pounding from the combination of the flashing and the force of being thrown against hard metal. Kitty considered herself fairly tall, but her feet didn't touch the ground as the corpse lifted her up, his concave head tilting. Its chest and stomach were still open, so blackened organs spilled from it, the flaps of flesh from the opening hanging loosely down. Despite its soft body, its grip was strong on her neck, cutting off her air supply. Its jaw, mostly intact, moved up and down, as if it were trying to speak. Due to the damage she'd done with her fist, no sounds came out.

Kitty grabbed its arm, her nails digging into it as she kicked the corpse hard. The arm tore off and the rest of the body flew across the room, landing with a wet thud. Kitty crashed to the ground, gasping for air through the mask and choking.

The lights finally stabilized, flooding the room. Cyrus was at her side in an instant, peeling the arm from her neck and tossing it aside. He stripped off the rubber gloves, putting a hand on her shoulder. "Kitty! God. Are you okay?"

Not a chance.

Kitty's gaze traveled across the room to the corpse, now a steaming pile of feral goo mixed with pure white ash in wet chunks across the tile floor. The medical examiner pressed herself against the wall, eyes nearly bugging out of her head.

Kitty looked down at herself, covered in dark blood and a few chunks of offal quickly turning to ash and crusting the fabric of her clothes.

"Well," she said finally, her voice faint, "do you think this is going to stain my skirt?"

BITCHES SHOULD HAVE BEEN EASIER to bully. Ryder assumed Kitty Swan would be like every other skank he came across—they could dole out unfair treatment but couldn't take it themselves. Unfortunately, it seemed his efforts were too insignificant for her to care. He didn't have many friends on campus, but money could buy him a few allies. It was easy to spread the word about the newest bitch on the block. The rumor mill would make his work seem effortless, but the skank refused to shed a tear. Hell, he got a group of girls to moo when she passed, and she looked at them like they were crazy!

Maybe he wasn't good at harassing others. Did that mean

he was a good person? He was too tired to figure it out. He stayed up late studying teen movies to figure out the best way to break her, but it seemed his research was for naught. Nothing he'd done so far elicited any sort of response. It wasn't as if he wanted to do these things, but her complete lack of emotion was infuriating. It only fueled his belief that she needed to be taken down a peg.

Which was why he found himself on the floor outside her dorm room in the early hours of the morning. He hadn't slept all night and was running on pure caffeine, but the payoff would be worth it. He made sure the security cameras weren't working before getting to work on her door. He knew there was a way to get to her—he just had to find something important to her and exploit it. After observing her for the past week, which was a nicer way to say he began stalking her, he made several observations:

1. Kitty lived with her sister.
2. Kitty cared about her siblings.
3. She also cared about her hair.
4. She almost had a breakdown at the sound of a text message coming through.

The other day, on the campus green, as she walked by, a ringtone sounded. She flinched. He tested the theory by purposely walking by and having his texts go off. The same thing happened, only this time she dropped her bag. For whatever reason, this startled her. It was a small detail, one most people would overlook, but Ryder noticed it.

If you wanted to break someone, you needed to destroy what they loved. So he would.

But first, he wanted to give her a message, clear as day, for everyone to see. He was no artist, but the red paint got his words across. "Go to Hell Communist Cunts" was admittedly uncreative and the handwriting wasn't his best, but hey. He could only do so much. The red letters were big enough to cover the entire door, and the paint was thick, so the message wouldn't wash off easily.

The faster he could get her out of Northeastern, the better it would be for everyone.

EIGHT

CYRUS HAD HER. Sitting on her abs, he pinned her wrists above her head with one hand and her throat with the other. Kitty wasn't bothered, lying beneath him like that. Her hair came loose from her elastic as they sparred, fanned out on the black mat.

"I met Dr. Woods," she said conversationally, as if she wasn't at his mercy. "She's a character, all right. And that's putting it nicely. Because I'm a nice person."

"Who?" Cyrus asked, still trying to catch his breath.

"Me," Kitty said, annoyed.

He snorted. "No, who is Dr. Woods?"

"You know, that feral researcher. The one Everleigh wanted me to talk to. I went to her office this morning and we had a long conversation about cultivation."

"Your parents were okay with that?"

"She's my mom's new boss," Kitty said. "Besides, I only reiterated what my parents already shared."

Originally, she wasn't very interested in talking about cultivation with yet another shadowborn researcher. But after the protest, the dog meat signs, and Chancellor Kinsey's complete refusal to acknowledge anything was wrong, she decided to take matters into her own hands. And, okay, the uptick in comments around campus and vandalism hadn't helped. Some asshole had crudely painted on her door; she'd had to clean it up before Noelle woke up and saw.

Normally, this type of childish bullying would mean kicking some ass. But after meditating on it and re-reading an annotated copy of *The Inner Garden: How to Manifest Happiness and Personal Growth*, she realized something. Maybe her parents were right, and the shadowborn were just ignorant. In that case, she *should* educate as many as she could, especially scientists who would be more willing to listen to reason, like Dr. Woods.

Kitty did a bit of research on the woman. She was involved in several projects at Northeastern and Southeastern, specializing in genetics studies, until recent years, when she shifted her attention to ferals. If anyone could convince the shadowborn world that the Swans weren't a threat, it would be Dr. Woods. And, admittedly, Kitty hoped to get more information about the moving corpse. She had nightmares about it, not that she'd ever admit it, and the whole thing was shrouded in secrecy.

"Did you get an ID on that corpse?" she asked Cyrus.

"No. The medical examiner took photos before it turned to ash, but so far we've got nothing. Nothing they'll tell *me*," he replied. His thumb subconsciously rubbed the side of her throat, feeling her steady pulse. He didn't squeeze, but his grip was firm.

"You think the school is deliberately keeping information from you?"

"No; Kinsey called in law enforcement to investigate. The SNPD."

"SNPD? Please don't tell me that stands for Supernatural Police Department."

"It's no secret truebloods are horrible at naming things," he said.

"You're right," she conceded. "How does the SNPD work?"

"They don't—not really. It's run by shadowborn, but truebloods have all the power. They prioritize cases where the discovery of the supernatural is risked, followed by the feral disease."

"Really? I'd think it would be the other way around." The disease was fatal, after all.

"Truebloods want to remain undetected in the mortal realm. They think if humans were to discover them, they'd be forced to go back to the Veil," Cyrus explained. "And no one wants to do that."

She understood why. The pollution in the Veil was horrible, and the beastbloods made it dangerous. "So the SNPD insisted on taking over this moving corpse case. They'll investigate at some capacity, right?"

"Think about it: no one's claimed the body, so there's no pressure from family members. I've been sworn to secrecy, and so have the other students who went on the hunt," he said. "This isn't an active threat, so while the SNPD has staked a claim over all the files and the investigation, it's mostly because they don't want anyone else digging into it."

But it *was* a threat. If Cyrus's theory was correct, then the feral disease had mutated and was able to spread much faster. Not only that, but shadowborns who became infected could potentially turn into zombies.

"You think they have something to do with it?" Kitty guessed.

Cyrus nodded slowly. "I've been thinking about this nonstop. How did the corpse get into the Veil? What was it doing, how did it get infected, who was it...? All these questions could be answered by chalking it up to a fluke, sure. But the likelihood of this being a huge coincidence, versus something intentional? Something fishy is going on."

"Intentional? Like, someone is experimenting with the disease?"

"Yes. It could be someone is trying to cure the disease. Or...using it for nefarious purposes."

"So basically, Resident Evil?"

"What?"

Kitty brought both her legs forward, clapping his ears with her feet. Surprised, Cyrus's grip weakened. She used this to her advantage, swinging her upper body up and freeing herself. She rolled to her feet, flipping her hair over her shoulder.

"Resident Evil. You know, the video games? Tyler used to be obsessed. Like, to the point where we'd be in his basement alone and he'd play on his PlayStation rather than make out with me."

"I think we've already established that he was an idiot."

"Totally," she agreed with a grin. "But I learned about the game. Basically, this company called the Umbrella Corporation makes this bioweapon that turns people into zombies 'cause they want to sell it to the government and make money off war."

Cyrus looked up at her from the mat until she reached out to help him up. His hand enveloped hers as she pulled him to his feet. But their fight wasn't over yet. He circled her, contemplating her words before replying. "Despite the differences between truebloods, there hasn't been a war in, what, a few centuries? Even if conflict started in the Veil, no doubt it would spread to the mortal realm, which would risk discovery. Truebloods don't want that, and frankly, with so many moving out of the Veil, there's not as much to fight over. Usually, it was land disputes or monarchies. Now, monarchies have been mostly dismantled or rendered politically powerless."

"I'm not saying the situation is exactly the same," Kitty said. "But money is a huge motivation for just about anyone. Even a trueblood. Let's say, though, that a scientist was trying to *cure* the disease. By accident, they ended up making it worse. Whatever the case may be, I don't think you should stop investigating."

He lunged for her, and they were locked in a grappling position once again. Their hands intertwined, and she struggled to keep her center of gravity as he forced her backwards. Her strength failed her completely, and she knew her powers were on the verge of flickering off, leaving her with diminished strength.

Cyrus managed to pin her to the mat again, this time face down. He held her wrists behind her back, his entire body weight pressed against her. With one hand, he swept her hair to the side and bent down. "Do you surrender?"

All of a sudden, she couldn't think straight. Maybe it was the fact that they'd been sparring for hours. Or it could be the part of her monthly cycle where she got...*antsy*, to put it politely. Or, most likely, it was because his proximity made her hyperaware of every place their bodies touched, and how much she liked it.

His lips ghosted the shell of her ear, and whether it was intentional or not, his hips pressed into her ass.

Silence stretched between them, and when she didn't reply, he asked again. His voice came out a bit rougher, breathier. "Do you surrender, Kitty?"

The rational part of her brain, growing quieter by the second, told her that this was bad. They were supposed to be friends, for God's sake! The horny part of her brain told her that she had zero interest in being rational, not when the most attractive guy she knew was practically humping her.

In the end, it was her pettiness that won out.

If you give in now, you lose.

Kitty Swan did not lose.

She slammed her head into his, the force of which was enough to help her free her wrists and flip him over, maneuvering her legs to give herself maximum leverage. She shot to her feet while he held his nose, bloodied from the collision.

Her breath came in pants, though she wasn't sure if it was from the exertion or from him. She preferred to think it was the former.

"I'm tired," she admitted. "Can we get something to eat? I bet they still have muffins in the cafeteria. We can go after you, like, stop bleeding."

Cyrus was silent, and for a moment she worried she seriously hurt him. But he let go of his nose and grabbed a towel by his water bottle. "Sure. Let me shower, and we can walk over."

He stood and wiped his face, not making eye contact. Was he mad? He'd never been upset with her for winning; he wasn't that type of guy. But something was the matter, and she had no idea what.

As he walked to the locker room, she tried to make sense

of what happened. She didn't know why she got so...whatever it was she got when he touched her. But it was distracting, and the last thing she wanted was to revisit their fling. Even if she suspected—judging by the hardness pressed into her backside earlier—that he was interested in a replay, too.

RYDER WEAVED through the hallway with a frown, remembering just how much he hated school. Especially a school his father ran. He felt trapped, and despite the number of cute girls roaming the halls—and guys, for that matter—he wanted to ride away on his motorcycle and put as much distance between himself and his father as possible.

He'd been too busy finding ways to harass Kitty Swan, observing (stalking) her every move. The more he observed, the more indifferent he felt toward her. First of all, she wore the shortest skirts known to mankind. Whenever she went to the pool, she sat in an inflatable tube with the world's tiniest bikini, like every other attention-starved skank, but worse. And after a quick Google search, he found a video of her dry-humping some guy at a party.

As if it weren't bad enough she was a total slut, she wasn't a very nice person, either. In the halls, she rarely smiled. She went to the main office again to complain about the wrong name on her ID one morning, and she tore down some sign in the cafeteria and ripped it up. Rude bitch.

He hated the way she walked, the way she talked, and the fact that he had to pay attention to her at all. He had his own life to live. At one point, he considered seducing her and dumping her—that would be the fastest way to get her out. But he couldn't stand the thought of having to interact with her. He already wanted to strangle her from watching her from afar.

Ryder opened the door to the main office. He pulled out a folder from his bag—he didn't want to leave a digital trail—and handed it to Liza, his father's secretary. The older woman had always been kind to him, even as a child, though he suspected being her boss' son had something to do with that.

"Oh, Ethan! Twice in one week. To what do I owe the pleasure?"

"Just doing some stuff for my old man." He flashed her a smile. "Can you make sure he gets this? Confidential stuff."

"Of course, hon. Anything for you," she chirped. "Hey, have you seen the school paper today? Dr. Woods published a very interesting article."

Had he seen it? He was the one who helped Dr. Woods *write* it. He turned down her offer for credit, though. He didn't need it traced back to him.

"There are free copies outside, right? I'll check it out. Thanks for the tip." Ryder left without saying goodbye, hurrying outside. He grabbed a paper on his way out and shoved it into his bag; he'd read it later. Right now, he wanted to get back to his dorm quickly and sleep. He needed it, badly. The Swan girl got up at the ass crack of dawn every morning for a run or a meditation session. Sometimes both.

He was in such a hurry, he nearly knocked another student to the ground as he exited the main building. He wasn't going to pay them much attention, until he heard the soft squeal of surprise. Definitely feminine.

He glanced at the girl on the ground, a redhead with emerald green eyes staring up at him. A slow smile spread across his face. "Well, well. If it isn't Veronica Halliwell."

"Ethan!" Veronica held out her hand and he helped her

up, picking up a fallen textbook. "It's been forever. How are you?"

"Doing well. It's Ryder, now."

She laughed. "Right, sorry. Ryder. I forgot that you go by your middle name nowadays."

"Ouch, Vee. I'm over here thinking I'm a memorable person," he joked. "You sure know how to humble a man."

"Sorry. You're still the caddy boy at my father's country club, in my mind."

That had been a horrible summer—at first. Dad had forced him to work over the school break when he was fifteen, to teach him the value of a dollar or some shit. He'd had to work on a golf course and ride around with the most obnoxiously wealthy old jackoffs he'd ever met. Now *those* guys were racists, always talking about how Mexicans stole jobs or something. It made Ryder feel a bit better about his own father. Not much, though.

After two days, Ryder had wanted to quit—until one of the assholes brought his daughter along to the course. Veronica. They'd spent the remainder of the month together, every day, hiding out in the pool house. They never fucked or anything, but she'd made that job bearable.

"Are you still with that bastard wolf? Blakey Blackie whatever?" Ryder asked her.

Veronica winced. "No. We're done. It was a pretty bad breakup."

"Sorry." He meant it. "Do I have to kick his ass? Because I will, happily."

"No. I just want to move on. I'm trying to, anyway."

"Well, if you need a rebound, I'm your guy."

She laughed, the sound sweet and light. "You're funny as ever. But I'm not looking for a hookup."

"Who says I'm only interested in hooking up?"

"Um, every single girl on campus you've hooked up with?" She crossed her arms, but she didn't look angry. "I know how you operate. You're a love 'em and leave 'em kinda guy. I'm not interested in casual sex, and I'm not ready to get serious again, not after what happened."

"Suit yourself," he said, "but you should know that it would be different with you. You're not some slut I'll forget about the next day."

"That's really flattering." She rolled her eyes. "If I didn't know you, I'd say you were genuine."

"I am. Let me take you out to dinner, and we'll see what happens."

Veronica hesitated, and he knew he had her. But then she said, "I can't tonight. I'm having a girls' night with my friend, Kitty. We're going to paint our nails and watch a movie."

"Kitty?" he questioned. "You're friends with that Swan chick?"

"Yeah. Why?" she asked, oblivious to his displeasure.

Veronica and Kitty. How'd she get suckered in to being that bitch's friend? Ryder didn't like the thought of Vee getting caught in the mess he was going to make with the Swan girl and her family. Maybe he could convince her to ditch Kitty.

Or maybe he could use Vee to get to Kitty. If the enemy of your enemy was your friend, then what did that make the friend of your enemy?

Ryder pulled the school paper out of his bag and handed her the article. "She said some pretty nasty things about our kind, Veronica. Maybe you should re-think your association with her."

Veronica scanned the article, her face scrunching. “This can’t be true.”

“Dr. Woods published it herself. And you know her. She’s one of the most respected scientists right now for her contributions to the feral research initiative,” Ryder said. “Why would she lie?”

“I don’t...” Veronica shook her head and handed him the paper. “I have to go. Sorry, Ethan- Ryder. I...I’ll call you, okay? Has your number changed?”

“Nope. I’ll be waiting for your call.”

As she hurried away, Ryder couldn’t help the satisfaction welling inside him. This whole ‘destroy Kitty Swan’ thing might turn out to be more fun than he thought.

NORTHEASTERN TRIBUNE

MONSTER IN OUR MIDST

In a world where supernatural abilities define our identity, the introduction of new, unorthodox elements into our midst demands rigorous scrutiny. My recent interview with Katherine Swan, a self-proclaimed 'Chinese cultivator', offers a disturbing glimpse into a practice that not only challenges the sanctity of the shadowborn community but also threatens the natural order of the mortal realm.

Upon delving into the Swan family's background, a troubling picture emerges. Discussions with an unnamed source within our admissions office revealed that the Swan siblings' applications bypassed the standard review process. Their acceptance, orchestrated directly by Chancellor Kinsey, came with full tuition waivers and board, a decision purportedly based on the 'research contributions' of the Swan parents. This revelation suggests a willingness to compromise our standards in the name of diversity, potentially at the cost of our own community's deserving members.

The Swan family, with no formal academic qualifications

to speak of, seems to have bypassed the rigorous standards we hold dear. This raises an uncomfortable question: Are we sacrificing quality for the sake of appearing inclusive? The idea of uncredentialed individuals who barely speak English robbing opportunities from more qualified, home-grown talent is not only disconcerting, but also undermines the hard work of our students and faculty.

Katherine Swan's interview revealed a disturbing sense of superiority inherent in her cultivation practices. Cultivation, as she claims, demands more effort than the innate abilities of shadowborn individuals, minimizing the worth and achievements of our core community. Such divisive rhetoric only serves to alienate and devalue the contributions of our shadowborn students.

The concept of cultivation itself strays into morally questionable territory. Ms. Swan speaks of manipulating 'qi', an alleged energy she claims is emitted by all living beings—a concept utterly alien and unverifiable in our academic realm. The pursuit of immortality, a central tenet of their practice, directly contravenes the natural laws governing life and death, edging dangerously close to paganistic ideologies.

The presence of the Swan family, under the guise of cultural tradition, could potentially introduce destabilizing factors within Northeastern College. Their unfamiliar and, by our standards, unnatural practices raise the question of whether their intentions are as benign as they appear.

In conclusion, while diversity remains a cornerstone of our institution, it is imperative that we remain vigilant against elements that might not only contradict our academic principles but also pose a potential threat to the very essence of our shadowborn community. The Swan family, while seemingly innocuous, may represent a more insidious challenge to the fabric of our society: a 'Mortal Monster' lurking in plain sight, threatening the natural order and our cherished values.

NINE

BY THE EVENING, Noelle had written five-hundred flash cards, covering the entire semester's vocabulary words and key points for Professor Evans's class. Doing well—and proving him wrong, by extension—would be a sweet victory on her part. Despite her sore hand, she smiled at the thought of him giving her an A at the end of the semester. She knew she'd do well on any test or quiz, and as for essays, she wrote excellent papers. She had this in the bag.

Deciding to reward herself, Noelle tucked the flashcards away in her desk and took out her phone. Turning on the sound and taking it off Focus mode, she went through the notifications she had missed while studying. She had twenty texts, most of which were from Melody. The general gist of her messages were asking about some sort of school article. Noelle didn't read the paper, so she clicked on the link Mel sent over.

It was a quick read, but Noelle read it twice, just to make sure she understood it properly. And she was simmering.

Why the hell would Kitty agree to an interview? She

wasn't good at speaking, specifically on the fly. She made the Swans sound horrible! God, did she have anything between her ears, or was her head completely empty?

In her anger, Noelle barely registered the sound of the door opening. Kitty entered the dorm in workout clothes, pulling out her headphones and throwing her bag on her desk.

"What did you do?" Noelle asked sharply.

The phone beeped again, and Kitty flinched. "Hey, can you turn that off?"

"Kitty! What the fuck? That interview with Dr. Woods! Why didn't you tell me you were going to speak with her? Have you seen the article?"

"Noelle, can you please turn off your phone notifications? And...I told Mā and Bà about the interview. They were fine with it," Kitty said. "What's the problem? The interview was straightforward. I didn't tell her anything she shouldn't have already known."

Noelle thrust her phone towards her sister, the article glaring back at them both. As Kitty's eyes darted across the screen, her expression became pinched.

"I didn't say that."

"Really? Because it sounds like something you'd say. God, did you really have to put the shadowborn down? Do you know where we are right now?" Noelle asked, trying to keep her voice level. "We are at a *school* for shadowborn. And you've insulted them. They already didn't love us, and you had to go poke the bear. What? Were you upset because you're not Miss Popularity anymore? Don't you understand what you've done, not just to yourself, but to our family?"

"I didn't say any of that!" Kitty insisted, pointing to the phone screen. "I swear, I didn't. I told her that cultivators aren't born, that we have to study and practice and meditate to advance. I didn't even mention the shadowborn. She twisted my words!"

"You shouldn't have talked to her in the first place!" Noelle exploded. "God, Kitty. Sometimes, you can be so stupid!"

Kitty jerked back, as if Noelle had slapped her. She grabbed her bag, shrugged it over her shoulder, and opened the door.

"Where are you going?"

"I'm going to find Dr. Woods and ask her why she published that article," Kitty said, scarily calm.

"You can't do that. What do you expect her to say? What if she writes another article?" Noelle demanded.

God. Kitty never thought ahead, never considered the consequences. It was always Noelle picking up the pieces and cleaning up the mess. She wished, for once, she didn't have to act like the older sister.

"I don't know what I'm going to do or say. But she practically spat in my face with this crap. I went to her thinking that... Hoping that... Fuck. I didn't say this."

"Kitty—"

"If our positions had been reversed, I would have believed you. And I would have never, *ever* blamed you, or insinuated that you did this because of your vanity, or called you stupid. I would never do that to you."

Noelle didn't have a response. Kitty walked out, and the worst part was, she didn't even slam the door.

For a few seconds, Noelle swore her heart stopped beating. She hated it, but admittedly, her sister *wouldn't* have done that. Guilt speared her, and she regretted her harsh words. She got her purse from the back of the door, shoved her phone and wallet inside, and followed after Kitty.

She was nowhere in sight, but Noelle knew where Dr. Woods worked—in the lab in the main building, with her mother. Actually, Noelle was pretty sure Dr. Woods was Māma's new boss. Which meant she *really* had to stop Kitty from doing something bad.

Noelle rushed across campus, scanning her phone to get into the building. She managed to catch Kitty just as she arrived, walking up to a woman inside.

The woman, who Noelle assumed was Dr. Woods, was older than her picture showed online. Her graying hair was pulled back in a bun and her hands were wrinkled and shaking as she stripped off her blue latex gloves. She wore a maroon blouse and slacks under a white lab coat, looking particularly small next to Kitty despite her heels.

"Miss Swan. What can I do for you?" Dr. Woods asked, as if she had no idea what Kitty could possibly be angry about.

Noelle understood immediately that she was a bitch. Call it a sixth sense, or spending too much time with Kitty, but she had the feeling Woods knew exactly what she was doing.

Māma looked up from her lab station, piled high with paperwork. "Kitty? Noelle? What are you doing?"

"Why did you write that article about me?" Kitty demanded, getting right in Dr. Woods's face. "'Mortal monster'? Are you fucking serious right now?"

"You know, foul language is a sign of an improper education. What, exactly, has your mother taught you?" Dr. Woods asked, feigning concern.

Yeah. Definitely a bitch.

Noelle stepped up, putting a hand on Kitty's shoulder. "Excuse us, Dr. Woods. We were just wondering why, exactly, you would publish an article that portrays us so negatively."

Dr. Woods blinked. "I don't think it was a negative

portrayal at all. And you must be Noelle. Your mother has told me all about you. You're a human panacea, are you not? Your blood could be very useful. It is too bad you refuse to donate it to the lab."

"Noelle doesn't have to do anything," Kitty snapped. "How could you stand here and claim you didn't portray us in a negative light, when you claimed in your article that we're only here because the school wants to up its diversity quota?"

"I didn't claim that at all. You must have misunderstood, dear. Perhaps it was above your reading comprehension level. Some students struggle when English is their second language. I'm sorry, but Northeastern doesn't offer ESL courses. You'll have to take some online. There are many free resources available."

Noelle held onto her sister tightly, in fear she'd lunge at the scientist and gouge her eyes out. Māma walked over, too, confused.

"What are you two doing here?" she asked.

"Damage control," Noelle answered.

Kitty didn't struggle, but her face turned bright red, a contrast to her white-knuckled fists. "Māma. She wrote an article about us saying that you are underqualified to work in this lab and barely speak English."

"She doesn't have a college degree," Dr. Woods reminded.

"She's over a hundred years old, and her contribution to this school—and to the feral research—is based on her cultivation knowledge."

"But if you cannot measure it, how can you validate it? You understand that I am a scientist, Miss Swan. I have several advanced degrees to show my years of dedication and study. I've worked hard to earn my place in a space typically reserved for men. I do not need a lecture on diversity, when I, myself, have fought against stereotypes in the STEM field. And frankly, I think it is quite rude to have you barging in here and disrupting the life-saving research we are conducting for these petty issues. There is a time and a place, Miss Swan. Surely someone taught you that, if not at home, then in school?"

Kitty opened her mouth, but before she could speak, Māma interrupted. "I am terribly sorry, Dr. Woods. May I please speak with my daughters outside for a moment?"

"Of course, Ariana. Please, go. It's the end of your shift, anyway," Dr. Woods said graciously.

Māma and Noelle practically dragged Kitty out the door. But they couldn't stop her from spinning around at the door, because she was Kitty Swan, and she always had to have the last word. "If ignorance is bliss, then you must be the happiest person alive."

Noelle hustled Kitty into a nearby classroom, empty and unlocked. Māma closed the door behind them for privacy, letting out a sigh. In Mandarin, she said, "Kitty, what have I told you about antagonizing others?"

"Only do it to win a fight?"

"Yes. But do not antagonize my boss. You know we need this job," she said. "The school paid off our debt. If we leave, we might have to pay it back."

"Why? You didn't sign a contract or anything. You did a ton of work for them last semester, too. How would they have the legal grounds to take back the money, which was a gift?"

"We can't afford lawyers, and it is clear this school operates differently than other institutions. Even if I didn't *need* this job, what Calista said was right. English *is* my second language, and I do not have a degree."

"That doesn't mean you're unqualified. It just means you didn't have the opportunities. And your English is fine, Mā.

She had no right to insult it, or mine, for that matter. She was just being a..."

"Cunt," Noelle supplied. She handed her mother her phone, with the article pulled up. "Actually, Mā, Kitty is right. The article paints us in a really bad light."

"Regardless, you cannot do this. Either of you. It is unproductive. I don't want to make waves here. I just want to do my work and leave. And you will do the same."

"But—"

"I wasn't asking, Kitty."

Kitty's lips thinned, but she didn't argue. It wasn't worth it.

"Both of you wash up. Bàba is making dinner tonight, and you'll join us, and we'll put this whole thing behind us. You're worked up because you're hungry," Māma said. "I'll meet you at the apartment."

"That's fine, Mā," Noelle answered for the both of them. Kitty sank into a chair as Māma left, the door closing firmly behind her. As the heat of the moment passed and Noelle's anger over the article cooled, she took a seat beside Kitty, thinking of the right thing to say. It wasn't easy. It was never easy. But she did it anyway. "I'm sorry."

Kitty shrugged, looking away. She didn't cry, nor was she on the verge of it, but she didn't say anything, afraid her voice would come out warbled. The sisters fought enough for Noelle to recognize this.

"I shouldn't have blamed you for the article or called you stupid. And you're right—I know that you wouldn't have done the same to me. I...I should have believed in you. I'm sorry."

Kitty reached over, putting a hand on Noelle's arm. "If

anyone says anything to you about this, or anything else, you'll tell me, right?"

"Kitty—"

"I can't stand the thought of something happening to you. Or to Jax. So you'd tell me, wouldn't you? If anyone was bothering you."

Noelle cleared her throat awkwardly. "Yes," she lied. "Of course I would."

"IN SOCCER, THERE'S NO BITING," Cyrus admonished.

"There's not," Kitty agreed, flopping down on the grass, "if you want to play the boring way."

He took the ball from her, and she was too tired to get up and fight him for it. Earlier that morning, he had come to her dorm to have breakfast with her. They both got up before eight, despite it being a Saturday. He'd brought cereal, and she'd turned on a movie in the common area. They were going through Amanda Bynes comedies from the 2000s, the golden era of romcoms.

Unfortunately, like with most things, Kitty and Cyrus couldn't agree on the best Bynes film they'd seen. He tried to claim it was *Easy A*, which didn't even count because Bynes wasn't the lead character. As the best Emma Stone film, it was a strong contender.

"You have zero taste if you think *She's the Man* is better than *What a Girl Wants*," he argued.

"God, what is your obsession with Colin Firth? Is it because he played Mr. Darcy, who is secretly your role model?"

"What? No!"

"*She's the Man* has way more action, with the soccer stuff," Kitty said.

"Soccer is overrated."

That launched them both into a full debate over the best team sport, causing them to let their cereal go soggy and, eventually, challenge each other to a five-game match. So far, the score was tied. Kitty beat Cyrus at field hockey and basketball, but he won their baseball game and football match.

Finally, they played soccer. By the time they were finished, the game was deadlocked, with neither able to make a single goal on the other. They lay in the middle of the empty field, storm clouds rolling in at an alarming pace.

"You lost," Cyrus told her. "You got too many fouls."

"I didn't lose! You're such a baby."

"Baby? I have half a mind to get a rabies shot, you animal!" He held up his arm, her teeth imprints clear on his bicep. "Do you like biting me or something?"

"You taste pretty good." Kitty realized as soon as the words left her mouth how suggestive they sounded. Of course, she tried to do damage control, making it much worse. "Well, I mean, not like... You don't taste good. It's not *bad* either. You know, the taste—your sweaty skin—isn't horrible, so I'd say it's okay. But also, not good. Like, not something I'd crave, if I ate people. That would be cannibalism. If you keep making that face, I'm gonna punch you for real."

"What face?"

She sat up and poked him between the brows. His nose wrinkled and his cheeks flushed, probably due to physical exertion. As annoying as he could be—like, younger brother levels of annoying—and as weird as he made her feel sometimes, when they had their arguments or competitions, he put a hundred percent into it. He never *let* her win, and he didn't hold back, which Kitty took as a sign of respect. She almost didn't mind that they tied.

"What do you say we take a break?" Cyrus asked. "It looks like it's about to downpour. And we still have a bunch of horror movies on our watchlist."

"Really? You don't feel like our real lives have too much horror in them already? We have to watch fictional characters get slashed?"

"Alright, we can do a funny one. Like *Scream*." He sat up, leaning on his elbow. "You're not still worried about the moving corpse, are you?"

"No," she lied, rolling to her feet. "How much mud is on my back right now?"

"It looks like you shit yourself."

"Nice. Take your sweatshirt off." She held out a hand as he shrugged out of his top, a thin white tee sticking to his torso. He handed her the Northeastern sweatshirt, grass stained but somehow not as muddy, and wrapped it around her waist.

As they started toward the dorm, a cold raindrop fell on her cheek and dripped down to her chin. Then another, and another, until the sky opened up and a torrential storm drenched the two of them in seconds.

They ran for the nearest building, the student science labs and astronomy center. Due to the chemicals in the labs, the building was locked for the weekend. All Kitty and Cyrus could do was seek shelter under the overhang, huddled together against the brick wall.

Kitty's teeth chattered as she wrapped an arm around herself. "You think it's going to let up anytime soon?"

"No. It might be worth it to make a run to the dorm," he replied.

"Is Blake going to be around?"

"I'm not sure."

"Can we hang out in the common area of your dorm, this time?" Things between her and Noelle were still weird, and Kitty wished she knew what to do to make it better. Noelle was smart, but sometimes, she lacked self-awareness. Regardless, Kitty figured all these new changes in her sister's life had her stressed and overstimulated. She wasn't angry about the article anymore, and she hadn't brought it up since, but the distance between the sisters stretched on. Like yesterday, when Kitty and Veronica were doing their nails and chatting, Noelle had left the dorm to study in the library. Every time Kitty walked into the room, aside from just before bed, Noelle left. They'd used to talk for hours before falling asleep, having shared a room all their lives.

Though, to be fair, the distance had built over the course of the summer. Ever since Kitty had learned the truth from her parents, it became increasingly difficult to speak with Noelle and *not* divulge the fact that:

1. They were fraternal twins, not born a year apart as they were brought up to believe.
2. The cultivation sect their parents were raised in thought female fraternal twins were a bad omen and practiced infanticide, which was why their parents had run away.
3. This apocalyptic prophecy may or may not be true, based on Kitty's own affinity for demonic energy.

Kitty was used to telling her sister everything, for the most part, but her parents had sworn her to secrecy over this. Coupled with the fact that Kitty's powers sometimes failed her due to the damage to her golden core, these secrets weighed heavily on her. Not that it was any better than her situation with Cyrus, but at least whatever was between them wasn't a secret.

Friendship would have been easier if his shirt wasn't currently transparent from the rain.

"Let's go to my room," Cyrus told her.

They made a mad dash for the boy's dorm, barely able to see through the storm. He let her into the back of the building, where Blake and all the other guys living in the dorm snuck girls in. Once inside, it was a hike to his floor. Blake, thankfully, was nowhere to be seen.

The room always smelled like lemon cleaning solution, sterile, and she had a feeling that was mostly Cy's doing. He crammed a lot of stuff into the small space but made the most of it by using clear plastic organizers on the desks and bookshelves. He had a label maker, too.

Kitty waltzed over to his closet, rifling through the hangers.

"What are you doing?"

"Helping myself to your clothes, and realizing chivalry is dead since you didn't offer," she replied, picking out one of three of the same sweatshirts, all navy blue with the Northeastern logo on it. "I'm going to take a shower."

"This is the guy's dorm. We have communal showers," he said.

"So you'll join me, then." They were both muddy, sweaty, and gross anyway. "Come on. Lead the way."

"This is a bad idea," he warned.

"You're being dramatic." She grabbed the clean sweatshirt off the hanger, and he tossed her a fresh towel. Bringing along his shower caddy, the two walked down the darkened hallway toward the bathrooms. Inside, stalls lined the left wall and a large shower section sat on the right. It must have been for the entire floor. In the girls' dorm, they had a single bathroom shared between three rooms.

No one was inside, since it probably wasn't a good idea to shower during a thunderstorm, but Kitty had been struck by lightning before. She wasn't particularly scared. Cyrus chose two showers beside each other, all the way in the back. The walls only rose to eye-level for Kitty, so if she wanted to, she could see into the next shower. Not that she planned on peeking; she wasn't a total degenerate, despite the thoughts running through her mind at the moment.

Stripping out of her wet clothes, she let them flop to the tile floor and turned on the hot water.

"Shampoo?" She held out a hand over the divider, and he squirted two pumps of amber liquid into her palm.

The hot water felt amazing on her back. Bruises began to bloom all over her body from today's activities, but she didn't regret it. Closing her eyes, she relaxed under the spray of the shower head, letting it run through her scalp. She finished and toweled off, slipping into Cyrus's sweatshirt. She'd imagined it would be cute and oversized on her, forgetting the fact that she wasn't much shorter than him.

"Uh, Cy?"

"Yeah?"

"Do you have a pair of bottoms I could wear?"

"What's wrong with yours?" he asked.

"Well, my skirt is muddy, and my underwear is soaked through."

He coughed.

"Are you okay?"

"Yeah," he managed hoarsely. "I just swallowed down the wrong pipe."

"That's what she said."

"Is this really the time?"

"It's never a bad time for a joke like that," she informed him. "Are you clothed?"

The shower stall creaked open, and he stepped out. His hair was still wet, but he dressed in a t-shirt and checkered pajama bottoms. "I'll run and grab you...something."

"I can wrap the towel around my waist—"

"No. I'll be right back, okay? Just stay put. If another guy comes in...you should use that move you tried on me the other day."

"The one that almost made you pass out?"

"Yeah."

She watched him leave, peeking over the stall. He rubbed the back of his neck, looking both ways before exiting. For a few minutes, the only sounds in the bathroom were the drips from the showers and the storm outside. Lightning lit up the sky, followed by a loud clap of thunder that shook the building. The bathroom lights flickered before going out, leaving her cold, wet, and bare-assed.

Great.

The door creaked open and someone entered. Unsure if it was Cyrus again, Kitty stayed completely still. Their phone flashlight nearly blinded her as he waved it around, looking for the stalls.

Not Cyrus, she thought, looking at the guy's head of blonde curls. Thankfully, it wasn't Blake, either. Kitty huddled against the door, perhaps using a bit too much force, and knocked the entire thing off the hinges. Due to the slippery tiles, she fell forward, landing flat on her face with a groan.

The student swung his flashlight over to her and screamed bloody murder, flying out of the bathroom like a bat out of hell. Kitty was a bit offended. There she was, pretty, naked, fresh from the shower, groaning in pain...with long, dark, wet hair...like Sadako...

Oh.

"I'm not even Japanese!" Kitty exclaimed, her voice echoing through the bathroom.

The door opened again, but thankfully, Cyrus had returned. His face, illuminated by his phone light, looked shocked to see her on the ground. "What happened? I was gone for two minutes!"

"Uh, if someone starts spreading a rumor that this bathroom is haunted, it's *totally* not my fault."

He handed her an unopened package of boxers and turned around. "Just change and let's go back to my dorm. Security doesn't care that much about girls in the dorm, but they have to keep up appearances. If they find you, we'll both be in trouble."

Kitty tore open the package and slipped a pair on. "You are a life saver."

"And you're a walking heart-attack."

"I'll take that as a compliment," she said, gathering her things. They hurried back to his room under the cover of darkness. "Where should I put my clothes?"

"Hang them to dry. Blake won't be back tonight," Cyrus said, slipping the dead bolt into place. "Sorry about the movie, though. Without power, there's not much else to do. I have an umbrella if you want to head back."

"Judging by the sideways rain hitting your window, I think I'll stay in, if that's okay," she said.

"You can sleep in Blake's bed," he offered.

"When did he last wash the sheets, and when did he last have a girl over?"

"Fair point. You can crash in my bunk, and I'll take the floor. Blake sleeps nude, and frankly, even staying on top of the sheets is unappealing to me."

"Don't be ridiculous. It's a tile floor, you haven't put a rug down, and it's freezing."

It was almost as if Kitty were having an out-of-body experience, watching herself formulate the most idiotic plan she'd ever concocted and propose it to Cyrus as if *he'd* be unreasonable for not agreeing. She wanted to shake herself and demand to know what her problem was. Then again, she wasn't sure she'd like the answer to that particular question.

"Fine," Cyrus agreed, climbing up to the top bunk.

She followed him up the ladder, sliding in beside him. It was an awkward fit, with both of them squeezed in while simultaneously trying not to touch each other. Eventually, they gave up the facade of propriety. He held her close to his chest, their legs tangled together. Kitty was sure they both felt the same way: confused, but also like she belonged in his arms.

Maybe her heart didn't understand how complicated things were between them, or maybe it understood perfectly and was willing to risk the inevitable fallout.

Either way, she was toast.

TEN

THE FERAL BIRD had eaten her own eggs, then regurgitated the embryos onto Charity's head. Two hours later, despite showering (and subsequently hyperventilating in the shower, because really, what had her life become?), she still felt disgusting.

She hadn't embarrassed herself by throwing up, thankfully. Wyatt had partnered with her on this hunt, and she wouldn't have been able to look him in the eye again, especially since he seemed so unperturbed. She'd come to the conclusion that he was just *cool*, in the effortless way all cool guys were. Everything seemed to come easily to him.

He leaned against the wall outside the medical office waiting to get checked for infection. Fresh from the shower, his deep brown skin glowed. A tight t-shirt clung to his chest, a Nirvana tee stretched and distorted from his pectorals. Charity waited beside him, a head shorter, fiddling with the straps of her tote bag. All she wanted to do was go back to her dorm and sleep, but she knew after this, she'd have to study.

The semester just began, and she already felt like she was falling behind with all these hunts.

"I want credit for my sacrifice, today," Wyatt told her suddenly. "I smell like bird, and I'm pretty sure I have feathers in places no human should have feathers. Not to kink-shame."

He was trying to make her feel better, but Charity couldn't smile. "What did Everleigh say about the flock?"

"I didn't talk to Everleigh. He's been up to his nose in reports. They even gave him a student assistant, and she looks stressed as hell too, running around his office. I don't think any amount of work study is worth it."

"Who did you speak to, then?"

"We have to report to Dr. Woods for the time being. She's..."

"An associate of my father's. So, a bitch," Charity supplied. "Did you see the article she wrote in the school paper?"

"My old man did. He went down to talk to her about it, and she doubled down. Not a great look for the school."

"If hunting means I have to deal with *her*, I'm just going to hold back for the semester. I have a lot of classwork as it is." As a junior, she was already gearing up for her senior year thesis.

"I wish. But with the colony of Blood Wasps, and now this flock of bird chimera, I don't think things will slow down."

He had a point. "What did Woods say about the flock?"

"Nothing. She just thanked me and told me she was busy."

She didn't comment at all on how weird it was that. First, a colony turned feral, and now an entire flock? Thank goodness the birds couldn't fly. This particular batch of monsters were three-headed cranes with wings, the long, scaled body of a reptile, two barbed tails, and eight legs. They moved in flocks of twenty, and the only reason Charity and Wyatt weren't bird food was an environmental advantage. They'd found a spot where they could strike while hidden behind rocks, luring the birds in one by one.

The most concerning part was the fact that the ferals moved as a group. They were supposed to be *mindless*, and most ferals attacked others on sight. With the Blood Wasps, colonies were psychically connected, so it made sense they didn't attack each other. The flock should have torn each other apart.

"I think Cyrus is right. The disease is mutating," Charity muttered. Just what they needed. "What do you make of what happened in the morgue?"

Wyatt perked up with interest. "What happened in the morgue?"

She briefly explained what she'd heard from Melody, who'd heard it from Blake, who'd heard from Cyrus. A moving corpse shouldn't have been more frightening than the zombified ferals they dealt with on a weekly basis, but for some reason, it was. Sure, it was less physically threatening, but... But it had been human, once. 'It' had been a 'he' or 'she' or 'they'. A person. And that hit far too close to home for Charity's liking.

Wyatt, to his credit, maintained his usual calm demeanor. His smile, however, dropped from his face. "And now the SNPD has taken over the case."

"Not necessarily." Ryder Kinsey appeared in the doorway, seemingly out of thin air. He wore his usual smug expression, his lips caught between a smile and a frown, his eyes laughing at a joke no one else was privy to. Charity had never liked the guy.

Ryder, Wyatt, and Blake were popular at Northeastern. It

was a small school, and the community of shadowborn were tight-knit, making it difficult for students and faculty alike to grow out of their more childish, clique-y mentalities. Cyrus could also be included in the lineup of sexy guys, coming from a good family, but there were a few girls who disparaged him, based on his mixed ethnicity.

Wyatt was known for being kind, but in Charity's opinion, he possessed a rare optimism that made him easy to get along with. He maintained a genuine image while radiating positivity. He also had washboard abs, which helped.

Blake was good looking—that was about the only thing he had going for him. He could be charming, but often times, Charity found his false niceties grating to watch. That didn't stop them from jumping into bed together.

Ryder, on the other hand? If you asked two different girls on campus, they'd give completely different responses. To some, he was Prince freakin' Charming. To others, namely Charity, he was a total jackass.

Exhibit A: "Hey Charity. Look what the cat dragged in. You still pining after that werewolf bastard?"

"It's nice to see you're still obsessed with him," Charity muttered.

"Hey, Ethan," Wyatt said, not smiling. "What are you doing here? I didn't think you came to campus that often."

"It's Ryder," he said. "You know that."

"Sorry. Ryder," Wyatt corrected, casting him an apologetic smile. "You back for good this semester?"

"Tell me more about this body you found at the Blood Wasp nest," Ryder asked, ignoring his question.

"Not much to tell."

"It sounds like an interesting story," he hedged.

Charity didn't know why he cared, anyway. He barely

cursed campus with his presence, thank God, and when he *did* deign to show his face, it was never to help. Perks of being the chancellor's son, she presumed: he got to sit on his ass and do nothing while the rest of them hunted ferals day and night. Blake, for all his faults, helped out for the betterment of the community.

Okay, so she was pretty sure he did it for the extra credit. But still, he helped!

Ryder had a particular distaste for Blake, though. Charity couldn't figure out why, aside from the obvious: they were both raging egomaniacs.

"There's not much to tell," Charity said, echoing Wyatt. She raised her chin, crossing her arms. "A colony of Blood Wasps were turned feral. Now, a flock of bird chimera. It's a mystery—and your father isn't doing anything about it."

"No surprise there," Ryder replied cheerfully. "So SNPD took over the investigation?"

"No. They took over the cover-up."

"Hmm." He shoved his hands in the pockets of his jeans. "Thanks for the gossip. I'll be seeing you two around, I guess."

With that, he departed. Just as well—it was Charity's turn to get checked for infection. But as she watched him leave, an unsettling feeling sunk into her stomach.

She heard that things usually got worse before they got better. In this case? Things were going to get worse—and it wasn't going to stop.

DAILY PROMPT: WRITE DOWN FIVE THINGS YOU ARE GOOD AT.

1. *Right hook*
2. *Kicking people in the face*
3. *Getting out of a chokehold*
4. *Styling outfits*

Kitty tapped her feather-tipped, pink glitter-gel pen to her affirmation journal. She couldn't think of a fifth item, and even her current list was lackluster. Three of the five had to do with fighting! And yes, she was proud of that; she worked hard to achieve her current skill level. But was that really all she had to offer? Being pretty and being strong?

She wasn't a nice person, despite her best efforts. Which was not to say she'd stop trying. But she had to be realistic about it. Kindness, generosity, selflessness...none of those things came naturally to her at all. Not to mention, she struggled finding the line between being good and being a pushover. Currently, she felt she leaned toward the latter. Google hadn't helped. She tried looking up a gentle way to tell someone to fuck off, but the results were mostly "hold your head up high and don't let it get to you". She knew she shouldn't have cared, but she didn't like being called names—out loud *or* on her things, which somehow kept getting vandalized with the most uncreative insults on the face of the earth.

And intelligence? She just flunked her first quiz in her Magic of Sociology class. She wasn't doing so great in any other classes either. It had been a week since the article had come out, and now, she felt like everyone on campus was glaring at her. Her first instinct was to go on the defense: So what if they stared? Let them! If they wanted to believe some racist junk, go ahead! But despite these thoughts urging her not to care, deep down, she had...feelings. *Gross*.

They were like a tangled jumble of yarn, woven together and knotted so tightly she could barely unravel a single string, much less see what lay at the center of it all. She tried cultivating, meditating, and writing in her affirmation journal to make sense of it all. Nothing helped.

She considered talking about it with someone, but who? She couldn't think of anyone, though that wasn't to say any of the people in her life were lacking. It was her fault entirely. She struggled to admit it even to herself, in the library alone in the middle of the afternoon. She sat in a secluded corner of the stacks, hidden among the shelves at one of the study cubicles near the window.

In the dead of night, as Kitty lay awake in her bed, staring up at the top bunk, her mind whispered traitorous things. Her thoughts turned, and she couldn't control them from slipping out: If she were to reveal her feelings and insecurities to anyone in her life, they would not see her as strong. And if even one person found her strength inadequate, then Kitty herself would too.

She scribbled out her entry in the journal, tore the page, and tossed it in the nearest trash can.

"You've got glitter on your hand," a young man pointed out. She didn't know when he'd snuck up behind her, but the knowledge that he managed to surprise her was yet another blow to her ego.

He wasn't particularly tall, though Kitty herself stood at 5'9" and often wore shoes with heels. He must have been a few inches taller, but probably not 6'. His skin was dark and smooth, and she could see the outline of his muscles from the tight tee clinging to his chest.

Ah, Kitty thought, recognizing him. He was in her Magic of Sociology class.

"I've never been a big fan of glitter. It gets everywhere," the young man continued, putting his phone down on the desk beside hers. "Props to you for being brave enough to deal with it."

"You're Wyatt, aren't you? Professor Ainsworth's son?" She had Ainsworth for her mandatory combat class.

Wyatt nodded. "And you're the most popular girl on campus, Kitty Swan. It's an honor to officially make your acquaintance."

"How'd you find me?" she asked.

He settled in the chair beside her, pulling it out enough so he could look at her while he spoke and not be hindered by the separators dividing each study cubicle. "What makes you think I was looking for you? I just came to study."

"I can see that by the numerous books in your hand," she replied dryly. He didn't even have a bag with him. Where did he keep his cell phone? "If you have a complaint about the article—"

"Nah. You wanna know a secret?" He leaned in. "Dr. Woods isn't nearly as popular as she thinks. Actually, *I* think that article she wrote only showed how desperate she is."

"For what, a lobotomy?"

He chuckled. "Truth is, Woods has only become prominent more recently, with this whole feral thing. The amount of funding she gets yearly would make most politicians jealous. So your parents coming in and actually bringing us a step closer to solving the illness? It's a threat to her."

"It all boils down to money?" Kitty asked incredulously.

Wyatt shrugged. "That, and good old-fashioned discrimination. The community has always had a problem with it, but no one likes to admit it."

"Oh my God. I thought I was going crazy!"

"You're not," he assured her. "My dad and I get it too. A lot of students on campus do—and not just for race. It's weird how shadowborn can acknowledge species-based discrimination; angel and demon shadowborn not liking each other, for example. But in a way, that almost *allows* other forms of discrimination to occur. 'Oh, they didn't beat you up because you're Black, they did it because you're an angel shadowborn. It's just the way things are.' That kind of shit."

So essentially, they can acknowledge one form of bias and shove everything else under that umbrella as a way of accepting it without doing anything. That sounded healthy.

Not.

"Funny how we're taking a sociology class and we're not talking about discrimination within the community at all." Their entire syllabus seemed to be an argument for why humans could never find out about magic.

"Species-based discrimination is tolerated because there are biological differences," Wyatt said. "That's what my old man tells me, anyway. Trueblood angels have wings whereas trueblood wolves can shift. Two completely different powers and physical attributes. They can argue whether one power is better than the other. That ideology transfers to shadowborn, despite the fact that among us, there's little variation. But you, Kitty Swan? You check all their boxes. It's like Bigot Bingo. You look different, you *feel* different in a way I can't quite explain, and your powers are foreign to them."

"This is all helpful information," Kitty said, "but why are

you telling me all this? You don't owe me anything, and we've hardly ever spoken before."

"I'm buttering you up," Wyatt admitted with a sheepish smile. "Trying to get on your good side and help you, so that maybe in turn, you'd agree to spar with me."

Kitty barked a laugh. That wasn't what she expected, but she wouldn't say no. Though this was the first time they were speaking, she knew she liked Wyatt immediately. He was personable, yes, but he made sense of what was going on around her. While the revelations were disturbing, no doubt, she felt a bit better knowing she wasn't the only one who saw what was going on. Her entire family seemed to be pretending the issues didn't exist.

"You want to fight me?" Kitty asked, her tone playful.

Wyatt nodded. "I heard from my dad that you're good at hand-to-hand. Better than *good*, actually. He says you're a tank."

"Thank you?"

"I hear you and Cyrus Ward spar together pretty regularly. And that you kick his ass most of the time." He stood, holding out his hand with a grin. "Would you do me the honor of allowing me to experience that firsthand?"

Kitty played into it. "Why, Wyatt Ainsworth. Are you propositioning me?"

"Absolutely, Miss Swan."

"I can hardly say no." She took his hand, allowing him to pull her to her feet. Gathering her things, her body buzzed with excitement. Getting to take on a new opponent, especially the son of the combat instructor, filled her with anticipation. But before they could make it out of the library, someone stood near the front door, blocking it.

Wyatt's expression dropped for a fraction of a second. "What are you doing here, Ryder?"

The young man standing in front of them approached with a grin befitting the Cheshire cat. "I'm here to challenge Kitty Swan to a duel."

ELEVEN

DAILY PROMPT: WHAT ARE YOU MOST GRATEFUL FOR?

The opportunity to give Ryder Kinsey a school-sanctioned beat-down.

Students and faculty alike crammed into the arena, everyone fighting for front-row seats to Kitty's humiliation. She kept her head held high, staring straight at Ryder as she waited for the referee to arrive. The room was in the basement, built like an amphitheater with a large glass dome covering the fighting pit.

"You sure you don't want to change into something a little more comfortable, Princess?" Ryder called, taunting her.

Kitty still wasn't sure what to make of him. All the self-help books spoke against snap judgments. But if she *were* to make one, she'd say that he was a total asshole. She had no idea why he wanted to fight her.

Maybe he just wants to spar with you like Wyatt, she told

herself, trying desperately to give him a chance. Her gut said otherwise. *He could just be socially awkward...*

But he didn't look it. He radiated arrogance, something Kitty herself could relate to.

"It doesn't matter what I wear; I could kick your ass in a garbage bag and *still* look fabulous doing it," Kitty shot back. "Let's just get this over with."

"With pleasure."

The referee, one of the physical education professors, came shortly after. He was a stout man, wearing slacks and a button-down. A whistle looped around his neck; it seemed out of place, given the rest of his attire. In a gravelly voice, he said, "Do you both know the rules?"

"Yes," Ryder replied.

"Explain them," Kitty said.

The professor nodded. "You will have twenty minutes for each round. Leaving the chalk circle—" he gestured to the circle drawn on the concrete— "will get you disqualified. Any shots taken after the whistle blows will also disqualify you. By agreeing to a duel, you agree that any consequences or long-term damage done is on you and not on the school. Likewise, any damage to your weapons is your responsibility to fix or replace, not on the school. You pin, you win. Do you understand?"

Kitty nodded. The chalk circle was wide enough to fit a full-sized school bus in, and the time limit was more than enough for Kitty to render most opponents she faced defeated. But she hadn't seen Ryder fight before, and looking at the crowd, she wondered if this could be an opportunity to prove to them precisely how wrong Dr. Woods's article was.

The idea of uncredentialed individuals who barely speak English robbing opportunities from more qualified, home-grown talent is not only disconcerting but also undermines the hard work of our students and faculty.

Uncredentialed?

Kitty could show them exactly how much she deserved to be here—by kicking this smug shadowborn's ass.

She grabbed her saber. The dark metal matched her eyes. The blade belonged to her grandfather, custom-made to be a cross between a traditional saber and a meat clever. They called him 'The Butcher'.

The weighty weapon was more than half her height tall and seven inches wide, blunt on one end and sharp as hell on the other. She held it as if it weighed nothing, a display of the strength cultivation provided her. Focusing her energy, she found the qi in the air and circulated it through her meridians to prepare herself. Strengthening her body further, the whistle blew, and Kitty darted forward.

Ryder only used a double-edged sword, and if he wasn't trained well enough, it could bounce back in his face when he attempted to strike. She wasn't cocky enough to play with him, but she wanted to get a taste of his fighting style so she'd know how to counter it.

Sure enough, he managed to block her with strength befitting of a shadowborn. She lunged forward several more times, not to land a blow, but to see how he would react in close combat. As expected, he wasn't prepared for it, and kept trying to push her back. His stance was solid, though. He never lost stability as they fought, but his moves were linear, back and forth like a pawn on a chess board.

"You're strong," he commented, his voice controlled. He wasn't tired at all. Maybe *he* was the one playing with *her*. "They said you would be."

"That doesn't sound like a compliment." Kitty blocked a blow, narrowly avoiding catching his sword with her face.

"It isn't." He blocked her saber again. "Jeez, don't you know the meaning of personal space?"

She took a step forward just as he did, swinging his sword to the side and arching it toward her arm. Kitty was fully prepared to block the blow, but when she moved to lift her saber, she found it was too heavy.

Not now, she thought. Of course, her powers had to choose the most inopportune time to crap out on her. She managed to deflect the strike somewhat, but the force of his strength brought her to her knees. She dropped the saber, now completely unable to lift it.

Damn it. She scrambled up, not bothering with the weapon anymore. It was no use—her powers wouldn't be returning before the match ended.

"Giving up so soon?" Ryder asked, almost like he hoped she'd say yes.

They both paused for a moment, and it was then Kitty noticed the crowd. She hadn't paid much attention before, and now was *not* a good time to start. But as her head swiveled around, seeing the leering face, she knew one thing: everyone in that arena was hoping she would fail. They came to see her defeated.

She wanted to throw up.

But Kitty would never give them the satisfaction. "I don't walk away from a fight, ever."

"Are you going to crawl away? That would be entertaining, to see that short skirt—"

She lunged. He wasn't expecting it, possibly because he had a sword and she had nothing. Why would an unarmed fighter throw themselves at their opponent?

She swung around at the last second, sliding to the ground and kicking him hard in the back of his knee. He went down easily, and while he was startled, she landed another blow to the space where his neck met his shoulder.

Kitty might not have been as strong as a shadowborn in her current state, nor was she as fast, but it hardly mattered. She had to win: not only for herself, but for her family.

She didn't let Ryder recover from her blows. She didn't spare herself much time to recover, either. She knew she had to hit hard, fast, and in the correct spots. Back of the knees. Ears. Throat. Groin. She was a blur of movements, and when she finally pinned him to the ground and knocked his sword away.

The whistle blew, but not a single person cheered. The room was stock silent, and while Kitty shouldn't have been surprised, a tiny part of her was hurt. But she brushed it away, reminding herself she didn't need validation.

Not from these losers, she told herself.

Taking a breath, Kitty released him and stood, brushing herself off. In a show of good sportsmanship, she held out her hand to help him up.

Ryder stared at her for a moment, a myriad of unintelligible emotions on his face. He took her hand, smiling without any humor in his eyes. "You're good, Katherine Swan."

"It's actually—"

Before she could finish her sentence, Ryder bent down and kissed her full on the mouth.

"I DIDN'T THINK I'd see you here so soon, Miss Swan."

Kitty hadn't expected to be in the chancellor's office again this quickly, either. But of all the emotions running through her right now, shame was not one of them. "I'm surprised you called me in here, too."

"You assaulted a student," Chancellor Kinsey pointed out. "You also called him names that I, as an educator, cannot repeat on school grounds."

"He kissed me against my will. Actions have consequences." And, in Ryder's case, said consequences ended in a slap in the face. With her *human*-level strength. "It's hardly my fault he was such a little bitch about it."

Yeah, she knew that wasn't a very nice thing to say. But screw being nice.

"You know, he ate broccoli before we fought. I could taste it," she said. "I *hate* broccoli."

"Miss Swan. Parents have been calling me for the past hour, complaining," Kinsey said impatiently. "They feel their children are not safe at an institution where students are ferociously assaulting other students after duels!"

"He assaulted *me* with his broccoli breath!" Kitty argued. "He shouldn't have kissed me. And he sure as fuck shouldn't have *won* because I slapped him."

"The rules stated that any blows dealt after the whistle was blown would disqualify you. You agreed to those terms, Miss Swan."

She had, and she suspected that was why Ryder kissed her. To provoke her, to make her break the rules. There was no chemistry between them, no prior rapport that could ever justify the kiss.

In truth, it wasn't even the kiss itself that bothered her. Though that was pretty gross, due to the aforementioned broccoli. Yuck. It was the way others treated her afterward, the way she lost, and now, how she'd been called into the chancellor's office for defending herself.

Suffice to say, her anger burned hotter than Satan's asshole.

"The board is very displeased with you," Chancellor Kinsey said gravely. "And due to the article you participated in, published by Dr. Woods—"

"The one riddled with *lies*?"

"Dr. Woods is a highly accomplished researcher. Accusing her of lying would not be smart, Miss Swan."

"When did I ever claim to be smart?" That was Noelle's thing. And far be it for Kitty to take that away from her sister. That was, like, the basis of her identity.

He gave her a stern look. "Parents and faculty are questioning the validity of your family's presence here. The situation does not look good for you. Of course, I think expelling you would be extreme. But I *did* come up with another solution, perhaps one that will benefit us both. You see, many think you are here because of your...ethnic background."

"That's the dumbest thing I've ever heard."

"Well, some of our largest donations come from these parents. Their words hold weight."

"Their *money* holds weight in your pockets, you mean," Kitty said, though she knew she really shouldn't have talked back to him.

"Miss Swan," he admonished. "It is believed that you and your siblings should undergo a trial, of sorts. You see, when the school was first founded, we had many students from various backgrounds. We needed a placement test to see who would be assigned to which level of combat classes. To do this, we held Blood Trials, a series of three aptitude tests designed to test magic and physical ability. They were retired fifty-odd years ago, but—with the board's permission—we're allowing you Swan siblings to complete each trial at your own pace."

"Oh. So nice that you're *allowing* us to take part in three tests no one else at this school has to take," Kitty scathed. "Do you even hear yourself?"

"You could just save us all the trouble and withdraw. Less paperwork," he suggested.

No. Jax and Noelle had just got settled, and Māma and Bàba were finally working regular hours. They couldn't go back to the way things were, and frankly, Kitty wasn't sure if the school would take away the money they'd already given the Swans.

She didn't want to leave, but she couldn't accept this treatment lying down, either.

So she said, through gritted teeth, "No. I'm not leaving."

He smiled. "Perfect. The first trial is a test of strength. That is all I can tell you; no one else will be able to help you, either. You'll only be given information once you come to the testing center—"

"I'll take the test in two days," Kitty interrupted impulsively. "If I beat it, I never want to see the inside of your office again."

Chancellor Kinsey chuckled. "You're very confident. But remember, there are a series of three trials."

"Whatever you need to tell yourself, buddy," she said. "I know you want me to be ashamed of who I am and where I came from, but I'm not. I don't care how many tests you throw at me or bogus articles your staff writes; I'm staying right here."

VERONICA STORMED into the medical office, slamming the door shut and startling the on-duty nurse.

"Don't do that," she admonished. "Some students are sleeping!"

"Sorry," Veronica muttered, the reprimand taking a bit of the wind out of her sails. But then she saw Ryder, and her anger renewed.

He sat on a bed by the window, overlooking campus. Holding an ice pack to his cheek and another to his eye, he looked like he might as well stick his head in the freezer. Not only was his eye starting to bruise, but he still sported a distinct red handprint on his cheek and a nasty split lip. The rest of him looked pretty battered, too, his arms and what she could see of his legs a smattering of bruises.

And he deserved every single one.

He lit up when he saw her, wincing as he tried to smile. "Vee. What brings you here?"

"You!" She hit his arm, not caring how hurt he was.

"Ouch! Harsh!" he said, though his words held no real bite. "I just got beat up by a giant baboon. Or would it be more appropriate to say panda bear?"

"You're a jerk, you know that?" Veronica yelled.

The nurse glared at her.

"How could you do that?" Veronica asked, lowering her voice. "You...you kissed my best friend!"

"Jealous?"

"You kissed her so you could get her disqualified." Veronica was certain that was the case. Not that Kitty wasn't beautiful—she was. But that was hardly the time or the place. No, Veronica suspected something else was going on, and Ryder was involved. "Why would you do something like that?"

"Come on, Vee. Don't read me the riot act," he groaned. "I already got beat up by your ex-boyfriend today."

That froze her in her tracks. "What are you talking about? Blake hit you?"

"Yeah. Well, his friend did. The dude is a monster." Ryder pointed to his split lip. "I thought he was gonna kill me until Blake pulled him off. I've already had a near-death experience today. Cut me some slack."

"What, were you embarrassed, losing to Kitty?" Veronica asked.

"I didn't lose. I won."

"Because she was disqualified."

"Hey, it doesn't matter *how* I won. I did." He shrugged. "I can't believe you're still hanging around that chick after that article came out."

Veronica couldn't believe him. "It was all lies. The Swan family is really nice—you shouldn't believe what people are saying so easily."

"The kiss didn't mean anything," Ryder assured her.

Her face turned bright red, and she took a step back. "Why would I care if it meant anything?"

"Because you like me," he said simply.

Veronica wanted to scream. What the hell? Her? Like *him*? Okay, so admittedly, he was attractive. But so were lots of guys at the school. Blake was attractive. Cyrus was attractive. Wyatt was attractive. Didn't mean she wanted to date any of them. (Well, if Wyatt asked her out, she probably would agree. But he had a girlfriend, so it was a moot point.)

It was clear Veronica didn't have good taste in men, so how could she trust herself to go on a date with Ryder? More importantly, he just kissed her best friend! It would be one thing if he kissed Kitty because he liked her. It was arguably much worse knowing that he only kissed her to manipulate the situation in his favor.

Veronica placed her hands on her hips. "I do *not* like you."

"*Sure* you don't. That's why you came all the way over here to find me and tell me off, right?"

"Yeah, that's exactly why I came! To defend my friend's honor!"

"Your so-called friend already slapped me across the face. And she's got the mouth of a friggin' sailor." He showed her his cheek, swelling by the minute. "Look, there's no shame in liking me, Vee. Lots of girls do. But you know the difference?"

Veronica didn't want to play his game, but she asked anyway. "What?"

"I like you, too."

TWELVE

WITH ALL THE gossip flying around campus, the last thing Melody Ward wanted to do was hunt ferals. Not only were hunts gross, physically demanding, and mentally draining, but as someone solely with an assist role, she was allowed (read: forced) to go on more than students who wielded blades. It was unfair, if you asked her. Just because she carried a crossbow didn't mean she stayed far from the action, or that her assists weren't just as valuable as other teammates' efforts.

Still, she continued to go on hunts because she didn't know how to refuse. Even thinking about saying no to Professor Everleigh induced anxiety so great, Mel nearly threw up. Ever since Rory had died, she felt such a profound guilt within her. She didn't have a single idea how to deal with it, despite the numerous Instagram pages she followed about mental health. But oh well.

Mel had a running list of things she didn't want to think about, and Rory topped it. But now, thanks to her brother, she added something new this afternoon: Cyrus's anger issues. She didn't get it at all. Hell, she thought he'd be *happy* to see

Kitty Swan and Ryder Kinsey fight. Watching Kitty, or any of the Swans, spar felt like watching an action movie. Sure, Ryder had given her a peck on the lips, but from what Melody could seen, it didn't mean anything. And even if it had, Kitty slapped him so hard he spat blood afterward. So, what exactly was eating Cyrus?

He looked fine after the fight. Blake, Mel, and Cy poured out into the hallway with the rest of the students. As soon as he saw Ryder walk out, holding his cheek from where Kitty hit him, a switch flipped in her brother. Blake and Wyatt had to pull Cy away; Melody was too shocked. By the time she came back to herself, Everleigh was dragging her down the hall with a last-minute assignment. She didn't even get to see how everything played out. Would her brother get in trouble? She hoped not. But, more than anything, she hoped this wasn't a sign he had residual feelings for Kitty.

Mel tried to focus on her current mission instead. The fog was thick in this part of the woods, and all she could see was Charity's blonde ponytail swinging a few steps in front of her. Mel gripped her crossbow, ready to fire should anything pop out at them.

They were hunting a chimera bear, this time. Sightings reported it had antlers like a deer, clawed feet like a big cat, hands with five fingers like a human, the body of a bear, and the head of a praying mantis. Oh, and it was covered in white fur, so it would blend in with the fog real nicely. Fantastic.

Seriously, she didn't know how the Veil ended up with so many freaky animal combos, and she wasn't sure she wanted to. Ick.

Charity stopped short, and Mel nearly punctured her back with an arrow. She yipped and swung her crossbow to the side just in time.

"Black goo," Charity murmured.

"Watch it," Mel snapped, though it lacked bite. She and Charity weren't friends, per se, but they were *childhood* friends, which was its own separate category. Charity and Cyrus always hung around each other—they were a trio, with Blake. Mel hung around on the outskirts of their little group, being Cyrus's annoying younger sister. Though, admittedly, Cyrus was kinder to her than any other older brother would have been; he never complained about her or left her out. And Charity, despite being withdrawn even as a child, was a steady presence in Mel's life. The girls wouldn't talk about serious topics, but they didn't mind each other's presence. The familiarity was comforting, in a sense. Of course, that comfort only went so far. Hunting a bear with an insect head in fog so dense she couldn't see her hand in front of her face? Yeah, Mel didn't feel very comforted, regardless of who her partner was.

Luckily, the fog started to clear by the time they walked a bit further, and Mel made out the outline of trees. Dead trees, but trees, nonetheless. She understood why her father left this hellhole.

Not that he ever talked about it. He rarely spoke about anything serious.

They followed the trail of feral goo, which went against every instinct Mel possessed. Suddenly, a roar echoed through the woods, shaking the ground. As the fog cleared, almost miraculously, another sound joined the *chorus* of growls surrounding the girls.

Laughter.

Human laughter. From a woman, by what Mel could tell.

Fear seized her heart and she readied her bow, while Charity's back slammed into Mel's. They circled the center of the clearing, eyes searching their surroundings. But nothing came forward. If anything, the fog looked like it had only dispersed around them, in a perfect radius.

Charity tensed. "What the hell is going on...?"

Melody didn't have an answer, focusing solely on not passing out. Funny, the frequency of these hunts made Cy a better fighter. They did nothing to curb Mel's apprehension or fear.

The laughter weaved through the trees, becoming so loud it sounded like someone had pressed their lips to her ear one moment, and then jumped ten feet away the next. For a shadowborn angel, Mel shouldn't have been scared of ghosts. They didn't exist...probably. But right now, especially after her brother's incident in the morgue, she was questioning everything.

"We need to push forward," Charity said.

"I would rather not, if that's okay with you," Melody replied.

"Don't be a baby."

"I'm not!" she said defensively. "I just don't think..."

She trailed off, on account of seeing someone through the trees. She couldn't quite make out the figure, pushing her glasses up. It was a woman, she thought, darting between the trees.

Melody didn't *enjoy* using her magic. It was rare, the ability of True Sight, and often overwhelming. But she used it then, almost on instinct. Her eyes went from olive green to completely white as she looked around, searching for an aura. Each person had one, unmistakably unique. Not that Melody could always *tell* per se. Some looked the same, but upon further inspection, there were small differences. Because the ability was so rare, Mel didn't know much about what determined it. The colors represented something, a reflection of the soul along with powers. Humans, for example, tended to have a duller aura. Truebloods had dark, jewel-toned auras; shadowborn auras were even darker.

Kitty Swan's aura was black—the only aura she'd *ever* seen that was completely dark, like a shadow. The rest of her family had bright auras, almost neon.

Mel searched the trees, her eyes focusing on a bright green aura. Like a flame, it rose and fell, coupled with the laughter she heard earlier. It flickered on and off, coming closer and farther away, almost as if someone was teleporting...

Which was impossible. It should have been, anyway.

Melody's eyes returned to normal, and she looked on as the figure drew closer. The girl—Mel was now certain it was a woman—peeked out from behind the tree. The features were too far away, but now, coupled with the aura, Melody knew who it was.

The girl's eyes, even from far away, shined a brilliant green. Just like Charity's.

Melody gasped, and at the same time, Charity whipped her ax at the girl's head. The girl disappeared as the ax sunk into the trunk of a tree.

"Charity!" Melody exclaimed.

Charity's eyes hardened, her fists clenched so tightly they'd turned white. "Mel."

Her voice was rough and low, unlike anything Mel had ever heard from the girl.

"Char, was that—"

"Don't tell anyone," Charity snapped abruptly, as if she didn't even want to hear Mel speak her sister's name. "Especially not Blake."

"YOU LET the girl beat you. How humiliating."

Ryder didn't dare admit that he hadn't 'let' the Swan girl win. Instead, he told his father, "It will inspire more hatred, Dad. Don't worry so much. I know what I'm doing."

Chancellor Kinsey looked at his son like he had two heads. "Really? Then why isn't she gone yet?"

"You had your chance. You should have expelled her after she hit me," Ryder argued.

"I couldn't. You are my son—the board thought I was acting 'too emotionally' when I suggested that. There are those who want her gone, it's true, but some of the others are intrigued by her," the chancellor said, disgusted. "You should have beaten her. You represent *me*. What will others think, now that you've been beaten by a little girl? She looks no more than twelve years old!"

Ryder thought it was an exaggeration, but he didn't dare say anything. In truth, he *didn't* know how the bitch had done it—and he despised her for it all the more. What his father said wasn't false; losing to a woman, especially one like that, was humiliating. Had she been beautiful, at least he would have enjoyed holding her body close as he pinned her. But everything about her was rough and hardened, as evidenced by the multitude of bruises on his body.

Maybe she cheated somehow. But a small voice in his head told him that wasn't the case, and damn it if he couldn't even lie to himself about it to ease his mortification.

Despite his growing distaste for the little cunt, he couldn't claim that she didn't belong at the school. Mortal or not, she had defeated a shadowborn. That spoke to something within Ryder, and had she been a man, perhaps he would have respected her.

Arrogance never looks good on a woman, he thought. *On me? It is even worse.*

"You fail to see the bigger picture," Ryder reasoned, making it up as he went. "By going against her directly, I've baited her. The crowd I drew with the duel knew very well who I am—shadowborn, like them. I fit in."

"Despite your absence."

"Well, yes. I am shadowborn, which means I'm like their representative. The Swan girl was my opponent...my enemy. And, by extension, theirs. I've made her into something that must be defeated." Something...*other*. Though Ryder intended to completely destroy her publicly, plans shifted. This also worked in his favor, given how many students hated her. It was amusing, in a way. The article set the stage, and those preconceived notions of her arrogance only fed into her poor reputation, an us vs. them mentality that was lovely to watch unfold. "You have her where you want her, now. She won't pass the trials."

"But if she does—"

"She won't." Not if Ryder had anything to say about it. "She can't possibly succeed, and that will be grounds for expulsion. Even if she doesn't fail, she can't do the trials and attend class at the same time. Whether she bombs the trials or flunks her classes, it's all the same. She'll be gone before the winter."

His father shook his head, letting out a sigh. "You'd better hope you are right about this."

"I am." Ryder was sure of it.

The phone rang, and the chancellor picked up in a swift movement. He didn't say anything, nodding as if the other person could see him. Finally, after two minutes of stone-cold silence, he rose and hung up the phone. "I'll be back in a minute. There's something Dr. Woods needs in the lab. Don't move—we're not finished with this discussion."

"I wouldn't dream of it." Ryder watched as the chancellor left the office, the fool. He waited several minutes, looking at the grandfather clock on the wall, before moving behind the computer. His father kept it locked, but didn't use double sign-on like he should have. His password was scrawled on a Post-It in the drawer.

Ryder shoved a memory stick in the port and dumped every folder he could onto the thing. His father wouldn't be back for at least fifteen minutes, having to walk all the way to the labs and then back. If Dr. Woods wouldn't speak over the phone, it would be a long conversation.

When the upload finished, Ryder took the memory stick out and left the computer as he found it. Slinging his backpack over his shoulder, he left the office.

"Can you tell my dad I'll see him later?" Ryder asked the secretary.

She nodded, smiling. "Goodbye, dear. You get some rest."

"Thanks." He sauntered out of the main office, scanning the halls. He had too much to do, and too little time to do it.

He headed straight for the girls' dorm, going in the back way to let himself in and taking the elevator to Veronica's floor. She would probably be home, this early in the day. Not like he could check. She wasn't answering his texts.

He knocked on the door, putting a hand over the peephole so she couldn't reject him outright. He needed her, both for her powers and for her connection to the Swan girl. And, admittedly, he liked Veronica. Perhaps not as much as he initially made it seem, but of all the bitches on campus, she was the most tolerable. He meant what he told her yesterday, though she stormed off before giving him an answer. He knew he should have given her space, but he wasn't patient.

She yanked the door open, eyes bleary from sleep. A loose t-shirt hung off her shoulders, skimming the top of her thighs. "What do you want?"

Ryder grinned. "You."

She began to close the door, but he slammed a hand against it and wedged his body in the doorway, forcing himself inside.

"Hey!" she protested, stumbling back.

"Are you going to accept my apology?"

"When did you apologize?"

"I'm apologizing now," he said. "I'm sorry, Vee. I don't want things to be weird between us."

Veronica crossed her arms, unaware that her sleep shirt rode even higher when she did so. "*I'm* not the one you should be apologizing to."

He groaned. "I was afraid you were going to say that."

But at least she didn't seem too angry at him. He needed her as an ally—*wanted* her to be, anyway. Not that he thought Vee was the type of person who would turn against her best friend so easily.

She was definitely the type that would be easy to manipulate, though. And she came in such a pretty package.

"You want me to tell the Swan girl I'm sorry? I'll do it," Ryder agreed.

"Try saying that again without sounding like you have a gun to your head," Veronica said.

"Will you help me?" he asked, taking a step forward.

She studied his face, putting her hands on her hips. "Fine. But we're going *right now*. And you're going to be sincere."

"Am I not always?"

She rolled her eyes and walked into her closet, picking out some clothes. "Turn around, please."

Ryder was...not a gentleman. But he didn't want *her* to know that, so he did as she asked. When she finished, the two walked to the cafeteria in silence. He didn't dare provoke her, though he wanted to, just to see her cheeks redden. Now was not the time.

When the pair arrived, he spotted Swan immediately. She held court in the corner of the cafeteria, sitting on the tabletop with her back against the wall. Two other girls sat with her, one Asian and another with pink streaks in her hair.

Veronica paused at the sight of Blake, but only for a second, before continuing. "Kitty."

The girl looked up, her stony expression melting into a smile. "Vee. And...oh. You."

God, the girl made every hair on his arms stand. Ryder stood at the end of the table, rooted in place. Veronica didn't have the same reservations. "He's come to apologize."

Kitty looked him over. "But he's not sorry."

"He is," Veronica insisted, nudging Ryder's side.

He could have swallowed his pride earlier, but now, standing in front of the little bitch, the last thing he wanted to do was apologize. Even if it meant earning Veronica's favor. He met the Swan girl's gaze, unflinching. She didn't intimidate him, even if she'd bested him once. It proved nothing.

"You throw a mean punch," Ryder said, "but it doesn't change the fact that you lost."

"You're as good of a fighter as you are a kisser, which is to say, you're severely lacking in both areas," she shot back, tossing her hair over her shoulder.

"You don't have to play coy with me. You can admit that you liked it."

"Is there a point to this? Or is your life goal to be as insufferable as humanly possible?"

He snorted. Pot, meet kettle. "Wow, you got my number."

"If I had your number, I'd throw my phone into a fire."

Bitch. "You know, kissing you wasn't so great, either. You've got lips like a dead fish."

"Ryder!" Veronica hissed. Yeah, he fucked that one up.

"Kitty, don't," the other Asian girl warned. She muttered something else in a foreign language, not that it mattered to Swan.

Kitty moved like a viper, her movements graceful and smooth as she stood from the table. She wasn't as tall as Ryder, but she tilted her chin up, looking him dead in the eyes. "You know what? *I'm* sorry. I'm sorry you're such a sore loser that you can't admit I'm not only physically stronger than you, but a better fighter."

"You aren't *better* than me. I won," Ryder said, annoyed. "Doesn't matter how—it is an indisputable fact that I won. And if you think you're stronger, then you're batshit crazy. But, well, you know what they say: You are what you eat."

THIRTEEN

DAILY PROMPT: REFLECT ON A TIME WHEN YOU HELPED SOMEONE ELSE, AND WHAT IMPACT DID IT HAVE ON YOU AND THEM?

> *I didn't tear Ryder's throat out with my teeth when he insinuated that I eat bats, exhibiting extreme self-control. The impact is, I'm not in jail and he's not rotting on a metal slab. I didn't give in to my angry impulses, and that probably makes me a better person. Even if I feel like total shit right now because I didn't defend myself and let him walk away smugly.*

Kitty put her pen down, resisting the urge to cross the entry out again. She already made a promise to herself not to tear any more pages out, but the more she wrote, the cringier the entries became. She knew that was *supposed* to happen, but it was a lot easier to respect herself when she gave one-word answers.

Nobody told her that being a nice person involved scrutinizing her opinions of *herself*. Wasn't it enough that she recognized she wasn't all sunshine and rainbows? Now she had to deal with this self-reflection crap. Thinking about her feelings in and of itself wasn't bad, but writing it down and re-reading past entries to see her own "mental growth" or whatever? Gag.

Before, she was concerned about being evil, and how it would affect those she cared about. Not just her family, but the friends she'd made. There was much more involved when one was a bad person, and Kitty learned that on top of being abrasive, over-competitive, and mean-spirited by nature, she was also a hypocrite.

Remembering the words Cyrus had thrown at her shortly after their first meeting—calling her vapid and shallow—she realized living a life unexamined felt far better than putting her emotions under a microscope. Or, at least, writing them down in pink glitter-gel pen.

In the beginning, her entries were comfortably short, pared down to a sentence at most. For example, her first entry:

DAILY PROMPT: WHAT ARE YOU LOOKING FORWARD TO IN THE NEAR FUTURE, AND HOW CAN YOU PREPARE FOR IT?

Showering; I feel gross.

See? Was that not a perfect response? Now, she wrote...*paragraphs*. Using words from, good God, her *emotional toolbox*. Thinking about it made her want to puke!

Sometimes, she wished she was an old man. It would be

socially acceptable for her to grunt out one-word answers, then. But she supposed she should be grateful she wasn't an old man, because she doubted she could pull off a micro-mini skirt quite so well.

She closed her journal and shoved it in her bag.

"Kitty!" Bàba called from the kitchen. "I could use some help!"

He and Māma hadn't spoken to her since she arrived. She figured they were angry with her for how she handled Ryder, and didn't want to press them, lest she delve into another argument. She needed to tell her siblings about the Blood Trials anyway and was prepared for a blow-out fight.

She hadn't *meant* to get them involved in her mess. If it were up to her, she would handle it all on her own. Noelle was just getting into the swing of school, and Jax...

Okay, so she didn't know what his deal was. The little brat —not so little anymore, she reminded herself—barely spoke to her. Was this 'teen angst'?

"Kitty!" Bàba called again.

Kitty rose and walked into the kitchen, where a symphony of smells greeted her. "You're doing Dim Sum?"

Bamboo steamers filled the counter, and Bàba handed her a small bowl with steamed spare ribs in a brown glaze. "You try! We have a special guest coming for dinner."

This was the first time she was hearing that. "Special guest?"

"Yes, yes. Uncle Stefan met someone and—oh, you'll see."

Māma entered the kitchen, and Bàba watched as she skirted around him to get to the dishes. She wasn't allowed near the food. "Kitty, you help me set the table."

Kitty nodded, gathering the bowls of rice and small plates while her mother got the cup of chopsticks. The pair began bringing food out and setting the dishes on the lazy Susan at the center of the table. Of course, the smell brought out the two vultures, Noelle and Jax. Thankfully, her siblings weren't completely useless, arranging the dishes and getting water cups, along with tea. They truly *were* having a traditional dinner.

"So, uh, I have something to say," Kitty announced awkwardly. "Before the special guest or whoever comes."

Bàba and Māma paused, giving her their undivided attention.

"I assume you heard about the duel...thing," she said. "With Ryder Kinsey."

"Ah. Yes," Bà said. "I wanted to speak with you about that."

"It's not that we're *disappointed*, Kitty," Mā began. "But Bàba and I were talking, and we realize we've been slacking. With all of you. We've been so caught up in the lab, we haven't had a chance to train together as a family."

"You fought well," Bàba said, "but after that boy kissed you... What do I always tell you kids?"

"Aim for the balls," the Swan children chorused.

"Always," Māma confirmed, settling at the table. "There are many other pain points that won't leave permanent damage. After dinner, we'll go to the gym and review. The goal is to maximize their pain while minimizing your own efforts."

"It is very satisfying to see your enemies writhing in agony," Bàba added cheerfully.

Kitty was relieved they weren't angry. Yet. "That's not all, though. Because of that incident, I spoke with Chancellor Kinsey."

"You didn't gloat about it, did you?" Noelle asked. "Bàba, can we start eating?"

"No, we'll wait for our guest."

"What did Kinsey say?" Jax asked. "Did you get expelled?"

"Do you think I'd be sitting here if I'd done that?"

"Yeah, you're a glutton and you would've been drawn in by the food."

"Like you aren't the same?" Kitty asked hotly.

He shoved her shoulder. "You always eat the last of everything! If there's one more cookie left in the pack, you take it without asking anyone!"

"You *inhale* sweets! Noelle and I are lucky there are even enough snacks left after you're finished going through the pantry! You'd eat us out of a house!"

"Let's calm down," Māma said, giving the kids a stern look. "Kitty, what did Chancellor Kinsey say?"

"He, uh, said that...the board and a bunch of parents don't think I deserve to be at this school," Kitty began, struggling to find the words. "He told me I could either withdraw —all of us—or we could take this sort of magic entrance exam. There is a series of three tests, and I kind of volunteered us to take the first one tomorrow."

"Tomorrow," Noelle repeated. "Huh. Why are you looking at me like that?"

"You're not pissed, are you?"

"It's just an exam. I'm great at those."

"And then maybe we'll get some respect around here," Jax muttered.

"What do you mean? Are kids being mean to you?" Kitty asked sharply. "Give me their names and I'll ruin their lives."

He turned red. "I don't need *you* to fight my battles for me. I'm bigger than you, now."

"What's that supposed to mean?"

"I can cook up a batch of Anus Annihilator," Noelle

offered. "That will solve both your problems. You give some to your classmates, Jax, and Kitty and I will take care of Ryder Kinsey."

"Anus Annihilator is *not* the answer," Māma warned. "You cannot solve all your problems with high-potency laxatives, Noelle."

"Really? I think it gets people to shut up relatively quickly."

"It also clogs our toilets when you test the batches on your sister."

"Touché."

The doorbell rang, and Kitty sprang up, eager to get away from the conversation, which started and ended on an awkward note. But when she opened the front door, she was *not* expecting who she saw.

She screamed, slamming the door closed. An extreme reaction, perhaps.

"What's wrong?" Jax and Noelle shot to their feet, rushing toward the door. If something made *Kitty* scream...

She pointed a shaking finger at the door. "T-There's a..."

"What?" Noelle demanded. She yanked the door open, only to have the same reaction as her sister: screaming and closing it again.

Jax rolled his eyes. "You two are so dramatic."

"We are *not*," Kitty hissed, though admittedly, he was right.

The sisters took a step back as Jax crowded the entryway, opening the front door for a third time. The stranger standing outside put a hand on the door, forcing his way inside. He wasn't being rude, per se; it seemed as though he was trying to prevent the door from closing in his face again.

He was, without a doubt, the most handsome man Kitty

had ever seen. In person or on television. Even more handsome than her celebrity crush, Charlie He. No, this guy was on a whole other level entirely.

"My apologies for the interruption," he said smoothly. Even his voice was sexy! He had a faint accent, similar to the Swan parents, but nothing that would hinder anyone's understanding of his English.

"You aren't interrupting. We were waiting for you," Māma gushed, rushing over. "Come in, come in."

"Thank you," the handsome stranger said. He wore black trousers, dress shoes, and a button-down, all of which gave him a somewhat luxurious aura unbefitting of their small apartment. He was so tall, he nearly had to duck inside. But despite his large stature and the muscles rippling beneath his shirt, he had a face that could only be described as *beautiful*. Smooth, creamy skin contrasted his jet-black hair, strong brows, and dark eyes.

The combination of all his features, each one perfect, made Kitty's brain turn to mush.

"This is Chen Jianhao. He'll be our research assistant this semester," Bàba announced, switching to Mandarin. "He is from the same cultivation sect we were part of, though he's defected as well."

He must have defected a while ago, since his English was so good. In the sect the Swan parents had grown up in, they'd only spoken Mandarin and used traditional Chinese characters for writing. The sect lived completely secluded from modern China and didn't even cook their food! They only ate raw vegetables, which was perhaps the reason why Bàba liked to play chef so often.

"Shībó told me all about you," Jianhao said, referring to Uncle Stefan. He turned to Kitty with a charming smile. "He said you were lovely, and I must agree. You would be a wonderful candidate to be my wife."

MELODY THOUGHT LONG and hard about what to do, and eventually, she found herself standing in front of Professor Everleigh's office door. Taking a deep breath, she pushed it open.

Inside, piles of books and loose papers were stacked on every available surface. They created a wall of paper with a single narrow path to his desk—quite the fire hazard indeed.

"Um, Professor? A-Are you busy?" Melody asked, her voice squeaking as she spoke up.

Professor Everleigh's head popped up over a stack of dusty spell books. "Melody. What brings you here? You're not having trouble in school, are you?"

"No, sir. I was just wondering if I could talk to you. About the Churchill family," Melody clarified, her heart beating a mile a minute. "You worked at the college when Tessa Churchill was..."

"Killed?" he supplied with ease.

Melody had been about to say, "a student here." He'd cut right to the chase. "Yeah. Were you on the hunt when she died?"

"They weren't hunts back then," he reminded her, sitting back in his chair. She couldn't see his face, but his voice carried over the mess. "The feral disease was a very new occurrence, and you must remember, three years ago, the problem was mostly contained in certain areas of the Veil. Kids from the college snuck out all the time to the Veil, usually on dates. Sometimes they would go on assignments—extra credit for science and the like. I believe Tessa had to gather some potion ingredients and sought to turn it into a date, inviting Blake Blackwood to go with her. He was still a high school student, I remember."

"He was a senior," Melody recalled.

"Yes. I didn't see the two leaving campus. Students could come and go as they pleased, not needing permission to go into the Veil. But when he came back, he woke the entire school up. Funnily enough, when I spoke with him, he didn't remember much. He spoke of a monster and was covered in her blood. We never found the girl's body—but we found the beast."

Melody winced. She remembered fragments of that time. She had been a junior in high school. She woke up one night to her parents pacing the kitchen, on the phone with Mr. Blackwood. Cyrus had demanded to go to the college and see what was happening. Eventually, Dad and Cy had left while Mel stayed with her mother.

The search for Tessa went on for days before she was declared dead. More attacks had begun to happen all over the country—reports of shadowborn being infected in the Veil and dying within twenty-four hours. After that, based on Blake's account, it was assumed Tessa had died as well.

"What if Tessa...mutated?" Melody asked. "There was no body, right?"

"The illness destroys shadowborn bodies, causing them to rot rapidly. It's possible there was nothing left of her."

"But the most recent instance, the Blood Wasp colony, that infected body didn't rot," Mel protested. "The nature of magic is fickle. Could it be possible that Tessa is still alive, somehow?"

"Excuse me?"

"I saw her," she blurted. "I saw Tessa. In the Veil. I...I know it was her."

"Tessa Churchill," Everleigh repeated incredulously. "You saw her alive and well?"

"Her eyes were unmistakable," Melody confirmed. "But I don't know how that's possible."

"It isn't. Perhaps it was a trick of the light, or a shapeshifter, or something else. You've been on quite a few hunts," he said.

"I know what I saw." But as she spoke, her mind became riddled with doubts. Many girls had green eyes, and yes, Charity's family had a very distinct and bright shade of green, but the figure they'd seen had been quite far away.

Still...

"What if Tessa is back?" Melody asked. "A ghost or...or something? What if there's more to this illness than we originally thought?"

"That could be so," Professor Everleigh relented, "but I assure you, Melody, despite all the changes that are happening right now? With the discovery of the Swans, the ferals, and more recent developments, one thing still holds true: the dead stay dead."

Melody hesitated. There was more she wanted to say, but no words came out. Finally, she nodded. "Yes. Of course, Professor. I was...being silly."

"It's alright, Melody," he said softly. "You know as well as I do that I wish that weren't true. But it is. It would be best if you forgot about that incident."

As if on cue, the door opened, and a young woman bustled in with an arm full of empty boxes. She was unassuming, with brown hair cut to her shoulders and dark clothes that could have been found on a mannequin in the Gap. The only reason Melody paused was the girl's eyes. She had one brown eye, and the other was pale blue, bordering silver. Heterochromia, it was called.

"Ah, thank you, Nora," Professor Everleigh said. "If that is all, Melody, I believe my assistant and I have some work to do here."

"Of course, Professor. Thank you," Melody said, excusing herself. She nodded at the girl as she squeezed past her on her way to the door. Nora's head swiveled, watching silently as Melody exited. Even after she closed the door, that one blue eye burned bright in her memory.

FOURTEEN

DAILY PROMPT: WHAT'S ONE PIECE OF ADVICE YOU'D GIVE TO SOMEONE YOU CARE ABOUT?

It's okay to be afraid of spiders, snakes, and clowns. But don't be afraid to stand up for what you believe in. (Unless, of course, what you believe in is world domination.)

The only type of dungeon Kitty feared was a sex dungeon. Everything else, she could deal with—or so she told herself.

The first trial was officially upon them, and while Kitty tried to go to sleep early, the anticipation kept her awake. Thank God for coffee... except now, she kind of had to use the restroom. Not that she could admit it as they walked downstairs.

She followed her parents down the stone steps, escorted by five board members and Chancellor Kinsey. Her siblings trailed behind her, and if they were afraid, they did a damn good job of hiding it. Better than her, pathetically enough.

You weren't the one who started this, she tried to remind herself. She just listened to a podcast about being kinder to herself over breakfast. *But you'll be the one to end it. And the only way to do that is to beat the trials, just like you said you would.*

They were led into a small stone room with only the light of sconces illuminating the space. Dust and cobwebs lingered in every corner. The only things in the room were two small chests.

"For your belongings," Chancellor Kinsey said, noticing her gaze.

Right. "We're not allowed to take anything with us for this trial?"

"I'm afraid not, Miss Swan. This is a test of strength, so you must rely solely on that to complete it. But the rules are fairly simple. All you have to do is pass through an obstacle course and locate the Chalice of Truth. This is an enchanted object, which we used—once upon a time—to determine how powerful a student's blood is. Drop your blood in the glass and make it glow to pass the trial. It should not be difficult for one such as yourself."

"Even if you were born mortal," one of the board members, a snotty brunette lady, adds.

Kitty bit back a disparaging comment and smiled. "Is there a time limit? Or anything that we should be careful of, in order to avoid disqualification?"

"There is an hour time limit. It began the moment you stepped foot in this basement."

Damn it. She knew there would be a catch. But she tried not to look panicked, shifting her weight to one leg and crossing her arms. "Let's begin, then. Where's the starting point?"

Chancellor Kinsey pressed a stone on the wall, leaving a handprint in the dust. Gross. The room shook and a portion of the wall slid away, revealing a pitch-black hallway. "After you."

"Kitty," Māma said, grabbing her arm. "What do you want for dinner?"

"Um, the clock is kinda running, Mā."

"This is a very important question," Bàba interrupted. "Sushi, meatloaf, eggplant...? You think about it."

Kitty nodded and turned toward the darkened doorway.

"After you," Noelle said.

Jax nodded.

Kitty strode forward, emptying her pockets—which, as it turned out, she only had a stick of gum—into the wooden chest. Darkness enveloped her and her eyes struggled to adjust to the low light. Pressing her elbow against the wall to guide her, she slowly moved down the hall. Noelle's hand rested on her shoulder, and Jax was behind her, making a train.

"I can't believe Northeastern made students do this. It's not like there are a ton of shadowborn anyway. I'd think they would need all the tuition money they could get," Jax muttered.

"It wasn't an entrance exam, back then; it was an aptitude test. A poorly designed one," said Noelle.

"It's an entrance exam for us, though."

The words surprised Kitty. She didn't think her brother cared, especially after she'd made such a big deal about it in their parents' apartment, while he seemed indifferent. "Did something happen at school?"

"No."

He wasn't a good liar. It ran in the family, apparently. "Jax. Tell me."

"I don't know. Just some stupid kids running their mouths. I can handle it."

"You can't beat up high schoolers, Kitty. That would be creepy," Noelle admonished.

"People already think I'm creepy. Why not give them another reason?"

The trio came to a wooden wall, which Kitty nearly smacked her face against. She nudged the wall with her foot, which creaked as it opened. The room before them wasn't much of an improvement in terms of lighting, but Kitty could make out the outline of a chest-height metal podium in the center of the room. She stepped inside, but as soon as her foot touched the floor, metallic whirring filled the air.

"What the hell?" she exclaimed, barely able to hear her own voice over the noise. It sounded like propellers or something.

And then the walls began to close in. Literally.

The three siblings ran to the podium, wiping the dust off the metal surface. There were three levers. Noelle pulled the middle one, which made the walls speed up. Kitty went for the left one, and Jax the right. Nothing happened.

"We need to get the correct combination," Noelle shouted, squinting at the engraving in the metal. "This is Latin! Do either of you—oh, what am I saying?"

Kitty raced around the room, trying to determine if there were any other clues written on the walls. This was just a test, right? The walls wouldn't actually crush them, right?

But she recalled the trials ended because students died during the trials. She couldn't rule out the possibility that this was real, and her siblings would be pancakes if she didn't figure it out.

Noelle read the engraving aloud, but it sounded like garbled nonsense to Kitty's ears.

"Jax, do you see anything?"

"No!" He pounded on the stone with his fist. "Damn it!"

Noelle pulled another lever, and the walls began moving even faster, the whirring sound so loud, Kitty thought her eardrums might explode.

And then she realized something. The sound was connected to the walls moving, which suggested the mechanics were powered by a machine, not magic. She shut her eyes, gathering any qi she could feel around her and pulling it inside her meridians, strengthening herself. Planting her feet, she pushed against the rough stone with her bare hands. The grinding stopped as the wall halted, the machine sputtering. Jax, bless his heart, got the memo and used his strength to keep the other wall at bay.

Kitty's arms strained and all her energy went toward not being crushed. It would have been easier in a place with more plants, but the dungeon was underground, which meant she didn't have as much qi to work with. She could draw it to her from quite a distance, though admittedly she never tested the exact limits. But it took a few seconds to reach her, and for this particular task, she needed it constantly circulating through her to maintain a superhuman level of strength.

That was another difference between the shadowborn and cultivation: shadowborn didn't need to bolster their strength with magic. Kitty was stronger than an average human, but she needed to use qi techniques to actively strengthen herself, if she wanted to reach her peak strength. That went for speed and agility, too. Whether that was an advantage or disadvantage, she couldn't say; it was just different.

Noelle pulled the levels randomly, her hands moving fast. She must have been guessing at that point. The only clue was in Latin, and without a way to decipher it, they were out of luck. But Kitty and Jax bought her enough time to try various combinations, until finally, the walls began retracting.

Kitty relaxed, pulling back to realize her hands were completely scraped up and bloody. Weird. She had been circulating qi to strengthen herself, but it also should have prevented these sorts of minor injuries. She tried to draw qi toward her again, but this time, nothing happened. She couldn't even feel it in the air, as she normally did.

Well, there went her powers. Perfect timing, too.

"You did it," Kitty said, turning to her sister. She couldn't make out Nell's expression, but she didn't look happy.

Another portion of the wall shifted on the far side of the room, revealing another dark hallway.

"Let's go," Noelle said, breezing past her siblings. Jax and Kitty exchanged a look, but ultimately said nothing as they entered the next chamber. The doorway sealed behind them, and lights blinked on—real fluorescents, not candles, like the other two rooms. Compared to the medieval-era stone and dust of the previous rooms, this one looked like something out of a sci-fi movie. Metal walls gleamed with polished chrome. Goosebumps rose on Kitty's arms as she hugged herself. First, they tried to flatten her, and now, she was being frozen?

"I'm starting to think this school doesn't like us," she joked, discreetly trying to wipe her bloody hands on her skirt.

Neither of her siblings replied. She supposed a sense of humor didn't run in the family.

The trio didn't move forward, first examining their surroundings. They had learned their lesson from the previous room. Apparently, the interior designer had been going for a minimal look, because there was nothing else in the room. No other doors, no levers. Nothing. The walls were covered in what looked like peepholes, and the tile floor was the most God-ugly thing Kitty had ever seen, a combination of gray, brown, and green squares. Each square had a different pattern on it, clashing with the metal walls.

"Maybe this is the challenge. Staying in a room hideous enough to induce madness," Kitty quipped. "I'm already there."

Jax kneeled and, carefully, pressed a hand to one of the tiles. Nothing happened. But when he touched the one beside it, something in the wall clicked, and a torrent of darts shot out from the wall, narrowly missing his head.

Kitty and Noelle stumbled back just in time.

"Well, at least we know how to activate it," Jax said in a low voice.

"Yeah, by almost dying." Kitty rubbed her forehead. "Any ideas, Nell?"

Noelle was staring intently at the patterns on the floor. "It's a puzzle. If you step on the right tiles, then you can advance to the next room. But if you step on the wrong ones..."

"You turn into Swiss cheese."

"Right. And the trick is, we don't know the pattern. It's not random, but the only way to figure out what the pattern is, is to test out the tiles."

"Do you find it strange that both this room and the last one are powered by machines, not magic? I mean, this is a magic school, isn't it?"

"I would have thought so, too. But think about it. Shadowborn magic is different from what you see on television or read about in fantasy books; it's much more limited in terms of what you can do. Destructive elemental spells are their forte, and long-range magic is challenging, even for some of the teachers."

"Wow, somebody's paying attention in school," Kitty commented.

Nell cracked a smile, finally. "If they used magic for these traps, they would have needed a bunch of teachers to maintain the spells."

"Huh. I guess machines really *are* replacing jobs."

"We'll have plenty of time to debate the future of automation when we aren't trapped here," Jax reminded them. "There must be some sort of pattern or sequence here. Noelle, can you tell what the tile is supposed to be?"

"Maybe... if I could find a starting point, then I could figure out the rest."

"Wasn't the starting point this tile?" Kitty tapped one of them with her foot. "Nothing happened when Jax touched it before."

"You're right," Noelle said. "But let's check the other tiles in this row, just to be safe."

The group went along each row, testing every tile. Kitty frowned, crossing her arms. "You know, if this is all mechanical and not magic, there are probably a limited number of darts. If we active them all a bunch of times, we could probably just walk across."

"That's not the challenge."

"So? The rules are getting to the chalice within an hour. There's nothing around how we pass, just that we do. We shouldn't waste any time."

"And if you're wrong?"

"Then we have to think of another idea. Look, I'm not trying to be a jerk, but it's pretty obvious that the board members and the school staff don't like us. They aren't going to go easy on us, so maybe we should think outside the box," Kitty said.

"What are you implying?" Noelle asked.

"What? I'm not implying anything. I'm just saying—"

"That you don't think I can do this. Is that it?"

What? "That's not what I said."

"No, but it's written all over your face," Nell accused. "What, you think you can do a better job? Because the last I recall, you're the reason we're in this mess."

Kitty had no idea where this animosity was coming from, and she certainly didn't expect it from her sister. "I'm not going to stand here and argue with you. We need to get through this, and we don't have time."

"No, you're right. We don't have time. You've wasted enough of it. *I'm* not the problem," Noelle snapped. "You are."

"Hey," Jax cut in. "I get that you're pissed off, but now isn't the time. Kitty, your idea is right, but we have no idea how many darts are in each hole. There are eight rows, and we pressed all the tiles in this row already. There are still darts shooting out, which means they aren't running out anytime soon."

Kitty didn't think he was right, but she was tired of arguing.

"Noelle, can you figure out the rest of the pattern?" Jax asked.

"Let me think!" Noelle exclaimed, rubbing her temples.

She paced back and forth, her footfalls echoing on the hard tile.

"Oh, God." Everyone was being so dramatic. Kitty stomped on the tiles two more times. Darts shot out, but the third time, she was greeted with a click and nothing more. She tried it again, just to be sure, and the same thing happened. "Out of darts. As I said. Let's go."

Noelle's jaw clenched, but neither of the siblings continued to protest. For each row of tiles, they activated the darts until they ran out. They were able to cross the room fairly quickly, and once they reached the final row, a door opened on the other side.

"See? Easy." Kitty strode ahead, into the next chamber. She expected the final puzzle to be the worst, but instead, she found herself in a dining room. Her parents, along with the chancellor and the board members, sat at a long wooden table, waiting for them. Tapestries lined the walls, and on the very top of the chandelier, a goblet encrusted in rubies sat in plain sight.

"That's the chalice?" she asked, raising an eyebrow.

"Yes. It's up to you to get it," Chancellor Kinsey said.

Well, that was easy.

"Now, you can use any object in this room to—"

Kitty threw her shoe at the chalice, hitting the goblet and knocking it off the chandelier. It landed on the ground with a thud, and Kitty retrieved it. The room was dead silent as she stooped down to pick it up.

"I just need to put my blood in it, right?" she asked.

Chancellor Kinsey was silent for a moment before nodding. "Yes. Yes...just a drop from each of you. One at a time."

Jax grabbed a knife from the table and wiped it on his t-shirt. He tossed it to Kitty first, who caught the handle and smoothly cut her finger. She squeezed a drop into the glass, watching as it swirled to the bottom of the goblet. However, after a minute, nothing happened.

"It's as we suspected," one of the board members, a stout old man, huffed. "They have no powers to speak of."

"The magic in the goblet is made to detect shadowborn magic," Kitty reasoned. "We've already determined—really, it was me—that magic from the Veil and cultivation qi is different. So it makes sense that this cup wouldn't be able to detect anything in my blood. Besides, that's not really how cultivation works; our blood is no different from a human's."

"Exactly! That proves my point!"

"They don't belong here," another board member murmured. "Northeastern has a curriculum based on the fact that its student body is connected to the Veil. If we allowed humans in, what is the purpose?"

"I heard Southeastern let a human in, and look what happened."

"We just have to make it glow, right?" Jax interjected. He stepped closer, looming over him and casting a long shadow on the table.

"Y-Yes," the man stuttered. "If it glows, you've completed the trial."

Jax picked up the knife, twirling it in his fingers. "Well, let's give it a shot."

He cut his finger, squeezing his blood onto the glass. Then, he handed it to Noelle, who followed suit. Using his bloody finger, he traced an array on the tabletop. Kitty didn't recognize it, not that she would have—she was always lousy at arrays, which required memorization of traditional Chinese characters. Jax, however, must have been studying up. He completed the array, a circular design, with his blood and placed the Chalice of Truth in the center. Sure enough, the jewels lit up like a disco ball, rising several inches into the air.

"There you have it," Jax said.

For the first time, Kitty marveled at how much her little brother had grown. She never considered using an array; she wouldn't have known which one to use. Standing in front of her now with a smug expression on his face, his arms crossed, he looked more like their dad than ever.

Pride surged through her chest and her face broke into a grin. "You're brilliant, Jax!"

He grunted in acknowledgment as she threw her arms around him.

"This doesn't count," a board member sputtered. "The chalice isn't glowing!"

"It looks bright to me," Bàba interjected. "The rules stated only that they have to make the chalice glow, and that's exactly what my children did."

"But it's not glowing the way it's supposed to! A student's blood would—"

"You are welcome to discuss the semantics, but in my opinion, it is glowing," Māma said.

"It's a loophole!"

"A loophole you failed to account for," Bàba said calmly. "Chancellor Kinsey, I believe my children have completed the trial. Do you disagree?"

Kinsey stared at Bàba, opening and closing his mouth like a fish. Finally, he said, "No. The Swans have succeeded in passing the first Blood Trial. But keep in mind that there are two more, and if they fail one, their admission to Northeastern is revoked."

"Thanks, Chancellor. But you don't have to worry about that," Kitty said. "I hope y'all aren't too embarrassed when we beat the rest of the trials, too."

She smiled and turned on her heel, her family following her out.

NORTHEASTERN TRIBUNE

A SWAN SONG FOR TRADITION

In a turn of events that has raised eyebrows and fueled late-night debates within the storied halls of Northeastern College, the Swan siblings—Katherine, Noel, and Jackson—have managed to pass the first of the Blood Trials. These trials have traditionally been the domain of the shadowborn, those born with magic in their veins. Yet, the Swans, who are of mortal Chinese descent, claim their place among us, sparking controversy and speculation.

It's a narrative we've encountered before, not just within the hallowed walls of our institution but in the annals of history. One cannot help but recall the echoes of Pearl Harbor, an unexpected attack on civilians by a foreign enemy.

Despite the lack of concrete proof, the circumstances surrounding the Swans' success in the Blood Trials whisper of a cleverness that skirts the edge of what is deemed acceptable. The faculty has scoured the rulebooks, looking for a loophole that might disqualify the Swans, but to no avail. The letter of the law has been met, if not the spirit, leaving a bitter taste in the mouths of those who hold the sanctity of our traditions dear.

It's no secret that the family are something of an anomaly. Some voices, perhaps too quick to extol the virtues of diversity, hail it as a breakthrough moment for inclusivity within the shadowborn community. Yet, this perspective fails to recognize that our institution is already a bastion of diversity. To equate the Swans' presence with progress is to misunderstand the nature of our world.

Allowing the Swans to remain among us under the guise of expanding diversity is a mistake, one that undermines the essence of what it means to be shadowborn. Their so-called success is not a triumph to be celebrated but a warning. It is a signal that our traditions are under threat, not from outside forces but from within, from the erosion of our standards and the dilution of our heritage.

We must ask ourselves what we value most. Is it the fleeting applause of inclusivity, or is it the preservation of our sacred traditions, the very traditions that have allowed the arcane arts to flourish for centuries? The presence of the Swans at Northeastern College poses a question of magical integrity. It is a reminder that in our quest to be open, we must not be so open that we lose what defines us, that we become so inclusive that the essence of being shadowborn is edged out.

In the end, the Swans' so-called success through the first of the Blood Trials has left us with more questions than answers. Indeed, something smells funny in the wake of the Swans' victory, and it isn't just the disgusting food they eat.

FIFTEEN

ACCORDING TO THE WEATHER REPORT, it would be the last warm day of the month, so naturally, Kitty went to the pool. After the first trial, she deserved a break! Donning her favorite pink bikini, she set her bag down on a chair and began applying sunscreen all over herself.

The water was a welcome reprieve from the heat. As she sank to the bottom of the deep end, she cleared her mind, trying not to think about the shitstorm swirling through her life at the moment.

Dealing with ferals was... Well, not *easy*. But she preferred using a blade to handle her problems than, God forbid, her mind. She could barely list out all her grievances—where would she begin? The protesting? Or did she sound like a broken record about that, by now? How about the vandalism, the nasty comments, the vague posters hung around the school that both didn't quite address her race, but at the same time, made her feel slightly uncomfortable? These minor incidents weren't a big deal—at least, not to her parents. They just shuffled it away in the recesses of their brain, like it didn't matter.

It would have been better if someone physically threatened her. She was strong enough to beat the crap out of anyone who tried, as evidenced by her fight with Ryder. She'd been in plenty of fights before in high school. Like that time she had rejected Kevin Farleigh's advances in tenth grade, only to have him drive up to her while she walked home and throw eggs at her. She had chased down his car, dragged him out, and made him cry in the middle of town—an easy solution. He had never bothered her again; wouldn't even make eye contact.

This was different somehow, and because she couldn't find the words to discern precisely *why* she felt the way she did, the problem kept her up at night. She couldn't help but think that perhaps, if she were smarter, she'd be happier.

Kitty never minded not being a straight-A student. She told herself she had other attributes, namely, being a kick-ass bitch. Bitch in a good way, of course. Being physically strong was obviously important to the shadowborn. So why didn't they respect her? Did the entirety of her being boil down to her face?

No. She was supposed to be clearing her mind, and God damn it, she was going to! But by the time she actually managed this, she was out of air. She kicked up to the surface with a gasp and realized she wasn't alone anymore.

"You can hold your breath for a while," Blake commented, sitting down on the chair beside her things. "I guess that boded well for your boyfriends."

Kitty wondered if he was doing this on purpose, making her hate him more than she already did. "What do you want?"

"I needed to talk to you." He sounded serious, which was so out of the left field, she was inclined to believe him.

Still, she stuck to her guns. "I'm not interested in whatever you have to say."

"You're still hung up on that Veronica thing?"

Kitty swam to the edge of the pool, peering up from the water. With the sun behind him, she couldn't get a good read on his face. Judging by his tone, he sounded almost...annoyed. As if she didn't have every right to be pissed that he used her best friend. "I don't have any interest in someone who hurts my friends."

"Since when are you anything more than a bitch to everyone?"

That was low, even for him. Kitty raised her chin, holding his gaze. He wouldn't intimidate her, no matter how uncharacteristically serious he became. So what if he was Cy's friend? He wasn't hers.

"Didn't your best friend in high school make a series of videos telling people how awful your personality is?" Blake continued. "And then, she released a sex tape of you and your ex—who she was seeing behind your back? Ring any bells?"

He was just trying to hurt her, now. But she was used to this behavior, and if her experience in a middle school locker room told her anything, he was lashing out to cover up his own insecurities, in hopes she would rise to the bait and change the subject.

It wouldn't work.

"That's not what happened, and it had *nothing* to do with Veronica and you," Kitty snapped.

"You don't know anything."

At this point, all the self-help gurus she followed would advise her not to engage further. But Kitty was a work-in-progress, because she said, "I might not know everything, but I know right now, I don't want to deal with you."

Once the words were out, she regretted them. Which was, if you thought about it, progress. Last year, she wouldn't have felt bad at all for hurting someone's feelings. In fact, she might have enjoyed it, if they deserved it. And Blake certainly deserved it, didn't he? So why, when a flash of hurt flitted across his face, did she want to apologize?

She didn't, though. As awkwardness settled in the space between them, she lifted herself out of the pool. Goosebumps rose on her arms, but she didn't care, grabbing her stuff and hoping to make a swift exit before anything else was said or felt. And she would have gotten away with it, too, if it weren't for Jax and Jianhao.

Damn. Not this guy again.

Kitty wasn't afraid to admit she was swayed by good looks. Sometimes, her own beauty influenced her when she looked into a mirror! But appearances only got you so far. Jianhao's hotness bought him about ten minutes before she realized he was a douchebag. Talking to him was like eating a brownie, only to take one bite and realize it was actually cow dung.

Suffice to say, his only good trait was that he showed his true colors right off the bat.

"Xiao Xing!" he called, smiling with those stupidly perfect white teeth. She physically cringed when he called her that. She asked him not to last night, multiple times.

"Sow sing?" Blake repeated, fumbling with the Mandarin.

"Xiao Xing," Jianhao said again, stopping in front of Kitty. He looked her up and down, his smile faltering.

"It's a nickname," Jax supplied, for Blake's benefit. He wore a pair of swim trunks and sandals, though Kitty doubted her brother had plans to swim. He hated the heat, but at least in the summer, he could get away with wearing bathing suits instead of real clothing. "'Xiao' means 'little' and can be added before the last character of a given name. Kitty's is 'Zixing.' So, Xiao Xing is her nickname."

"Are you sure it's appropriate to be wearing that?" Jianhao asked.

"Yes, just like I'm sure it's *in*appropriate to police someone's clothing choices," Kitty replied politely, showing her teeth in what was meant to be a smile. It looked more like a grimace. She was never good at faking her emotions. "It's a pool. I'm in a bathing suit."

"I can see your nipples." It wasn't a lecherous comment, rather, a criticism disguised as advice. Like he was *helping* her by pointing it out.

"Take a picture, it'll last longer," she said, feeling like a true New Yorker. Still, she crossed her arms over her chest. "What do you want?"

"There's no need to take that tone, Xiao Xing."

Yeah, she was fairly certain he was only calling her that to piss her off. "My name is Kitty. Not even my parents call me by my Chinese name."

Mostly because Kitty and Noelle had very similar names. Kitty was Zixing, with the character "star" in her name, while Noelle was Ziyue, written with the character "moon."

"It is not your 'Chinese' name," Jianhao said gently. "You *are* Chinese. It is just your name. 'Kitty' is your white name."

"Kitty is my name—full stop," she argued back. Again, she realized it would have been easier to let him believe what he wanted—to just agree and escape his scrutiny. Certainly, it would have saved her the headache later. "I really don't appreciate everyone at this goddamn school ignoring me when I—"

"You should be grateful," Jianhao cut her off. She hated when he used that voice—like he was calming a child in the midst of a temper tantrum. "Jax is not as fortunate to have a proper name."

"There's nothing wrong with my brother's name!"

Jax shrugged, like it didn't concern him at all. "Are you coming over for dinner tonight? Bà is cooking."

"I don't care *what* he's cooking. If he's going to be there" —Kitty jabbed a finger at Jianhao—"then I'm not coming."

"Very mature."

"We didn't come here to argue," Jianhao soothed. "Xiao Xing, I was looking for you because your parents suggested we spar together. A test of your abilities."

"No thanks."

"It wasn't a request."

Kitty's hands fell to her hips. "And what makes you think you can order me around?"

"I am your shīxiōng," he said plainly.

Blake, trying to follow the conversation, repeated, "See song?"

"It means 'older brother' when used in the context of a cultivation sect," Jax explained again. "In Chinese, we can call those who aren't related to us 'brother,' 'sister,' 'aunt,' 'uncle,' and what have you as a way to show familiarity or respect. There are a lot of honorifics."

"As I told you last night," Jianhao said, "I wouldn't mind if you called me gēgē."

"And as *I* told you last night, there's not a chance in hell I'd *ever* call you that!"

It was too embarrassing! "Ge" was a more acceptable way to call a slightly older male figure "big brother" outside of a sect, but "gēgē" sounded cringey and childish!

She found it ironic that he wouldn't honor *her* request to call her Kitty, yet he made a bunch of outlandish nickname requests to her. Regardless of his association with Uncle Stefan, they were complete strangers! And that was the way it would remain—she hoped so, anyway.

But admittedly, the thought of sparring with him interested her. She hadn't had the opportunity to fight with any cultivators outside her family, and Jianhao had grown up in the same sect her parents had. He was probably a very skilled fighter, not to mention, he was a level above her in cultivation.

"When do you want to spar?" Kitty relented.

Jianhao grinned. "How about right now?"

NOELLE ARRIVED AT CLASS EARLY, settling into her usual seat in the front row before anyone else had a chance to enter. It wasn't that she liked Magic History in particular, or even Professor Evans. On the contrary, she thought the man was a troll. But still, she wanted his approval, which would be a victory in and of itself. Now, it was proving to be a Sisyphean task.

It shouldn't have been as difficult as it was. She was clearly the smartest in the class, something Professor Evans affirmed yet again when he started class today by handing back their tests. Noelle glanced around at her classmates' scores, seeing a mix of 70s and 80s. Blake got a 69. She wondered if he planned that.

Noelle, on the other hand, got a 98. She beamed, for although it wasn't perfect, she was confident it was the highest grade in the class. Not only was she intelligent, but she raised her hand for every question posed. She looked up to see Professor Evan's expression, searching for any sign of approval she could read on his face, but he'd already moved on to the front of the class.

Well, whatever. It was still early on in the semester; there would be plenty of time to earn his favor. She couldn't wait until he admitted how wrong he was about her!

But she'd settle for a lecture for today, at least. Professor Evans began to talk about early shadowborn settlements among the mortals, stuff she had already gone over in the textbook. She could give an oral presentation on the subject right now, if he asked her to.

"It's almost October. Time passes quickly," Professor Evans remarked. "For your next assignment, you will be paired up. I expect a presentation outlining one of the following topics on the screen. If you can all turn your attention to the slide—get off your phone, Blackwood—you will see your topic and partner. And before you ask, *no*, I will not be changing your partner. They are assigned at random. If you email me and ask to switch, I will give you a zero for this assignment. Is that clear?"

Noelle scanned the PowerPoint slide for her name, but horrifyingly enough, she found it right next to Blake Blackwood's.

"Looks like we're partners," he said. He always sat beside her, and while he admittedly didn't bother her, his very presence was irksome. It was as if he emitted some sort of noxious gas that subconsciously disgusted Noelle on another level. She would have loved to tell him as much, but that was something Kitty would have done. Correction: that's something Kitty *did* do.

So instead, Noelle said, "It seems we are."

"If you aren't careful, you're gonna break that pencil in half."

He was being dramatic; Noelle was barely gripping it. "You don't have to worry. I'll do all the work. If you could just follow some note cards for the presentation, we'll do fine."

Blake frowned. "I'm not an idiot. I can help. The topic is *shifter* communities, and I'm a werewolf shadowborn."

"You've also been getting consistently poor scores," Noelle pointed out.

"We've had two knowledge-check quizzes that don't even count toward our grade," Blake protested, his brow furrowed.

"So? Just because it doesn't count doesn't mean you should flunk it."

"You're nuts."

Noelle turned back to the board. It was no use arguing with an idiot. There wasn't a doubt in her mind that his contribution to the project would be lackluster at best, and misinformative at worst; he would probably tell some personal story and pass it off as fact. She didn't need him to go through the motions just to be stuck with the project incomplete the night before their presentation. It would be easier if she did the whole thing, so she could control the quality.

"You can't shoulder everything by yourself," Blake told her, but this time, it sounded like he was talking about more than just the project.

Noelle took a deep breath, making sure not to lose her temper before answering in her calmest voice, "I can, and I will."

THE DOOR to the greenhouse shed hadn't done anything wrong, but in Kitty's eyes, it might as well have murdered her mother. Her blood splattered across the aged wood, her breathing heavy. She'd been out here for most of the day, and nothing she did was working. She couldn't meditate properly, her mind consumed with Jianhao, and now, her powers were malfunctioning too. Her frustration reached its boiling point. All she was left with was a torn affirmation journal, bloody fists, and a boatload of emotions, none of which she could find on her Feelings Wheel.

God, how pathetic.

Cyrus had the worst timing. He walked up to her, having somehow found her despite her efforts to hide from the world. "What did that door ever do to you?"

Kitty turned away so he couldn't see her face. She wasn't in the mood to talk to anybody, much less him. But he didn't get the memo.

"I've been looking for you. You haven't answered my texts. Or Jax's."

"I know," she answered evenly, staring at the crumpled paper talismans torn on the ground, along with pages in her affirmation journal. "I just need some time to think."

"Anything you want to share with the class?"

"Alone," she emphasized.

"We're alone."

"Alone, as in, solitary. Single. On my own."

"You're not going to break out into song, are you? Because I've heard you sing and..."

Her glare could have pierced a diamond.

"I brought you a chocolate bar." He pulled a Cadbury chocolate bar out of his backpack, and Kitty knew immediately that she couldn't push him away again. Mostly because she wanted the chocolate, and she knew he hadn't got this bar on campus. They only sold Hershey at the school store, which was the tragedy of the century.

Kitty held out her hand and he placed the bar on her palm. She tore it open, through with pretenses, because she hadn't eaten since yesterday's lunch. Since she'd fought Jianhao.

"It's not usually like you to go MIA when you're upset. I figured you and Veronica would have sped off to the mall or something for some retail therapy," Cyrus continued. He pulled a first aid kit out of his magical bag of tricks, wiping the wounds on her knuckles and spraying her hand with disinfectant. She didn't flinch at the sting, too preoccupied with the rich British chocolate to give a shit about anything else. "What happened?"

"My parents got a research assistant, and he's a total douchebag."

"Yes, Noelle mentioned."

That surprised her. "When did you speak with my sister?"

"When I was going around campus looking for you," he said.

"Why?"

"Why do you think?" He wrapped her bloody knuckles with a bandage. "You would make a great spy, Kitty, because if you were captured? Not even pulling teeth could get information out of you."

"I never really got that. Like, why would you torture information out of someone by injuring their mouth?" Kitty derailed. "I'd pour something hot in one ear, or seal their eyes shut with gel nail polish and cure it under a UV lamp."

He gagged a little at the thought. "We're not talking about the gross and unnecessary torture methods you'd use on someone."

"Why not?"

"Because you're going to tell me what happened."

"Nothing happened," she insisted. "Jianhao and I sparred,

and then I decided to meditate. That's it. Are we done with the third degree?"

Cyrus tended to her other hand. "Jax said that you stormed off afterward."

"He's so dramatic," Kitty said. "I didn't *storm* off. I walked away. I mean, I know I look like a model when I walk, on account of my long legs and all, but God. That was not 'storming'. 'Strutting', maybe."

"And this is?" Cy gestured to the litter on the ground. "Running away to the greenhouse, beating up a door?"

"I'm trying out gardening."

"Is that what they're calling it these days?"

"Why are you so concerned about this?" she snapped. "It's none of your business."

"I don't know. Maybe it's because you seem like you've gone off the deep end?"

"I have not! Stay away from me. I don't need, nor do I want, your help!" She knew he didn't deserve that, but she couldn't bring herself to stop.

"What's the deal with you, Kitty?" he demanded, throwing up his hands. "You're acting like—"

She grabbed him by the collar of his shirt, her bandaged hands making this more difficult than necessary, and kissed him. It wasn't a gentle kiss, either. Why would it be? She was angry, and by trying to help, he only pissed her off more. He wasn't happy with her, either, and she wouldn't have been surprised if he shoved her away. Instead, he pushed her up against the shed. His hands dug into her hips, pulling her flush against him. She could feel his annoyance, matching her own, but there was an undercurrent of something else: a hunger neither cared to deny at the present moment.

She wasn't sure which of them started undressing, first.

Keyword: Started. They hadn't finished, only taking off the absolute minimum amount of clothing needed. Her safety shorts—a thin layer of fabric attached to her skirt, just in case the wind decided to be a jerk—tore easily and landed in a heap in the dirt. Thankfully her shirt remained on, otherwise she would have gotten splinters from being shoved against the wall of the shed.

It wasn't sweet or loving. They weren't tender with one another, but she didn't care. The anger was still there, and the only way to release the tension was with rough hands and demanding kisses. Kitty had no problem with that.

"You're so fucking frustrating," Cyrus panted, breaking their kiss to move to her neck. "All you had to do was ask, and I'd do anything."

"Ask for what?"

"Whatever the hell you want. It's always got to be a fight with you."

She couldn't argue with that, so she didn't try.

After it was over, Kitty was thankful for the wall behind her, because her legs felt like jelly. Thankfully, she couldn't see her reflection. Her lips were swollen and her hair was a tangled mess, and the dirt on her clothes would need to soak in a tub of stain remover. She also couldn't find her underwear, which would have been less of a problem, had her safety shorts still been intact.

She couldn't bring herself to regret it, though.

"You're going to need to wear a turtleneck for the next few days," she commented, trying to sound casual. It would have been more dignified, had she been able to stand on her own. Her fingers traced his neck, a hickey forming on the side. "Sorry about that."

"Well," he muttered, "so much for being just friends."

SIXTEEN

DAILY PROMPT: WHERE CAN YOU ADD MORE JOY TO YOUR DAILY ROUTINE?

Sex with Cyrus Ward.
Unintended ethical crises may occur.

Kitty could think of a hundred excuses for her behavior in the greenhouse. The subsequent incidents afterward? Well, she had no justification for what she'd done. Part of her knew how wrong it was, especially when they were both angry. But the volatile emotions made everything more...intense.

There was nothing remotely romantic about their interactions. That made it easier to accept. The only word Kitty could come up with to describe it was raw.

She knew for certain that they weren't a couple. But their tryst in the greenhouse blurred the lines between their friendship. Their unspoken agreement hadn't just been broken; it shattered. And now they couldn't keep their hands (or other body parts) off each other.

"We should really get back to studying," Kitty admonished, shrugging her cardigan back on. They were in the back of the library, at a table between the shelves. No one else was there, or she imagined there would have been some sort of noise complaint. "You really need to learn some self-control."

"Me?" Cyrus sputtered, buttoning his pants. "You're the one who shoved me into a bookshelf. That hurt, by the way."

"Oh please. I'm the one who ended up against the microfiche. I'm going to have button indents in my ass for the next few days."

"I'll give you a massage."

"How generous of you," she said sarcastically. She settled back into a chair, examining one of the books. "Damn, you wrinkled the pages!"

"I'm sorry you find me irresistible."

"You must mean incorrigible." She sighed. "Let's get down to business, already. Where did we leave off?"

"You were complaining about not being able to Google the Blood Trials."

"Right." Because the magic community was a secret, she couldn't just find information about the trials online. She had to—gag—go to the library and open a physical book. Oh, the horror of it all!

Even worse, she had a feeling Kinsey had purposely hidden all the books on the trials. She looked in the library catalog and most of the records had either been removed, were missing, or were already checked out by other students!

Cyrus had a different idea. Instead of checking out books that had "Blood Trials" specifically in the name, he looked up student records from the time the trials were conducted. He then cross-referenced the names with articles written by the students in the school paper, along with any research papers for senior capstones and graduate theses. What they ended up with were first-person accounts of how the trials had gone. Unfortunately, none of them went into detail about what each trial entailed. She had a vague idea, though.

The first trial was a test of magic, though Kitty and her siblings essentially strong-armed their way through it. The second would be a test of courage. And finally, a test of intelligence.

Power and courage, sure. Fine. Intelligence? Her chances weren't promising.

She didn't have a choice in the matter, though. At least there was no official deadline, but she figured the sooner she got them over with, the better. Maybe once she passed, her school life would be easier.

Her classmates still avoided her, even after passing the first trial. She refused to believe it hurt her, even a little, but she couldn't deny being treated like a social leper...wasn't the best feeling. Sure, when she started middle school, she wasn't instantly popular. But she'd turned things around fairly quickly. Here, at Northeastern, it seemed she had to put in a lot more work for minimal results. The only professor who actually seemed to like her was Professor Ainsworth.

You don't need them, she reminded herself. *You don't need anyone.*

Once she had gathered the information she needed about the trials, or lack thereof, she began putting her things away. Cyrus watched, looking like he wanted to say something. Whatever it was, she didn't want to hear it.

She worked faster, shoving the books back on the shelves and rolling the microfiche into the corner where it belonged. But she wasn't fast enough to avoid the inevitable question.

"So," Cyrus hedged, "you wanna talk about what's bothering you?"

She resented the question, and him, by extension. No, she absolutely did *not* want to talk about anything that had to do with her personal feelings. "Nothing's bothering me."

"Really?" he asked dryly. "Every time I ask about the Jianhao thing, you jump me."

"That's not true," she said, knowing very well it was. They were heading toward dangerous territory, and she knew she was slipping up, but she couldn't find the willpower to stop. Maybe that was why she could never improve herself, why the self-help books weren't working as well as she hoped: Because she couldn't stop the toxic things from coming out of her mouth. "It's not like you haven't enjoyed it."

"That's not the point. I already talked to Jax. I know what happened. Look—"

"What do you gain by harassing me about this? You think you're going to be my knight in shining armor or something?"

"No," he gritted out. "I'm trying to talk to you, as a friend."

"As a friend? Or as something else?" she accused. "Newsflash: Just because we had sex doesn't mean you're my boyfriend, or anything close to it. I don't expect you to hold my hand or tell me everything's going to be okay, so save it. Got it?"

He looked taken aback, and honestly, she felt a little surprised at herself, too.

"Yeah," he said finally, grabbing his bag. "I got it."

He stood up and walked away, leaving her alone.

Just like she wanted. Right?

IT WAS her first day back in the lab since the semester began, and Noelle was glad to get back to work. Classes were too easy, and she needed to feel challenged and productive in her spare time. Her parents needed *someone* to help them, and let's face it, her siblings weren't up to the task. No, it had to be her; she was the only one well-versed in alchemy and foundational knowledge of cultivation. She was also smarter than both Jax and Kitty combined, by a large margin. She doubted either of them knew how to properly use a microscope.

She prepared slides for Bàba while he scribbled down notes at his station, looking uncharacteristically serious. His face was drawn, and she almost didn't recognize him without a smile.

"What is this from, Bà?" Noelle asked, handing him a completed set of neatly organized slides. "The Blood Wasp hunt?"

He shook his head. "They're from a different hunt but taken from feral insects. Creepy, isn't it?"

"Yeah." She knew how much he hated bugs. Māma was the insect killer in the family. Bàba mostly screamed. "Bà, if ferals are cultivating and qi deviating, then why are we still researching them like this? Don't we already have the cause?"

"They are cultivating, but there's an element we're missing," he said. "Qi deviation happens when using demonic energy to cultivate. Theoretically, it might be happening to these beastbloods if they are using Veil magic to cultivate. Either way, it doesn't explain how the disease is infectious. Qi deviation isn't—so how is this spreading through body fluids?

And how is Veil magic in general being used to cultivate? It doesn't make sense."

On top of that, how had Kitty managed to escape infection? That was a question that nagged at her, but neither of her parents had an explanation. And Kitty herself simply shrugged and said, "Because I'm, like, superwoman or something," when Noelle asked.

No matter. Noelle continued to work, helping clear Bàba's workstation and type up all his notes, written in a mix of English and Mandarin. The lab was bright and sterile, with a plexiglass divider separating the room. She and her father worked on one side while her mother worked on the other.

Dr. Woods walked in at six, which should have been the time her parents got off work. Noelle had mixed feelings about the woman. She was well-respected in the community, and it was clear everyone else in the research facilities respected her. But on the other hand, that article she'd written was...bad. While Kitty had a tendency to misspeak, Woods's opinions in the article were clearly biased.

Her parents didn't speak negatively about Woods, but that didn't mean much. They came from a cultivation sect, where it was frowned upon to voice any sort of dissent about those ranked above you. How they managed to defect—from a mental standpoint—was beyond Noelle. When you spend most of your life conditioned to believe that a single way of life is the only way, it's nearly impossible to deviate from that.

Sometimes, she got the feeling that there was more to it than they let on. And Kitty knew more, too. She had been acting strangely ever since last semester ended, and while Noelle wanted to chalk that up to all the changes going on in their lives, Kitty had shown a side of herself Noelle had never seen before. She just couldn't pin down a word to describe it.

She wasn't maturing, exactly. It was more like she was hiding something.

"Can you explain this to me, Ariana?" Dr. Woods's voice cut through the quiet lab; her tone cool.

Māma looked up from her station. "The data analysis? I followed the standard protocol, but it seems there was a slight discrepancy in the sample volumes—"

"A 'slight discrepancy'," Dr. Woods echoed. "You do understand the importance of precision in our work, don't you?"

"I double-checked everything. It was a minor oversight that I've already corrected."

Woods chuckled, the sound grating on Noelle's ears. "We operate at a level where even the smallest mistake can have significant consequences. I would have expected you, especially, to be careful. Surely, you've heard what people think of you here? Don't you want to prove them wrong?"

"And what, exactly, do they think?"

Uh oh. Noelle recognized that tone. It was the same one Kitty used, right before she freaked out on somebody.

Bàba was quick to intervene, forcing a smile. "Ah, yes. We're committed to high standards in our research, Dr. Woods. It won't happen again."

"I certainly hope so," Dr. Woods said, staring up at Bà. "Everyone in this lab is here, not because they know someone or because they check a box on an affirmative action plan, but because they've *earned* their place. And if I were in your shoes? Well, let's just say I'd work twice as hard to make sure no one thought I was given a position due to the slant of my eyes."

MĀMA AND BÀBA returned to their apartment at ten. Kitty stayed up for them, using the spare key to get in. She sat at the dining room table, staring at the wall until they returned.

"Kitty? What are you doing here?" Bàba asked, turning the lights on. "Are you pretending you're in an emo music video again?"

"No, Bà. I only do that when it's raining in the car," she admonished.

Māma threw her bag on the chair and settled on the couch, swinging her feet up. "Aiya! I am so tired. I could fall asleep right now!"

"Do you want something to eat? I just bought a panini press," Bàba added. "Kitty?"

"Have you talked to Jax?" she asked nervously. "Recently, I mean?"

"Oh no. What happened? Did you argue?"

"You should be kinder to your little brother," Māma reminded her.

"No. I just... The other day," Kitty said, faltering. "I-I fought Jianhao. He told me you wanted us to spar, so I did."

"Oh?" Bà walked into the kitchen, opening the fridge. She could hear the sizzle of butter on the panini press.

She looked down, almost unable to say the words out loud. As if admitting it to her parents would cause the world to end. It certainly felt that way. "I lost."

Humiliatingly fast. He had her pinned in no time at all. And he did it repeatedly. It wasn't even that Kitty was unprepared or lost on purpose. God, she tried her hardest. She had her powers, used her saber, thought of every technique she could possibly throw at him—and she lost.

There was no excuse, no justification that could possibly

explain it, other than she hadn't been good enough. And Jianhao wasn't even at the same level as her parents, yet he'd still beaten her.

Maybe she'd grown arrogant, having defeated Cyrus so many times. Or maybe, in general, she'd gone soft. But she had a feeling the truth was much worse: she simply wasn't good enough.

"Do you want ham or turkey?" Bàba asked.

"Did you hear what I said?"

"Kitty, you're getting shrill," Mā commented. "We know you lost."

"We figured you would. But did you have fun?"

"He's handsome. I would think you'd find some enjoyment being pinned under him."

"Māma!" Kitty screeched.

"I've seen him shirtless, Kitty," Bàba said seriously, poking his head from out of the kitchen. "He has a very nice body."

"And he waxes his chest. I think that is popular nowadays," Mā added. "Do you prefer hairy men, Kitty?"

"Oh my God, please stop," Kitty begged.

"You aren't upset about it, are you?" Bà asked. "Ah. I have some chocolate lava cake in the freezer. You will be happy after you eat."

"Bà, now is not the time for chocolate."

Bàba dropped his spatula. Māma got up and sat beside her daughter at the table, taking her hand.

"This must be serious," she murmured, pressing a hand to her forehead. "Are you feeling okay?"

"I'll go to the store," Bàba announced, grabbing his coat. "Ice cream will help. Rocky Road or cookie dough? Oh, what am I saying? I will get both!"

He was out the door before Kitty could protest. She didn't need ice cream. She didn't know *what* she needed. She just...

She wiped her eyes with the sleeve of her sweater. "I hate Jianhao. I already hated him before, but now? Now I hate him even more."

"You lose to me and Bàba all the time," Mā said awkwardly, putting an arm on her shoulder. "Why does it matter this time? Jianhao is a level above you in cultivation, and he is much older. It is only natural he is stronger. We didn't want you to spar to humiliate you. We thought it would be a good learning experience."

"Yeah, I learned something all right. You know, all my life, I've been stronger than everyone. I've lost to you and Bà, but that's only natural—you're my parents, and my teachers."

"So, you lost *once*. It isn't a big deal," Māma soothed. "It should motivate you to train harder."

"Will it even matter?" Kitty exploded. "I know I'm not a good person, okay? No matter how many affirmation journal entries I write or self-help books I read, I still suck. I'm stupid, something Noelle never fails to point out. The only reason why anyone wants to be around me, outside of familial obligations, is because I'm strong. That is the single redeeming quality I have, the only reason anyone could respect me. It's who I am, who I've always been. Take that away, and what's left? Some vapid, selfish loser."

Mā grabbed her face, squeezing her cheeks between her hands. She squished Kitty's mouth so much; she couldn't form coherent words. "Don't talk about my daughter that way. She is kind, because she can recognize her own faults and try to better herself. She is brave, because even when the world is against her, she stands up for what she believes in. And she is strong, not because of her cultivation or because she wins fights, but because she does the right thing even when it is hard. I may not always understand her, but I am proud to call her my daughter. Don't insult her like this again. Got it?"

Kitty managed to nod.

"Good. Now, you're too skinny," Māma said sternly, releasing her face. "There are leftovers in the fridge. Let's eat a proper dinner before your father gets back."

SEVENTEEN

DAILY PROMPT: WHAT ARE YOUR PERSONAL GROWTH GOALS?

Stop being a selfish bitch, and put others first, for once. Even if it hurts.

Kitty suspected her father's sudden desire to celebrate the Mid-Autumn festival stemmed from wanting to show off his cooking skills. He created a two-page menu and everything. The Mid-Autumn Festival was a big deal in China, as the second largest holiday behind New Year—following the Lunar calendar, of course.

"Wow, Mr. Swan. These dishes look incredible," Veronica complimented. She and Kitty sat in the living room, giving each other pedicures. "I can't wait to try them all!"

"We got permission from Professor Everleigh to use one of the club rooms in the main building on Friday," Māma said. "We'll invite all our coworkers. You invite your friends, too!"

"Friends?" Jax snorted. "Kitty only has Veronica and Melody. That's not exactly a crowd, Mā. Bà is going to cook all that food for nothing."

"I'll invite people," Veronica assured him. Her eyes darted to Jianhao, a notable distraction in the corner of the room.

Kitty, on the other hand, was doing her best to ignore him. She didn't blame her friend for staring, but his blasé attitude only served to annoy her. "I will, too. I'm sure plenty of people will show up, Bà."

"Yes. Māma and I have been thinking about what you said, Kitty. We would like it very much if our coworkers learned more about Chinese culture. And what better way to teach them than through food? The way to the heart is through the stomach, right?"

"No, that isn't right," Māma said with a frown. "If you want to reach someone's heart, you have to maneuver around their rib cage."

"It's an expression, dear."

"Xiao Xing, why don't you invite your boyfriend?" Jianhao teased. "That blonde werewolf boy?"

Veronica's head snapped up. "Um, what is he talking about?"

"Blake was bothering me by the pool. I told him off, and Jianhao interrupted before I could make my exit," Kitty explained.

Veronica's lips curved. "You told him off?"

"Every chance I get."

"Well, that's sweet," she said, "but you don't have to do that. I'm really okay, Kitty. And I know you're friends with Cyrus, which makes Blake hard to avoid."

"It's pretty easy, actually. I got into a fight with Cy too."

"You always argue."

"This time was different. I messed up," Kitty admitted. "But I have a plan."

"Are you going to share with the class?"

"Maybe one day."

Jianhao smiled. "It would be far easier for you if you accepted me, instead."

"Shidi. It would be best not to press the matter," Bàba said lightly. "Kitty doesn't like being told what to do. The more you try, the more she'll dig her heels in. Trust me."

"Of course, shīxiōng. I will listen to you," Jianhao immediately agreed. "I apologize, Xiao Xing."

"Kitty," Bàba corrected. "It's Kitty. It means 'pure'. We chose that name because we thought it suited her."

Jax laughed—a little too hard, if you asked Kitty. She grabbed a pillow and chucked it right at his face. "I'm a *treasure*!"

"Kitty, will you help set up the room? You are very good at decorating," Māma interjected.

It was a blatant attempt at changing the subject. Still, Kitty took the hint. "Sure, Mā."

"I'll help, too," Veronica promised. "It'll be fun, right?"

Fun was *not* the word that Kitty would use to describe preparing for the Mid-Autumn festival. She ended up having to order all the decorations online and rush shipping. Her mother insisted on getting involved in picking stuff out, which made the experience ten times longer than necessary, all because Māma didn't know how to use a shopping app.

Then, she accompanied Bàba to the grocery store to buy the ingredients for the food. She wheeled around two carts full of stuff. She tried to tell herself that the food would be worth it, but after two hours, she wasn't sure *anything* was worth the pure torture her father put her through. He read every single label in the store, it seemed, breaking out a calculator to evaluate the prices per ounce. And, when they were on the way out, he saw the grocery flier with coupons, and they went back for price adjustments.

She hadn't even thought about her plan on how to apologize to Cyrus yet, even though she told Veronica that she had one. True, Kitty had *something*, but it wasn't a plan. It was a piece of scented printer paper with scrawl in pink glitter gel pen.

By the time Friday actually rolled around, Kitty was prepared to drop into a coma. Thankfully, all of the decorations came on time. She got Jax and Noelle to help her bring all the boxes to the empty club room in the main building. They had to leave right after for classes, so she was left to set up on her own. No matter.

After setting up all the folding tables and chairs and putting tablecloths down, she still had three more boxes of supplies to go through when the door creaked open. Cyrus walked in, the last person she expected to see. She briefly looked out the window and wondered if jumping out would be a viable option.

"Veronica told me you'd be here," he explained.

Two stories. I could make it, she thought.

"Do you need help?"

"With what?" she asked blankly. He gestured to the boxes. "Oh. Uh."

She really hadn't been prepared to see him so soon and couldn't gauge whether he was still pissed. She imagined he was, especially since she wasn't groveling for forgiveness. She'd never been quick to get on her knees.

"Do you need these hung?" Cy held up a back of paper streamers.

She managed a nod. "Um, twist them and tape them up around the room. Please."

He did as he was told. Her eyes followed him across the room, unabashedly staring. She knew she needed to apologize, but she'd never been very good at it. And knowing that it needed to be done but being unable to do it made everything worse.

"Jax told me that you were celebrating the Mid-Autumn Festival," Cyrus began, "which is unfortunate, since your brother doesn't even like me, and yet the only updates I get about you are from him. You know, I've never been the clingy type. Not in any sort of relationship. But you might just have a hidden superpower, Kitty—making others worry about you."

She winced. "I'm sorry. I didn't mean to make you worry. I just...had a lot going on and needed time to process some things."

"And? Have you processed them?"

"No," she said honestly. "I think the one thing that I've learned from this whole situation is that I'm a work in progress in every aspect of my life. And I'm sorry that I lashed out at you. You didn't deserve that."

He turned toward her, looking her in the eye for the first time since entering the room. "Don't you know you can rely on me?"

"I have this problem where I know things in my head, but not in my heart. And that isn't an excuse for how I treated you. I'm not the easiest person to deal with. As you said—I'm very high maintenance."

"And yet, here I am."

"Yeah. I think you must be a masochist. Or one of those smart people who just aren't good at social situations."

"Hey, now."

She reached into her backpack and pulled out a piece of paper. Her face heated, and she was almost tempted to turn tail and run. "Here. I went to Bath & Body Works with Veronica and sprayed it. Now, it smells like cotton candy."

"And you used glitter," he commented.

"I thought it added a certain je ne sais quoi."

Cy scanned the page. "Have you lost your mind?"

"Yeah, I thought we already established that."

"A friendship treaty. This sounds like a horrible idea, taken straight out of a rom-com."

"I've thought about that, but there's a very important difference," Kitty argued. "In the rom-coms, they make these agreements *before* doing anything. We've already fucked."

"Multiple times."

"Exactly! Just because we're never going to get married, have kids, and buy a house with a white-picket fence, doesn't mean we can't have sex."

"You're asking me to be your fuck buddy?"

"Don't say it like that! It sounds crude. We're friends who sometimes sleep together. After having sex."

"I'm pretty sure that's the definition of a fuck buddy," Cyrus drawled. "But if that's how you want to think about it, sure."

"Then we're on the same page?"

"We're in the same library, reading the same book, on the same page."

She looked at the clock. "Okay, so if we finish setting up quickly, we'll have time to kill before the party."

"Are you serious?" he asked incredulously. "Aren't your parents coming over later?"

"What, are you scared of my mom?" she mocked.

"I'm *terrified* of your mother. She looks at me like I'm a criminal."

"Nonsense. She's probably just thinking about the most effective way to dispose of your body, should you ever break my heart."

"That is not reassuring!"

She waved a hand, dismissing him. "Just hurry up and finish decorating. There's a perfectly fine closet in the back of the room, if you're that worried about getting caught. It's a tight squeeze, but I'm pretty sure we could make it work."

"You know, we really need to work on your definition of romance. Because this isn't it," he retorted, but he picked up the pace, nonetheless.

"WHY IS THERE a bandage on your head?"

Kitty gently touched her forehead. "Uh, I slipped getting something from the supply closet."

That wasn't like her. Veronica tilted her head, trying to assess her friend's face. She was clearly lying, but the question was why. She looked almost...*guilty*. "You're usually pretty coordinated."

"Yeah, well, we all have our moments. Hey, did you get dumplings?"

She was deflecting, but Veronica had actually gotten dumplings.

The aroma of Mr. Swan's cooking filled the air, and she couldn't choose just one thing. She picked a little from each tray. There was something about his food that tasted like home. Every time Veronica visited Kitty at her parents' apartment, the Swans stuffed her with food. Kitty said it was a cultural thing. Those two kept Vee better fed than her own parents! The first time she had gone over, to drop a textbook off for Kitty, Mr. Swan had reeled her in with egg tarts. Of course, to be polite, she had told him that they were the best thing she'd ever tasted. And yes, they were delicious. But ever since, when she came over, they had egg tarts for her.

"You are such a nice girl," Mrs. Swan would say, fussing over her.

Veronica couldn't help but feel a bit jealous of Kitty for having such loving parents. It was a stark contrast to her own parents: a mother who was a narcissist and a father who didn't have any interest in her at all. And maybe that's where the root of all her problems stemmed from: her parents being incapable of loving anyone but themselves. That's what a therapist would say, if her parents would send her to one, but of course, no one in the Halliwell family could go to a shrink; what would the neighbors say? So instead, her therapist was Reddit, with a healthy dose of Wikipedia.

After filling her plate, Veronica turned around and realized Kitty was gone, which left her awkwardly alone. Noelle wasn't there, and Mr. and Mrs. Swan were talking, or *trying* to talk, to their co-workers. It didn't look like they were doing a great job. Mrs. Swan smiled and walked up to a woman, only to have her make eye contact and walk away. What the hell?

Honestly, the turnout for the event was really low, even with the free dinner. Veronica told a handful of classmates, but she figured it would be packed. She should have made flyers or something—she thought Kitty would have done that.

Veronica counted about fifteen people, most of whom

barely touched the food and stood huddled in groups, ignoring the Swans. Jax and Jianhao Chen, someone Kitty made clear was person-non-grata, discussed something by the window with their faces drawn. Cyrus and Blake—ew—were by one of the doors. Veronica quickly looked away, hoping Blake hadn't seen her. But how could he not have? At least he had the decency to avoid her. Unfortunately, he was *smiling*. Genuinely, she suspected. Was it because of Cyrus?

Maybe they should just date each other, Vee thought bitterly.

Melody walked in, wearing a baggy grey hoodie and cargo pants. She was the opposite of her brother, whose clothes were always clean, wrinkle-free, and perfectly fitted. She was going for the 'effortless, casual' look and ended up with 'hobo chic' minus the 'chic' part. Last year, Veronica wouldn't have even *thought* to initiate a conversation with Melody.

Mel, Charity, Blake, and Cy had all grown up together, and part of Veronica resented them for it. It wasn't their fault—they lived on the same street. Of course they would be childhood friends! But Charity and Mel were too close to Blake for Vee's liking. And it turned out her suspicions were correct—he had cheated on her, and dumped her, for Charity.

Melody, on the other hand, had a reputation for being arrogant and childish. After getting to know her better, Vee had realized Mel was just painfully awkward. And what could Veronica really complain about, in that regard? She was just as bad!

But they were both at the age where they weren't quite adults, yet they were desperate not to be written off as children. Neither had been able to figure out who they wanted to be yet, and the growing pains had social consequences.

Namely, neither had many friends. It only made sense that they'd befriend each other.

"Hey, Veronica, how have you been?" Melody asked, approaching with a smile.

Oh no. She was using *that* voice—the pitying one Vee had heard all too much since the start of the semester.

She forced a smile. "I've been good. Really good. Better than ever."

"That's great," Melody said, though she didn't sound convinced. "Where's Kitty?"

"Around here somewhere," Veronica said, gesturing to the room. "Hey, has she said anything to you? She's been acting weird lately."

Melody grabbed a paper plate and began going around the table, serving food for herself. "I haven't talked to Kitty that much. And she never answers her phone. But I think she and Cyrus get dinner together regularly. They have that weird food-sharing thing. I don't know what to call it, but it freaks me out."

Veronica knew exactly what she was talking about. "Is there something going on between them?"

Melody laughed. "I doubt it. They can barely stand each other. Eating habits aside, they're always arguing over the dumbest shit. Or bragging about themselves. 'I bet I can run faster than you.' 'I bet I'm a better soccer player than you.' Blah blah blah."

She had a point. Besides, Kitty had enough to think about with the Blood Trials...and Ryder. It was a topic neither of them really expanded on, but Vee knew the results of the fight bothered Kitty.

If Veronica were a good friend, she would hate him. He was awful, and he'd kissed Kitty just so he'd win the duel—on a technicality. Not only that, but he couldn't properly apologize for it. What did that say about his character?

Despite all the red flags, Veronica admitted, in the depths of her heart, that she was attracted to him. It must have been the same part of her that wanted Blake's attention, even after what he'd done.

Kitty had frozen Blake out after what he did. It was only fair that Veronica do the same, and stick by her friend's side.

Even if maybe, just *maybe*, she was overreacting.

THE WARD-SWAN FRIENDSHIP TREATY

(DRAFTED BY KITTY SWAN, REVIEWED AND SIGNED BY CYRUS WARD)

Our Little Secret: We're not telling anybody what we may or may not be doing under the covers.

No Jealousy Clause: We are free to date, flirt, or hang out with whoever we want. (But I totally reserve the right to judge whoever you bring into the friend group. If she has a bad perm, I'm going to comment on it!)

Condoms, Condoms, Condoms: We're not doing anything without them!

Romance is Off the Table: Keep it PG in public and NC-17 in private. I don't need flowers and chocolate. (Well, I'll make an exception about the chocolate.)

Keep It Light, Keep It Moving: No shared pets, tattoos, or anything that screams "We're together!" Especially since we're not.

Honesty Policy: If one of us starts feeling like this arrangement isn't working, we speak up immediately. No ghosting, no icing out, and no passive-aggressive nonsense. (I will find you and kick your ass if I feel like you're playing me. You know I hate games like that.)

Exit Clause: If this arrangement starts feeling like a rom-com gone wrong, we shake hands like two lawyers closing a deal and walk away. No drama, no mess. No feelings, aside from friendship!!

Our safe word is "glitter" if things go too far.

NORTHEASTERN TRIBUNE

HARVEST FESTIVAL OR DEVIL-WORSHIP?

In an ostentatious display that veered more towards the bizarre than the celebratory, the Swan family recently hosted what they called a 'harvest festival', a tradition from their homeland. Yet, what was intended to be a showcase of cultural richness quickly devolved into a spectacle that left many guests questioning the palate, and perhaps even the sanity, of our hosts.

The Swans, ever eager to parade their heritage around, laid out a spread that was as alarming to the eyes as it was offensive to the taste buds. Dishes that bore more resemblance to the aftermath of a particularly troubling stomach flu than to any recognizable cuisine were presented with a flourish. The highlight, if one might call it that, was a centerpiece that looked suspiciously like vomit. The only good thing to come out of China was a fortune cookie.

The entire affair reeked of heresy, or at the very least, a complete and utter disregard for the sensibilities of the refined palate. One could not help but draw parallels to the gatherings of pagans or devil worshippers, who delight in flouting convention and embracing the grotesque. The Swans, it seems, are no different.

But perhaps the most egregious affront was the implicit expectation that guests should not only partake in this culinary travesty but also express gratitude for the opportunity. It brought to mind a recent venture to a Korean restaurant—a concept I use loosely—where the 'chefs', if one could even call them that, had the audacity to expect patrons to cook their own meat. Such laziness! It's a trend, it appears, not limited to the Swans but endemic among immigrants, who seem to operate under the delusion that mere participation warrants acclaim, and that the novelty of their presence excuses a lack of effort and quality.

In reflecting on the evening, one is left to ponder the broader implications of such events. Is this what we are to expect as the norm, a future where the richness of tradition is replaced with the shock value of the foreign and unfamiliar? Where the hard work and culinary craftsmanship are sidelined in favor of spectacle and novelty?

The Swan family's Satanic festival has provided food for thought, indeed, though it's a meal that, much like their offerings, leaves a sour taste in the mouth.

EIGHTEEN

SO, Veronica was back to red.

Charity liked that. It wouldn't be so jarring to look at her anymore.

They hadn't run into each other since the semester began, mostly because Charity was doing her best to avoid her...niece. Yeah, it was a strange relationship. She wished her father would be like other, more normal, truebloods and only reproduce one generation at a time.

Many truebloods aged much slower than their shadowborn offspring. Her father, fae, would look to be in his thirties for the entirety of her life. As such, he cycled through wives like tissues, each one needing to be young and fertile. Once they disappointed him or showed a wrinkle? Hello, divorce.

You'd think, given his propensity for womanizing, that Charity would have learned from it. That she would have known to avoid getting hurt and falling for men who resembled her father. But, if anything, she gravitated toward them even more.

God, it was *textbook*—which was currently what she was

hiding behind to get a glimpse of Veronica. She weaved through the aisles, plucking a few spell books from the shelves. When she turned, suddenly, her eyes met Charity's. She tried to duck, but it was too late.

"Hi," Veronica said, approaching.

Charity tried to keep the scowl off her face, failing miserably. "Uh, hi."

"How are you? I haven't seen much of you since the semester started."

"I have. You've been going around with Ryder Kinsey, haven't you?" Charity saw them together in the cafeteria just that morning.

"Yeah. He's a...friend."

Some friend. She didn't say anything—it wasn't her place. But if she could speak freely, she'd rant about how awful an idea it was to consort with Ryder. Not that Charity herself had much experience with him, but from the few interactions they'd had, he wasn't very pleasant.

Despite all her flaws, she had self-awareness. She wasn't *working* on any of her issues, but she knew about them! Ryder, on the other hand? Purely delusional. He must have thought himself a brooding antihero. Charity just thought he was a jackass, and arrogant beyond measure.

Kitty Swan was like that too, but at least she had some skill to back up her giant ego. What Ryder had pulled during their duel was cheap and, frankly, creepy. Speaking of...

"Aren't you friends with Kitty Swan?"

Veronica stiffened. "Yeah."

Oh. Charity could tell she wasn't ready to talk about it, and certainly not with her. "You should be careful. Ryder is up to something. He only ever returns to campus on Kinsey's orders."

"He's rough around the edges," Veronica admitted, "but he might just be misunderstood. There are so many rumors about him around campus. Who's to say what's true and what's not?"

"Don't fall back into old habits." There were rumors about Blake, too—and they were all true.

Now Veronica looked upset. Charity knew she had gone too far, and prepared herself for an inevitable blowout, but it never came.

"I'll be cautious," Veronica relented.

Charity tried to hide her shock. "Alright, then."

There was nothing more to say. She turned to leave, having gotten what she needed from the library, but Veronica put a hand on her arm. "Wait. I want to ask you something. If I can."

"What?"

"It's about Tessa."

Charity froze, her entire body, seeming to ice over.

Veronica must have sensed something was wrong. "I'm sorry. I didn't mean to—"

"The less you know about her, the better," Charity said, her voice clipped. "I'll see you around."

And as she walked away from her sister's doppelgänger, she could almost hear Tessa laughing.

THE PROJECT WAS SHAPING up to be a total disaster. It was time to accept what Noelle had known all along: she and Blake made a horrible team.

Professor Evans seemed to think so, too. After their presentation, during which Blake merely stood there looking out the window, the two were called to stay after class was over.

I knew it, Noelle thought bitterly, glaring at Blake. He had ruined it all.

Sometimes, it seemed Professor Evans looked for excuses to single Noelle out, whether it was when she gave an incomplete answer, or she raised her hand too much, or she spoke too loudly without enunciating. Now, he had something that would actually affect her grades.

She was aiming for a 4.0 GPA this semester and damn if she'd let Blake stand in her way! She'd whip up a special batch of Anus Annihilator, just for him!

"Do you know why I asked you both to stay?" Professor Evans said condescendingly.

Blake rolled his eyes. "I can take a guess. Miss Perfect over here thought I was too stupid to help out!"

He had the nerve to jerk a thumb at Noelle.

"Excuse you! I *knew* you weren't going to do any work. Why would I wait until the last minute to figure that out?"

"You didn't even give me the chance—"

"Silence. You're getting a zero for this project. This was a group assignment," Professor Evans admonished. "You didn't follow the rules."

Ugh. Wasn't it more resourceful on her part that she did everything? Why was she being punished because Blake was lazy? Noelle felt the sting of tears, which was stupid, since it was just a project. Just an...F.

"You should give us another chance," Blake told him. "We can redo it by next week. We'll pick a different topic."

"Another chance? You don't get second chances in the real world," Evans said.

"You're right. I'm sorry. Please, let us fix this. Even if we can't get full credit, there are still other groups presenting, right? We'll go again, and it will take five minutes, max."

Noelle had never heard Blake apologize before. She guessed Professor Evans hadn't, either.

The older man looked thoughtful for a moment. "Fine. By next week, then. You're presenting first thing."

"Thank you." Blake nudged Noelle. "Come on. Let's get started."

Everything happened so quickly, Noelle could barely process it until they were in the hall. Blake turned to her, frowning.

He wouldn't make this expression at Kitty. He would smile, even if it was fake.

"This is all your fault," Noelle said finally.

"My fault? Are you insane?" he growled—literally growled. It must've been the werewolf genes. "You're the one who refused to work with me. You didn't answer my texts, you wouldn't set up a date to work on this, and now you're blaming me? You think I'm an idiot, don't you?"

"So? You think I'm ugly," Noelle shot back. "You think I'm just Kitty's ugly sister."

"*What*? What world are you living in?"

"You do! That's why you're all smiles around her, but for me? You don't give a shit, because you don't want to fuck me. And girls who aren't dating prospects are nothing to you. That's it, isn't it?"

He looked at her for a long minute. And then he laughed. *Howled*, to be more accurate.

Noelle never wanted to punch anyone more than she wanted to punch him, right then and there. "What's so funny?"

"You know," he gasped, "when we first met, I thought you

were going to be some boring, whiny loser. But you've proven me wrong today. You're entertaining after all, Noelle. Because you're jealous of your sister. I love catty girls, you see. They're funny to watch self-destruct. I thought Kitty would be the queen of that, given her name. But you? You take the cake. Don't worry, babe. I way prefer you, now."

Noelle's face turned red as a tomato. "I...I'm not jealous!"

What did she have to be jealous of? Kitty was stupid. Strong, physically, but not mentally. Just the other morning, Noelle's phone had buzzed and Kitty'd had a near panic attack. She was still hung up on something that happened *months* ago. She could never let things go! Plus, she farted in her sleep, was an ugly crier, sweat like a pig in the heat... There were plenty of things wrong with Queen Kitty! It wasn't that Noelle was jealous of her sister. She loved her, of course. But sometimes, it felt like everyone saw this perfect version of her, and they forgot she was human. Imperfect, smelly, and very human.

"You're jealous," Blake confirmed. He straightened, giving her a smile without humor. "Kitty's a cunt, plain and simple. But you? You're like an onion, Noelle."

"Are you quoting Shrek to me right now?"

"You've got layers," he continued. "And that makes you all the more interesting. Better yet? You have *zero* self-awareness. Maybe it's because your only interactions, for most of your life at least, have been with your family. And I'm sure that no matter what you did, no matter how insufferably egotistical and self-righteous you behaved, they still loved you. But this isn't your home anymore, sweetheart. Here? Nobody gives a shit about you."

IN ANOTHER FIVE MINUTES, Melody would be calling campus security. Her brother was late, and he hadn't called. He *never* did that, especially not to her. Something must have happened. What if he'd fallen into a well?

No. Mel shook the thought out of her head. There were no wells on campus. And also, this wasn't an episode of *Lassie*. Or *The Ring*, for that matter.

Just as she reached for her phone, there was a knock on the door. Melody sprang up, not checking the peephole before letting her brother into her dorm room. She had a double, but no roommate. Any other girl on campus would be elated with the situation; Mel essentially had a single room! But she didn't *want* a single room. It got cold, and frankly, a bit scary at night. There was a rumor going around about a ghost in the shower room of the boys' dorm. What if there were ghosts in the girls' dorm, too?

Cyrus's cheeks were flushed, and his hair was slightly damp, smelling strongly of lavender and lemongrass. Melody knew the scent from somewhere, but she couldn't quite put her finger on where.

"Sorry," he muttered, shuffling inside with his book bag. "I got, uh, caught up in—with—something."

"Something more important than your sister? Your own flesh and blood?" Melody asked, only half-joking.

He softened, unable to take a joke. "Of course not. I'm sorry, Mel."

"Geez, I was kidding, you big idiot." She gestured to the empty desk beside hers. "Sit. Stay a while. I have energy drinks and granola bars."

"Didn't Dad send you money for a mini-fridge?"

"Yeah. It's stocked with energy drinks and granola bars. Would you like Watermelon or Peach?"

Cyrus put his backpack down with a sigh. "Can you just do me a favor and go down to the cafeteria once in a while? Eat a salad or, I don't know, something not from a can?"

"Yeah, yeah." Typical of her brother. *He* was the one who needed help, and apparently, it was serious enough that he couldn't put it in a text like a normal person. He insisted on scheduling an appointment—with his own damn sister—to talk in person. Then again, he'd always been a bit strict, with himself most of all. "So, what was so important that you needed to make the long trek all the way to my dorm?"

"It was hardly a trek," Cyrus said wryly.

"Don't avoid the question."

"Remember when Kitty asked if you tried to look at the aura of a feral? Did you ever end up doing that?"

Melody frowned. As a shadowborn, it was rare to inherit psychic powers. Generally, psychics were seen as the weakest descendant of a trueblood, due to blood dilution.

Shadowborn had a standard set of abilities: heightened strength, faster healing, better stamina, and heightened senses. Mel had got the short end of the stick there—she wore glasses to correct her vision. Her prescription was low, but most shadowborn had *better* than 20/20 vision, not worse.

To make up for that, the universe had decided to 'gift' her with True Sight, the power to see auras. Not many had the power historically, so little was known about it. All Dad had told her was that auras were unique signatures everyone had. While there were slight shifts in their appearance over time, Mel had never seen one change drastically. Then again, she didn't use True Sight often. She didn't know what the auras meant, not exactly. And when she looked at them, she couldn't see much else. All in all, it was a useless skill.

"No. I haven't used it on ferals," Melody replied. "I would

have to get close enough to one to use it, and I wouldn't be able to defend myself. It's dangerous, especially now that they move in groups."

"I think we should take a trip to the Veil together, then. I'll protect you," he said hastily, as if it wasn't already a given. "But I need to know how the auras compare to regular beastbloods. Kitty was onto something with her suggestion."

"This wouldn't have anything to do with the moving corpse in the morgue, right?"

"It does."

She was afraid he'd say that. "You're not Nancy Drew, Cy. The SNPD took over the case. Let it go."

"You and I both know they're not doing anything about it," Cyrus said firmly. "Also, Nancy Drew has a male equivalent. The Hardy Boys. That would have been a more accurate parallel."

"You want me to call you a Hardy Boy? Gross, you're my brother."

"Get your mind out of the gutter. Anyway, whenever the SNPD gets involved, it means a cover-up is taking place. I looked into their previous cases. They only come to conclusions after newspapers, private investigators, and others in the supernatural community speak out. It seems like their only function is to buy time."

Why? Most truebloods recognized the gravity of the ferals. The issue affected everyone in the community; the SNPD had very real reasons to want to solve the case, just as much as anyone else. There was no treatment or cure, so it wasn't like anyone made money off it. Except the researchers, Mel supposed.

"Ever since Dr. Woods arrived, things are being kept very

hush-hush. At least Sabine Everleigh publicly published her findings, or lack thereof, in the school paper."

"Sabine was responsible for the release of the horde," Melody pointed out.

"Probably," he conceded, "but that doesn't mean her transparency with her research is a bad thing. Dr. Woods is the opposite; I have no idea what she's working on. I tried to go to the lab yesterday and ask, but she wouldn't tell me. I even lied and said I was working on an article for the paper. All she said was her work is confidential. I don't even know if she's concerned about the happenings in the Veil. It sure as hell doesn't seem like it! I asked Chancellor Kinsey, too, and he kept trying to change the subject. Something is very wrong here."

Melody wasn't sure why he was pressing so hard on this issue, but it was clearly important to him. And if it was important to him, it was important to her. She just didn't understand what possible motive anyone would have to delay the research. Money aside, it wasn't as if Woods—or any of her researchers—were immune to ferals. They could get attacked at any time on campus, and if they were infected, they'd die like every other shadowborn.

"The moving corpse is just one piece of the puzzle," he continued. "What about these groups of beastbloods becoming infected? It used to be, the disease wiped out entire packs at once. It didn't spread fast enough for a beastblood to turn feral—usually, it would be killed before it reached that point. If the incubation period is becoming shorter, then what does this mean for the Veil as a whole? And beastbloods? The entire realm could be at risk."

"If I were a therapist, I'd say you're catastrophizing. But you have a point." And that unsettled her. She agreed with what her brother was saying, and on top of it, there was the Tessa issue.

Mel knew Professor Everleigh denied the possibility, but the more she thought about it, the more she was convinced it really had been Tessa Churchill in the Veil that day. But why would Everleigh be so quick to shut her down? Did it relate back to Rory?

She winced at the thought. Everleigh had, understandably, changed since the death of his son. Not only had Rory died, but Sabine's involvement had her locked up God knew where.

"I did some digging." Cyrus unzipped his backpack and dropped a full binder on the desk with a dramatic thud. When he opened it, a row of colored and labeled tabs allowed him to quickly find what he was looking for. It looked like a page of mumbo jumbo to her. "These are all Dr. Woods's papers published from the start of the feral illness."

"You read all this crap?"

"It's not crap. Well, it is. But it's important. See?" He pointed to a chart.

"Numbers."

"Yes, but they don't add up. I ran her raw data sets—which I was able to track down, thanks to the librarian—and she manipulated the results in her conclusions on about seventy percent of these published research papers. She's gotten recognition from major scientific shadowborn journals. How has no one caught this?"

Maybe they're not neurotic busybodies, Mel thought. "Aren't you in your third year of pre-med? How did you have time to do this?"

"Coffee. That's not the point. The point is, Woods profits off these papers. She gets grants, recognition, and she was even hired here to conduct more research. She's profiting off the ferals, in a sick and roundabout way. It *does* benefit her to continue studying them. And the more she alters her findings, the more headlines she gets in shadowborn news outlets. In a twisted way, I can understand *one* person being stupidly greedy enough to try and turn a profit on something that could easily affect them. What I can't figure out is how no one caught this. She has an entire research team working with her on every project she's overseen, and they're making a pittance compared to her."

"Even Everleigh is working with her." And, of all people, Melody doubted Professor Everleigh would get involved in an academic dishonesty scandal.

"This was a long way of saying: I need your help, Mel. Can we go to the Veil this weekend and hunt?" Cyrus asked. "I promise I'll keep you safe. I wouldn't ask if I wasn't desperate."

"You don't have to wait until you're desperate to ask me for favors." They were siblings; helping him was a given.

While Cyrus was the older brother—and, therefore, expected to take care of her—Mel always felt some sort of responsibility for him as well.

She wasn't an idiot. She knew she had a reputation for being immature around campus, and for the most part, it was true. But she liked to think that, in some ways, Cyrus needed her too.

HOW MANY TAS did it take to change a lightbulb?

Just one, as it turned out.

Nora screwed the bulb in, letting it flicker on before skirting around the edge of the desk. The bookshelves loomed against the walls, casting long shadows in the room. They were ancient, creaking things stuffed with volumes that had seen better days. Their leather spines were faded, and their pages yellowed, each one carrying a strong musk.

The office suited Professor Everleigh, filled with brilliant articles, but completely disorganized. Papers littered every surface, piled high on the desk, the floor, and even the windowsill. Among these piles were notebooks filled with scribbles, loose papers with hastily jotted notes, and even old photographs.

As she went through the list of books Everleigh wanted removed and destroyed, she came across a particularly old tome, its cover worn to the point of being nearly unrecognizable. She pulled it out, a cloud of dust puffing into the air, making her cough. Wiping away the dust, she opened the book to find it filled with intricate drawings and notes in Latin.

She glanced at the door, half-expecting Everleigh to burst in and catch her... What? Snooping? She was doing her job. But even holding the book in her hands, something felt off. She couldn't put her finger on what.

Thank God for cell phones.

Nora opened her translation app and took photos, page by page, until she finished the first chapter. It was an introduction, detailing the contents of the book on death curses.

Why would Professor Everleigh have a book on that? Blood magic, especially magic like this, was forbidden.

The more she read, the more she realized the rarity and value of the knowledge ensconced within its pages. Professor Everleigh had mentioned, in passing, his intention to clear out some of the older, less useful texts from his collection. The fate of many would be the recycling bin or, worse, the shredder. A pang of desperation hit her—the thought of such a unique book being destroyed was unbearable.

Nora told herself that Professor Everleigh wouldn't miss this one book. With a glance around the silent room, as if to ensure the shadows themselves held no objections, she slipped the grimoire into her bag.

NINETEEN

"YOU KNOW this place is haunted, right?"

Kitty turned. Jianhao stood behind her, leaning against a tree. She didn't know how long he'd been there, but as soon as she saw him, she got up to leave. Meditating wasn't going well, anyway, and the sun would set soon. She needed to get to the cafeteria before the dinner rush.

Jianhao stopped her, putting a hand on her arm. "Where are you going, Xiao Xing?"

"Away from you," she retorted.

"In the middle of a conversation? That's not very polite, is it?"

"There was no conversation. You were monologuing about a ghost, and I was thinking about food."

"Still angry that I won our little sparring match? Don't be too hard on yourself," he told her. She could have slapped that smug grin right off his face. "It was bound to happen eventually. Everyone loses at some point. It's the only way you can become a better fighter."

She knew that—but she didn't want to hear it. Especially not from him.

Talking with her parents had made her feel better, but it hadn't changed her animosity toward Jianhao. He bruised her pride and her ribs, that day. She knew he'd be insufferable about it, so she avoided him like she avoided white clothes after Labor Day.

"Are you going to run away again?" he asked, drawing closer. Screw him and his stupidly perfect hair and deep brown eyes. His hotness didn't negate the fact that she didn't like him. "Or will you stay and listen to me?"

"Listen to what? Your thinly veiled insults?"

"No. You misunderstand me—I sparred with you at the request of your parents. They wanted me to see how far along you are in your training, and, after a proper assessment, I could help you."

"How magnanimous of you," she bit out. "I don't want to be your charity case. My uncle might have asked you to help out, but why don't you just focus on assisting my parents with their research and leave me alone?"

"I didn't think you would be so prideful. Don't you want to improve?"

"Not with you."

"Ah," Jianhao said, as if he cracked the code at last. "You're in love with me."

Kitty's mouth fell open. "Excuse me?"

"You're afraid to be around me. You're constantly running away from me, and your cheeks flush in my presence. You're in love with me, and you're afraid that if you let me help you, you'll fall for me even more."

"You're insane!" Kitty screeched. "Like, actually certifiable. I should have you committed—to the morgue!"

Jianhao laughed. "I knew you'd be shy about your feelings, but there's no need to hide from me."

"You have a very skewed version of reality," Kitty informed him. "I'm not in love with you. I hate you."

"Hate and love are two sides of the same coin, qīn'ài de."

"Do not call me that!"

"There's no need for concern," he said generously. "It's only natural you would be shy, given how much more attractive I am than you. I'm not offended, if that's what you're worried about."

"I can't even... How... What..." Kitty's brain was short-circuiting. The words that were coming out of his mouth were too preposterous for her to comprehend. The only thing she could conceivably do was hit him as hard as she could in the face.

Unfortunately, she wasn't fast enough. He ducked, grabbing her arm and pulling him toward his chest. "Even if you're not my type at all, I'm willing to train you."

"Get your hands off me," she growled.

"Only if you agree to let me help you. There's a lot I can teach you. Like, for example, how to improve your qi efficiency. A little goes a long way, you know."

That made Kitty pause. "What do you mean?"

"You only need about a fourth of what you're actually using to have the same effect. Your technique is good, but you need to work on refining it. You can be much faster and stronger, if you make a few tweaks," he explained.

"Why would I trust you?"

"I don't care if you trust me or not. I'm merely stating the facts. I can help you, if you let me, Xiao Xing." He switched to Mandarin, his voice taking on a deeper baritone. "Don't you want to be immortal? To heal your golden core?"

Kitty had no idea that her parents had told her uncle what happened, or that Uncle Stefan had told Jianhao. She hadn't confided in anyone, not even Cyrus, about the golden core issue. Her parents weren't worried, and she didn't think the matter was worth mentioning. It wasn't as though she was dying or anything, so she kept it to herself.

"I can fix all the things you're doing wrong, if you'll let me help you."

Kitty nodded. "Fine. If you can help me improve, even a little, in the next hour, I'll let you help me."

As haughty as it sounded, she didn't doubt he would actually be able to train her. She'd seen his skills up close and personal; he wasn't just blowing smoke. And that scared her more than anything. As a smile slowly spread across his flawless face, Kitty couldn't help but feel like she'd just made a deal with a demon.

JIANHAO HAD A VERY PUNCHABLE FACE. That was Cyrus's first thought as he stepped into the greenhouse.

He had come looking for Kitty, to tell her about his plan to go into the Veil with Melody. Instead, he was met with a sickening scene: she was cheating on him.

Alright, she wasn't *cheating* per se. They weren't together, and even if they were, she hadn't done anything technically wrong. She and Jianhao were on the grass, beating each other senseless. He straddled her, his hands wrapped around her neck while she punched his stomach repeatedly.

Kitty was Cyrus's sparring partner. She should have been

punching *his* stomach! Not some...stupidly muscular pretty boy! Fuck, did he have to be so hot? Kitty mentioned it, but Cyrus thought she'd been exaggerating. Unfortunately, if anything, she undersold it. Jianhao was like a work of art, and damn if that wasn't a shotgun to Cy's ego.

More importantly, he had always been the only one to spar with her. She was vicious, and she liked to win. That meant she had to have an outlet. If it wasn't him, then who the hell was she going to beat up? Was Jianhao going to replace him as her punching bag?

Not if Cyrus had anything to say about it!

"Hey, Kitty," he greeted her, trying to play it cool. She and Jianhao looked over at him. Kitty's face was flushed, her breathing ragged. A flash of unreasonable anger coursed through him; he was the only one who should have the privilege of seeing her like that. "I've been looking for you."

Jianhao hopped off her, offering her a hand up. She took it, standing and dusting off her knees.

"Oh?" she asked, not sounding particularly concerned.

Cyrus wasn't sure if her indifference was because of Jianhao's presence or because she'd been distracted. "Yeah."

"You must be Sirius," Jianhao said with a smile.

"Cyrus," he corrected.

"Right."

He did that on purpose.

Cyrus thought Kitty hated the guy. She specifically described him as a pompous, crusty asshole who she'd rather throw out the window of her dorm than speak with. So what the hell?

And no, he was absolutely *not* jealous. Because that would have gone against that stupid friendship treaty Kitty wrote up, and he wasn't going to risk their arrangement by doing something so petty and childish. (Probably.)

"Cy, are you alright?" Kitty asked.

Cyrus realized that he hadn't responded, instead staring daggers at Jianhao. "Oh. I'm fine. What were you two doing? Training?"

"Yes," Jianhao answered for her. "Kitty is a talented fighter. I'm teaching her a few techniques. Would you like to join us, Sirius?"

"Cyrus."

"Right."

Kitty glared. "Don't be an ass, Jianhao."

"My apologies." Jianhao didn't sound apologetic at all. "That will be all for today. We'll meet again tomorrow, Xiao Xing. Think about what I said, about the qi circulation. It should help you a great deal in the upcoming trial."

"I will."

Jianhao kissed her hand—the one punching him moments earlier—and left, whistling some cheery tune as he did so. Cyrus wanted to kill him.

"What was that all about?" Cyrus asked once he was out of earshot.

Kitty shrugged. "He wants to help me with the upcoming trial."

"Really?"

"No. I think my parents sent him to babysit me." She rolled her eyes and wiped the back of her hand on her skirt. "But he knows what he's talking about when it comes to cultivation, so I have to take advantage of the opportunity. Even if it means putting up with his bullshit."

Cyrus raised an eyebrow. "And what about me? I'm a good sparring partner."

"You are."

"He's handsome," he hedged.

"Yeah. Want me to set you up?"

"No!" Cyrus snapped. He coughed, trying to cover it up. "I just... You and I were training partners."

"We still are," Kitty reassured him. "Don't worry. It's nothing romantic. Even if it was, you and I are just friends."

"I know," he mumbled.

"Are you jealous?" she teased, pinching his cheek. "Because that would be cute. Against the treaty, but cute nonetheless."

He couldn't look her in the eyes. "Glitter."

"What?"

"The safe word," he clarified, reddening.

"Oh, right." She laughed. "You're such a dork."

"If I was jealous, would you consider ending this friends-only arrangement?"

Kitty was taken aback. She studied his face carefully, her eyes narrowed. "Are you serious?"

"No, I'm Cyrus."

"Har har."

"Would you?"

"No," she said. It sounded as painful to say as it did to hear, which was strange. It shouldn't have hurt. Cyrus knew what this was, and told himself it was alright as long as he only had a crush on her. Crushes were fine. He'd had plenty of those before, and he got over them. Anything more than that, however, was a dangerous territory.

Kitty was protecting his heart as much as her own with her answer. That didn't make it any easier.

"I didn't think so," Cyrus said, forcing a laugh.

"Cy—"

"I just came to tell you that Melody agreed to look at feral auras in the Veil. I could use some backup this weekend. Do you want to join us?"

"Absolutely," Kitty replied without hesitation. "But, Cy, if you're really upset about the Jianhao thing—"

"I'm not."

"Really? You're not angry because he's objectively hot, and he's had his hands all over me?" she asked, crossing her arms. "It doesn't piss you off, knowing that I could conceivably date him and not you? My parents definitely approve of him. They would probably love for me to date a cultivator from the same clan, who has the same goals and ideals. And—"

"Kitty." He shoved her to the grass, pinning her down. He didn't have her strength, but she was so startled by his actions that she didn't react right away. It was an opportunity he wouldn't get any time soon. "Are you trying to make me mad?"

"Maybe," she admitted. "Look—"

He didn't let her finish, slamming his mouth onto hers. The kiss was sloppy, rough. He bit her lip, tasting blood. She gasped, giving him the chance to slip his tongue into her mouth.

She pissed him off more than anyone else. But that was what attracted him in the first place. She challenged him, and she didn't pull punches. She was an equal match for him; he wouldn't want her any other way.

They had an agreement, and not just that stupid piece of perfumed paper. They both knew the reality of their differing lifespans. And logically, he understood her reluctance to get too close. But when faced with a very attractive man who had the same lifespan as her, and who also had her parents' approval...

Cyrus' chest tightened, and from that point, he couldn't

stop himself. He was jealous, and he didn't want to talk about why. All he wanted was her.

Anger and jealousy were easy emotions. They were familiar. He knew how to work with those. He didn't know how to work with the pain that came with loving someone he couldn't have.

Shit.

He hadn't meant to think of that word. Once he did, he couldn't take it back. He loved Kitty, and not in the platonic sense. It was a big, messy, inconvenient love. One that was so deep and wide and intense, it made him do dumb things. Like, say, have sex with her in a glass greenhouse with bushes and prayers as their only shield.

When it was over, and they were both panting and sweaty, Cyrus knew there was no turning back. He didn't have to admit it to her, and she didn't have to acknowledge it, but there was no denying what he felt.

"I think we should make an amendment," she said finally, rolling off him.

He watched her get redressed. Her fingers trembled as she buttoned up her blouse and smoothed her hair.

"Oh?"

"Yeah. We should be exclusive. For the purpose of STIs," she said quickly. "Nothing serious. I'm not suggesting that we start dating or anything. I just... think we should play it safe. You know."

"Play it safe."

"Yeah."

Cyrus sat up and pulled his pants back on. "That's a very sensible suggestion. For safety purposes. Not because of any feelings."

"Well, I do care about you," she admitted. "As a friend. I

wouldn't want to risk your sexual health. Besides, it makes things less complicated."

Less complicated?

He disagreed.

TWENTY

SUNSCREEN WOULD HAVE BEEN a good idea, but it was too late now.

The moment Kitty stepped through the rift, sunlight blinded her momentarily. She stood stock still on the other side, having forgotten to move out of the way and let the others through. As a result, Melody stumbled into her, and Kitty found herself landing face-first in the dirt.

She was usually more coordinated, but lately, things hadn't been going well for her. It seemed the more effort she put into the gym, the worse she got. Even her parents had noticed. Māma said Kitty was doing too much physical activity and tiring herself out; she needed to cultivate and meditate. The problem was, Kitty always cultivated in the greenhouse. And whenever she went into the greenhouse, Cyrus stopped by, and she was no longer in the mood to meditate.

"Are you okay?" he asked, helping her up.

She blinked rapidly, her eyes adjusting to the light. "Fine. Just...clumsier than usual, these days."

"That's good, considering we're going on a dangerous hunt," Jax said, crossing his arms.

"No one asked for sarcasm."

"No one *ever* asks for sarcasm. Doesn't mean they're not gonna get it."

Kitty rolled her eyes. She didn't know why her brother had insisted on coming. It was just supposed to be her, Cy, and Mel. That was enough. But Jax caught the trio as they headed to the campus green to create a rift and invited himself along. For once, Jianhao didn't come along and spoil everything.

Kitty still didn't like him, but damn if he didn't know what he was talking about when it came to cultivation. They trained every day, and she already saw herself improving. Even her golden core felt better.

When they weren't together, he was busy in the lab, working on research with her parents that seemed to be going nowhere. He spent time with Jax, too. They were attached at the hip, something Kitty abhorred. What if Jianhao's bad attitude rubbed off on her baby brother?

...Well, maybe it was too late to worry about Jax's personality.

"The climate here sure is strange," Jax noted, brandishing his sword.

Kitty agreed. If they walked west, they'd hit a humid jungle area and beach. East was a dense, chilly forest. There were buses into town up north, though that was a long walk, and marshes down south. It was as if the land followed its own rules.

"Let's just find a feral and get out of here," Kitty announced. "Lead the way, Fred."

"We'll go to the woods first, Daphne," Cyrus responded.

"What?" Jax asked.

"You know. Scooby Doo," Kitty said.

"You two are so weird."

"In a good way, right?"

"Whatever you need to tell yourself."

"Let's end this fast," Melody said, adjusting her glasses.

The group followed Cyrus into the trees. Fog inexplicably swirled on the ground, growing denser as they headed deeper.

According to Cy, hunts only used to take place when there were feral sightings. Now, thanks to the horde, the Veil was lousy with ferals. Walk a little and you'd certainly bump into one. But Kitty felt a pang of guilt settle in her stomach as they continued, knowing what she had to do.

She could cure a feral. Using her powers, she could help one in exchange for her own immortality. It wasn't logical and she knew it would do more harm than good, but she couldn't help feeling villainous for participating in these hunts.

"Do you smell anything?" Melody asked.

Kitty frowned. "A little. Whatever it is, it's not close."

"What, exactly, is the plan here?" Jax asked, jerking a thumb toward Mel. "We see a feral and keep it occupied while this one gets a look at it?"

"Can you not point at me, please?"

"I'll be the one playing with it," Kitty said. "You and Cyrus are going to be protecting Melody. She can't defend herself while using her powers."

He grunted, which she guessed was in agreement. She couldn't tell.

Her nose scrunched as they took another step forward. A smell hit her like a freight train, overwhelming enough to make her stumble. Rot and decay filled her nostrils and she gagged.

The boys were immediately on alert, unsheathing their

swords. Kitty's hand wrapped around the handle of her saber, and she held it up, unlatching it from the case on her back. The polished blade gleamed, the dark gunmetal color matching her eyes.

A roar tore through the trees, and the ground shook as the feral drew closer. The fog obscured her vision, but a shadow passed over the trees. A second later, they bent as the creature came into view, forcibly carving a path through the forest.

"What the hell is that?" Melody asked, her voice trembling.

"A sign we should run," Jax replied aptly.

And run they did. The feral was unlike anything Kitty had ever seen, in real life or in movies. It was as if a child's description of a nightmarish monster came to life. The closest thing she could compare it to was a furry dragon, which stood about as tall as a standard basketball hoop. From there, though, she wasn't sure what to think. And she didn't plan on sticking around to study it.

A long, leathery tail covered in dark slime swept them all off their feet. Kitty was hyperaware that her new jeans were ruined even before she hit the ground. Rolling to her back, she jumped up and pulled Melody with her. She couldn't see Cyrus or Jax anymore, though that didn't necessarily mean much, with the fog rising around them. The monster came fully into view, its two necks twisted around each other. One head hung limply, its eyes glazed and sunken into a nearly skeletal face. It squelched as it walked forward, dragging along a train of decomposing intestines with it.

Kitty coughed, backing up slowly. The living head swiveled, watching her with its eight glowing eyes. Its mouth opened with a creak like an old staircase, and out slithered a silver snake in place of a tongue. God, what the fuck was in the water here? How did such a creature even exist, on a biological level?

"I'll use True Sight," Melody said quickly.

"What? No! Don't use—"

She stilled, her eyes turning white. The creature roared again, charging at the girls.

Kitty was moving before she could think about it. Gripping her saber, she darted to the side. The monster focused on her, lunging. It grabbed at her with human-shaped hands, catching her leg. It dragged her toward it quickly, scraping her body on the forest floor. Getting a better grip on her legs, it threw her body up and opened its mouth wide.

She spun mid-air, swinging her saber down to guide her movements. The blade sunk into the creature's skull, causing it to hiss and cry. The smell was even worse close to its mouth. The head jerked as it died, shaking Kitty around. She held tight to the grip, her body dangling. Finally, the creature shuddered and went limp.

"Jax?" she called, rolling safely to the ground. She yanked the saber out of its head, gagging when more goo gushed from the wound. "Cy? Mel? Where is everyone?"

"Kitty?" Melody's voice rang out. "Where are you?"

"Mel? Kitty?" Cyrus yelled.

The fog was getting thicker. They ended up regrouping back at the starting point, where they originally stepped through the rift.

Kitty's shoulders relaxed when she saw her brother exiting the forest. "Are you okay?"

"We encountered a feral. Didn't you hear me calling for you? I was worried sick!" Jax replied.

Cyrus put his hands on Mel's shoulders, examining her. "Neither of you were infected, were you?"

"I'm fine," Mel assured her brother. "Kitty led the thing away and killed it."

"We also killed a creature. What did yours look like?" Jax asked. "Ours looked like a scorpion and a kangaroo had a baby. An ugly, mentally traumatizing baby."

"Aren't beastbloods supposed to be, like, Bigfoot and unicorns and stuff? Not monstrous abominations?" Kitty asked, strapping her saber to her back. "Ours was a furry, two-headed dragon with no wings and human hands. Creepy as hell!"

Cyrus frowned. "A dragon?"

"Sort of. It had the body of one. Then again, the fog made it difficult to see all the nitty gritty details. But what I don't get is how all these different creatures could even exist in the same habitat," she complained. "Like, aren't kangaroos and scorpions from hot climates? Why is it in a forest with a dragon?"

"What?"

"I just don't get it."

"No, no. Repeat what you just said," Cy urged.

"Uh, scorpions are from hotter climates? I think. Look, I don't know a lot about the animal kingdom—"

"You're right. I can't believe I didn't see it before. We were so overwhelmed with the horde and the missing students, I don't think anyone cataloged what type of monsters were coming through the rifts," he said, speaking a mile a minute. "Look, you know how rifts work, right? For every location in the Veil, there's a relative location in the mortal realm. So if I open a rift on campus, I will always land within a certain radius in the Veil. But we're seeing creatures that aren't even local to this area here."

"Well, if Sabine Everleigh's lures worked, couldn't that have attracted ferals from different areas?" Jax asked.

"No. They would have needed a huge reach, and Sabine isn't nearly powerful enough to bring beastbloods across continents. I don't even know if that's possible."

"Do you think they're migrating?" Kitty asked.

Cyrus shook his head. "No. Why would they migrate to an area they aren't even acclimated to survive in? I don't think they're coming here of their own free will. I think someone is purposely bringing them to this area."

"Why? And how?" Melody asked, dumbfounded.

"Kitty and I were cornered by a hydra in the greenhouse last semester. And didn't she encounter a chimera at the mall in New Jersey?" He turned to Kitty. "You were trapped in a loading dock and the creature just appeared out of nowhere. Even just now, how was it that we were separated within seconds, you didn't hear me or Jax, and we didn't hear you?"

Kitty had a bad feeling. "You think someone is doing all this, for what?"

"I don't know. But I intend to find out."

ALL HE NEEDED WAS a good fuck.

Blake tried to convince himself of that as he trudged across campus, clean from his latest hunt, but exhausted. It was the fourth time this week he'd gone to the Veil, and at this point, he was sick of complaining about it. He knew Cy, as his roommate, felt the same. Of course, Cyrus was too polite to say anything. Blake wondered if that was a bad thing. Friends shouldn't be polite toward one another—they should just say whatever comes to mind, right? Especially friends as close as Blake and Cy. But the two boys hadn't spoken much this semester.

They weren't arguing. They were simply busy, and their coursework was now more major-focused, so they no longer shared classes. When they weren't in class or on hunts, Cyrus was studying in the greenhouse. Blake would have joined him, but he hated studying. Besides, he'd heard the greenhouse was haunted. People reported spooky noises coming from the shed.

Blake's loneliness was compounded by his lack of female companionship. He'd slept with a few girls since the semester started, but none more than once. Which was strange; he usually had no trouble finding a warm body.

It wasn't that girls weren't interested. With his looks, there was always a naïve freshman out there waiting to be invited back to his room. Nor was it a problem with his appearance; he was still handsome as ever. Inside, however, he was a mess.

He knew why. But he preferred to lie to himself, to feign ignorance, because the truth opened Pandora's Box.

He missed Veronica.

Blake didn't love her. Probably. He wouldn't have hurt her if he did. But she had been reliable, at least. Whenever he was upset, more so than usual, all he had to do was pick up the phone and text her. She'd come running. Or, sometimes, he'd do the opposite—ignore her until she came to him. She'd be pissed, but she'd still show up.

Going to Charity wasn't the same. She wasn't one to be manipulated; they knew each other too well for that. There was something honest and raw about their fucking, and it scared Blake. Not because he was in love with her, either—God no. But sometimes, Charity was better than nothing. Which was how he found herself outside of her dorm room.

"You have no shame," she said, opening the door. Her curls were still damp from the shower, and a thin white t-shirt stretched over her chest. Long plaid pajama bottoms covered her legs, and Blake knew immediately the outfit would be easy to remove.

"You have no roommate," Blake replied smoothly, wearing a smile like an ill-fitting hat. He pushed his way inside, not bothering with an invitation. She'd never say no, regardless of how much she hated him.

Which, he was pretty certain she did. Hate him, that was. Even when they had sex, she looked at him like he was garbage. Surprisingly, that only made him feel better about it. She hated him, and yet, she didn't refuse him.

She had every right to. He would have left her alone, if she indicated she didn't want it. He knew she didn't want *him*. But he figured that, in her moments of weakness, even the great Charity Churchill wanted to get fucked.

"I didn't say you could come in," Charity complained. But she always complained a little, at first. Blake could read her like a screenplay; he knew what she would say next. An insult, probably about his personality. "You're so obnoxious, Blake. Why are you here?"

"There's only one reason I'd be here."

Charity stared at him. He hated her stare, just as piercing as any sword. Even when they were kids, she always seemed to see right through his act. "Get out. I'm serious."

"Alright. I see that you're in a pissy mood."

"It's not a mood. I don't want to see you at all."

"What's your problem?" he asked. "You were the one who pursued me. You practically begged me to fuck you, and you're the one who said it would just be a physical thing."

"My problem? My problem is that you used Veronica as a stand-in for my sister."

Who told her that? It was true, but Blake wondered if

Veronica went off blabbing to everyone, even Charity, about the situation. "So? You only wanted me because you wanted to feel closer to your sister, right?"

Silence.

For a few seconds, Blake thought Charity would go into her closet, get her ax, and hack him to pieces. He knew he'd said the wrong thing but couldn't retract it now.

"Why would I *ever* want to emulate Tessa?" Charity asked finally, raising her chin. She was trying to act strong, but the tremor in her voice gave her away. He was afraid she would start crying. In all the years he'd known her, she'd only cried in front of him once—when her father beat her so badly, he broke her hand. She spoke again, slower now, as if trying to control the emotions coursing through her. "You know something, Blake? I find it kind of funny how we remember the dead. We have wakes and funerals, showcases for the living. Everything is a performance, and mourning is no different. It doesn't matter who died or why. It just matters that they're gone, and you're supposed to be sad. I'm so tired of it. I'm tired of Dad ignoring her existence, and of everyone else revering her just because she's gone."

"Charity—"

"She was a bitch," Charity snarled, her rage making a rare appearance. It was enough to make Blake take a step back. Her fists clenched so tightly; her knuckles grew white. "I hated her. I was happy when she died. She was a sadistic, cold-hearted narcissist, and everybody treated her like she was a god amongst mortals. You, especially. You knew how she made me feel, and you worshipped at her feet anyway. You still do."

"So what? You're jealous, because of her?"

"Jealous? No. Bitter? Yes. I thought when she died, things

would change. But no—the world still revolves around her. Your world, at least."

"And why does that matter?" Blake mocked. "You hate me. Sometimes, I think you always have."

"Hate you?" Charity was taken aback. "I loved you, Blake. Before I even knew what it *meant* to be in love. You made me laugh even when I felt like crying. You made me feel like I mattered when my father told me I was nothing. You were the only person who understood me. And then you chose my sister. I told you all the awful things she'd done, and you picked her anyway. And you know what? I learned to accept it, because you were happy. And then she died, and your mourning took precedence over my own. She must have infected you with her narcissism, because you didn't ask me *once* how I was doing. Everything revolved around you and your guilt. I told myself that you had every right to feel that way, because if it had been you... I would have been devastated too. But you kept choosing her. Even now, you're putting a dead woman above everyone else, including yourself. So maybe I do hate you—because the person you've become is the antithesis of who you were. You're just—"

"Don't." The single, sharp word cut through the room.

Charity's eyes narrowed. "You're just like your father."

Blake didn't remember what he told her after that, if anything. All he remembered was slamming the door behind him as he walked out. The last glimpse he caught of her; she was on the verge of tears. And, for many reasons, most of which he couldn't name, he wanted to cry too.

RYDER HAD Veronica in the palm of his hand, and he knew it. She probably knew it too, which was why she let him into her dorm room on the first knock.

"I like it when you wear your hair like that," he commented, tugging her long ponytail. "Looks sexy. Now, are you going to let me in?"

Veronica shook her head. "I shouldn't."

"But you will anyway," he said. "Because you like me."

"I don't," she said fiercely, stepping aside.

He waltzed past, unable to stop a smug grin from spreading across his face. Her room had a pink color palette, with a big, fluffy blanket and an assortment of pillows on her bed. Photos decorated one wall, and fairy lights lined the ceiling. The cute, feminine room was exactly what he expected from her.

"What are you doing here?" she asked, leaning against her desk.

Ryder sat on her bed, sinking into the cushions. He fished for the USB drive in his pocket and held it up. "I have something for you that you might find interesting."

"What's that supposed to be?"

"A list of all the students who vanished during the horde attack. I got it from my old man's computer. No remains were found for any of these kids. I thought you might find it interesting, is all. I certainly did. Do you know my father funded a research facility in Tennessee? Partially-funded, anyway. It's owned by some bigshot trueblood in the South, yet my father spent three million on it. Curious, isn't it?"

"Not exactly," Veronica said, crossing her arms. "Ryder, if you're just using this as an excuse—"

"There have been a series of robberies and strange incidents happening around the area near the facility. Funny how the footage released of some of the perpetrators look like the students on this list." He shook the USB. "The missing students."

Hook. Line. Sinker.

"That's not possible."

"Think about it. The corpse that attached Cyrus Ward in the morgue? No one ever claimed him. I didn't see a photo, but I bet he was one of the missing students, too. Just a guess. He disappeared during the horde attack, and reappeared in a Blood Wasp nest," Ryder said. He'd done hours of research pouring over this, going as far as to drive two towns over to use the library so his father wouldn't track his school computer. He was fairly confident in his research. "I think we should follow up on this. Care to take a trip with me?"

"You're insane."

"Am I?" he asked. "Or am I just unraveling this mystery?"

Veronica moved to sit on the bed with him, but must have thought better of it and paused in the middle of the room. Her cheeks reddened slightly and she looked away, out the window. "Okay, so let's say you *do* discover something. What would that mean? The students are still alive somehow and, what, committing crimes in Tennessee because...?"

"I don't know about the crimes. But if they are alive, it means they didn't actually disappear during the attack. Obviously. What if the horde attack was done on purpose? A distraction?" Ryder theorized. "My father has been up to something, ever since this whole feral business began. And the Swan's presence at the school has only made it worse."

Veronica shuddered. "We need to tell someone. We need to—"

"You can't tell anyone," Ryder cut her off. "Who are you

going to tell? Everyone in the school is in my father's pocket. Or they can be bought, if they're not already."

"Kitty or Cyrus would have a good—"

"No. I don't trust the Swan girl, nor do I trust her beefy boyfriend."

"Cyrus isn't her boyfriend." Veronica paused. "He's not 'beefy' either."

"He punched me in the face. I'd say he's beefy, and if he's not her boyfriend, he wants to be. But that's not the point. We need to go to Tennessee. You can either come with me or stay behind, but either way, I'm going."

"This is insane," she repeated.

"Yes," he agreed, "but you're going to join me anyway. Because if I leave, and I do this without you, you will never know the truth about Rory Everleigh."

TWENTY-ONE

OF ALL THE people Noelle thought would wait outside her dorm, Blake was the last person on her list.

"What are you doing here?" she asked, point-blank.

He looked up, sliding to stand. "I came here to talk."

"Why?"

"Because you don't like me. And I don't like you," he explained, his voice dull. "I needed someone I could be honest with."

"You can be honest with me because we don't like each other? In what world does that make sense?" But she opened the door and let him in, anyway. Kitty wasn't around, probably meditating in the greenhouse as she'd begun to do every night. She wouldn't be back until much later.

"I don't know," Blake confessed. "I guess, I just can be honest with you because you won't care either way. You already hate me, so it's not like telling you anything else will change your opinion of me. And, as the saying goes, the truth sets you free."

"Are you looking for a therapist or an audience?"

"Both."

And then, Blake told her—completely unsolicited—his story.

BLAKE BLACKWOOD HAD KILLED a total of three people in his life. The first two were unintentional. The third wasn't, but he regretted it all the same.

Trueblood werewolves valued males over females, and no number of social movements or protests could change that. It was an immutable fact to them: males were stronger in every aspect. Anything a female could do, a male could do better. Blake's father taught him that, when he bothered to show his face.

The first time Blake saw his father, he didn't recognize him immediately. Blake was only five, but he distinctly remembered coloring on the back screened-in porch with his nanny, Martha. Their quiet afternoon was interrupted by the squeal of the screen door, and a tall man standing in the doorway with a scowl in his face.

"Is this him?" Loren Blackwood said, pointing a finger at Blake.

Blake stared back at the blonde man in the suit, who looked oddly familiar. But before he could open his mouth and speak, Martha stepped in front of him. She trembled like a fawn, her shoulders hunched. Blake thought she would burst into tears right then and there. He wanted to comfort her, but Loren stepped toward them and flung Martha against the wall like a rag doll. He picked Blake up by the collar, shaking him about.

"You look just like *her*," Loren snarled, all wolf. He threw

Blake to the ceramic tiled floor and walked toward the door. Blake didn't see him for another five years after that, and in that time, he replayed the scene constantly in his head. He had no idea that the man was his father until Martha explained it to him. And he didn't know what his father had meant—*You look just like her.*

He said it like it was an insult. But who was "her" in that situation?

Blake had an otherwise normal childhood. Aside from his lack of parents, he had nannies and housekeepers and chefs to take care of him. And of course, his neighbor, Malcolm Ward, was like a father to him. More so than his own dad. Malcolm treated Blake like one of his own. He was well known in the neighborhood for taking in the stray kids. Malcolm was the reason Blake met his second victim.

That's the first one he remembered, though at the time, he never thought she would die by his hand. Tessa Churchill had a smile like sunshine and long, golden hair like Rapunzel. He thought she was a princess when he first met her. She was kind enough to be an older sister who took care of the neighborhood kids. And Blake, being raised as a werewolf, thought it was his duty to grow up strong and protect a woman like that.

But all childhood dreams have to end at some point. Blake's shattered when his father returned from a trip. Blake was ten, and, laying perfectly still in bed, he heard the front door open. He thought his father would come in to speak to him. Instead, Loren went into the other room and had sex with a new pack member. It was an initiation, Blake later learned. Nothing more, nothing less.

The next morning at breakfast, only Loren appeared in the kitchen with a tall glass of orange juice and the morning paper.

"Your training begins today," Loren told his son casually. He didn't even greet Blake—he just gave him an order.

Blake did not know what the training would involve until the end of the day, when he thought his life would truly end. In the light of the moon, his father stood over him with a bloodied silver sword. Blake never forgot his words, echoing inside his brain from that point on like a curse.

"You murdered the only woman I ever loved—your own mother. You took her life, and *this* is what you do with it?"

Blake didn't know it at the time, but an odd sort of feeling grew in his heart. As if someone had opened up a small hole, and instead of healing—over time—it grew bigger.

The training continued for two months before Loren left again, in the dead of night. And, when Blake was sure his father was gone, he began asking about his mother.

He'd never considered he even *had* a mother before. All he knew were the staff members. Most of his friends didn't have mothers, either. Not biological ones. The Churchill girls had countless stepmothers.

But perhaps that was his biggest mistake. He'd made so many, it was hard to keep track. They say curiosity killed the cat, and Blake wondered what would have happened if he never asked about his mother. Would he have gone on to kill his other two victims?

Eventually, at fifteen, Tessa found out where his mother's family was. Tessa had always been a loyal friend, but Blake never expected her to go out of her way and find his maternal family. Finally, he could get answers.

The two boarded a bus and traveled all the way to Virginia to meet them. But when they arrived, Blake was not expecting such a cold reception. He'd always seen touching reunions on television, and while he never admitted it to anyone but Tessa, he dreamed that one day he would also have one. His father wasn't exactly warm, and the staff members who raised him were Blackwood employees. But a maternal family? Maybe he'd finally found the place he belonged. A family might actually have filled the void Blake felt in his heart ever since his father said those fateful words.

You murdered the only woman I ever loved—your own mother. You took her life, and this *is what you do with it?*

Blake wanted his mother's family to tell him that it wasn't true—that his father was lying. He *didn't* kill his mother. How could he kill her and not even remember it? Of course he couldn't. But he needed the affirmation from them.

He got his affirmation. The moment they opened the door, they knew who he was. At fifteen, Blake had begun to resemble his father. They had the same hair, the same eyes, and *that face*. Had they been the same age, they could have been twins.

The woman who opened the door was short with graying hair and a hand-knitted shawl across her shoulders. For a moment, Blake imagined her to be his grandmother. He began to smile, stuttering an introduction.

"What the fuck are you doing here?" the woman hissed.

"I-I.... My name is Blake Blackwood, and I'm here to see—"

"I know who you are. I know why you're here." The look of anger on the woman's face was unlike any Blake had ever seen before. "You are the reason my daughter is dead."

Another woman rushed to the door, locking the screen with a glare. "Mom, please calm down—"

"Tell this bastard to get off my property right now!" the

old woman snarled. "He murdered my daughter! She would be alive if it weren't for him. I told her to abort him—I told her that she would regret it, carrying the child of a rapist. But she didn't listen to me, and now she's dead."

Blake realized then and there that touching reunions weren't meant for a person like him. He was tainted even before his birth. He couldn't even refute the old woman, his grandmother, who spat at him through the screen and slammed the door in his face. He stood stock still as she called the police and had him escorted off the property.

The hole in his heart grew bigger that day.

Blake wasn't sure how to fix it. His father wouldn't help. He considered going to Malcolm Ward. He even went to the Ward house and found himself standing at their door, his finger hovering over the bell.

But what would Malcolm think if he knew I was only born because my father raped my mother?

What would he think if he found out I'm the reason my mother died?

Blake was a coward. He ran from the house, his heart hammering in his chest.

I'm the reason my mom is dead.

He didn't even get a picture of her. Even if his maternal family wouldn't accept him, Blake had hoped to get a photo and know what she looked like.

By the next morning, Blake pretended as nothing happened. He had no choice, if he didn't want to be discovered. The only person who knew what had happened was Tessa, and she understood. Her father also mistreated women, albeit in a different way.

As time passed, Blake realized he had fallen in love with Tessa. She was beautiful, yes. But she also understood him.

When he was with her, the hole in his heart didn't feel so big. And, most importantly, her very presence made all the voices in his head go away.

You murdered the only woman I ever loved—your own mother. You took her life, and this *is what you do with it?*

She would be alive right now if it weren't for you.

I told her to abort you.

You're the child of a rapist.

You're tainted.

You should just die.

Tessa made everything bright again. And then Blake killed her, and his life had been shrouded in darkness ever since.

It was just supposed to be a normal hunt. High schoolers weren't even allowed to come, but Blake was an exception, because he was in a college prep course, and he begged to go. An overnight trip to the Veil with his girlfriend—how exciting! He looked forward to it all month, thinking about all the places he would take Tessa.

Blake didn't actually *remember* her death. It was his fault, though—an indisputable fact. He went to hunt with Tessa. Both of them left the campgrounds. Only Blake returned, bloody and battered and dazed. He'd failed to protect her. He didn't even remember where the feral had appeared, so her body couldn't be recovered. But they found her blood, and they found two feral corpses. They pieced together what happened.

The Churchill family buried an empty coffin. The father didn't attend the funeral, and neither did his current wife. No one blamed Blake, either, though that hardly mattered.

You murdered the only woman I ever loved—your own mother. You took her life, and this *is what you do with it?*

You're the child of a rapist. You're tainted.

She would be alive right now if it weren't for you.

If it weren't for you....

You should just die. It should have been you. You should have just died.

The hole in Blake's heart returned, becoming a gaping black hole from which nothing could escape. He didn't know how to fix it this time. He felt like an empty shell of a person, unable to smile or laugh or feel anything at all. All the light in his life had disappeared.

And, in the darkness, Blake had a lot of time to think. He realized that everyone had been right about him all along. He was born tainted, and he could never get rid of that for as long as he lived. So why bother? He didn't need someone to understand. He didn't need to get close to someone else. They would just leave him in the end. All he needed to do was make himself feel better.

He wouldn't be like his father, who assaulted women. Women would come to him because he was handsome, and they wanted him. Even if it was just a night, sleeping beside someone else made him feel just a little bit warmer.

And then he saw her across campus: his third victim.

Veronica Halliwell truly disgusted Blake. The first time their eyes met, a blush appeared across her cheeks, and he wanted to vomit. How dare she? How dare this disgusting girl feel flattered by him, with a face so closely resembling Tessa's? Blake wanted to hurt her. For the first time, he wanted to hurt someone else more than he wanted to hurt himself.

Veronica was easy. After a few compliments, he got her into bed after just a week. Slut. Tessa would have never done something like that. No, Veronica wasn't like Tessa at all. She was more like the women his father brought home, just a warm body to fuck.

As disgusted as he was by Veronica, the morning after they slept together, she smiled at him. Her smile was so similar to Tessa's, Blake realized that he could make use of her. Because Veronica, he'd learned, was desperate for attention. And those bitches were the easiest to manipulate.

Blake didn't feel bad about stringing her along. She wanted attention, and he gave it to her. Made her feel like a princess. In return, she dyed her hair and acted as a replacement for Tessa.

At first, Veronica made Blake feel better. Sometimes, when they were in bed together, Blake would truly feel like Tessa was with him and his heart would feel a little bit better. He was warm again.

But compared to Tessa's sunlight, Veronica was fluorescent. A cheap imitation. And she began telling him about herself.

Her story was different from Tessa's. Blake didn't want to hear any of it.

Stop making that face.

Stop looking like Tessa.

Stop making me feel sorry for you.

Stop making me fall in love with you.

Blake knew he had to end it. Charity came to him as an opportunity, and he used her to break Veronica's heart. But surprisingly, Veronica's hatred was much more digestible than her love. So Blake began playing with her more. He would be kind to her one day, and downright cruel the next. He thought that she would eventually kill him for it and end it all. He deserved it.

It wasn't until later that Blake realized that he had killed Veronica, too. She was alive, but hollow. Before, even if she was just a florescent, she still lit up. Now she was shrouded in darkness, just like him. She was his third victim, and certainly not his final one.

Someone really needed to stop him.

TWENTY-TWO

DAILY PROMPT: WRITE A PERSONAL PROMISE TO YOURSELF.

I will beat my second trial, no matter what. (And then I will reward myself with an ice cream sundae.)

The universe was actively working against her today. First, her hair dryer broke—a tragedy if there ever was one. Then, her favorite pink tennis skort tore at the side seam. She was forced to wear black leggings instead. At least she would be going to the Veil, and no one important would see her. Oh, and most notably, her powers crapped out. Because why wouldn't they choose the day of the second Blood Trial to fail on her?

As much as she hated to admit it, the power outages, so to speak, were happening more frequently than before. She didn't know what she'd done wrong. She followed her parents' instructions, cultivating regularly and not going near ferals.

She even had a smoothie yesterday for breakfast. With *kale*. Yuck.

This was how her body chose to repay her?

Regardless, she put on her best face. What else was she supposed to do?

Kitty sat in the shade of a tree, waiting with Noelle and Jax as Chancellor Kinsey and his minions sluggishly marched across the campus green. They were to meet by the school sign at exactly noon, and while the Swan siblings arrived early, Kinsey was fifteen minutes late. Kitty reckoned he kept them waiting on purpose, as a power play. It's exactly what she would have done in high school, which was to say, Chancellor Kinsey was acting like a sixteen-year-old high school girl.

When he finally stopped in front of them, he wore an ugly smile, tinged with arrogance. She had the feeling he just finished talking about her with his little cronies.

The board members joining the Swan Family Humiliation Show were two women, both in their forties, and five men from their early thirties to late fifties. By appearance alone, Kitty wouldn't have known how to group them; they looked like pieces from different puzzles. Still, she knew not to judge based on appearances. Whether they were shadowborn or truebloods, they had power here she could not easily dismiss.

That didn't mean she'd show an ounce of submission.

"Ah, Miss Swan. Lovely day, isn't it?" Chancellor Kinsey asked.

She wasn't in the mood for small talk. "Where do we need to go?"

"We'll be taking a trip to the Veil. And I see you've followed my instructions." He glanced over the siblings, none of whom were permitted to carry a weapon. That was the only upside to having a power outage at the moment; without qi to supplement her natural strength, she couldn't lift her saber.

None of the Swans could open a rift, so Kinsey did it himself. He withdrew a pocketknife from his jacket pocket and slashed it through the air with gusto, failing to impress any of the Swans. Grasping the sides of the rift, he pulled it apart, revealing a tear in the seam of space. The board members filed in, their silence eerie. Were they robots or something?

Kitty stepped through the rift, a slight wind blowing her hair back as she found her footing on the other side. Jax and Noelle followed, and the Chancellor entered last. He snapped the rift shut, cutting off the flow of warm air.

Immediately, the chill of the Veil settled into Kitty's bones, causing her breath to come out in little puffs. The sky overhead was a hazy blue, and the forest around them was a dark blur. She couldn't make out the individual trees, not that she cared to. Somehow, it was winter here, and snow crunched underfoot as they walked.

"You can see the entrance to the trial grounds up ahead," Chancellor Kinsey said.

Kitty wasn't sure what to expect, but she certainly wouldn't have guessed the entrance he spoke of would be a dingy cave: a hole in the side of a steep hill, looking like a mouth open in a silent scream.

"Are you sure we're going to the right place?" Jax asked.

Chancellor Kinsey looked offended. "I would never lead you astray. This is the correct location."

"Let's just get this over with," Kitty muttered.

"The trials are sacred. They are not something you 'get over'," a board member scolded.

"Sacred? Come on now. That's a bit of an exaggeration,

isn't it?" Kitty said. "What does a bunch of people crawling around a cave have to do with being shadowborn?"

"This is a test of courage, Miss Swan," Kinsey explained. "You will have three hours to return here. Simply go into the cave and come back, and you will have completed the trial. However, be warned: this is a Nightmare den. The creatures inside will show you your deepest fears, and your greatest weaknesses."

"We just have to go in there," she pointed into the darkness, "and come out within three hours?"

"Exactly. Best of luck. Your time begins now."

JAX DIDN'T LIKE the dark. The first trial was bad enough, with that dim lightning. Now, they were going into a cave where they knew monsters lived, off to face illusions of their greatest fears. His heart raced as he walked into the darkness. He knew nothing could hurt him. Not physically, at least.

The silence was deafening. He wasn't sure how long he walked, but finally, he came across a heavy metal door. He pushed it open and entered a well-lit cove. The sun shone bright and hot overhead, and the air smelled like pine and wildflowers. Ahead was a wide-open field of lush green grass. He walked across it, wondering how a place like this could be someone's worst fear. But as he continued walking, it was almost as if the ground beneath him sunk. The grass grew taller, as did the trees swaying around him.

"Jax!" Kitty ran up to him, her saber strapped to her back. "There you are!"

"We've been looking all over for you," Bàba called, as he

approached. But there was something wrong here. Kitty towered above him, as did their father. Jax only reached her hip, which should have been impossible, since he was standing upright. He looked down at his body, just to make sure.

"Come on. We need to get inside. The shadowborn are almost here." Kitty picked him up like a child, cradling him against her chest. Her heartbeat was calm, unlike his.

"No! Put me down. I can walk by myself," Jax yelled.

"Stop kicking. We need to hurry," Kitty insisted, carrying him toward the house. "Don't be so difficult."

"I'm not a child!" he insisted, trying to push out of her grasp. She was so much stronger than him, and she held onto him firmly. "Kitty! Put me down!"

She finally did, once they got back to the house. She settled him on the sofa and gave him a juice box. "There you go, buddy."

"This isn't real. Kitty never calls me that," Jax snapped.

"Don't worry. It'll all be over soon." She dropped a kiss on his forehead and ran out the front door. Jax rolled to his knees and looked outside. They were all there: Kitty, Noelle, Māma, and Bàba. Their weapons drawn, they stood against what appeared to be an army of shadowborn. There were so many of them, Jax couldn't see the end of their ranks.

He tried to go help them, but he was too short to reach the doorknob. Was he still shrinking? Or was the house getting larger? He didn't know. All he could do was watch the window as the battle began.

Jax knew it was just an illusion, but the details terrified him. Noelle shot at her enemies using her needle gun, while Kitty fought hard with her saber. The Nightmare captured their fighting styles perfectly, as if it had scanned Jax's mind in seconds and reproduced the scene from his memories.

The fight was fierce, and Jax watched his family take down enemy after enemy, while also taking a beating. Blood poured from Noelle's shoulder. Jax winced, but his sister didn't seem to notice. Kitty took a hard kick to the gut, which nearly doubled her over. Bàba and Māma were fine, but the fight was long and brutal.

Noelle was the first to fall. It was a blur. All Jax saw was a sword, sticking out of her neck. Her eyes went wide and blood pooled around her, spilling into the earth. Kitty let out a blood-curdling scream and leaped at the enemy. He'd never heard a sound like that before, so full of anguish and pain. It sent chills down his spine, even though he knew it wasn't real.

He wanted to close his eyes. He wanted the illusion to stop, but he couldn't look away.

Bàba was next. Jax turned away, but he still heard the screams, as if his ears were trained on his father's death. Māma's followed soon after. Kitty fought like a madwoman, cutting down shadowborn after shadowborn. Covered in blood and gore, she stood alone, her chest heaving.

"Kitty!" Jax yelled, banging his tiny fists against the window.

It was always like this, wasn't it? They were out there, and he was inside, safe. Useless.

He was an adult now, or close enough to it. So why didn't they rely on him more? Why didn't they trust him? He wasn't the baby of the family anymore.

And yet, there he was, trapped in the safety of his home while his family suffered. He couldn't save them. In the end, as always, he was left behind.

NOELLE SHIVERED as she walked into the cave. Her thin sweater wasn't made for the frigid weather of the Veil.

She could hardly see her hands in front of her face, but the ground was smooth and flat. While she continued her walk deeper into the cave, her surroundings became darker. She felt her way along the wall, her hand pressed flat against the rough stone.

A soft glow appeared ahead. She walked toward it, curious, and found an archway, illuminated by a single torch. But when she stepped through, she was back at Northeastern, in one of the lecture halls. Students sat around her, watching the teacher speak.

Has she just woken up from a nap or something? She wiped the drool from her mouth and sat up.

"Does anyone know the answer?" the professor at the front of the classroom asked. Several hands shot up, but he pointed toward Noelle. "Why don't you go, Miss Swan?"

Noelle's eyes widened. Was this her fear? Failing academically? That was a little pathetic, but at least it was easy to get through. She wouldn't have to fight a spider monster or anything.

But as soon as she opened her mouth, someone else behind her answered.

"X equals zero," the girl replied.

Noelle turned, her eyes widening. It was...her. Another version of herself. Beside her was Kitty, both of them dressed in matching outfits consisting of a button-down and plaid skirt. Side by side, they'd never looked more different. While Kitty was polished and gorgeous, not a hair out of place, Noelle had a rounder, flatter face. The clothes didn't suit her at all, like they were too tight, or perhaps her body was shaped differently.

Still, Noelle knew this was really how she looked. The Nightmare didn't exaggerate anything about her appearance.

"I'm sorry, Miss Swan. Miss Swan, do you want to try?" the professor asked, turning to Kitty.

Kitty nodded. "The answer is X equals seven."

"Very good! I see why everyone says you're a genius."

"I am," Kitty replied with a bright smile.

"That's right. You're the most intelligent student this school has ever seen. Everyone knows you're going places," the professor gushed.

Noelle frowned. This was it? She knew she had some image issues, and some trouble when it came to her sister, but it seemed like the Nightmare wasn't able to tap into her fears after all. So how the hell was she supposed to leave?

"You really think you're above everything, don't you?"

Noelle turned. Kitty looked directly at her, a friendly smile on her face that didn't quite match her words. "Are you talking to me?"

"What do you think your fear is, Noelle Swan?" Kitty asked. But it wasn't Kitty, not really. It was the Nightmare, directly speaking into Noelle's mind. She didn't want to play its games, but the creature laughed. "We can sit here all day and stare at each other, or you can tell me. I have an idea, of course, but I want to hear it from you."

"I suppose I have some insecurities around my sister," Noelle acknowledged. "It's petty and stupid. We're two different people. But the world seems to compare us, and sometimes I don't measure up."

"That's the wrong answer, Nell. And you know it deep down, I think." The Nightmare tilted her head to the side. "Why don't you try again?"

Noelle shook her head. "I don't know what you're talking about."

"You are not afraid of your insecurities. You are afraid of what you truly are: a fraud. If your siblings surpass you, your position is threatened. They won't need you anymore, and you'll have to redefine who you are. It's comfortable, isn't it? Being the smart one."

"It's not, I assure you. It's a lot of pressure," Noelle defended.

"Yes. But you love it. You enjoy having them rely on you. That's why it hurts so much when they don't need you anymore, isn't it?" the Nightmare asked. "And they don't. You didn't contribute at all during the first trial. I can see your memory, so I know that's true. You celebrated their victory as your own, when the truth is, you wouldn't have passed if it wasn't for your family. How many more times will they save you, Nell? How long until you have to stand on your own, and realize you are a failure, an imposter?"

Anger burned in her chest. "Shut up."

"Your identity, your sense of worth, is tied not just to your intellect but to your role within the family. Because your family is your entire world. If they don't need you to be the 'smart one', then what is your place? The spoiled brat? The baby sister? What about the black sheep?"

"Shut up!" Noelle yelled.

"That's the answer, isn't it? You're afraid of being an outcast, especially among your siblings. You'd do anything to prove your worth. Even kill for it. Isn't that right?"

She froze. "That was self-defense."

"If it was self-defense, why did you continue to explore that power? Didn't you get a thrill out of it, of getting to put people in their place? You pride yourself on your advice, on your maturity, but when the chips are down, you're the one making questionable choices, reveling in the very acts you'd condemn in others."

"That's not who I am," she whispered, but the conviction was gone. The Nightmare was peeling back layers, revealing uncomfortable truths she refused to acknowledge.

"Yes, it is. When you're at your lowest, your judgment falters. You can guide others with wisdom and clarity, but you're blind to your own failings. You're so afraid of losing your place in your family that you're willing to do anything it takes to hold on to it. You would rather hurt people, even your own siblings, as long as it meant maintaining the status quo. You're selfish. You're a hypocrite. And the worst part is, you know it and you don't care. Because your happiness is all that matters. Right, Noelle?"

She shook her head. "None of this is real."

"I can see your memories. I can see your emotions, your denial, your fear. I have seen into the minds of many, and yours is no different. In life, everyone has rules they must follow and trials they must face, choosing either to accept the rules or challenge them. And the choices we make during the most difficult of times lead us down paths we never would have imagined, and our lives change forever. The path you walk is one many monsters tread. Are you prepared for what's ahead?"

KITTY WALKED for what felt like forever. It was hard to tell in the dark. But she was starting to suspect she'd missed the exit and was simply wandering the caverns. She should have marked her way with some chalk, or breadcrumbs. Then again, didn't Hansel and Gretel get screwed in the end of that folk tale?

Finally, the light ahead gave her hope. She rushed toward it, eager to get out of this godforsaken cave. But when she stepped through the archway, she wasn't outside.

Mirrors lined a narrow hallway, each one distorted in its own way. She could see herself perfectly reflected in one, and in the next, she was bent and twisted. Some showed her as a monster, while others reflected her normal appearance. She could almost feel the Nightmare's presence, a malevolent entity lurking nearby. But she had no choice; she had to move forward.

"Hello?" she called. Her voice echoed through the maze as she weaved her way through the mirrors.

"Hi, there."

Kitty twirled around. She didn't see anyone, though. Just her reflection.

"Katherine Swan. That's what they call you, isn't it?"

Kitty took a step backward, her eyes widening. It was her voice, coming from her reflection. "Um, actually, it's Kitty."

"No one at Northeastern seems to care about your preferences, do they? They don't care what you choose to call yourself, nor do they want to see the truth of who you are. They think you're Katherine, and so, that is who you are—and nothing can change their minds."

"Katherine doesn't even suit me," Kitty complained, peering into the mirror.

"It's deeper than that. It's a rejection of the person you are, how you define yourself."

"Or, it could be, they're so jealous of me because I'm pretty. I've been told I could be a foot model, you know. Sure, the guy who told me that was a creepy teacher in high school, but, like, it still counts, right?"

"And there it is. The airhead act. The one you put on to hide from the world. You think if you're dumb enough, the truth can't hurt you. But look at me, and I'll show you the truth."

"Nope. I'm good." Kitty started to walk away, until her reflection stepped out of the mirror.

"It's not like the truth will hurt you, Katherine. Your ego is so large, nothing can penetrate it."

Kitty scoffed. "Is this supposed to be my fear? Myself? Maybe I should be afraid—of being a total cliche! Like, seriously. Did you run out of ideas? This is *so* embarrassing for you!"

"You are afraid of yourself. More specifically, what you are destined to become: the mortal monster. The world-destroyer, the mistress of demonic cultivation. But that is not a new fear, because even before you learned of your cursed destiny, you were terrified of being immortal. To be immortal means to outlive those around you. And yet, if you choose mortality, you will disappoint your family. Your mother and father, who have sacrificed everything for you."

Alright, that struck a chord within her. Kitty would have loved denying these claims, to pretend that the Nightmare twisted her memories and thoughts into being more than they were. But the truth was...

"You're right," Kitty acknowledged. "I'm afraid of what's going to happen. But, if you haven't noticed, I'm a really busy person. I have these trials, school, my social life, the problems in the Veil... There's a lot of other stuff to worry about, and worrying about things that haven't happened yet is kind of useless. I can't turn off my emotions, and some situations are just out of my hands. All I can really do is move forward and trust that the people around me will keep me grounded. Right?"

"You don't believe that."

"Sure, I do." Kitty shrugged. "To be honest, if you really wanted to scare me, you should've shown me embarrassing stuff. Like, farting during an assembly or something. But it seems like you're running out of material, so I'm going to go now."

"Don't walk away. The nightmare is only beginning."

"Yeah, but I'm done talking about my feelings. I need to get back, before Kinsey blows a gasket."

The reflection's smile turned feral, her teeth sharpening. "This is just the beginning, Katherine—"

Kitty punched her reflection in the face, which was more satisfying than she would have thought. The hallway, along with the mirrors, fell apart around her. For a moment, it felt like she was falling. She blinked, and suddenly, she was lying flat on her back in a damp cave. A woman stood over her with hollow eye sockets and a thin mouth, straggly hair hanging down her face. Her skin glowed in the dark, illuminating the space.

With a bony finger, she stroked Kitty's cheek. "You might be able to walk out of this cave, Kitty Swan, but you cannot escape the fate that awaits you."

"You could've just showed me your real face, instead of the whole mirror sequence crap. Do people actually fall for that?" Kitty asked, sitting up.

The nightmare wore no expression, tilting her head to the side. "I may look like a monster to you, but to me, you are the monster."

"Yeah, yeah. I've seen that Twilight Zone episode." She rolled to her feet, shaking herself off. "Where are my siblings?"

"They have not passed their trial."

"They'll pass if they leave the cave. We could walk out with you dead or alive. Your choice. But since you've seen into my head and all, I think you know how serious I am about this."

The Nightmare studied her face before hobbling toward the other end of the cave. Two more Nightmares crouched on the ground, beside Noelle and Jax's prone forms. The trio of Nightmares looked at each other before retreating, leaving the Swans behind.

Kitty knelt and shook her siblings awake. Noelle had tears on her face, while Jax sniffled and rubbed his nose. They both seemed a little worse for wear, but otherwise, physically fine.

"Let's get out of here. I don't think I'll be able to get the stench out of my clothes," Kitty joked, helping them up. She extended a hand to Noelle, who slapped it away. "Hey!"

"Don't touch me," Noelle muttered, wiping the tears from her eyes.

"What did you see?" Kitty asked.

"Something I'd rather forget."

Kitty frowned. She didn't want to pry, but the coldness in Noelle's voice bothered her. She wondered what the Nightmare revealed to her. "Whatever it told you, it was just messing with you. You're not—"

"I don't want to talk about it. Let's just go." Noelle stalked off, her footsteps heavy.

Jax sighed, looking up at her. "She'll be fine."

"And you?"

"It was a nightmare. Just...a really vivid nightmare," he explained.

Kitty wasn't convinced, but she decided not to push the matter. As they emerged from the cave, Chancellor Kinsey was waiting, along with the board members.

"There you are. Your three hours are up," Kinsey said.

"We passed the trial. Let's go home."

"Did you kill the Nightmares?"

"We walked out, and they didn't stop us. So, I'd say we won."

"Typically, if the trial is passed, the Nightmares are killed," one of the board members explained.

Kitty shrugged. "Oh. Well, too bad."

"How can we know for sure that the Nightmares were defeated?"

"Um, they let us walk out. That was the test. We faced our fears and came back before the time limit. Unless you mean to tell me that you used to force students to invade the home of Nightmares, attack them for sport, and then drag their corpses back, like trophies, to prove they won?"

"That is not what I'm saying. However, it is how the trials were typically conducted in the past."

"Well, we're not doing things like they were in the past." Kitty smiled. "And thank God for that. This is supposed to be a test of courage, right? I don't think it's courageous to slaughter creatures in their own home because we provoked them. We walked out alive, and they didn't try to stop us. That's all there is to it."

"I suppose we have different ideas of bravery, then, Miss Swan."

"Yes, our problem-solving methods are definitely different. It seems to me like you and your board members think killing things makes you brave, that making a group of students you deem different pass a series of trials no one else has to face is somehow not discrimination. But it's fine. You're never too old to learn, right? And I'll be happy to teach you the lesson you so desperately need."

NORTHEASTERN TRIBUNE

MISS SAIGON? TRY MISS SWAN!

Once again, the Swan siblings have skirted the edges of tradition and honor, this time in the second Blood Trial: a test of courage. This trial requires participants to confront and slay a Nightmare, a creature as grotesque in nature as it is powerful. In a move that has become characteristic of the Swans, they have managed to advance without fulfilling this fundamental requirement, finding yet another loophole in our ancient laws.

Their failure to kill the Nightmares is not just a deviation from tradition; it is proof of their unworthiness to stand among the shadowborn. The task is designed to test one's mettle, to prove one's strength and resolve in the face of darkness. By sidestepping this challenge, the Swans have shown that they lack the very qualities that define us.

Katherine Swan, the eldest sibling, whose frequent training sessions with an unnamed male shadowborn have not gone unnoticed. The nature of their association has raised eyebrows, with some suggesting that Katherine has resorted to using her feminine wiles to influence her shadowborn mentor into teaching her our ways. This would not be surprising, given the historical precedents set by her people. One is reminded of the tragic figure of Miss Saigon, or the tradition of geishas in Japan —examples of women using their charm and guile to navigate situations to their advantage. It seems Katherine may be employing similar tactics, exploiting whatever means necessary to ensure her and her siblings' advancement.

This shadowborn mentor has also come under scrutiny. His willingness to be swayed by Katherine's manipulations suggests a deficiency in his character or, perhaps more disturbingly, his bloodline. It raises the question of what flaws might lurk with those of us with muddied heritage. The blame, therefore, may not lie solely with the Swans but also with those among us who fraternize with foreigners.

Are we to stand by as our traditions are unraveled? Or will we take a stand to preserve the sanctity of our rites and the purity of our lineage?

TWENTY-THREE

BLAKE SHOULD HAVE JUST HAD a key to the Swan sisters' dorm, at this point. When Noelle returned from her shower down the hall, her hair dripping down her back, he was there, leaning against her door.

She was too tired for this shit. After the second trial, none of the siblings wanted to talk to each other. Specifically, Jax and Noelle didn't want to speak to Kitty. So they all went their separate ways.

Noelle dreaded thinking about what would happen when her sister came back for the night. What would they even say to each other? If Kitty didn't ask, Noelle would be annoyed. But if she did...Noelle would also be annoyed.

And she knew how insane she was acting. Of course she knew. She was the smart one, right?

Ha. No—she was the joke of the Swan siblings. And soon enough, her brother and sister would realize it.

Kitty was supposed to be the fuck-up. She was supposed to be the impulsive one, the one who needed to read self-help books because she was such a bitch. And yet, today, she was the hero. The spotlight wasn't stolen from Noelle, because in truth, she wouldn't have passed the test of courage had Kitty not woken her from the Nightmare. And that was a bitter pill to swallow.

Noelle was the one who had special powers, not her sister. So why was she floundering while her sister succeeded? If you could even call it that.

"Hey," Blake said, noticing her. "What happened to you? How was the trial?"

Noelle unlocked her door and stepped inside. "It was a trial."

"Very descriptive."

"I know. I've always said I should become a novelist." She stepped into her closet and Blake turned while she changed. "What brings you here? Another therapy session?"

"Is that what we're calling it, now?"

"Do you have a better idea?"

"Begrudging friendship, maybe."

"Don't flatter yourself," Noelle said, pulling on a sweatshirt. "We're acquaintances at best."

"You look upset."

She ignored that. "You're going to take me back to your dorm."

"With anyone else, I'd take that as an invitation. But with you, right now, it seems more like...a threat," Blake admitted.

"I *do* have Anus Annihilator in the drawer."

"Let's go back to my dorm, then. I have a stash of cookies hidden from Cyrus. He says no snacks should be in our dorm because he doesn't want bugs, or crumbs, but I have them anyway."

"How rebellious." Noelle followed him out of the room. She didn't want to be there when Kitty got back, and sadly, she didn't have anyone else to turn to. Kitty and/or Jax could be at their parents' apartment, and Noelle didn't have any friends on campus. Melody and Veronica were Kitty's friends.

"So, you gonna tell me what's wrong, or am I going to have to torture the information out of you?" Blake asked as they walked down the hall.

Noelle considered ranting to Blake about her problems. Venting might help, and he certainly wasn't Kitty's number-one fan. But the problem was, despite not liking her on a personal level, he respected her. Noelle wouldn't know what to do if he defended her.

So she said, "It was a Nightmare den. That was the trial."

"Yikes. That's rough for anyone, shadowborn, trueblood, *or* cultivator. But you passed, didn't you?"

Humiliation speared her. "Yeah. Technically, we passed."

"What's the problem, then?"

"Kitty is the problem," Noelle found herself saying, despite her better judgment. "If it weren't for her, I would still be in that cave, feeding the Nightmares with my fear. These trials were supposed to be easy for me. They're tests; I test *very* well. This was a chance to highlight my strengths. Instead, all they've done is expose my weaknesses."

"It's not a competition."

"No, but I've made it into one. The Nightmare told me all kinds of things, painting me in this awful light. And I can't help but wonder if that's how others see me. It saw into my memories." It knew her, intimately. And it put into words the feelings she had tried so hard to deny.

It wasn't right, she reminded herself. *It twisted the truth to scare me.*

"And what did it say?" Blake asked.

Noelle took a deep breath as they exited the dorm building, heading toward the boy's dorm instead. "It told me that I am the type of person who needs to feel secure in my role. I center my identity off my intellect, and if someone else threatens my place, I tear them down."

"Huh."

"What?"

"Do you think it was wrong?"

"You didn't hear the way it phrased things," Noelle insisted. "It made me seem like a child. Like I'm jealous of Kitty or something. But what's there to be jealous of?"

"If she's doing well during these trials, maybe you feel like you're the one who should be the star of the show, and when you're proven wrong, it makes you feel insecure."

She hated how calm he was, and how confident he was in his assessment. "I'm not insecure."

"Really? Because you seem to care a lot when you think others are comparing you to Kitty. And you care what Professor Evans says, even though he's a bigoted ass. You've been kissing up to him despite his disparaging remarks."

Noelle's mind spiraled. "What do *you* know? You're an idiot!"

"I am," Blake acknowledged, "but that doesn't mean what I'm saying is wrong. Clearly, academic excellence isn't a measure of emotional intelligence."

"Oh, like how you're so emotionally intelligent?" She wasn't sure why she didn't stop and turn on her heel. Maybe she couldn't stand letting him get the last word in. They stood in front of his door, arguing in whispered taunts. "Let's see. Were you emotionally intelligent when you fucked Veronica over? Or when you hit on my sister, despite her clear refusal? Or maybe, it's when you decided to tell me your life story, which turned out to be a pity party of cliches. Blaming everything on your father and your dead girlfriend. Guess what? People lose their loved ones all the time. People have shitty parents. And somehow, they don't turn into sociopathic narcissists who revel in bringing others down with them."

Blake was silent for a terrifying moment, and she held her breath. She was hoping he'd say something equally as emotionally devastating. But instead, he almost looked...hurt.

Fuck.

Now she looked like a bitch. Even though she was right.

Aren't I?

Or was she just trying to hurt him, because what he and the Nightmare said held a grain of truth?

No. They were lies. All lies. These people don't know me, Noelle tried to convince herself. *They aren't psychologists. It's a dumbass college student and a cave-dwelling monster.*

You're smarter than them, which means you're better than them.

Finally, Blake said, "I think you should go."

He was dismissing her. As if *she* were the one in the wrong. But she wasn't the one telling lies.

Blake had a habit of tearing others down to build himself up. He was a jealous person—he had admitted it himself!

And yet...

Noelle was rooted to the spot. Somehow, it felt wrong to end things this way.

Blake unlocked the door, ready to disappear inside and leave Noelle standing there, trying to come up with something to say so she'd at least have the last word. Instead, the two were greeted by a horrific sight.

"N—Oh my God!" Noelle screeched.

Cyrus was in bed, a thin sheet covering his bare form. He jolted up when he heard Noelle's voice, and the lump beside him nearly tumbled off the bed. With a curse, he grabbed an arm, pulling the girl back against his chest.

Kitty peeked out from under the sheets, and Noelle didn't have to be a genius to tell that her sister was buck-naked under there.

"What the fuck?" Noelle exclaimed. "Kitty, what are you doing?"

She pulled the covers up to her chin. "Um, we were just wrestling."

"Naked?"

"On a bed?" Blake added, his jaw hanging open.

"The removal of clothing is really...symbolic in some cultures," Kitty fumbled to explain.

"Symbolic? Of what?" Noelle asked, crossing her arms.

"Uh, horniness?"

Cyrus groaned. "That's the best you could come up with?"

Despite his tone, he didn't actually sound angry. He sounded *relieved*.

"How long has this...." Blake waved his hands in the air, unsure of what to call the tryst.

"Unholy union," Noelle supplied. "How long have you two been dating?"

"We're *not* dating," Kitty clarified quickly. "We're just fuck buddies!"

"Acquaintances, really," Cyrus added. "This is purely physical."

"A stress reliever."

"*Barely*."

"We don't even know what to call it, it happens so rarely. Once a month, maybe."

"How did this even *start*? I thought you hated each other," Noelle said.

"He came onto me," Kitty replied, without missing a beat.

Cyrus looked at her incredulously. "Me? *You* came onto *me*."

"Psh-Sh. Like I would ever do that! You're the one who brought up the whole kissing thing in the first place."

"You suggested we make a competition of it!"

Kitty turned to him with a scathing glare. "You shoved your tongue in my mouth first!"

"You *enjoyed* it!"

"Oh my God, please stop!" Noelle shouted.

Kitty rolled her eyes. "Come on, Nellie, don't go clutching your pearls. My mouth is the *least* scandalous place his tongue has been."

"I'm going to hurl!"

Blake shook his head in disgust. "Where do you two even do it?"

"Noelle spends some nights in the lab, and you have your own dalliances that keep you away overnight," Kitty explained. "But there are plenty of other places we go. The greenhouse, his car, behind the bleachers, in the arena..."

"You did it in the greenhouse? The walls are *glass*, Kitty!" Noelle's eyes widened. "Oh my God. The rumors of the greenhouse being haunted..."

"It's not, don't worry," Kitty assured her. "We go there, like, once a week to hook up. I've never seen any ghosts."

"You *are* the ghost, you dumbass!" Noelle cried. "God, students had reported rustling and moaning, but I never thought... *EW*!"

"Once a week?" Blake asked. "You said once a month before!"

"I have been *very* stressed out lately. You can die from that, you know," Kitty said.

"You're a cultivator. You're going to be immortal! How the fuck are you gonna die from stress?"

"You're making a big deal out of nothing," Cyrus cut in. "It's none of your business whether Kitty and I see each other twice a week."

"Wait. Is this the reason my condoms have been going missing?" Blake demanded. "You dog!"

"More like rabbits," Kitty joked. "Get it? Because we're fucking like—"

"We don't use your condoms *every* time. Just when we run out," Cyrus defended. "That's been, what, two times?"

"We wouldn't have run out if you had just sprung for the container," Kitty said, looking up at him. "A hundred for forty bucks. That was a great deal!"

"You aren't taking into account the specs or the brand."

"This is the most repulsive and unnatural thing I've ever heard of," Noelle said flatly. "I can't believe you two are having sex."

"Only sometimes," both Kitty and Cyrus insisted in unison.

"We can stop whenever we want to," Kitty added.

"Then stop right now."

"I said whenever *we* want to. Besides, it's not like we did it in *your* bed."

"We have bunk beds, Kitty. Your bed and my bed are technically the same piece of furniture!"

"I'm not going to take any more of this grilling!" Kitty declared. "I'm leaving!"

"You're naked."

"Then *you* leave."

"I'm not leaving," Blake said. "This is *my* room."

"You're going to leave. You're not going to see my girlfriend naked," Cyrus said.

"Girlfriend? I thought you were just fuck buddies!"

Cy reddened. "It was a slip of the tongue."

"I'm *not* his girlfriend. But you're going to be dead meat if you don't get out of here in three seconds." Kitty swooped down, reaching with her long arms to yank out the clock on the nightstand.

Blake knew she would really throw it, so he quickly ushered Noelle out the door.

But, on the other side, he could still hear their muffled conversation.

"Girlfriend?" Kitty questioned, hopping down from the bed. "Really?"

"You know what I meant," Cy grumbled.

"Glitter."

"What?"

"Glitter!! And I want my panties back!"

AFTER SPENDING MOST of the plane in the bathroom, Veronica was not excited to be stuck in a car with Ryder for the next hour to get to their hotel.

Tennessee was colder than she expected. She should have looked at the weather report before they took off, but she assumed the southern states were all significantly warmer than New York regardless of the time of year. Wrong.

Ryder rubbed her arms as they stepped outside with their luggage, grinning. "The car will be here, soon."

"Car?"

"I ordered one. Better than taking a taxi, right?"

"Who are you trying to impress?" she joked.

"You. Is it working?"

Veronica wanted to say no, but the word wouldn't come out. She shook her head instead.

This wasn't a romantic getaway; they were supposed to be investigating the missing students. So far, though, Ryder hadn't gotten the memo.

Before she'd got nauseous in the cabin, the duo drove to the airport from campus. He paid for club passes to a lounge, which offered free refreshments and snacks. Their seats were in first class, which made Veronica feel bad not only because of the money, but the amenities were wasted on her, considering her fickle stomach.

Now that she had two feet planted on the ground, she felt better, physically. Mentally, she wondered what the hell she'd gotten herself into. She tried to tell herself that she was here for purely altruistic reasons, such as, finding out what was really going on at Northeastern. Ryder made it very difficult to feel good about their mission when he did things like compliment her, tuck her hair behind her ear, hold doors open, and help her with her bags.

When the car came around, he gently put her luggage in the trunk and helped her in the back. "So, what do you think? Are you impressed, or should I be doing more to earn your approval? I can try and get the hotel to send up a bucket of ice and a dozen roses, if you want."

"You're ridiculous," she informed him.

"And you love it."

"I really, really don't."

"So, I'm getting somewhere?"

"Not even close." The lie tasted bitter in Veronica's

mouth. She didn't want it to be true, didn't want to like him. Not in that way. Because between Blake and Ryder, though the two would never admit it, they had something in common: they made her feel special.

Blake was a womanizer; Veronica had known that going into their relationship. But the fact that he chose to be with her made her feel important and valued. She was a prize to him, the girl no other man could win. With Ryder, though, Veronica was the only one he wanted. The dichotomy between the two had her confused, and she wished she had someone else to talk to about it.

Kitty would have been her go-to, but she was not an option. Veronica felt like a traitor for even entertaining Ryder. Just because he treated her well didn't mean he was a good person. And yet, there she was, sitting in a car with him.

"What's on the agenda today?" Veronica asked, trying to bring the focus back to the investigation.

"We'll go to the shops where the break-ins occurred and see if any workers saw anything," Ryder said. "From what I've read, it sounds like a string of gas stations were hit, all at night, and all within the past two months. we'll interview some of the employees and see what we can find."

"And what if we find nothing?"

"Back to square one, then. But if we find something...this could be the beginning of the end."

"The end of what, exactly?"

Ryder only smiled.

When they pulled up to the hotel, Veronica tried not to react. It was a five-star resort, and the parking lot was full of high-end cars.

"Are you sure this is where you made the reservation?" she asked skeptically.

"Yep. They have an indoor pool, a sauna, a gym, and the restaurant is amazing. Supposedly," he added. "I booked us a suite, so we'll have our own separate bedrooms."

"How can you afford all this? I thought you said you were keeping this off your card, since your dad has access to it."

"I am. This is all on my savings."

Veronica raised an eyebrow. "And how long have you had your savings, exactly?"

"Since freshman year of high school," Ryder replied, looking amused. "Why? Are you afraid I'd be paying for your Swedish massage with blood money?"

"I'm not getting a massage. This is a work mission, not a vacation."

"It's a little bit of both," he protested. "You deserve a chance to relax. After all, we don't know what's coming. And the hotel is already paid for."

"Can I ask you something? Why are you doing all this?" She waved her hands around. "Digging into your father's computer, coming to Tennessee, spending so much time on what could just be a coincidence."

"Not for any noble reason."

"Then, why?"

Ryder opened the car door for her and retrieved her suitcase from the trunk. "Simple. I hate my father. I want to see him ruined. The byproduct of that just so happens to be helping expose a conspiracy theory."

"It's just a theory. This could be one massive coincidence."

"But it's not. And you know it, don't you? In your heart, you know something is going on at Northeastern," Ryder said. "And we're going to figure out what it is."

TWENTY-FOUR

'WHAT HAPPENS in Tennessee Stays in Tennessee.'

An apt saying for the t-shirt. Veronica considered buying it, until she saw the price tag, after which she put it back neatly and quickly walked out of the gift shop.

"Nothing stands out to you?" Ryder asked. She'd had doubts about her feelings for him, complicated further by this trip. Aside from concerns about him being less than pleasant to her best friend, the more she learned about him, the more his 'cool guy' persona cracked. Which was, of course, a problem.

On any other guy, a belt buckle with a pinata and the words 'I'd Hit That' etched in silver would have looked ridiculous. And, okay, it looked dumb as shit on Ryder, too. Regardless of his handsome face and nice hair, and those deep brown eyes...

"Eyes up here, Vee," he told her.

Her face burned. "I can't believe you bought that."

"I had to. It was practically a steal!"

"You stole it," she pointed out.

"Well, that old lady deserved it," he retorted. "She was rude to us."

"She was just asking us if we wanted to buy anything," Veronica insisted.

"She asked if we needed any help five times within, like, three minutes. She was obviously trying to get us out. And besides, the way she looked at me, she must have thought I was a criminal or something."

"You stole from her; you are a criminal!"

"Psh. Take her side, why don't you?"

Vee rolled her eyes. "Come on. We've hit up all the places that got broken into, and nobody saw or heard anything. We should just go back to campus and face the fact that we've hit a dead end."

"No way. We have one more day here. Why not enjoy it?" he cajoled, wrapping an arm around her waist.

Admittedly, she let him for a few seconds before coming to her senses and pushing him off. "Seriously?"

"Look, we've got one more place to check, and then we'll go back to the hotel. We can relax and, if you insist, study, before heading to the airport tonight. What do you say?"

"That we're not going to find anything. If the cops couldn't catch whoever did it, we're not going to," she said. "This is crazy. We're working off a few fuzzy shots and a theory, not real evidence. What if we're wasting our time here, and there's some big thing going on back home?"

"It's a calculated risk," Ryder said. "Besides, what do you think you're missing back at Northeastern? A slumber party with your friends? Actually, I wouldn't mind—"

"I get it, you're not exactly a fan of Kitty. She can be a bit much," she conceded with a half-hearted shrug. "But she's still important to me, you know?"

"Some friend. She's been ghosting you for weeks. Ignored your texts, ditched your plans. Doesn't sound like much of a friend to me."

Veronica bit her lip. "She's...busy."

What exactly, Veronica couldn't quite pin down. She was aware of the Blood Trials, of course, but her offers of help were always politely declined by both the Swan sisters. It left her wondering—did they not want help at all, or was it specifically her assistance they could do without? Being a magician had its merits, but next to Cyrus's shadowborn abilities, with whom Kitty seemed to spend countless hours, or her recent sessions with sexy cultivator, Jianhao, Veronica felt sidelined.

She couldn't deny her physical limitations, compared to the shadowborn, but her skills weren't negligible. Her talent in spell casting was better than most other magicians at school, and she had been instrumental in creating the lures last semester. What changed? Was Veronica suddenly not good enough, anymore?

Or maybe she never had been. Maybe she'd just been a placeholder, until Kitty found more interesting people to spend her time with.

"Are you okay?" Ryder asked her.

"Huh? Yeah. Of course," she lied.

"Because it seems like you're about to cry."

"I'm fine. Let's just head to the last gas station."

He hesitated, staring at her for a long moment, then nodded. "All right. Let's go."

Ryder called a rideshare and they drove a few miles out to a remote gas station. It was the furthest place hit, and also the most heavily damaged. The cameras were busted, the windows were smashed in, and the door was hanging off the hinges. According to the reports, anyway. The break-in had happened a few weeks back, and everything looked fixed, for the most part. The duo walked in, the little bell on the door tinkling.

A woman with short brown hair and tired eyes glanced up at them. "Can I help you?"

"Hi, yes. We're with the *Tennessee Times*," Ryder said, flashing a fake press badge. Because sadly, while they could both use magic, making a fake badge online was easier than using a spell in these cases. "We're writing a story about the string of robberies that occurred recently and were hoping to talk to anyone who may have witnessed something."

"You and everyone else. The cops already came and went, and so did a bunch of other people. You're a little late," she informed them.

"I apologize for the inconvenience," Ryder said smoothly. "If you could tell us anything, any information, really, it would be very helpful."

The woman sighed. "There's not much to tell. I was on shift, taking out the garbage at night. No cars were in the parking lot, and no one had come through for at least three hours. The trash is just outside, and the door was shut when I left. I must have locked myself outside, because the back door wouldn't open. I walk around the front, and the place is trashed."

The building wasn't very large. It would have taken less than a minute to walk around it. Veronica asked, "You didn't see anyone?"

"Security camera footage, along with a kid in a hoodie. I didn't recognize them, though. It looked like a boy from a local high school, probably." The woman shrugged. "Not my problem, though. My boss says he didn't even take anything—the kid just broke shit."

"Did he leave anything behind?" Ryder questioned.

"Not that we could tell."

"And you didn't hear anything?"

"That's the weird part—I didn't. No explosions, no glass breaking. I just saw it, and that was that. I called the cops, they took the tapes, and nothing's came of it."

"You can't think of anything strange about that night?" Veronica prodded.

"Nothing beyond the obvious." The clerk paused, clicking her tongue. "Well, there was one thing that seemed strange. There was, like, this neon green Pixy Stick powder on my clothes. But we don't sell that candy, and I didn't have any with me. It's probably nothing, but, you know."

Ryder looked at her. "Pixy Sticks? Are you sure?"

She shrugged. "That's what it looked like. I don't know. I only got a glimpse, but it was bright green."

"Thank you," Ryder said. "That was really helpful."

"If you say so."

Ryder and Veronica exited the gas station and started walking down the street, back toward the main road.

"What are Pixy Sticks?" Veronica asked.

"Colored sugar in a paper straw. A sign that you had a fun childhood—or, in your case, didn't," Ryder replied. "But they don't make neon green ones. The powder is more pastel. You know who does make neon green powder one could mistake for Pixy Sticks?"

"No?"

"Southeastern. They use a memory potion there on humans, if they've seen too much. My cousin goes there, and he's used it a few times."

Memory potion? "I thought that didn't work. And it's dangerous to inhale," Veronica said.

"Oh, it works. But yeah, it's not great to inhale. Anyway, my bet is, someone from Southeastern is involved."

"Why?" She still didn't understand what anyone would have to gain from these robberies, if they weren't stealing anything. But to come prepared with a memory potion, to go purposely to an area with humans... It didn't make sense.

"Think about it. We've got a string of cases where no money or anything of value was stolen. The buildings are trashed, and there are no leads."

"Except for a high school student in a hoodie, which could be anyone," she added. "I know you said it looks like one of the missing students, but we have no proof."

"True. But if I had to guess, these incidents weren't about stealing to begin with. It's a test of sorts. The gas stations were isolated enough, and in each case, only one or two workers were on shift."

Veronica considered this. Why would Chancellor Kinsey be connected to a research facility in Tennessee? It made sense if he had colleagues at Southeastern, given he was the Chancellor of Northeastern. And how did the missing students and these gas station incidents fit into everything?

"Were there any cars seen in the security footage clips?" she asked.

Ryder shook his head. "I didn't see any, but it's hard to say. These clips of the actual incidents were only a few seconds long. I was lucky enough to get a freeze frame of any faces, to begin with."

"How did you even come across that? I understand how you got the USB drive of missing students, but the gas station videos?"

"A magician never reveals his secrets."

She gave him a droll look, putting her hands on her hips. "I want to see the videos."

TWENTY-FIVE

VERONICA AND RYDER weren't the only ones investigating. Cyrus had his own suspicions against the SNPD, but so far, he'd found nothing. He hit so many dead ends, he considered giving up.

He had hoped it wouldn't have come to this, but in the end, his hands were tied. He had to speak to Mr. Swan.

As he waited at the door to the Swan family apartment, he prayed to God, or any higher power listening, that Mr. Swan didn't know about his relationship with Kitty. Noelle wouldn't have mentioned it, would she? He wasn't about to walk into a minefield, right?

Because seeing the father of the girl he was casually screwing would be suicide. Cy knew that behind Mr. Swan's pleasant smiles and cooking escapades was an alchemist who would happily turn him inside out if he ever got wind of the truth. Cyrus liked his organs on the inside of his body, thank you very much.

After two painful minutes, the door opened. Mr. Swan stood there in his 'Kiss Me, I'm Irish' apron, holding a meat clever. "Come in, come in! Kitty isn't here, but I'm making chicken dumplings. Would you like some?"

"I'm not that hungry—"

"Sit down, make yourself comfortable!"

Cyrus slipped off his shoes and walked in. Listen, when a man tells you to do something and he's holding a big knife, you do it. No questions asked.

Mr. Swan put a plate of cheese and crackers on the Lazy Susan and returned to the kitchen.

"Mr. Swan, I actually came because I wanted to talk to you," Cyrus said.

"Ah, Kitty's too young to get married. She needs to wait a hundred years, at least."

"Not about that," he said quickly.

"Is my daughter not good enough for you to marry?"

"No, not—"

"Ha! I kid. Sit, eat. Tell me what's bothering you, Cyrus."

"I wanted to ask about the feral research, and how that's coming along. I know you and Mrs. Swan, and Noelle, are working hard, but there seems to be a lot of new developments when it comes to the monsters." Cyrus took a cracker off the plate, nervously eating. "It's been getting more and more dangerous."

Mr. Swan hummed, setting the oven timer. "Yes, there are more ferals, more deaths. It's troubling."

"But we've been hunting all summer, bringing back bodies to autopsy. It's hard to believe no new developments have been made."

"That's not entirely true," Mr. Swan said, wiping his hands on a dishtowel. "There have been some. They just haven't been shared."

"Like what?"

"My wife and I suspect the ferals are engaging in a form of cultivation, using Veil magic. However, we believe they're going about it the wrong way—essentially, they're doing it incorrectly. Righteous cultivation involves aligning with qi, which comes from nature. The backbone of cultivation is Taoism and harmony. However, when one deals with demonic cultivation, the energy comes from death and negativity," he explained patiently. "While this energy is powerful, it is also dangerous and difficult to control. One can...overdose, so to speak."

"Qi is life energy," Cyrus said slowly, "and because you're alive, there's some sort of balance there. You can't get sick from it because you also produce it. But with demonic energy, it's like two opposing forces."

"Exactly. The demonic energy will fight with the qi a living cultivator naturally produces, causing imbalance. It is very difficult to control, but it is also hard to tell when you are losing control until it is too late. Qi harmonizes with nature and one's self. Demonic energy clashes; it is chaos and ruin. It is very difficult to keep these energies stable. This is one reason why it is against the Immortal Rules to cultivate with it. The other reason would be, using a power which naturally benefits from death is seen as immoral."

"But you have to be taught to cultivate. You wouldn't just happen upon it, right?"

"Correct."

"So would it make sense that someone is teaching these beastbloods how to cultivate?" Cyrus asked.

Mr. Swan nodded. "Yes. I think the beastbloods originally began using a form of cultivation, using your Veil magic. But Veil magic and qi are different; we have already established this. While cultivation draws qi inside the body of a cultivator directly, Veil magic requires users to channel external forces to commit supernatural feats. The magic doesn't actually penetrate your body. It is like holding a cup of water. A cultivator would take a sip and spit it out. A shadowborn would throw the contents of the cup directly in your face. Do you understand?"

"Yes, there's no need for a demonstration," Cyrus said quickly.

"Ariana and I are exploring the idea that beastbloods began cultivating, trying to conduct our research ethically, but it's challenging. Gaining the necessary approvals is proving difficult, as much of what we need to do falls outside standard practices. We're hitting barriers every step of the way, struggling to proceed with our research. And that woman isn't helping, that Calista Woods. She sends my wife on coffee runs and forces her to do organizational tasks. I collect data. When we have time, we try to look over autopsy reports, but many of the files are restricted access."

"What if I helped you? What if I could bring back samples or feral corpses, and you could—"

"You would get in trouble. They watch us closely, not because they believe we are 'underqualified', but because they know we are not. They fear knowledge, and I have lived in the sect long enough to understand that those frightened of knowledge are the most dangerous. Those people do not want to understand or be understood. They want power and control. I think a great darkness looming, and it is not the ferals. They are the symptom, not the disease."

Cyrus stared at the table. Who would want to create ferals? He knew Mr. Swan was probably right, about everything—but he still couldn't wrap his mind around why. "You've given me a lot to think about. Thank you, Mr. Swan."

"You remind me of my Kitty. You would risk yourself blindly for others. My daughter believes she is strong enough to save everyone. But what is your reasoning? Why do you fight?"

"I'm not sure." No one had ever asked him that. "I guess it's the same reason I want to be a doctor. I want to be useful."

The timer went off, and Mr. Swan removed the bamboo steamers from the stove. He prepared a plate and settled down across from Cyrus at the table, handing over a pair of chopsticks and a plate.

The dumplings were the best Cyrus had ever had, savory and tender. "This is amazing. Kitty said that you weren't allowed to cook in the sect. How did you learn?"

"I was not very good at first," Mr. Swan admitted. "But cooking and alchemy aren't so different. And I know I needed to do something. My wife and I fled China with very little. Our friend helped us gain entry and citizenship, but we had to take a loan out to afford our house. Our jobs were demanding, and I worked a schedule opposite Ariana. Our only time together as a family, all five of us, was often dinner. I wanted to make it special; it was the only thing I could give my children. I know that, growing up, I must have been a great source of shame for my kids. I could not provide them with the same opportunities their peers had. Kitty had to work since she was fifteen in order to help pay off our debts, and she's been caring for her siblings since she was young. Sometimes, I wonder if she resents me for it."

"She loves you. More than anything." This, Cyrus knew with absolute certainty.

"Hmm. That may be. She is a good daughter. I could not

give her everything she deserved, but I always made sure she ate well. It is the best I could do."

"That's very admirable, Mr. Swan."

Mr. Swan nodded. "I kept Kitty fed, and I trained her to defend herself. If I could not be there to fight her battles, I wanted to ensure she could handle herself. I am very confident in my daughter's strength. She can defeat ferals, yes. But she can also beat traitorous friends, school bullies, protestors...and young men who break her heart."

Cyrus gulped. "Right. I'll keep that in mind."

JAX READ the cultivation manual until he went cross-eyed, attempting—and doing quite a poor job at—to decipher the traditional characters, written with a hurried hand and a shaking brush. He was studying different forms of arrays, specifically ones that could be laid on the ground like mines.

Noelle excelled in alchemy, and Kitty fought like a beast when it came down to it. No one in their family specialized in arrays. That's where Jax would come in.

That was, if the goddamn author of the cultivation manual could get his act together! The members of the Qingshan sect couldn't drink alcohol, so Jax knew whoever wrote this hadn't been drunk. They had the misfortune of awful handwriting. Or, rather, it was Jax's misfortune.

He transferred what he could glean in a spiral-bound notebook, written in a garbled mix of Chinese and English. It reflected the inner workings of his brain perfectly.

Jax thought predominantly in English, and eighty percent of his dreams were solely in the language. The other twenty percent were in a mix of Mandarin and English. But when it came to cultivation, a lot of phrases didn't translate easily. Luckily, the grammatical structure of both languages wasn't obscenely different. He did his best to express his ideas, but when he looked back at his notes, they were only intelligible to him.

"What are you working on, Jax?" Jianhao asked, appearing out of thin air.

Jax nearly had a heart attack. He both hated and envied how silently Jianhao moved, and he was pretty sure the older boy did it on purpose. He hadn't quite figured out the technique, but he guessed it involved using qi to muffle his movements.

"Shīxiōng," Jax greeted, attempting to sound nonchalant. He failed at that, too. "What are you doing here?"

When Jax told him that he was going to the greenhouse to study and cultivate—he figured being surrounded by plants would help—Jianhao said that he heard rumors it was haunted. Jax didn't believe in ghosts...but that didn't mean he would tempt fate, either. So he settled on the campus green instead, out in the open, where there were plenty of witnesses should he be attacked or dragged off into a well.

Jianhao claimed he was going to work in the labs today, with the Swan parents, but it was only three in the afternoon. Were they finished already?

"Noelle came to work, so your parents asked me to check on you and impart some wisdom," Jianhao explained. "What are you looking at?"

Jax hesitated. "I'm trying to figure out some arrays for destruction. I know a few, but this manual is more about theories. If I can learn about the creation of arrays, I thought maybe I could—"

"Create one?" Jianhao laughed for a good minute. Jax didn't join him. "Oh, are you serious?"

"I was."

"You are not a bad cultivator. You've done a lot, with what little you have. But you can barely speak Mandarin—you and your siblings." He picked up Jax's notebook with a condescending smile. "You can barely read traditional characters. How would you expect to create an array without even being able to understand the basics?"

Jax's cheeks burned with embarrassment. "I can understand. The handwriting is just—"

"The handwriting is not the problem," Jianhao interrupted, switching to Mandarin. "You didn't even begin speaking to me in our native language, just now. Then, I suppose it's not native for you. Until you form a better connection with your heritage, your cultivation will never improve. You are too...white-washed."

The words felt like a physical blow, and though they might not have been intended to wound, they did. Deeply.

When Jianhao had first come into the picture, Jax was overjoyed. Finally, there was another cultivator in his midst, one other than his sisters. He thought Jianhao would be a true shīxiōng, helping him improve his cultivation. And, perhaps more importantly, Jax thought he had finally found someone he could relate to.

Growing up in Parker Ridge hadn't been easy. The Swans were the only Chinese family in town, it seemed, and no one knew about cultivation. Hell, they didn't even know about anime outside of Pokémon! Sure, he had his sisters, but it was different with them. Kitty cultivated, but she didn't want to talk about it outside her training sessions with Mā and Bà. Her idea of leisure involved boys, fashion, and gossip. Meanwhile,

Noelle didn't mind talking about cultivation, but she always brought the topic back to alchemy, her own specialty. She had always been the type of person to put down or be indifferent toward things she didn't excel at. Sometimes, it felt like Jax was the only sibling taking this seriously.

He didn't have many friends in school, either. Geeky and awkward, not even the kids interested in martial arts liked him. Whenever they had group projects, no one wanted to work with him, and until high school, he ate lunch alone.

Kitty tried to help, in her own way. If anyone bothered him, something inside her unleashed, and she attacked in a flurry of fists and, most harshly, words. It was humiliating, having your big sister fight a battle you were terrified to face. How could Jax think of himself as strong when he had to get help from his sister? In a mini-skirt and kitten heels, no less.

He preferred being alone, or so he told himself. Because being a cultivator made him special...and it also isolated him from his peers. When Jianhao had come, he thought he had finally found the missing link to his heritage. Instead, he discovered the truth: he wasn't special at all. He was inadequate in every single way.

"White-washed?" Kitty screeched. She wasn't even close to them, standing on the sidewalk with her hands on her hips. Her legs blurred, she moved so fast, until she was right in Jianhao's face.

Jax knew she didn't like him from the start—and apparently, the feeling was mutual. Because, while Jianhao kept his arrogant smile, something in his face tightened.

"Ah, Xiao Xing." He said the name like an insult. "I was merely speaking the truth. I apologize if I offended you."

"And I'm sorry you smell so bad, on account of having your head shoved up your ass," Kitty retorted in English. She switched back and forth, so angry she wasn't aware she was doing it. "What's your problem?"

"Me? I don't have a problem. It just seems like none of you have much of a connection to your heritage. And your parents wanted me to help you, to turn you into true Chinese cultivators. You are learning cultivation, but it seems you are not as adept at being Chinese."

"Why? Because you're the paragon of what a Chinese person should be? Please, don't make me laugh. Actually, you're not very funny, in the first place." She stabbed a finger at his chest. "You don't get to decide how Chinese I am. I wasn't raised in mainland China and sure, my Mandarin isn't perfect. And guess what? I *love* Chinese takeout. Kung Pao Chicken? Fortune cookies? Sign me up! I don't care what you or anyone else thinks. It doesn't change how I feel about myself."

"It seems you're in a bad mood," Jianhao said, as if indulging the tantrum of a child. "I will take my leave. We'll speak when you're more reasonable."

"If you're waiting for me to be reasonable, you'll be waiting forever!" Kitty shouted after him.

"You just roasted yourself," Jax muttered.

"I know, but at least I had the last word." She crossed her arms with a scowl. "I hate that guy."

"Yeah, you made that clear when you said he had his head up his butt."

"You hate him too."

Jax's head snapped up. He didn't think Kitty, of all, people, would be so accurate in her assessment.

She wasn't dumb. At least, not as stupid as everyone else seemed to think. But she could be self-centered, which made it difficult for her to read others.

"How do you know?" he asked.

"Oh, I was totally taking a shot in the dark. And you fell for it." She threw her head back with a laugh. "You really hate him? That's *hilarious*!"

"How so?"

"I thought you two were BFFs. I'm glad you aren't. He's a hairy pube on a malnourished tarantula."

"Do tarantulas have pubes?"

"If they do, Jianhao is one of them!" Kitty sing-songed, plopping down beside him. He knew immediately that she must have pitied him, because she was wearing a pale pink skirt and she still sat in the grass with him. "You know what he said is a total load of shit, right?"

"Is it? Or did he have a point? I've been studying this manual all day, and I still can't figure it out." Jax flung the notebook away.

"We're at a bit of a crossroads, aren't we? The shadowborn are accusing us of being too Chinese, too different. And Jianhao, a Chinese person from Mainland China, says we're not connected to our heritage. I call bullshit. Who is he, who are *any* of them, to determine if we're enough?"

Jax eyed her suspiciously. "Did you get that from a self-help book?"

"Yes," she said, unashamed. "But it's true. What makes someone more Chinese than another? What makes someone more American than another? These labels have value, but I don't think they're based on arbitrary things outsiders define. I might not speak perfect Mandarin, but I know I'm Chinese, and nothing that rat-faced bitch Chen Jianhao says will ever take that away from me. And, no matter what articles are written, or gossip is whispered, we're American, too."

"How can you be so..."

"Pretty?" She batted her eyelashes.

"No."

"Interesting? Special? Intelligent? Mature? Gorgeous?"

"Self-assured," he said.

"Well, normally I live by the phrase 'fake it 'till you make it'," she said, "but in this case? I would say, 'I am who I am. And everybody who says otherwise can get fucked.'"

TWENTY-SIX

THE RUMOR about the greenhouse being haunted was quite effective; Cyrus never saw anyone in there at night—except Kitty. She took to studying there and cultivating. Or sleeping. It was hard to tell, when she leaned against a tree with her eyes closed.

The moment he drew near, her eyes popped open. "Oh, it's you."

"Who else would it be?" he asked, hoping the answer wasn't Jianhao.

"I don't know. An elite assassin sent to torture information out of me?"

"What information? About cultivation?"

"No, my haircare secrets," she said seriously. "Unfortunately for them, my only secret is my genetics."

He sat next to her on the checkered blanket she laid down. Both had agreed fairly early on that, should they fool around in the greenhouse, they needed some sort of protection against grass stains. "Halloween is coming up."

"How could I forget? It's one of my favorite holidays!"

"You like dressing up? Isn't that kind of childish?"

"Oh my gosh, you don't dress up? You're, like, *so* mature," she replied sarcastically, stretching her legs. "Yes, I like dressing up. Plus, I'm good at sewing—one of my many talents—so making costumes was always fun. It really encouraged my creativity."

"Is that so? And what kind of costumes have you done in the past?"

"Slutty nurse, slutty nun, slutty policewoman, slutty postal worker, slutty firefighter, slutty Alice in Wonderland..." she rattled off, counting on her fingers. "The list goes on. You know, I could help you with a costume this year."

"No thanks, I don't think I'd look good as a slutty nurse."

Her eyes raked over him. "You've got nice pecs, so I think we could work something out."

"That's quite alright."

"Suit yourself."

"Halloween *is* a big deal around here, though," Cyrus began. "You'd think truebloods would hate it. They don't like humans very much, so having them dress up as supernaturals... But apparently, imitation is a form of flattery. All the shadowborn colleges across the country have this huge week-long extravaganza. Last year, Kinsey went all-out on carnival games, hay mazes, and apple bobbing. At the end of the week, there's a dance with a costume contest."

"Are you inviting me?" she asked.

He couldn't gauge whether she wanted it to be an invitation. "That would be in violation of the rules, wouldn't it?"

"Yes."

"Then, that's not an invitation. Just a PSA."

"Got it. But if I happened to go," she said, "and you

happened to go, separately, of course, and we met *there*, then... that wouldn't be breaking any rules."

"Rules *you* made," he pointed out.

"Regardless of whether or not I made them, the consequences of breaking them are..." She offered a tight smile. "Anyway, *maybe* I'll grace you with my presence."

"I look forward to it."

She inched closer. "So, was there another reason you came here? Other than to extend a non-invitation to the dance."

"Yeah. I'm having dinner with my parents, tonight." Halloween week was like Homecoming week, and many parents—even the trueblood ones—came to campus. Kinsey hosted a gala specifically for parents and alumni, though he hardly needed more money to line his pockets and fund his son's debauchery. Regardless, Malcolm Ward had driven up with his wife earlier, and the two were settling in a hotel nearby. Cyrus planned on meeting them for dinner with Melody.

He would have invited Kitty—his father would find her interesting, for sure—but that would be against the rules, or close enough to it.

They talked for a little while longer before he got up to leave, crossing campus in a hurry to get to the parking lot. Melody was already waiting, leaning against his car with headphones over her ears. As he approached, she slipped them down to hang around her neck. "You're late."

"Not really."

She checked her phone. "Yeah, we're supposed to meet them in five. We'll probably be there in fifteen, if you speed. Which you don't. What were you doing?"

"I lost track of time," said Cyrus, which was the truth. The siblings got into the car and headed toward the restaurant, an upscale burger joint in Park Haven, the closest town to Northeastern. As predicted, he didn't speed, and they arrived in twenty minutes.

Malcolm was a tall man, standing at 6'5" with a mop of chestnut brown hair and green eyes. Beth, his human wife, had similar coloring. At one point, perhaps they could have been mistaken for siblings. Now, though, they were relatives at best—or siblings with a large age gap.

Some species of truebloods aged slowly, angels being one of them. Malcolm only looked to be in his late twenties. Beth had let her hair go silver and, while she still looked stunning, she was in her late fifties, and she looked it.

Once they got past the standard round of greetings—because really, it wasn't as if they'd been separated long; two months, maybe?—they were seated at a large booth in the back of the restaurant.

"So," Beth said, clapping her hands together. "Tell me what's going on. How's this semester been treating you?"

"Classes are so tiring. I have two labs," Mel complained. She went on about classes until their food came, which was a welcome distraction. Cyrus hoped she would talk the whole time, so he didn't have to. He didn't consider himself particularly taciturn, but when it came to his parents, the less they knew, the better.

"I've heard there's been some trouble at Northeastern," Beth said. "You two haven't gotten caught up in anything bad, have you?"

Her tone was teasing, but the question was serious.

"What do you mean?" Cyrus asked.

"You know. Protesting, fights, things of that nature."

"A certain article has been circulating around trueblood circles, causing a bit of upheaval," Malcolm added. "You haven't gotten caught up in that, have you? Because you know, your studies are the most important thing right now. Especially for you, Cyrus. You'll be applying to medical schools soon and taking the MCAT next semester. You need to buckle down; you can't afford distractions."

"Blake isn't pulling you out every night, is he?" Beth asked.

"I'm doing fine in school. My grades are great," Cyrus said, hoping they would drop the subject. But, of course, once med school was mentioned, his father dug his talons in and wouldn't let go.

"Cyrus has the highest record of hunts in school. He's tied with Wyatt Ainsworth," Melody added, because she thought she was helping. In reality, she just made things much worse.

"It's very noble that you want to hunt," Malcolm told his son, "but you aren't going to be a warrior. You'll be a doctor. You should get an internship at a hospital instead."

"It will be safer," Beth added, putting a hand over his.

Cyrus shoveled a forkful of mac and cheese into his mouth, wishing someone was there to split it with him. He was beginning to have food regrets; the dish was too rich all on its own.

His parents stared at him, waiting for him to finish chewing so the conversation could continue. Damn it.

"I'm balancing hunting and schoolwork just fine," he said. "It's not about preparing for my future career; they need hunters, desperately. Maybe if your trueblood colleagues stepped in and helped, we wouldn't be in this situation."

"I agree. The truebloods are, by and large, unorganized," Malcolm said, "but I'm sure there are plenty of students who can handle hunting. You've done enough, this summer. It's your junior year, buddy—I just want you to focus on your future. You know? Be a little selfish. It wouldn't kill you."

Selfish? By focusing solely on studying for the MCAT?

Beth took a sip of water, changing the subject. "Have you met that Swan family? Those humans parading around the school?"

"We read the article Dr. Woods published. It's concerning."

"None of it is true," Melody said, quick to jump to the Swan's defense. "I mean, that article was full of racist undertones, Dad."

"It didn't mention anything about race. It simply argued that they are receiving special treatment despite being academically underqualified to work at Northeastern."

"Everleigh was the one who asked them to come and help, because they possess a special set of skills and knowledge no one here does," Cyrus explained, hoping he sounded calm. "They're good people. And Kinsey is forcing their kids to go through the Blood Trials to prove they belong, even though their powers are equal to ours."

"Equal? But they are not born with them, are they? They are not shadowborn, nor do they descend from the Veil," Beth said.

"Equality doesn't mean identical, Mom. And frankly, it's a stretch in this case," Cyrus said, "because Kitty is not only physically stronger than me, but she's a better fighter. And her parents are even more powerful. Maybe more than you."

Malcolm's eyes narrowed. "Be that as it may, public discourse is against them. If you are seen associating with them, your name could be dragged down with them. Getting a job in the shadowborn world is all about connections, son."

Yes, Malcolm had done his best to remind Cyrus of the

importance of his future since birth, practically. And Cy knew he didn't have a leg to stand on when it came to complain about his parents—they were great, truly. He loved them, and he knew they loved him. But his father's constant pestering about his future, all under the guise of concern, was irritating. The man could write any behavior off as done out of love, and Cy was forced to accept it.

He felt bad even *thinking* about this. It wasn't as if Malcolm and Loren Blackwood could be compared. Good God, that man was a monster. Cy knew what he had done to Blake, mentally and physically. But his children weren't the only ones to suffer at the hands of the trueblood werewolf; he used women like tissues. And Mr. Churchill? The coldest SOB Cyrus ever met.

Malcolm loved both his children and provided them with a stable home life, love, and resources to grow and pursue their interests. But he also had an uncomfortable level of control over Cyrus, specifically. And sometimes, it bothered him.

"I think what your father means is, being cautious wouldn't be a bad thing—at least at this point in your life," Beth added, forcing a smile. "Fight the system from the inside, and whatnot."

"Exactly. This year is crucial for your future—"

"*Every* year has been 'crucial' to my future," Cyrus cut him off. "I'm not a child. I can manage my time just fine."

"Cyrus, we're just concerned about you."

"Why? What reason have I given you to be concerned?"

"You've made excellent choices," Malcolm said, "but the world is unforgiving, son. Just one mistake, and your entire life could be ruined. You, especially... Well, people could mistake you for being one of them."

"Are you trying to imply," Cyrus said, his voice dropping,

"that you don't want me associating with a Chinese family on campus who are being unfairly treated because I'm half *Vietnamese* and you think, because of the way I look, people will mistake me for one of the Swans and treat me poorly?"

Beth winced. "Honey, no one is saying that. Right, Malcolm? I mean, you look very...much like your father. And your, ah, eyes are..."

"You look like me," Malcolm confirmed, almost proudly.

And Cyrus knew he needed to leave, then and there, before he said something he would regret later. But when he stood up and shuffled out of the booth, blocking out any further questions from his parents, Melody stood with him. Both siblings left the restaurant and drove back to campus in silence.

He felt his sister looking at him the whole ride home, but what was there to say?

Somehow, he found himself back at the greenhouse. He didn't realize he was heading there; he should have just gone to his dorm.

Kitty glanced up at him, sitting in the same spot she'd been in since he left her. "That was fast."

"What do I look like to you?" he asked, fumbling over his words. Smart as he was, he didn't have the proper language, if such a thing existed in the first place, to speak intelligently about race and ethnicity.

Before he could clarify what he meant, she said, "Ice Prince with a dash of Hot Nerd."

"Wait, you still think I'm an Ice Prince?"

"No, I think you look like one. 'Cause your face is usually like this." She frowned, furrowing her brows. "Don't worry, you have a really cute butt. Hence the moniker of 'Hot Nerd'."

"I mean ethnically. Do you think I look Vietnamese?"

"Is this a trick question?" Her eyes widened. "You *are* Vietnamese, aren't you?"

"Yes."

"Then what does it matter what *I* think if you look it or not? You are." She shrugged, as if it were a simple matter.

And maybe it was. Maybe he was overcomplicating things for himself. In truth, he hadn't thought much of his heritage, or his biological mother.

"Besides, I'm not sleeping with you because you're Asian," Kitty continued. "Or because you're an Ice Prince/Hot Nerd hybrid. Which is rarer than one would think, in the wild. I'm doing it because you have a big—"

"Heart?" he finished with a grin.

"I was going to say penis. Your heart's not that big. Don't flatter yourself."

Cyrus laughed in spite of himself. Lowering himself to his knees, he sat at eye level across from her. "Are you still studying?"

"Nope. Writing in my affirmation journal. The prompt is, 'What's your favorite unusual self-care idea?' Hell if I know."

"I think I have an idea."

"Oh?" Her brows lifted. "Share with the class, Mr. Ward."

His hands gripped her calves, and he dragged her closer to him, so both her feet were planted on either side of his knees. Her skirt pooled at her hips, and she looked up at him, surprised.

"What are you doing?" she asked, though from her heated gaze, she had a pretty good guess.

"Do you remember when we first came here together?"

"You mean, when I stumbled upon you, we argued, and then we fought a hydra?" She snorted. "Yeah, I remember."

"You told me that when men like you, they fall at your feet and worship you," Cyrus said slowly. "This is me, worshipping you."

CHARITY WASN'T the only sister her father hit. She thought she'd find solace in that, but over the years, such comfort waned until it was almost non-existent. And then, it disappeared entirely, worn down by the brutality of his belt.

She understood perfectly why, despite no longer fearing his strikes, she fell into line. If he said "jump", she didn't ask how high. She just did it, repeatedly, until he was satisfied. Somehow, despite hating the man to her very core, she still wanted to please him. Or, at the very least, keep him content.

Even that seemed to be too much to ask for.

She milled around the campus green, waiting until she finally spotted him. He was hard to miss. They had the same emerald eyes—the striking color ran in their family. He wore a suit and kept his blonde hair neatly trimmed, cropped close to his head, unlike her unruly red curls.

He looked her up and down as he approached. "Is this what you've chosen to wear?"

Jeans and a light sweater? It was getting colder in New York, but she didn't feel the need for a jacket in the daytime just yet.

"Women should present themselves well at all times. What happened to the dresses your stepmother bought you?"

"They're for summer." And for children, given the unflattering style teeming with ribbons, ruffles, and lace.

"You are a Churchill, which means you represent me and our family. You should always strive for perfection."

Charity didn't have anything to say to that. What could she possibly tell her father that would change his mind, about anything?

"You've been keeping up with school, haven't you?" he asked.

She nodded. Her grades were good, as per usual, and her record of hunts was among the top ten. Her father shouldn't have had anything to complain about, but no doubt he'd look anyway, and find something asinine she'd overlooked. Even after living her entire life under his thumb, as a trueblood fae, his moods changed frequently. She still hadn't given up attempting to predict them, though she knew it was moot.

"Let's not keep the chancellor waiting any longer."

The two men were meeting, most likely about the donations the Churchill family made to the college.

Charity walked toward the main building, trying not to look at the man who had raised her. When she got to the door, her foot caught in the pavement, and she slammed face-first into the door as another student kicked it open. Knocked back on her ass, she stilled, stunned at what just happened.

"Sorry," the young woman said nervously, holding out a hand. "Are you okay?"

Mr. Churchill sneered at his daughter. "Clumsy and inept, just like your mother. If you're this incompetent simply walking, I wonder how you look on the battlefield."

Charity knew better than to say anything, standing and dusting herself off as the young woman skittered away, deterred by Mr. Churchill's glare.

"If I had a son, I wouldn't need to send my daughters into the Veil," he said under his breath. "Maybe then, you could have ranked first and ousted that insufferable Malcolm Ward's child from his position. But instead, the fates have cursed me with daughters, each more useless than the last."

Hatred burned through her veins, along with the blood they shared. But she couldn't bring herself to say a single word against him. Coward.

The door swung open with such force, it banged into Mr. Churchill's legs and sent him stumbling. He righted himself before he fell, his head swiveling toward the offender. His eyes narrowed to slits, and Charity's heartbeat quickened.

"Sorry," Mrs. Swan said, walking out of the building. She didn't look sorry at all. "I didn't see you there."

"Are you blind, then?" Mr. Churchill snarled. "Or simply a bumbling buffoon?"

"Why don't we find out?"

"Excuse me?" Anger rolled off him in waves, but the woman before them didn't seem affected at all. That, or she had a mean poker face. "You're...you're that woman, aren't you? The mortal monster?"

"Let's duel," she suggested. "We can determine who the real monster is in the arena."

TWENTY-SEVEN

ARIANA SWAN SURVEYED HER SURROUNDINGS, taking stock of what little advantages she had. Mr. Churchill was physically larger than her, though that was nothing special. She wasn't a tall woman to begin with, and her frame was considered 'slight' here.

"You are sure this is a smart idea?" her husband asked in Mandarin, falling back on their native tongue. Ariana didn't mind English, and she was fairly confident in her fluency, but there was something comforting about Chinese. Or, perhaps, it was the man speaking it.

She glanced up at her husband. George was tall and skinny, like a string bean. He wasn't built for fighting, not like her. On her wedding day, her father had mentioned how mismatched the two appeared. As if he'd forgotten the fact that he was the one who had arranged their marriage.

"I will win," Ariana said, with confidence she didn't quite feel. But he squeezed her hand, and she knew then and there that losing wasn't an option.

There were no words left to say between them. He left to

stand outside the glass dome with their children, his silence a sign of his faith in her.

Ariana took a deep breath. Mr. Churchill spoke to a professor she didn't recognize, who would act as a referee. His daughter stood beside him, her face a mask of terror.

Oh, what Ariana's shīgōng would say if he saw her now! This went against all the sect rules—she would be fighting a stranger, not out of necessity or self-defense, but to sate her own anger. It had been simmering ever since she began working under Calista Woods. That woman pushed every button Ariana had, and Ariana was a *mother*. She loved her kids, of course, but damn were they annoying when they were younger!

Calista might have been an adult with a lab coat and fancy degree, but her insufferable arrogance made it hard to view her as a person deserving of empathy or respect. Which was to say, Ariana hated her guts on a primal level and fantasized about doing awful things to the bitch. It wasn't very Taoist or enlightened of her.

A crowd gathered, filling the seats outside the dome as Ariana prepared herself. She wasn't sure what to expect from a trueblood, but she had confidence in her abilities. And, if it came down to it, her dirty tricks. But she was rusty, having not had time to train in the last twenty years. She rolled her shoulders, shaking her head from side to side.

"We'll use swords," Mr. Churchill called from across the dome. "Though I'm told you people prefer your hands, let's do something different and attempt to act civilized for once."

Blah blah blah, Ariana thought immaturely. "Alright. Please state the terms of our fight."

"Very well. We are adults, and not students here. We will fight until our opponent is unable to."

"That sounds dangerous." *For you.*

"Well," his lips curled into a smile, "this is the only way we will see who is truly the superior species."

"This is not about who is 'superior'," Ariana corrected. She was just a woman; how could she represent all cultivators?

"Then what is this about, Mrs. Swan? Clearly, you were looking for a fight when you approached me."

"Yes," she agreed. "Let us fight."

He didn't wait for her to grab a weapon. He took a sword from the rack and lunged at her. The sword pierced her shoulder, pinning her to the mat. His knee sank into her stomach, and he leaned down, his hand gripping her chin. "Do you see all those people watching us, Mrs. Swan? I hope you realize that, whether you win or lose, they don't care. They will continue to hate you and your kind regardless of how many matches you win or how many trials your savage children complete. There is nothing you can do about it. So, if this is your attempt to prove yourself, I think you'll find that you are wasting your efforts."

She knew that better than anyone.

For most of her life, she was Sun Xiaoyan, written with the character "dawn" because she had been born at daybreak in the middle of winter. It was an icy one, too. The weeks before her birth were filled with snow and sorrow, but her father said that on the morning she finally came into the world, the clouds parted and the snow stopped. Finally, the sun rose above the mountain, and all was calm.

Her mother hated the name Xiaoyan, and her by extension, but there was little to be done about either issue. She was born prematurely, one of many things her mother blamed her for. It was the night of her gift-giving ceremony, a tradition similar to a baby shower in the States, where all the mothers in the sect would gather and offer symbolic gifts. Ribbons for beautiful hair; chopsticks so she would never go hungry; furs so she would have a warm heart. The most important one was a sword, with a name approved by the sect seer engraved on the blade. Since Xiaoyan's sword had been stolen the night of her birth, the seer deemed it would be bad luck to use the name her parents originally intended. And so, she would be Xiaoyan instead.

Her mother never liked her very much. The pregnancy had been difficult, but it would have been worth it if Xiaoyan had been born a boy. Instead, she'd come out a worthless girl. And not even a *pretty* girl. Her mother always had to add that in. She was never as thin as the other women in her sect, never good enough at dancing or calligraphy or guzheng to catch a husband.

"The matchmaker will never find a girl like you a husband," she would say with a sniff. "It is a simple fact; not only are you ugly, but you have done nothing to compensate for it."

Xiaoyan preferred her father, basking in his attention.

He was more progressive than other cultivators in the sect. When she turned thirteen, Xiaoyan was allowed to take swordsmanship lessons along with her brothers.

She trained every single day. She practiced her form until it was perfect, until her muscles ached, and her fingers bled. Even when she embroidered, she pretended the needle was a sword and she was in the field, cultivating. So what if her hands grew calloused and she got a tan?

"You should have milky skin. Men like that better," her mother always said.

Xiaoyan was too consumed with being the best. She had

to prove to her father that she was worth the effort, and in doing that, she surpassed all her siblings. Even her brothers.

But Xiaoyan had a secret. Despite wanting to honor her father for the gift of education, part of her didn't care about any of it. Not her father, not becoming powerful...not even immortality. She strove for excellence in part because she wanted to prove her mother wrong.

You think I'm worthless?

I am a cultivator. You *are the worthless one. Your whole life was wasted on being someone's wife.*

Xiaoyan had loftier goals than that. She looked around her at the women training to be wives, fussing over their needlework and instruments. Useless. Were those skills going to help them attain enlightenment? Would they help those foolish girls live forever?

No.

She would be different. She would become great, just like her father. A respected member of the sect.

She would become the first female immortal. And then her mother would be sorry.

Xiaoyan thought she was above them, unable to recognize that she had been afforded opportunities they had not. Her father's praise blinded her to everything, until her mother died.

Madame Sun grew ill. Xiaoyan visited her out of obligation, though she waited until all her sisters left before finally entering her mother's chambers. She lived away from their family home, on the outskirts of the sect. Later, Xiaoyan learned that this was where women went to live out the rest of their lives, when their husbands couldn't bear to look at them anymore.

And her mother who had been so beautiful, with long

dark hair and clear eyes, had grown *old*. Xiaoyan hadn't seen her mother in many years, but now, as she looked at the wrinkled, white-haired lady in the bed, and felt an ache in her chest.

"Xiaoyan." Madame Sun never called her by a nickname or a term of endearment. "You came to see me."

"What happened?" Xiaoyan asked, shocked.

"I am dying," she said plainly. "This is what happens when mortals age."

Xiaoyan had seen people in her sect die before, usually during hunting trips. But she had never seen someone die of old age. She almost preferred watching a decapitation; at least it was quick.

This was long. Slow. Painful.

"Once you reach a certain age, they will lock you up too," Madame Sun said. "Men can get old. They can grow their beards and let their hair go grey. But it is not the same for women. Old men are wise. Old women are hags. Our usefulness has run its course."

"How long have you been here?"

"Three years, confined to this room. My time is thankfully almost up." The woman looked at Xiaoyan, unsmiling. "This will be your fate too, my daughter. And all I wish is that your suffering is ten times greater than mine."

After Xiaoyan left that day, she went into seclusion to cultivate. When she came out, she learned that her mother had lived for another five years before dying alone in the middle of winter, the season she so despised.

Her father remarried a month later, to a woman young enough to be Xiaoyan's granddaughter. When she questioned him, Master Sun said, "A woman is like a flower, Yan'er. When they are beautiful and in full bloom, they are meant to be plucked. But when you pluck a flower, it withers and dies."

Xiaoyan shook her head. "Then why not let it grow free?"

"Oh, Yan'er. Flowers are *meant* to be plucked," Master Sun said. "They want to be. If they are not, it is an insult to them."

"Even if they die?"

"They *want* to die. They do not want to become immortal." He frowned. "You understand, don't you? Your cultivation is good, but it will never be great. You cannot change your nature as a flower, my daughter. You might have a prolonged lifespan, but eventually, you too will be plucked."

"But what if I become immortal?"

He laughed at her, then. Right in her face. "Whoever said you would become immortal?"

"You allowed me to cultivate—"

"So you would stay looking younger for longer." He shook his head. "Do not be foolish. Women are not meant to become immortal. You have natural talent, from me. But you won't get much farther than this. Do you know why there are no female cultivators, my daughter? It is because cultivation is, ultimately, about how much effort one puts into training. How much discipline one has. And I'm afraid females are incapable of such things. You are the more delicate sex. You do not know what it means to work hard, or to suffer for what you want. It is not in your nature."

Xiaoyan could only nod. But she wondered now if her father had changed, or if he had always been so...

Difficult.

He was the person who taught her everything she knew. And if he was wrong about women as flowers, what else could he be wrong about? She grew angry with him as the days passed, humiliated by the man she thought cherished her above all others. It was all just a game to him, her life, her desires. She wanted to prove him wrong so badly, she continued to cultivate. She broke through various stages, fought beasts, and defeated some of the best cultivators in her sect. And yet, her father said the same thing.

"Are you not tired, Yan'er?" he would ask. "You should quit now, while you still have some value left. Otherwise, no one will want to marry you. And I'm afraid I can't have you living at home as an adult for much longer. Where will you go then? Feminine housing, with the other leftover females?"

No matter what she did, no matter how hard she tried, nothing would ever compensate for the fact that she was born a woman.

She hated people like that. People like her parents, and this Mr. Churchill, who were desperate for sons and disregarded their daughters. The look in Charity Churchill's eyes mirrored Ariana's own, once upon a time. Back when she was still Sun Xiaoyan.

But now, she was Ariana Swan.

"I understand that no one is cheering for me," she said quietly, meeting Mr. Churchill's eyes. "I know they wish for me to lose. But I do not care. Because this is not about proving them wrong, or even proving *you* wrong. It is about me, beating you."

She kicked him hard in the stomach and rolled him off in one swift motion. Kitty was right—these shadowborn weren't as well-versed at fighting. Had his footing been more stable, it would have taken more effort to put distance between them. Pulling the sword from her shoulder, Ariana circulated her qi through her meridians. The bleeding stopped, and any pain she felt faded, allowing her to stand.

Perhaps the difference was in the level of power we started with, she thought. Cultivators were born mortal, with no powers. They could only progress through training, which involved combat lessons. Every cultivator *had* to have some basic combat training, even at the first level. A trueblood, on the other hand, could conceivably never train a day in their life, and they would still be able to use the magic they were born with.

It was not that Ariana thought herself, or any other cultivator, as *better* than truebloods. Rather, their unique methods for gaining power differentiated them. Perhaps this was the issue with the ferals, too. If one were to start with power, if they were *used* to it, then perhaps it would be difficult for them to gauge their limits. Cultivate too quickly, especially with unstable demonic energy, and one would qi deviate.

Animals could cultivate in China. There were many folk tales of creatures cultivating and attaining human forms, and while she hadn't witnessed it firsthand, she knew it was possible. But animals, like human cultivators, started out with no supernatural abilities. These beastbloods could use magic, but most had the brain function of animals. If they didn't truly understand what they were doing, it would be easy for them to qi deviate.

Mr. Churchill rose to his feet with a glare. It seemed he had some tricks up his sleeve too, because he vanished before her very eyes. Had he teleported? No—invisibility.

Ariana focused on her surroundings. She heard his breath, felt the air shift as he moved toward her. He wasn't careful, nor did it seem as though he was accustomed to fighting like this. She reached him before he could attack, grabbing him and throwing his body to the ground. Hard.

He coughed, reappearing as he lay flat on his back. She

could have shown off, could have played with him more, now that she was confident she would win against his skill level. But that would be a poor example to set for her children, so she simply aimed for his pressure points, exerting only as much force as needed to make him pass out. She hit a special spot on his neck, making his body go limp and his eyes shuttered closed.

Ariana stood, dusting herself off. And for a moment, the entire room was still, as if the audience collectively held their breath. As Mr. Churchill had so kindly pointed out earlier, none of the students or parents watching appeared happy with her victory. Instead, through the glass, all she saw was a sea of faces filled with disgust and resentment. As if, by challenging their preconceived notions about her, she committed a grave sin.

How dare she make them question their belief that true-bloods were superior! Shame on her!

But then, the cheering began. No, not from the shadow-born. This wasn't a movie. Ninety percent of the audience was still glaring at her; just because she won one fight didn't mean they automatically liked her. Not by a long shot.

Instead, when she turned toward the source of the noise, she saw her family. Kitty, Noelle, and Jax cheered and shouted wildly, smiles gracing their faces as they jumped up and down. It didn't matter that no one joined them.

George, on the other hand, was already gone. He'd taken off toward her, entering the glass dome and picking her up. He lifted her off the ground, twirling her around in his arms. Ariana's face smushed against the hard planes of his chest, and even though showing such affection in public was a foreign concept, she didn't mind it now. Not when he was smiling at her like she was the sun.

"You did it. I knew you would," he said, setting her down. He cupped her face in his hands, holding her like he didn't want to let her go. It had been so long since they had such an intimate moment. From the day the girls were born, their lives were utter chaos. When they weren't raising their kids, they were working or worrying about money. Even now, at Northeastern, all they seemed to do was work or eat in silence. And there was comfort in that, in knowing she had a partner who she could rely on.

Ariana couldn't deny the heat radiating from her cheeks either, caused by her husband's gaze alone.

"Sir!" the referee shouted, racing toward them. Oh, so *now* he decides to show an interest! "You cannot just run in here and interrupt a match. It is against the arena rules! The fight only ends when I blow my whistle. This disqualifies Mrs. Swan—"

"Here you go," George said cheerfully, sticking an acupuncture needle in the man's neck. Ariana had no idea where he produced it from, but she wasn't surprised. George might not have been the strongest cultivator in their sect, but he always had a trick up his sleeve.

"Was that needle dipped in Anus Annihilator?" Ariana asked, wrapping her arms around her husband's midsection.

He grinned. "Of course, qīn'ài de."

The term of endearment, one she hadn't heard in decades, made her smile. "You poisoned him with a high-powered laxative just because he was going to disqualify me?"

"I would give a *thousand* men violent diarrhea, just to see you smile."

That was both the sweetest and most disturbing thing she'd ever heard. But she'd come to expect it from him.

Ariana didn't know how to tell her husband how much

she loved him. She'd *never* heard her own parents express love for each other, and certainly not for her. Culturally, she supposed she was raised never to express those types of feelings with words. Even with George, in the years they spent together, she couldn't remember *ever* explicitly telling him "I love you."

So she said it in her own way, the only way she knew how. "Have you eaten yet?"

MĀMA REQUESTED Italian after her victory, so Bàba prepared a pasta dinner that night. He put three large ceramic bowls of different-shaped pastas on the Lazy Susan, surrounded by smaller dishes of chicken, shrimp, sauces, and cheese. Regrettably, Kitty had the cheese, which meant it was going to be fart city tonight!

As much as Noelle enjoyed her father's cooking and spending time with her siblings, she mostly loved seeing her parents together. After dinner, they sat on the couch curled up beside each other, watching the news.

"You know there are other options, right? You don't have to limit yourself to just news channels anymore," Kitty said.

"We like seeing what is happening in the world," Māma replied.

"They have a segment about dogs on the top of the hour," Bàba said. "Maybe we should get—"

"No."

"But—"

"No," Māma said firmly.

Noelle finished putting everything in the dishwasher and grabbed her bag. She was ready to shower and go to bed, fully aware that she still had class the next day. "I'm going to head out. Kitty, are you coming?"

"I'm going to be late tonight. You head over without me," she called from down the hall.

"Okay." Noelle said her goodbyes and left, walking back to the dorm alone. She enjoyed the quiet for once, and while she knew this incident would surely come back to bite them, she couldn't find it in herself to care that much.

As the elevator doors opened to her floor, the lights automatically turned on. Blake was slumped against the door of her dorm, his head leaning against the frame. He smelled like a brewery, and immediately, she knew her night would be upended.

Strangely, though, this didn't dampen her mood. Despite the way they'd left things, she was actually *glad* he'd shown up.

"I heard about the fight," he said, his eyes cracking open. "I wish I could've seen it. Did he cry?"

"No. But Māma beat him quickly," Noelle said, standing over him. "Where have you been? I hope you didn't drive from town like this."

"I wouldn't. My old man demanded we have dinner together, and it went about as well as expected." He rose, steadying himself against the doorframe. "I don't know why I ended up here. It's not like I wanted to fuck you or anything."

"Maybe that's exactly why you came—because you *don't* want to have sex with me." Noelle opened the door. "You can come in if you promise not to puke."

"I'm jealous of you, you know." He filled the door, not coming inside, yet not leaving. "Your mom was fighting for you, today."

"She wasn't. Mr. Churchill just pissed her off."

"No. She was clearly fighting for you, to prove a point.

Even when I first met your parents, I knew immediately that they would do anything for you. And I hated you all for it. Happy families...they're awful. No one should be that happy," he said. "You grew up in backward South Carolina in the middle of the woods. Your house was small, you were poor as shit... Where's your resentment toward each other, Noelle? Where's your bitterness?"

"Blake..."

"You really disgust me. All of you. I hate you," he blurted. "I really hate you."

Noelle was taken aback by the admission. "I hate you too, asshole."

"What?"

"You're an idiot! You're barely passing your classes, and worse, you don't care at all! Me, on the other hand? I'm smart. My grades are practically perfect. And yet, you were right about me," she said, her voice rising. Everyone on the floor could hear her, but she didn't care. "It used to be easy, at home. No matter how much I bickered with my family, we always made up. Here, nobody owes me anything. In fact, most of the time, I feel like my peers actively hate me. I try to tell myself that it doesn't matter, that I'm better than my sister because I'm not concerned about popularity. But part of me *does* care, and it pisses me off. Worse, you saw it. If a dumbass like you could see so clearly where I'm lacking, who else has noticed?"

Blake looked down, and it was the closest to ashamed she'd ever seen him. "You're not lacking anything."

"Oh please. You said it yourself, didn't you? I have no self-awareness. I can give advice, but I can't take my own. And I'm not as pretty or strong or courageous as my sister. If it hadn't been for her and Jax, I wouldn't have passed the trials."

In the end, she wasn't nearly as good as she thought she was. And the only thing worse than being useless was knowing that everyone else could see how useless she was.

"I never called you ugly," Blake said. "And just because you're not the most self-aware person out there doesn't mean you're not smart."

"I guess."

"It's not your fault that everyone around here sucks. Myself included," he added, running a hand through his hair. "I...I don't hate you. Not really. I hate that you have something I want, which proves your point that I'm an ass."

"I called you an asshole, which is different from an ass. Because an ass would be the entire butt, and the hole is just the rectum."

"You make it really difficult to compliment you, you know that? Why can't you let me apologize like a normal person?"

"Because you're drunk. And while you're saying nice things, I'm pretty sure it's because of the alcohol," Noelle pointed out. "Do you want to go down to the cafeteria with me? Maybe you can get some food and sober up a bit."

"I'm good. I'm just going to sleep it off." Blake straightened, wincing as he moved.

Noelle's eyes narrowed. "Hey, are you okay?"

"Fine," he managed, his face twisting in pain. "I'll see you later."

"Wait." She reached out, tugging on his shirt. She didn't think her grip was that strong, but the material tore, revealing a patch of dark bruises over his ribs.

"Shit."

"Oh my God." Her jaw dropped. "What the hell happened? Is that from your dad?"

"What? No!"

"You're a worse liar than Kitty," Noelle hissed, dragging him back into the room. "Come in and sit down before you hurt yourself."

He groaned but followed her. "Look, it's not a big deal."

"Yes, it is." Noelle pushed him into her desk chair and ran to the common area's kitchenette for ingredients. Throwing fresh herbs into a bowl, she returned to the dorm and squeezed aloe into the mixture to bind it.

"What are you doing?" he asked.

"Helping you." She pulled out her first aid kit. "Lift your shirt."

"Noelle—"

"Don't make me knock you out. We're doing this."

He rolled his eyes, but relented, and Noelle began her work. The bruises were deep, but nothing seemed to be broken.

Her blood was the final ingredient, and Noelle cut her finger to complete the mixture. She rubbed the salve on Blake's side, careful not to hurt him. As she did, he relaxed beneath her touch. Tomorrow, the bruises would be gone. She covered the salve with gauze, wrapped around his torso, and secured the ends.

"You're good at this," he said softly.

"I used to do this a lot at home, when I was younger. Kitty and Jax were always getting hurt, and they weren't advanced enough in their cultivation yet to heal themselves. Māma and Bàba didn't really need it, but my healing abilities worked on them, too, so I always had a use. Maybe that's part of the issue, though. I felt secure in knowing that my siblings could rely on me for my intelligence, and at the very least, my blood. But here, they don't seem to need me at all. I'm useless."

"I wouldn't say magical healing is useless," he said. "Thanks for this."

"Do you want to talk about it?"

"Not really. I'm going to head out. You can bill me for your services, Doc."

"It's on the house," she said, leading him to the door. "Get some rest."

"Yeah, I'll try."

When he left, she locked the door behind him and returned to her room. She was suddenly exhausted. Between the fight and Blake, she hadn't had much time to process. But she was glad to see him, which was horrifying in its own way.

He was a rude, womanizing, insufferable jerk.

But maybe she was more like him than she cared to admit.

NORTHEASTERN TRIBUNE

DUEL DISGRACE: THE UNRULY CONDUCT OF ARIANA SWAN

In what can only be described as a shocking lapse in decorum, Ariana Swan recently took it upon herself to challenge the esteemed Gwyn Churchill, a trueblood fae of noble lineage and a luminary within both the arcane community and the esteemed halls of Northeastern College. The incident, which culminated in a duel fraught with controversy, has sent ripples of disbelief and disapproval throughout our community.

The duel, which onlookers hoped would be a display of skill and honor, quickly descended into farce, marred by tactics on Mrs. Swan's part that strayed far from the noble traditions of shadowborn combat. Witnesses were aghast as Swan managed to momentarily gain the upper hand against Churchill—a feat that, while surprising, was short-lived. The match was brought to an abrupt and unsatisfactory conclusion when Swan was rightfully disqualified for her unorthodox methods. However, the spectacle did not end there; in a display of uncouth behavior befitting a tavern brawl rather than a noble duel, Swan's husband launched an unprovoked attack on the referee, further staining the family's already questionable reputation.

Churchill, a respected member of our community and a generous benefactor to Northeastern, has conducted himself with the grace and restraint befitting his station throughout this ordeal. His contributions to our society extend far beyond the financial, embodying the virtues and traditions that have long defined our magical world. In contrast, Swan's actions and her subsequent disqualification serve as a reminder of the gulf that lies between those who uphold our values and those who seek to undermine them.

Reports from those familiar with Swan paint a picture of a person out of step with the norms of civilized society. Tales of her eschewing the use of a fork and knife in favor of sticks to consume her meals evoke images of a savage. Having grown up in the wilderness, she might as well be an ape in a dress.

TWENTY-EIGHT

HAVING two men fight over you was overrated, in Veronica's opinion. If she had known—before she opened the door—that the source of the noises outside were Blake and Ryder, she would have just stayed in bed.

The two young men—boys, really—were currently brawling in the hallway. It was too early for this shit. Blake had Ryder in a headlock, while the latter was punching his sides. The pair rolled on the floor, cursing and flailing. You'd think they would be a bit more civilized at twenty years old; apparently not.

Veronica leaned against the doorframe and watched with a mix of amusement and annoyance. She entertained the idea that they were fighting over her, but it was more likely a male ego thing. Veronica was not looking forward to the inevitable clean-up after they were done. She cleared her throat, causing the boys to freeze. Ryder was on his knees and Blake had one hand wrapped around his throat.

Sadly, he looked good. Like really good. What nerve! His skin was sun-kissed, and he smelled like the ocean—which was funny, since the school was nowhere near the ocean. Even after the fight, if you wanted to call it that, he looked disheveled in a sexy way. Unfortunately, she could easily picture him without a shirt on.

"What do you two think you're doing?" she asked causally, trying not to stare at her ex.

He let go of Ryder, who fell back on his ass.

Veronica could have helped him up, but instead chose to cross her arms and watch.

Blake, the bigger of the two, straightened up and adjusted his t-shirt, which was riding up, hinting at defined abs. He must have been doing this on purpose.

Standing before her, the reasons behind her intense dislike for him became muddled, overshadowed by an intense attraction. Despite the heartache he had caused, a part of her yearned for him. However, pride was a formidable contender; she wasn't willing to take him back without a significant show of remorse. On the darkest nights, she fantasized about him groveling for her forgiveness, though she knew well that Blake Blackwood at her feet was a scenario confined to her imagination.

Veronica's anger towards him diminished. This wasn't an indication of readiness to rekindle their relationship, by any means. She was more disappointed than angry, mourning her wasted time and crushed hopes. Recognizing that their parting was likely for the best did little to quell the complex brew of emotions—resentment, affection, and everything in between—that still tethered her to him, the exact nature of these feelings she couldn't quite pinpoint.

For once, he didn't seem cocky; in fact, he didn't appear happy at all to see her, even though he was the one who had come to her building and was standing outside her door.

While it was possible he was there for a neighbor, Veronica had a feeling he had come to speak with her. She wasn't sure why —there was no basis for it, other than her intuition. The last time she sought closure from him, she was sorely disappointed. She feared she would be let down once again.

"Vee, I've been wanting to talk to you," Blake said.

Ryder shoved a hand in Blake's face, pushing him away. "You don't have to listen to anything he has to say."

"Don't you have someone else's girl to harass?" Blake said, shoving him back.

"She's not *your* girl, dick."

Veronica rolled her eyes and shook her head. She wasn't a fan of this caveman behavior, but her interest was piqued by Blake's statement. He had a lot of nerve coming back after all this time and declaring that he wanted to talk. Or insinuating that she was his. She hated the part of herself that was secretly pleased, not just by Blake's declaration, but by Ryder's.

"I'm not *anyone's* girl," she interjected.

Blake smirked. "See? She's not yours either, Ryder. So go back to whatever hole you crawled out of and leave her alone."

"I came to tell her something important. What did you come here for, a quick fuck?" Ryder sneered.

"Yeah, I'm sure what you have to say is so important."

"What are you implying?"

"I don't know what your problem is, but you really think you're better than me? You're not. At least I can admit what I am. You, on the other hand?"

"Admit what? That you're a bastard?"

Veronica was getting tired of their exchange, but it was entertaining in a way. It was nice to know that she was worth fighting over.

"Oh, please," Blake said, laughing. "I may be a bastard, but you're a hypocrite."

"Is that the best you can do?"

"I'm not wasting my time with you."

"Alright, that's enough. You two need to cut it out." Veronica looked from Ryder to Blake. "It's early, and you're making a lot of noise."

"I came here to talk to you in private," Blake said in a low voice.

"I have nothing to say to you. I think everything between us has already been said, and you made it very clear a few months ago how you really felt about me."

"I know, and I owe you an apology."

"I don't want to hear it. I'm done with you," Veronica said. "Please leave. I actually need to speak with Ryder."

Blake looked between them. He seemed like he wanted to say more, but finally, he acquiesced. "I'll come again when you're alone."

"Don't bother," Ryder sneered.

Blake left without a fight, but Veronica wondered if he really didn't intend to apologize. She tried not to dwell on it, though she wasn't even sure the words "I'm sorry," would make her feel better. She had a feeling they wouldn't.

When the elevator door closed, Ryder turned to Veronica. "Can I come in?"

Veronica nodded.

"I want to apologize for showing up like this."

"You can't come to a woman's home uninvited, especially when it's early in the morning," she joked. She stepped aside as he entered, suddenly very aware of the skimpy tank top and shorts she was wearing.

Sure, they had gone on the trip to Tennessee together, but

not much had come of that—not in terms of their investigation, anyway. Aside from the last gas station clerk who had given them information about the green powder, they hadn't found out anything else. However, they had spent enough time together for Veronica to get to know Ryder a bit more. She wasn't exactly sure what to think about him. There were times when he could be so kind, sweet, and attentive, making her feel special. But then she doubted whether she was really a good judge of character, especially when it came to men. Could she ignore the fact that he had displayed some unsavory personality traits toward her friends and others? Didn't how he treated other people matter, even if he treated her differently? These were all questions, and Veronica had none of the answers. And part of her didn't want to explore the answers because it felt so good to have his exclusive attention.

Veronica sat on the edge of her bed and crossed her legs. "So, what's so important?"

"I brought the security footage you asked for. We can go through it together, if you want," he offered, taking the seat at her desk.

She nodded and started up her laptop, plugging the USB in. "Where did you get the footage in the first place?"

He hesitated. "You're not going to like this."

"But you're going to tell me anyway because we're partners in this investigation."

"Like Booth and Bones."

"What?"

"From the show 'Bones'," he clarified. "When we have more time, we'll watch it together."

Her heart fluttered at the thought of him making plans for their future. She tried not to let it show how it affected her as she pulled up the footage.

"A few months ago, someone messaged me," he admitted, his tone serious. "This was after the horde attack, but before my father told me to come back to Northeastern. I was traveling when I received this tip in the mail. I don't know how they found out where I was staying. I was in a hotel and hadn't told anyone my location aside from my father, but obviously, it wasn't him. It was an unmarked letter, telling me to come back to Northeastern. I would've dismissed it, had it not been for the USB drive included. It contained tapes of robberies, along with photos comparing them to the missing students and stills."

"How is that possible? You got this USB drive in the summer, but these robberies, if you even want to continue calling them that, took place a few weeks ago."

"I know. I didn't say this made sense at all."

"But time travel isn't real," Veronica countered. A lot of things with magic weren't possible. She learned all about the limitations of magic in class, and there was no spell that she knew of that could turn back time, even with blood magic.

"I haven't figured out who sent the tapes to me or how. All I can say is that they somehow knew something was going to happen."

Veronica clicked on the footage. As it played, she noticed a few things. First, it was in black and white. Second, there was no sound. She watched the time stamp in the bottom right corner count down, wondering if the perpetrator was wearing a mask. The video was grainy and shaky, but the perpetrator appeared to lack any sort of face covering. Stupid, unless you knew you wouldn't get caught.

Suddenly, the windows in the store exploded. She didn't understand how, but glass flew everywhere, and the footage cut to black.

It didn't take a genius to guess the perp was using some sort of magic.

"So, they made the windows explode and then left," Veronica said, trying to connect the dots. "That might explain the use of a memory potion. Maybe the clerk witnessed something, and they needed to erase her memories. But this spell is basic. It's the first thing we magicians learn."

"Yes, but the perpetrator wasn't a magician." Ryder clicked on a photo, zooming in on grainy footage of the perpetrator's face, then comparing it to a clear school photo. The resemblance was there, though hard to pin down—the young woman looked to be the same person. "She's cataloged in my father's directory as shadowborn. And shadowborn can't perform the spells that you can."

"That can't be," Veronica whispered, disbelief lacing her words. "Unless..."

"This was an experiment. The missing students were abducted and experimented on... and their abilities were enhanced."

COSTUMES FOR DUDES WERE LAME, so Blake didn't dress up. He chose slacks and a white button-down, with the sleeves rolled up casually. If anyone asked, he was a bartender.

He didn't know why he was attending the dance. Maybe it was just an excuse to get away from his father, who was still on campus and had grown increasingly volatile. As if it were possible for the guy to be more of a jackass than he already was.

Loren was probably out tonight on the prowl, strolling

along campus near the girls' dorms to pick out his next bride. Fucker.

Literally, in his case.

Blake scanned the room. Black and red streamers hung from the gymnasium walls, along with crystal decorations and dark swaths of velvet. Nothing was overtly scary, rather, the party theme was more of a gothic fairytale. Attendance was high, as expected for these types of events. Blake made his way through the crowd, looking for a particular girl.

He figured she'd be easy to spot. He'd only guessed she would show up, and he was correct; she stood in the corner, a wallflower in an elegant black dress falling to her knees. She rarely wore makeup, but tonight, she swept her hair up in a simple chignon.

Blake weaved through the crowd toward her, an involuntary smile spreading across his face. "Care for a dance?"

Her head rose, along with a single eyebrow. He didn't know how she did it, but it was impressive, nonetheless. "Me?"

"Yes, you."

"Blake Blackwood, asking little old me for a dance?" she asked sarcastically, laying on a fake Southern accent. "Why, I never!"

"I didn't take you for a theater dork."

Noelle rolled her eyes. "I don't know how to dance. Why don't you ask someone else?"

"It's not that hard," he said. "I'll lead."

He didn't expect her to say yes. He hoped but didn't expect. So, imagine his surprise when she actually took his hand.

"If I step on your feet," Noelle said, "remember that you asked for this."

"Of course, m'lady."

"Call me that again and I'm gonna vomit all over you."

"Alright, point taken. Jeez."

They stepped onto the dance floor, and as promised, Blake led. Though it was a faster song, they danced slow, completely out of sync with the partygoers around them. He didn't care, and neither did she. Everything else seemed to fade away, and he marveled at how natural it felt, being around Noelle.

He thought, after everything he shared with her, he'd be embarrassed and never want to see her again. But the opposite was true—he wanted to be around her, wanted to talk to her more. Although they both had their own set of issues, none quite overlapping, there was a rare level of honesty between them.

"I tried to talk to Veronica," Blake said, resting his hand on her back.

"And? How did it go?"

"Ryder punched me in the face. I'm wearing concealer right now."

"You want me to stick a needle of Anus Annihilator in his neck?" she offered, half-serious.

"A little," he admitted, "but I don't think giving him diarrhea is going to solve my problems."

"You'd be surprised how many snafus diarrhea has gotten me out of," she said with a straight face. "Are you gonna stop trying?"

"No." He wouldn't. Even if Veronica never forgave him, he owed her a genuine apology. Or some closure, at least.

He didn't want to get back together. They wouldn't be good for either of them. But he couldn't walk around wondering if she blamed herself for what happened, all because of some cruel words he threw at her. He didn't want to be the cause of her misery.

"I'm sorry if I was too harsh on you before," Noelle said. "I was angry because you were right. Partially. Maybe."

"Partially, maybe?" He grinned. "What spurred this on?"

"It makes me uncomfortable when others confront me. Clearly. I realized that insulting your intelligence didn't make what you were saying any less true. And as much as it...hurts," she admitted, "I can't keep denying that I don't always see the truth, when it comes to myself. Because the truth is hard—it's scary."

"Are you afraid now?" Blake asked, his tone soft.

"I am. But maybe, if it's you telling me these things, I won't be so scared. Because underneath all your bullshit, I think it's possible you aren't totally irredeemable. Like, a twenty percent chance."

"Only twenty?" he asked, acting shocked. "Is there anything I can do to convince you?"

"Hmm. Maybe."

Blake bend down, cupping her face with his hands. He kissed her, softer than he'd ever kissed any other woman. It was just a brush of the lips, but it felt like it lasted forever. And when he pulled back, his eyes meeting hers, he knew.

"Wow."

"I know," Noelle said, touching her fingers to her lips.

"No chemistry whatsoever," he concluded.

"Yeah. I thought my first kiss was going to have fireworks or something," she agreed. "It was kind of like putting my lips on a piece of wet ham."

"Gee, thanks."

"You really should brush your teeth before you go kissing people."

"Well, that sucks," Blake muttered. "So…friends?"

"Yes, but don't make eye contact with me for at least a week." Noelle paused, looking around. Thankfully, no one seemed to be paying attention to them. "And don't tell anyone we did this. I don't want my family to lose respect for me."

"Deal."

They shook hands with a laugh. Relief washed over him, glad that nothing would come of this. It felt like a natural next step, but when they actually took it…

Awful.

He didn't need another girlfriend, anyway. He just needed Noelle, as she was.

But whatever lingered between them didn't last as Loren Blackwood's voice cut through the air. "What do you think you're doing?"

Blake froze and turned. His father stood before them, his cold blue eyes glaring down at Noelle. To her credit, she met his gaze easily with her own fierce expression.

"I asked," Loren said, "what you were doing."

Blake's initial shock gave way to fear, a reaction that was as involuntary as it was intense. The presence of his father, not intimidating in stature but formidable in aura, seemed to dwarf everything else around them.

"I was just dancing," Blake managed, his voice betraying his nerves. "I didn't expect to see you here."

"With her?" Loren pointed in Noelle's face.

Blake moved between them. "She's my friend."

"Friends do not stick their tongue down their friends' throats. Any idiot would understand that," Loren scoffed. "Do not make a scene. Let her go. There's no use wasting your time with someone like her."

"What do you mean by that?" Noelle asked coolly. She

wasn't putting on a front—she truly wasn't afraid. She hadn't seen what Loren was capable of just yet.

"I think you know exactly what I mean."

Blake wanted to say something, to stand up for Noelle and reclaim some semblance of control. But the words wouldn't come, choked off by a lifetime of learned helplessness in the face of his father.

The tightness in his chest escalated into a suffocating pressure. He recognized the signs of a panic attack—something he'd experienced in the shadows of his interactions with his father before. But never had he felt it so acutely, so overwhelmingly, in public.

Loren turned to Blake. "Of the two female monsters, why would you choose the uglier one?"

"I—I..." Blake stammered, fighting for air, for words, for courage. But the words wouldn't come, his tongue heavy and useless in his mouth.

"Excuse me." Someone tapped Loren's shoulder. He turned, revealing a very angry, very scantily-clad Kitty. "What the fuck did you just say about my sister?"

TWENTY-NINE

CINDERELLA'S COACH became a pumpkin at midnight. Melody turned into one a little past nine, and regretted it as soon as she got to the gymnasium.

Not because she thought she looked stupid, though she did. Her costume was as cumbersome as it was unsexy, but she didn't mind. The pointed green hat, meant to represent a stem, and cumbersome velvet sphere strapped to her body made for a fun outfit. The only problem was how difficult it made getting food. She could barely reach down and grab a cupcake without knocking over the entire display. And punch? Forget about it.

She hovered over the table of food, hoping that maybe some of the crumbs left on the napkins would fly up into her mouth. Why couldn't she had been gifted with telekinesis instead of aura-reading? The former would have been a more useful power. Clearly. Aside from the fact that reading auras left her vulnerable, her inability to decipher what the colors meant rendered the power practically useless. The college didn't even find it worth studying, since the power was so rare. She didn't know where to start when it came to testing it.

Melody stood there, mouth open like a catfish, until she was bumped to the side by a couple of kids trying to get a closer look at the table. She stepped aside to let them pass, slightly annoyed at herself. She wanted to ask for help, but part of her was concerned they'd say no. And yes, she knew that a stranger's rejection wouldn't mean much in the grand scheme of things. She wasn't looking to befriend them, she just needed someone to help her get some damn food.

She felt a hand on her shoulder.

"You're blocking the table."

She looked up. There stood Jax Swan, looking delicious as ever. Puberty had been kind to him. Could she even call it puberty if it hit at seventeen? She felt like a creep, because despite being only two years older than him, she was acutely aware he was still in high school. Not that he looked too young for her, or anything. He was tall, with muscles cording his arms and a face chiseled from stone. His cheekbones were high, his lips full, and his eyes were a deep brown, so dark they were almost black. It was a far cry from the scrawny kid she met earlier in the year.

He wore a white t-shirt with a yellow circle on it and a headband with devil horns.

"Let me guess," Melody said. "You're a deviled egg?"

He didn't smile. In fact, she couldn't remember ever seeing him smile. If he wasn't scowling at something Kitty said, he wore a neutral expression, almost bored, as if he had better things to do in every situation. It didn't take an empath to tell he wasn't interested in anything but studying cultivation, which was admirable in a way.

"You are the first person to get it," he told her politely. He had two modes: bratty brother and distant but cold. When his siblings weren't around, the defaulted to the latter. Perhaps he was like Cyrus, in that way. "Do you need help?"

"Huh?"

"With the food," he gestured.

She hadn't expected him to offer. They weren't friends, not by a long shot, and she knew he wasn't exactly a people-person. But she really wanted a cupcake. "Yes, please."

To her shock, he prepared a plate for her. "Here."

"Thanks." She accepted the food, feeling her cheeks turn pink. "Aren't you hungry?"

"No. Bà cooked dinner earlier." He helped her to a table and, when she sat down, he pushed in the chair. It was such an old-fashioned thing to do, like something out of a movie. She wondered if his mother had trained him to act that way, or if he had picked it up elsewhere.

Melody tried to reach for her cupcake, but she couldn't bring it to her mouth. Maybe she'd died and gone to hell. She tried again. The cupcake refused to meet her lips.

Jax frowned. "Here, let me help."

Before she could react, he grabbed the cupcake and pressed it to her lips. Her entire face flushed. What was he doing? Did he know how this looked? He fed her the dessert, and she tried not to choke. The boy had no tact, but the cupcake tasted sweet. After a few bites, he brought the punch to her lips. This was humiliating.

"I'm not helpless, you know." She tried not to snap.

"No," he agreed, "you just didn't think this costume through."

She sighed. "I really didn't. I'm glad someone is here to help me, but don't you think people will get the wrong idea?"

He set the cupcake down. "About what?"

"You feeding me," she lowered her voice.

He looked at her like she had two heads. "What are you talking about? I'm just helping you eat. It's not like we're doing something dirty."

She was speechless. The kid was clueless. "You really don't think it looks like we're dating?"

Jax choked on air, his face turning cherry red. "No!"

"Gee, thanks."

"I didn't mean it like that," he mumbled.

Melody rolled her eyes. "I know. I'm just messing with you. Thanks for the food. You didn't have to do that."

"Sure."

"I—" She stopped. She didn't even know what she was about to say, but it wasn't nearly as important as the girl standing by the double doors on the left. The blonde smiled, waving as if beckoning Melody over. Her hair was loose around her shoulders, the curls brushing her elbows. And then, she turned and pushed the doors open.

Melody jumped to her feet, racing after her. Jax was hot on her heels, barreling through the sea of costumed students. When they reached the door, it was locked. Melody circled around to the main entrance, sprinting outside. Jax chased after her, his boots thudding against the ground.

"Where are you going?" he demanded.

"Did you see her?"

"Who?"

"Tessa," she breathed. "I swear, it was Tessa Churchill."

She knew it was impossible. Tessa was dead, long dead. But after the incident in the Veil, Melody had her doubts, regardless of what Professor Everleigh claimed. She knew in her bones that she had seen Tessa Churchill, or her doppelganger. And the look in her eye, the smile on her face.

The message had been clear.

"Find me."

THE PLAYBOY BUNNY thing was Kitty's idea, but Veronica didn't see her friend anywhere when she entered the gym.

The party was in full swing by that point, and admittedly, she'd run late putting on her makeup and squeezing into the blue satin bodysuit. It hugged her almost to the point of indecency, and Veronica hadn't quite realized how much of her cleavage would be on display until she put it on. The pain was worth how great her boobs looked. Apparently, her peers agreed, because several wolf whistles followed her as she wove through the crowd.

Was there anything more uncomfortable than coming to a party where none of her friends showed up? She saw a handful of her classmates she recognized, but none of the Swans were there. Mel should have been a spectacle in her stupid pumpkin costume—she'd turned down the Playboy Bunny idea, saying something about not wanting to objectify herself.

Veronica tried not to feel too disappointed. She floated toward the snack table and popped a few cookies into her mouth, along with a cup of punch. If no one was going to show up, she'd head back to her dorm and change out of her costume. Maybe take a shower and put on a sheet mask before bed.

"Veronica."

She turned. Ryder stood behind her, dressed in black pants and a black t-shirt that showed off his arms. "Where's your costume?"

"It's a funny story, I was going to be a Playboy Bunny, but I changed my mind. Good thing, or you would have been pretty embarrassed," he joked, his eyes roving down her body.

"I don't know," she replied, trying not to let the heat rise to her cheeks. "I think I make a pretty good Playboy Bunny."

Ryder's lips curled upward. "You certainly do."

A beat of silence passed between them.

"You want to get out of here?" he asked.

"I just got here. And I'm supposed to meet Kitty."

"I saw Kitty leave earlier. Her sister, too," Ryder added. "She and Blake left together."

Noelle and Blake? That was a match made in hell. Veronica couldn't help but snort. She liked Noelle but wasn't concerned—those two were like oil and water.

Wait. Why was she even sizing up Noelle as a potential rival for Blake? Veronica and Blake weren't together anymore. He was free to see whomever he pleased. Old habits die hard, indeed.

"Alright," she found herself saying. If Kitty wasn't going to show up, then Vee might as well leave. She felt ridiculous standing around waiting. "We can talk about what you've found out regarding the facility in Tennessee."

"I don't know how much talking I feel like doing," Ryder murmured, taking her hand. She allowed him to guide her out the back and down the sloping path toward the football field. This part of the campus was deserted, and Veronica suddenly felt self-conscious in her scant attire. She didn't know where they were heading but was content to let him lead the way.

It wasn't very empowering of her, but she had always appreciated when Blake, and now Ryder, took charge. It relieved her from the burden of indecision, from the fear of making the wrong choice regardless of how simple it seemed.

Letting others steer her was, in a way, Veronica's safety net. It absolved her of the responsibility and the subsequent guilt when outcomes fell short of expectations. She could deflect blame, sparing herself the harsh introspection that came with acknowledging her own misjudgments.

It felt as if, when push came to shove, she feared where her choices might lead. Once decisions were made, it led her down paths that weren't easily altered, and she was uncertain when another opportunity to choose differently would arise. It was easier to rely solely on others for her happiness, or in most cases, her misery.

Once they reached the center of the field, Ryder stopped and faced her. His expression was unreadable, but she'd have to be a real idiot to not realize he wanted to kiss her.

Veronica couldn't deny she was a bit tempted, though it would likely be a mistake. But all her doubts swam to the back of her mind as Ryder cupped her face in his hands, and she lifted her chin, allowing her lips to brush his.

The kiss was soft at first, as if Ryder was unsure, but as Veronica melted against him, he deepened the kiss. He tasted like peppermint and chocolate, and he smelled like expensive cologne. One of his hands moved down to her waist, and the other remained cradling her cheek. She thought of Blake, and how he used to kiss her. Now, she knew he was thinking about someone else. But Ryder? He was all hers, and he was kissing her with abandon.

Blake had come to her dorm the other day to apologize, though. Or was that another excuse to get her back in his bed? No, she couldn't trust him, not after what he had done.

And why was she thinking of Blake anyway, when Ryder was kissing her?

The thought caused her to pull away. "Ryder... What is this?"

"What is what?"

"This. Us."

Ryder smiled and shrugged. "It's whatever we want it to be. I told you, didn't I, Vee? I like you. A lot. I can't get you out of my head."

A rush of pleasure coursed through her at his admission. So he thought of her as special, after all. It was nice to be wanted, to be desired.

"I like you, too," she admitted. "But I can't... I can't promise anything right now."

He pressed his forehead against hers. "You don't have to promise anything. We're friends, Vee, and we can be more—if you want. But you can set the pace. I'll follow wherever you lead."

"You mean it?"

Ryder nodded; his expression serious. "Of course."

And, in that moment, she wanted to believe him. So, she did.

THE PLAYBOY BUNNY costume was one she already owned. She'd worn it two years ago, her senior year of high school, and it had been a hit.

She looked good, and she knew it. The pink satin body suit gave her curves she normally didn't have, and the sheer tights made her legs look nice. Shallow as it was, she enjoyed the attention, and the compliments that came with the outfit.

Of course, reality had a harsh way of humbling her. Not even an hour into the party, and she was ready to rip her ears off and stuff them down the throat of the first person who muttered something about prostitution under their breath.

"...looks like a whore..."

"I bet she'll spread her legs for anything that moves..."

"Did you see her cleavage? Or lack thereof?"

"If I saw her on the street, I'd call the police."

Kitty was no longer a mean girl—trying not to be, anyway—which meant she couldn't call anyone a troll-faced skank, Billy Bob bitch, or any other insult that sprang to mind. Instead, she pretended she couldn't hear them, and hoped they'd choke on their own saliva.

Yeah, not very nice of her.

She was just killing time until Veronica got there, anyway.

She scanned the crowd, searching for Veronica's red head, when she saw her sister. Kitty smiled, making her way over, when she heard an ugly voice.

"Of the two female monsters, why would you choose the uglier one?"

Kitty didn't close her eyes and count to ten like she was supposed to. She didn't think at all. "Excuse me. What the fuck did you just say about my sister?"

The man turned, and immediately, she knew this had to be Blake's father. The two looked identical, save their expressions. Arrogance set in every line of his face, his cold, calculating eyes reminding her of a snake. Meanwhile, his son looked like he was going to pass out.

Kitty never saw Blake like this, and it took her a few seconds to realize he was afraid of his father.

"Kitty." Noelle touched her arm. "Let's go."

"No," she said, not breaking eye contact with the old bastard. "No one talks about you like that. Ever."

"Haughty, aren't we?" Mr. Blackwood commented. "But I

suppose, if the article Dr. Woods penned is to be believed, you both think you're better than us, don't you? Even though all you are is mortal trash, with no higher brain capacity than an ape. You should know your place."

"I know yours—at the bottom of the fucking ocean like the scum-sucking bottom-feeder you are."

"Ah, and when the monster is confronted, she resorts to violence. How typical. I didn't realize they let uncivilized mongrels into Northeastern. It seems the standard has dropped."

"Dad, don't—"

Mr. Blackwood raised his hand. Kitty could've sworn Blake flinched, and that pissed her off. "Don't interrupt."

"Kitty!" Noelle grabbed her arm. "Stop it, right now!"

"Nell—"

"No! You're embarrassing me. Can't you see that?" Noelle looked around, her voice dropping low. "Do you have any idea how many people are watching this?"

Kitty didn't care. She had already learned to ignore the stares, the pointed, judgmental looks that hadn't stopped since she stepped foot on campus and only worsened with time. "I can't let him talk about you like that. It's not true, and it's—"

"You're worse than him! Do you understand that? Do you know how small you make me feel when you 'defend' me like this? It's humiliating."

"How is it humiliating?" Kitty demanded, unsure where to direct her anger and frustration, a volatile tangle of emotions knotting in her stomach. "I'm defending you. He's the one who started it."

Noelle laughed sardonically. "He's an asshole. I don't care what he thinks. I'm eighteen, Kitty. I don't need you to swoop in and fight my battles for me, like a child!"

"I-I'm just trying to help you," Kitty stammered, the fight draining out of her.

"And what exactly do you think you're helping me with?" Noelle's lip curled. "You're making me look weak. I can stand up for myself. But you don't get it, do you? You never have."

Kitty shook her head, not knowing what to say. Her hands were trembling, her throat tight. She felt sick.

"I wish you weren't my sister." Noelle spun around, stomping through the crowd, shoving her way out.

Kitty watched her go, feeling numb. She had to leave. She couldn't stay here, with people looking at her like...

She pushed through the throng of people, ignoring the whispers that followed her as she made her way out. She needed air. She felt claustrophobic, like the walls were closing in on her.

Noelle and Kitty had fought before, plenty of times. And of course, Nell had thrown those words around. But this time, there was weight behind them, and Kitty knew her sister meant every word. Worse, Kitty was more certain than ever that she had a point.

Her parents told her constantly growing up that she needed to protect her siblings. She was the oldest; she had to be strong for them, emotionally and physically. But now that they were older, had her care turned into control? Did Jax feel the same way?

Kitty found herself on the roof of the main building, staring at the stars, wishing she was one of them—a billion miles away from Earth.

"Well, that was...something."

She didn't bother turning around, instead, pulling her knees closer to her chest. "You saw?"

"Mmhm. An angry bunny girl is hard to miss," Cyrus said, sitting beside her. "You okay?"

"Yeah." She wiped at her face. "No. I think I'm a horrible person, and no matter how much effort I put in to change, I'm naturally just...awful. Sometimes I wonder if I'm not trying hard enough; other times, I wonder if it's impossible to fight something so innate. I wanted to help my sister, but instead, I've hurt her."

"I guess. But from my perspective, she was being kinda harsh. What were you supposed to do, stand by and do nothing?" he asked. "I don't know if Noelle would have been happy with that option, either. It seems like her reaction was less about you and more about something she's trying to work though herself."

"It still hurts."

"I'm sure it does," he agreed, rubbing her back. "And I'm sorry about that. She'll come around, especially once the adrenaline has worn off."

"You think?"

"Yeah. Regardless of what she said, she really loves you. Anyone can see that."

Kitty sniffed. "You aren't supposed to be doing this, you know. Comforting me. It's against the rules."

"We're friends. I can comfort you as a friend," he pointed out.

"I don't like being...vulnerable. Especially not in front of you."

"Why 'especially' me?"

She didn't answer. For the first time since he arrived, she turned to look at him. It was a mistake. He wore a tailored suit, black and slim, his hair neatly combed. She wanted to run her hands through it, to kiss him until he was breathless. A sash hung across his chest, reading 'I'm Sorry'.

His costume was a formal apology.

Kitty burst into laughter. "You're the worst. In so many ways."

"What? I thought you'd like it," Cy said with a grin.

"You're so lame."

"You love it."

Her smile faltered at the word, forbidden between them, even in jest. But it was too late. It was already out there, floating between them. "If I were really a good person, I'd end it. I'd walk away, and I wouldn't look back."

She didn't have to clarify what she was talking about.

"If that's the case, then I'm the most despicable person to walk the face of the Earth," Cyrus said, "because I wouldn't let you go."

"Don't say that," she warned. "Glitter."

"Kitty..."

"I mean it. I'm already bending the rules for you. Don't make this harder than it has to be," she said.

"You won't even let me say the words?"

Words they both felt in their souls, words they both knew were true and dangerous in equal measure.

"What would be the point?" Kitty asked. "We know how it will end."

"I know," he said, frustrated. "I just...wish things were different."

"Yeah. Me too." But they weren't, and it was high time Kitty accepted it before things went too far. Though, she had a feeling she was already beyond saving. "I don't think we should see each other for a while. In any capacity."

To her surprise, he nodded. "You're right. Maybe we need to cool down. Take a break."

Her chest hurt, and she didn't want to agree. But she had to, because if she didn't, she was going to do something stupid. And that wouldn't be fair to him. If she were truly going to be a better person, a kinder, less selfish individual, this was how it had to be.

"Can you give me a minute?" he asked. "Let's just... pretend that the world is going to end in sixty seconds, and whatever happens next won't matter."

"Sixty seconds," she repeated. What was the harm in that?

When he kissed her this time, she really did feel like the world was ending around them, crumbling like sand.

THE MUSIC from downstairs was muffled. Nora hardly paid attention as she snuck into the apothecary's closet for spell equipment. It wasn't difficult. In some older parts of the main building, the storage rooms still used a lock and key. She swiped the key from Everleigh when he wasn't paying attention and had it copied. Voilà.

Her phone screen glowed bright in the dark room, illuminating the shelves filled with ingredients. She had a list of what she needed and set about gathering them, careful to take only what she needed and shove it into her bag. She didn't want to take excess, since a professor might notice and figure out what she was up to.

No one knows what you're up to, Nora thought. *How would they guess?*

Being a magician, Nora knew that blood magic was forbidden. Death curses, hexes, they all had a chance of going wrong, but at this point, she didn't care. She knew what she wanted and she was going to go for it: for her father, and for the greater shadowborn community.

She read the articles, the news, and knew that things were going to hell. All because of Kitty Swan.

Blood magic might have been forbidden, but this? This was community service.

Nora began mixing the ingredients as soon as she got to her dorm room. She didn't have a cauldron, so she used a coffee mug. She poured the liquids in, one at a time, following the instructions as she added each new ingredient.

It wasn't a difficult potion, but the ingredients were rare, and the timing was precise. The last step was adding a drop of her blood. Her hand was steady, the blade sharp. She held her finger over the mug, watching the crimson drop form. She let it fall, and the liquid changed colors, turning pure white.

The color of death.

A plume of smoke blew in her face, stealing the life from her lungs. She coughed, fanning her hand to clear the air, but the potion settled inside her, stealing her life force as the final step.

For a life to be taken, one must be given. And once Nora Kemp's heart stopped, and her corpse tumbled forward onto the carpet of her dorm, Thompson Everleigh stepped out of the shadows and looked down at the bloodless body before him. He bent down, reaching for the only thing left in the coffee mug: a scrap of paper, hastily written but still legible.

"Kitty Swan."

The death curse was complete.

NORTHEASTERN TRIBUNE

HALLOWEEN AT NORTHEASTERN: A NIGHT OF FUN MARRED BY MISJUDGMENT

The annual Halloween dance at Northeastern College, a beloved tradition that marks the height of the fall semester, was celebrated with much fanfare this past weekend. The evening was a ball of ghoulish delight as students donned their most creative and spine-tingling costumes. Yet, amid the success of the event, a shadow was cast by choices that veered sharply from the spirit of fun and into the realm of the inappropriate.

In a surprising lapse in judgment, some students opted for costumes that left little to the imagination, notably embodying figures such as Playboy bunnies—a choice that has sparked a conversation about the image we project to the wider shadowborn community, especially with parents in attendance. Among those at the center of this controversy is Katherine Swan, whose costume choice has raised eyebrows and drawn criticism.

Katherine has been the subject of numerous harsh articles in recent times. Her choice, while questionable, highlights a broader issue of cultural assimilation and understanding. Coming from a background vastly different from the typical American upbringing, her faux pas sheds light on the challenges faced by foreigners across the country.

It is crucial to approach those different from us with empathy rather than judgment. The costume, undoubtedly, was in poor taste. However, this misstep offers a teachable moment, not just for Katherine but for all of us. It underscores the importance of cultural sensitivity and the role of education.

No one should be judged solely on aspects of themselves they could not control, such as race and gender. As the more sophisticated civilization, it is our duty to teach those beneath us advancements so they may one day strive to assimilate.

THIRTY

"SHE DUMPED YOU IN A BUNNY COSTUME," Blake repeated incredulously. "You know, man, that would only happen to you."

"She didn't *dump* me," Cyrus grumbled. That would have implied they had been dating, which they hadn't been. In his own words, it was a purely physical relationship.

He wished he could go back in time and punch himself in the jaw. Maybe then, he could prevent himself from agreeing to that stupid treaty, and...

And what?

Cyrus shook his head. It didn't matter. Time travel didn't exist, and if it did, there were bigger problems than the fact that Kitty had ended their...whatever the hell they were. He knew it was for the best, that she wanted to save them both the heartbreak later on, when he began to age and she stayed exactly the same. But...

Did she have to be dressed as a Playboy Bunny when she did it?

He sighed, trying not to think about it and failing miserably.

"You look like you could use a stiff drink," Blake said, sitting down at the desk in their room.

Cyrus snorted. "You offering?"

"Oh, God no. I don't have any alcohol. I was just making a comment about the general unpleasantness of your expression." Blake rummaged through his bag, placing what Cyrus hoped was lemonade on the table. "It's warm."

"Appetizing." He didn't need cheering up; it made him feel like a loser, moping around about something he'd known from the start was a bad idea. Oh no, the consequences of his actions actually hurt!

Idiot.

"When's your dad leaving?" Cyrus asked, changing the subject.

Blake snorted. "Not soon enough. Though I kind of hope he sticks around for a little longer. Maybe he'll run into Mrs. Swan and she'll beat him up, like she did to Mr. Churchill. Damn, do I wish I could've seen that. Noelle didn't film it, sadly, but she told me all about it."

"You talk to Noelle?" That was news to Cy.

"We're...friends."

"Oh, you got a new best friend? Should I be jealous?"

"Don't worry. No one could *ever* replace you," Blake said, batting his eyelashes.

Cyrus rolled his eyes, but in truth, he was surprised at the unlikely pairing. He thought they hated each other, and at a glance, they were different as night and day. "I'm honored. You're sure she doesn't see you as more than a friend, though?"

"Well, I kissed her last night, and we both agreed it was

gross. So it looks like we're just friends. My first platonic female friend. How exciting."

"And what was Charity?"

A complicated look crossed Blake's face, and Cyrus was certain he would change the subject or evade the question with a crude comment. Instead, he said, "You're right. Charity was my friend. But I think I screwed the pooch on that one."

Cyrus stepped closer, peering into his friend's eyes. "Who are you, and what have you done with Blake Blackwood?"

"Screw you," Blake snapped, but the corner of his mouth was turned up in a smile. "I'm allowed to be deep and introspective. And maybe a bit philosophical."

"Uh-huh."

"Hey, can I ask you a question? Like, a private question?"

"What happens in the dorm stays in the dorm," Cyrus agreed solemnly.

"Really? Is that the rule? Because if so, I told, like, a lot of people that I caught you and Kitty bumping uglies."

"Dude."

"Sorry, should I have told them you were smashing? Shagging? Bow-chick-a-wow-wow?"

"I hate you."

"No you don't. You love me, because I'm your BBF: Best Blake Forever. Or should it be BBL? Best Blake (for) Life?" he mused. "Whatever the case, friends don't steal their friends' condoms. That's like, bro code. You could've just asked like a normal person."

"If I said anything, you'd have been a dog about it."

"I can't help it! It's in my DNA," Blake insisted. "But come on. You and Kitty? That's something out of a bad porno. The geek boinking the cheer captain? Of course I would have needed all the details. I still do, actually."

"Boinked," Cyrus repeated.

"You're deflecting."

"Whatever. It just goes to show that we haven't talked much since the semester started."

"That's on me," Blake admitted, his lips twisting to a frown. "I know I've been an ass lately. I also know you've been putting up with me, even though you shouldn't have to. And I'm sorry about that. I'm not going on some self-help binge like your girlfriend, but I've been talking to Noelle, and it's enlightening, to say the least. To say the most, she's a total bitch, but in a good way. Runs in the family, I guess."

"One, Kitty was never my girlfriend, and she's not a bitch. All the time. Two, I have to ask...why Noelle?"

"She hated me. Her opinion of me couldn't have gotten lower. There was some comfort in that. But disappointing you?" Blake scratched his head. "Don't make me get sappy on you."

"So you had a heart-to-heart and realized the error of your ways?"

"Something like that. To be honest, some things are difficult to accept. And Charity is one of them." He paused. "She told me she loved me."

"...And you were surprised?"

"You knew?"

"It was obvious." Charity didn't usually show her emotions, but there was a tenderness in her eyes when she looked at Blake. You didn't have to be a genius to put two and two together. "Why do you look so unhappy?"

"She compared me to my dad."

That was the worst insult she could have thrown—and she'd said it knowingly. "That's bullshit."

"Is it?" Blake let out a bitter laugh. "We have the same

blood. Same genes. I've got the same temper, the same penchant for cruelty, and the same lack of moral compass. He treated women like trash, like they were subhuman. When I was with Veronica, I only thought of myself. Charity, too. They were just bodies, just tools to make myself feel better. Part of me can't even comprehend the amount of damage I've done to them. I fucked up, bad. And I don't think I can fix it with an apology. Even if I do...what's stopping it from happening again? I'm my father's son."

Cyrus shook his head. "I don't know if they'll forgive you, but the fact that you're trying means something. Maybe, in time, you can find a way to make it up to them."

"And you?" Blake asked. "Will you forgive me for being an irredeemable ass?"

"Will *you* forgive *me* for stealing your condoms?"

The boys shook hands. "Deal."

CHEN JIANHAO WAS the last person Noelle expected to see. It was five AM, and Noelle had been doing a pretty good job of avoiding her siblings. Three days had passed since Halloween, and she knew she owed her sister an apology. But she was afraid she would apologize for *everything*, when really, the only thing she was sorry about was the very last part. It was a childish, hurtful thing to say, and Noelle hadn't meant it. Not in the way it had sounded, at least.

Kitty meant well, Noelle had to give her that. But her 'help' was often belittling, bordering on smothering. And, when Nell had tried to explain this to her parents after the argument, they didn't understand. Or they pretended not to. They never got in the middle of the siblings' arguments, preferring to have the kids settle their own fights. Regardless, they let her sleep in their apartment so she wouldn't have to return to the dorm with Kitty.

Noelle hadn't seen her since Halloween, spending as much time as possible in the library or working in the lab. Jianhao flitted in and out, so she was familiar with him, but they hadn't conversed extensively. Usually, he hung out with Jax. Noelle suspected her parents put him up to it. He also bothered Kitty from time to time; Nell might as well have been invisible. Classic for the middle child.

"A'Yue," he greeted, using the prefix "Ah" and the last character of her Chinese name, Ziyue, to form a nickname. "I'm glad we've run into each other."

"Are you?" She crossed her arms. "What can I do for you?"

"It's not what *you* can do for *me*. It's about what *I* can do for *you*."

"Said every sleazeball salesman ever." She continued walking, but damn him and his model-long legs, because he kept pace easily.

"I heard you had a spat with Xiao Xing at the dance the other day. It's a shame she embarrassed you."

"And what do you want, exactly? Are you gonna tell me that I need to be a better sister to Kitty, since she's older and I should respect her?" She didn't have to grow up in China to know how hierarchical society could be.

He surprised her. "Not at all. She may be older, but of all you Cao siblings, you have the most potential. You speak the best Chinese, are the most intelligent, and you are a diligent student."

Noelle blinked. What was the catch?

"You can't get ahead when your siblings are dragging you down," he said. Ah, there it was. "You would have broken through to the Core Formation stage, had your attention not been split between cultivation and caring for your sister. It's a full-time job, making sure she doesn't get into trouble, right?"

"It isn't like that," she protested, although his words echoed some of her earlier thoughts.

"Isn't it?"

"*No.*"

"Oh? You don't feel like she's always the center of attention, like she outshines you when really, she's not that special, is she?" Jianhao smiled. "The last character of your names is interesting. Yours is 'moon' and hers is 'star'. From where I stand, the moon outshines the stars. If only others could see that."

"How do you know my family is the reason I haven't cultivated as fast as I should?" Noelle demanded. "Maybe I'm not as dedicated or as diligent as you think."

"Come, now. You and I both know you are entitled to more than this paltry life. You're a human panacea; you're *special.* Yet your family continues to hold you back. They will never realize your potential. They will never understand, not like I do."

"You understand me?" she mocked, crossing her arms. Just where did he get off?

"I do."

"Really? So, you're an empath?"

"I've seen many like you. You are driven, talented, born with a gift. But your family, they are a weakness. I offer you a solution." He handed her a velvet box. Her breath caught. Was that an engagement ring? But no. The moment she opened it, her hands shaking, she saw a pearl no larger than her pinky sitting on a velvet cushion. "It's a refinement pill. I made it myself. It will give you the extra push you need to break through to the third level of cultivation. From there, your progress will continue uninterrupted."

"This is a pill?" Noelle asked, picking up the pearl to inspect it. "Why would you give me this?"

"Because I want to see you flourish. Your uncle sent me to help you, and that is exactly what I intend to do."

Why? She had yet to figure out Jianhao's relationship to Uncle Stefan, and what his motives were for helping. She should have walked away from the conversation outright, but found herself intrigued by his words nonetheless. "This is cheating, isn't it?"

"Of course not. Many cultivators use refined pills to assist with their journeys. They are not 'cheating', as you call it, and cannot spontaneously cause one to advance," Jianhao promised. "Think of it as a gift, A'Yue."

Noelle swallowed, her mouth suddenly dry.

He is manipulating you, a voice inside her head warned. *Just because you aren't paying for it now doesn't mean it is free—everything has a price, and you don't know enough about refinement pills to understand the true cost of the magic he promises.*

She knew that, damn it. And yet, she failed to refuse him immediately, too enamored by the other voice inside her head, the one whispering, *What if it works?*

"You can either continue on, living in your sister's shadow despite knowing that she is not nearly as strong as you are, or you can seize the opportunity, the gift, I am offering you. You may keep the pill and think on it."

But Noelle didn't think. It was easier not to.

It was easier to put the pill in her mouth and swallow.

"WHAT ARE we going to do about the dead girl?"

Jax was always very tactful. *Not.*

Melody stood in the doorway of her dorm, bleary-eyed. She hadn't slept the past few nights, having fallen down a rabbit hole of obsession, reading forums and watching videos about resurrection. Of course, humans who knew nothing of the shadowborn had created this content, so none of it was applicable. Didn't stop her from consuming every morsel of information she could find.

"What?" she asked. It was too early to entertain visitors, much less visitors like Jax Swan.

"The dead girl we saw. Tessa." He shouldered his way into her room, because apparently having two older sisters hadn't taught him about personal space. "What are we doing about that?"

She didn't think there was anything *to* do, except maybe go back to bed. She had already tried to tell Everleigh the first time she saw Tessa, and that was a dead end. How could she be insistent on something that seemed so impossible? Everleigh would only dismiss her if she brought it up again, and no other faculty member earned her trust like he did. Moreover, explaining what happened without sounding insane was a challenge in and of itself. "Hey, I know Tessa Churchill has been dead for nearly four years, but I think I saw her!" Yeah, that'd go over well.

Melody shook her head. "Nothing."

"Why would we do nothing?"

"We *can't* do anything."

"Of course we can," he argued. "Did you tell Charity?"

No way. Charity and Tessa never got along, and that didn't change just because the girl was dead. Melody knew that much. "Look, it's really not a big deal."

"Think about what's happening. The moving corpse that attacked Kitty, the groups of beastbloods turning feral, the increase in ferals as a whole...it's all very fishy, isn't it?" Jax insisted. "I think we should talk to your brother and my sister. Maybe they can figure out what's going on."

"In what universe is that a solid plan? If Cy finds out, Blake will catch on, and then... Kaboom!"

"Kaboom?"

"Yes, that was the entire world exploding." Did she not do a faithful job making the sound effect? "I don't even know for sure if it was her, or just someone who looked like her."

"You wouldn't be so freaked out if you didn't know for certain it was her."

He was right. Melody was almost positive it was Tessa. But the implications of that cast a shadow of apprehension over her, for the answers surrounding this mystery were likely complex. It was like a house of cards—if one fell, the entire structure would surely follow.

But on the other hand, if she did nothing, then what? Tessa couldn't have been up to anything good. Melody had no gripe with the woman—she barely knew her—but look at what she'd done so far. She'd made herself known, but only just enough. She hadn't asked for help; she laughed and lured, as if she wanted to lead Melody somewhere else.

Mel had seen enough horror movies to know that when a ghost wanted you to follow them, they weren't taking you to get ice cream and pet unicorns. They were guiding you to your doom.

Whether the entity *was* Tessa or merely looked exactly like her, its intentions were likely malicious. And that was cause for concern, wasn't it?

"Fine," Melody relented. "I need five minutes to change. Then, we'll talk to my brother."

"And Kitty," Jax added, not wanting to leave his sister out.

"Fine." Though she agreed, getting Kitty and Cyrus together wasn't the best idea. If Blake's gossip was to be believed, the two were in an awkward stage of their relationship. Or, non-relationship, since they'd broken up. Sort of. The details were hazy, and frankly, Mel tried to know as little about her brother's sex life as possible.

She changed and washed up, trying and failing to feel put together. It didn't help that the only clean shirt she had in her drawer featured SpongeBob. Five minutes later, she found herself barging into Cyrus's dorm.

Kitty had already taken a seat at the desk, looking rough around the edges. Maybe the cafeteria was out of coffee or something. Mel explained what she had experienced, with the occasional snarky comment from Jax, while their siblings listened. She tried her best to be succinct, but her thoughts jumbled and she had a tendency to ramble.

Cy's expression was grim by the end of it. "You haven't told Charity about the second incident, have you?"

"She's an ax-wielding fairy so tightly wound, she's ready to snap any second. Do you really think I'd risk getting chopped up, Lizzie Borden-style, on something I can't even confirm?"

"Borden was acquitted, for one," Jax chimed in unhelpfully. "Do you think she could be undead, like the moving corpse in the morgue?"

Cyrus considered it. "The body in the morgue was decaying. You're saying Tessa looked fine, though?"

"I didn't see up close," Mel said.

"She wasn't mostly bone, so I think it's safe to assume she looked more or less normal. She's been dead for years, now."

"We can't take anything we've observed and assume it applies here. The rules are changing, clearly."

"Not logically, either," Kitty added, blinking rapidly. She seemed worse for wear, dark circles ringing her under eyes. She leaned on her hand, propping her head up. "Nothing's natural about any of this."

"We go to a school for *super*naturals," Cyrus reminded her, trying not to be obvious about his concern. He didn't dare go near her, rooted to his spot by the window, but his eyes flicked to her every few seconds. He wouldn't linger, but somehow, that made his feelings more obvious. At least, to Mel. She doubted her brother recognized the feelings he held for Kitty, and if he did, her heart ached for him all the more.

"It's all a conspiracy. Someone's doing this." Kitty gestured, though her hand movements made as much sense as the words coming out of her mouth. "It's like...alien probes."

"Alien probes," Jax repeated.

She nodded. "They're testing."

"Testing what?"

"My patience."

Mel shook her head. "She has a point, though. Think about everything that's happening, and all the answers we lack. Cy, you think ferals are being led to this area somehow—ones who are not native to this portion of the Veil. The weather's been insane there, too. Moreso than usual, I mean."

"My parents think that ferals came to be because they're using improper cultivation techniques," Jax added. "But who would have taught them how to cultivate in the first place?"

"Evil scientists," Kitty answered. "You know. Like in a zombie movie. The government is trying to cure a disease or make super-soldiers or something, but it went terribly wrong, and now, wham! Undead uglies."

"You're basing your theory on fictional movies?"

"Non-fictional movies," she defended.

"Kitty, that doesn't even make sense. Are you okay?"

"Sleep deprived," she muttered. "Nothing serious."

Melody took what her friend said into consideration. "Alright. So let's assume they are doing experiments, and our school is a test site, of sorts. Why? And who's running this, the school? The SNPD?"

"Could be either," Cyrus acknowledged. "Northeastern and Southeastern are fairly secluded. But maybe the difference is the chancellors. Southeastern is run by Chancellor Aeynore, who is childhood friends with Lady Torren."

"Who?" Jax asked.

"Lady Toren is an elf trueblood, once part of the elven noble lineage, hundreds of years ago. The monarchy was dissolved, but she still had a ton of money, and she used her private wealth to fund initiatives to aid shadowborns. She started the shadowborn schools in America," Melody explained. "She took a step back from running things in the last century, though. But she and Chancellor Aeynore, being elves, can tell when people are lying. It's like, their special power."

"If anything shifty was going on at Southeastern, Aeynore would know about it. Chancellor Kinsey is not a trueblood, though. And, let's face it, he's not the most trustworthy administrator," Cyrus said. "I'm more inclined to believe he'd be bribed, by money, power, or both. But still, even if Northeastern is a test site, what are they testing?"

"Either they're testing a cure for the feral illness—unethically," Kitty said, "or the feral illness is a result of the testing. For super-soldiers."

"Against who? We're not at war," Cyrus said.

She snorted. "Clearly, that doesn't matter. If I've learned anything since coming here, it's that anyone different will be perceived as a threat and harassed to oblivion."

His brow creased. "Have people been bothering you?"

"The way the feral illness operates is interesting," Jax interrupted. "Infected bodies decompose rapidly. If whoever is running these experiments were to kidnap a few students under the guise of a horde attack, no one would question the lack of corpses."

"Kidnap them as test subjects? Now you *really* sound like you've got anime brain rot," Melody commented.

"As opposed to your regular brain rot?"

"Get bent."

"Children, please." Kitty held up a hand, her manicure chipped. "I'm gonna go out on a limp and say that Chancellor Kinsey is either involved, or is getting paid off."

"Limp? You mean limb?" Cyrus asked.

"That's what I said."

"No, it isn't." He shook his head. "But I agree—Kinsey is in on it, to some capacity. But what can we do? Ask him about it?"

"No, we sneak into his office and steal his shit. Duh."

"Yes, let's waltz in and ask him to hand over his evidence—or else," Jax said sarcastically.

"I bet Wyatt Ainsworth can get you in. And Chancellor Kinsey won't be there when we do the third Blood Trial. He has to proctor it."

"This isn't the soundest plan ever," Melody pointed out.

"It isn't," Cyrus agreed, "but it's all we've got."

THIRTY-ONE

RAPPING her knuckles on Kitty's door, Veronica assumed her friend would be awake already. She usually went by the gym early in the morning, and with the Blood Trial coming up tomorrow, Vee predicted Kitty would be finishing her shower right about now.

It was unusually quiet around campus, a lull following the Halloween party and the end of the midterms. Parents were still making their way home after a week of visits—her own her notably absent.

Veronica had used her spare time wisely: obsessing over the footage Ryder had shared, trying and failing to piece together what it meant. She needed more context, more information than what a few stills and fuzzy videos could offer. And, while she could have gone to Ryder and talked through her thoughts, she refrained.

Not out of pride, or anything silly like that. But after thinking it over, she realized the obvious: he was holding things back from her. He might have requested her assistance in Tennessee, but there was another game afoot, and part of her wondered if he really needed her help at all with this, or if it was just a ploy to get close to her.

Because he likes me.

The thought was more flattering than it should have been. Ultimately, however, she didn't trust that he would be upfront if she questioned him. Perhaps her relationship with Blake had poisoned her against all men. Either way, she didn't have time for a round of psychoanalysis. When the men in her life failed her, as they so often did, she turned to her female friends.

Admittedly, she hadn't been the best when it came to supporting what few women graced her life. Kitty didn't make it easy, being all but unreachable by phone. Which was why, on that early Saturday morning, Vee waited outside her door. However, when Kitty finally answered, she looked—and smelled—awful.

Veronica couldn't just come out and *say* that. Kitty would flip a shit if she knew how sallow she looked, or that her hair wasn't as shiny as it used to be. And to mention her smell? She'd probably throw herself headfirst out the window!

"You look like you haven't slept in days," Veronica blurted.

"I haven't," Kitty said, annoyance clear in her voice. "What do you want?"

Veronica scanned her up and down. Oh no. Her socks didn't match. Something was *seriously* wrong here!

She hobbled—*hobbled*—back into her room, tripping over her own two feet. Her movements were sluggish and lacked her usual grace. Alarm bells went off in Veronica's head, and she decided then and there that her friend needed help. And a shower.

"Come on. Let's get you cleaned up," she said gently. Kitty complied, following Veronica to the bathroom.

The two girls entered and Veronica started the water. She

made sure it was warm and began pulling off Kitty's clothes. Her friend was too out of it to resist. After the shower, Veronica dried her hair and helped into a comfortable track-suit. At that point, she was practically limp in her bed. Her eyes remained unsettlingly open, hardly blinking.

Just what happened that would make her so...

"Is this about Cyrus?" Veronica had heard the gist from Melody. She tried very hard not to confront her friend immediately, but inside, she was a bit hurt Kitty didn't tell her about it. They were supposed to be best friends. Not that they owed each other secrets, but... Was Veronica so unreliable that Kitty couldn't confide in her?

Veronica ended up bringing her to the nurse's office; no easy feat, given Kitty's size. She wasn't much taller than Vee, but her muscles were more developed. When they got there, Kitty didn't protest at all. Veronica had never seen her so docile before, and briefly wondered if this was an Invasion of the Body Snatchers situation.

However, when it was their turn to be seen by the nurse, the older woman wrinkled her nose. "She just looks a touch tired, is all."

Veronica struggled to keep her friend upright. "*A touch tired?* She looks like she's about to keel over. Can't you give her a magic sleeping potion or something?"

"No can do," the nurse said without hesitation.

"Why not?"

The nurse sighed, putting a hand on the counter. "I have a lot of students to take care of, and for someone like her, I wouldn't even know if the potion would work. I don't have time to waste on someone who could come back and sue me if the potion failed, or worse. Just take her back to the dorms and get some Nyquil in her."

"You won't even examine her?"

"I can see her just fine. And there's nothing to indicate anything else is wrong, aside from the lack of sleep."

"This is ridiculous. We're at a magic college, and you're suggesting I run to the school store for *Nyquil*?"

The nurse frowned, folding her arms across her chest. "You're right; Northeastern is a magic college. And yet, they allow someone like *her* in our ranks. If she were a normal shadowborn, I could treat her. But she's not. If she gets sick, her people should be helping her, not me."

Veronica fumed, but there wasn't anything left to say. She could hardly force the rude nurse to take care of Kitty, so she decided to go to the next best person: Professor Everleigh. While he wasn't a medical doctor, he knew his way around a potion, and he wouldn't refuse care to anyone.

Veronica hadn't seen him since last semester, and she wasn't sure how to approach him since Rory's death. But with Kitty's health at stake, she had little choice in the matter.

The office door was open when the girls arrived, which was a good thing, since Veronica didn't have a spare hand. Professor Everleigh sat at his desk, reading a book. His face lit up at the sight of her.

"Veronica!" He closed the book and set it on his desk. "And...Katherine? My, she looks quite sick. Should she really be out of bed?"

"I tried to take her to the nurse," Veronica explained, struggling to keep her friend standing. Everleigh guided them both to the chairs in front of his desk. His office was cleaner than Veronica had ever seen it, the shelves dusted and the papers filed. His TA this semester must have worked overtime to get the place spick and span. "Can you look at her?"

"Of course," he said, kneeling before Kitty. "Katherine, are you able to hear me?"

"My name's not Katherine," she muttered. She said something else, but Veronica didn't quite understand her slurred speech.

"Is she talking gibberish?" Professor Everleigh asked.

"Yeah," Veronica replied, concerned. "I think she's suffering from some sort of stress-induced insomnia."

"Perhaps she's more concerned about the Blood Trials than she let on."

No, that wasn't it. Kitty had passed the other two trials pretty easily—according to her, at least. Was her friend downplaying the difficulties? Or was there another reason why she couldn't sleep? Maybe it had something to do with Cyrus.

"I'm sorry," Kitty said, looking around. "Where am I?"

"I brought you to Professor Everleigh's office," Veronica explained patiently. "You don't remember?"

"No..."

"That's troubling," the professor muttered, stroking his chin.

"Do you know what's going on?" Veronica asked him.

"I think she just needs a good night's sleep. I'll give her something for that. Why don't you two wait here while I gather the ingredients?"

He left the room, leaving Veronica alone with Kitty. She slumped in her chair, shutting her eyes.

"Someone's been watching me," Kitty croaked. "I can feel it. The qi is off in my room."

"What?"

"They're watching," Kitty reiterated with a weak insistence. The randomness and gravity of her statement left Veronica bewildered. Who could be watching? And for what purpose? Was Kitty's sleep deprivation causing hallucinations, or was there a more sinister element at play?

"*Who* is watching?"

Kitty could only shake her head, her expression a mix of frustration and fatigue.

"Do you remember anything else?"

She shook her head again. Veronica sighed, rubbing her temples. Why was everything so damn complicated these days?

Professor Everleigh returned, carrying a steaming mug. "Drink this. It will help."

Kitty accepted the drink, and without question, guzzled it down.

"What was in that?" Veronica asked.

"Something that will knock her out, and hopefully, keep the nightmares away. You should get her to her room before it kicks in," he said.

"Do you think she'll be okay for the trial tomorrow? Maybe it's better if she postpones." If Chancellor Kinsey would let her. Veronica had a feeling he wouldn't; the man was overly rigid with his rules.

"The potion will give her the boost she needs," Professor Everleigh assured. "Do you need help carrying her?"

"She can walk on her own." Mostly.

But halfway to the dorms, Veronica regretted not taking his offer. She somehow managed to get Kitty back to her room, though she did knock her head against a few walls. As soon as she laid her friend down, the exhaustion set in, and Kitty closed her eyes.

Convinced that Kitty was out of the red for now, Veronica retreated to her room. With Kitty recuperating, she was left to pursue the mystery solo. But the path forward was anything but clear. Who had sent Ryder those videotapes? What was the purpose of the facility in Tennessee?

The supposed reappearance of the missing students remained the most perplexing issue. The grainy footage was the only evidence of their survival, but was it really enough to go off? The resemblance was there, but not conclusive enough to act on without further proof. Veronica was cautious about jumping to conclusions, but how could she verify the students were alive with such scant evidence? And, even if she could prove it, did that mean Ryder's theory about the horde attack being a cover for kidnapping was correct?

And, the most important question, who had sent these tapes to him in the first place?

Then, an idea struck her with such clarity that she stopped in her tracks. Northeastern was rife with shadowy dealings, but what if the key lay in revisiting the horde attack? If the heart of the mystery traced back to that initial incident, maybe all subsequent events surrounding the ferals were somehow connected to it. Seeking answers from the one person behind the attack in the past could shed light on the present dealings.

But getting information out of Sabine Everleigh posed its own set of challenges. The first major hurdle was, the woman had been locked up Maryland. Even if Veronica could make the drive to see her, would she be willing to talk? Given Veronica's involvement with Rory's death, and knowing Sabine's complex character—despite her flaws, her love for her son was undeniable—Vee feared the visit would end in failure.

That didn't stop her from grabbing her keys and getting in her car. It was time for a road trip—solo, this time.

THIRTY-TWO

THE TATTOO APPEARED on her back five days after her insomnia began. Intricate black lines traced down her skin, crossing her shoulder blades in bold ink. She struggled to see it in the bathroom, mirror, but from what she could tell, it was a circle of sorts.

Kitty wasn't sure if it was real, quite honestly. She'd been hearing things all morning, whispers of her name when she was alone, for instance. She was almost certain it was the sleep deprivation. She looked it up, and auditory hallucinations weren't uncommon in cases of severe insomnia. Well, she was pretty sure she looked it up.

It took her an hour to get ready for the third trial. By the time she made it to the designated meeting spot, she resolved to go back to the nurse's office and ask for stronger sleeping pills. The ones she got the other day weren't working well, obviously. Maybe she'd ask about the tattoo, too.

Wait. Did she get the pills from the nurse? She vaguely remembered Everleigh's office. But no—the office she'd visited had been too clean to be his. Probably.

Her brain wasn't doing its job remembering.

"Kitty?" Jax's voice cut through the haze of her mind as he put a hand on her shoulder. Her eyes took a moment to focus on him. "What's wrong with you?"

A lot of things, none of which he needed to point out. "Did I make it?"

"What?"

"To the trial," she slurred.

"What's wrong with you?" he repeated, looping an arm around her. He sat her down in the grass and felt her forehead. "You don't feel hot."

"I'm *very* hot, thank you very much. When does the trial begin?"

"In a few minutes," he answered.

"Is she drunk?" Noelle asked from far away.

"What? No!" Jax shouted. He leaned closer to Kitty, whispering. "*Are* you drunk?"

"No." She closed her eyes, but it was like her eyelids weighed a ton each. "I haven't slept."

"Why not?"

"I don't know," she sobbed, her tears surprising her. She knew, somewhere in the back of her mind, that she shouldn't have been crying. Not in public, anyway. But she could hardly help the burst of emotion hitting her.

Jax looked around. "Maybe we should take her back to her room."

"And miss the trial?" Noelle demanded, walking over to them. "She's just a little tired. She'll be fine. She's just being dramatic."

"But..." Jax looked from her to Kitty. "You look awful."

"I'm okay," she told him.

But the time between blinks felt like an eternity, and when

Chancellor Kinsey showed up, she could barely comprehend what he was saying. Jax nudged her several times to get her to pay attention, but she was simply incapable of processing the words.

When she came back to herself, she was in the Veil. Violet clouds rolled overhead, and a rotting smell punctuated the air. Jax pushed Kitty along, Chancellor Kinsey's back teetering forward deeper into the forest, his movements jerky and unnatural.

Kitty. She turned. There was no one behind her. And yet, she swore she heard her name, felt eyes on her back. Then again, she'd been hearing and seeing a lot of things, lately. It didn't mean anything.

Kitty.

Cao Zixing.

She pivoted again until Jax twirled her around so fast it made her head spin. "Get it together."

She nodded her head. Again, probably. There seemed to be a major disconnect between her brain and reality, and she didn't know how to bridge the gap. It wasn't a good time to lose her marbles, but then, when was?

Chancellor Kinsey stopped at a tree with a trunk so wide she wouldn't be able to touch her fingers if she wrapped her arms around it. Not that she had a habit of hugging trees.

Why was it sideways? Jax pulled her to stand, now fully supporting the entirety of her weight. And, when she blinked, he was gone.

Cao Zixing.

NOELLE EYED HER SISTER. While Kitty imbibed occasionally, she'd never touched illicit drugs, nor did she drink to the point of...whatever *this* was. Jax held her upright, but her head still lolled from side to the side. Her eyes remained open, as if she was sleeping awake.

Surely the chancellor noticed, but she doubted he gave a shit. He'd made it clear he didn't want them to pass the trials.

"Come on," Noelle muttered, supporting Kitty's other side. The fact that she didn't protest the assistance spoke volumes about how serious her condition was.

Together, the three of them followed the chancellor, though Noelle had no idea where they were going. The board members hadn't shown up for the trial this time; it was just the Swan siblings and Kinsey. No weapons, no phones—just them. Those were the rules, which Kinsey had been kind enough to spell out beforehand.

The trial this time would be a test of intelligence, which meant it was Noelle's time to shine. She already felt better after eating the pill Jianhao had given her, and with Kitty incapacitated, the competition was already in her favor.

They walked for miles, though Noelle could never be sure of the actual distance when it came to the Veil. The forest looked the same everywhere, the path indiscernible. They could have been traveling in circles, for all she knew. Finally, they stopped by a freestanding door.

Kitty stood on her own feet, her head clearing up somewhat. Her gaze focused, and she looked around, her brow furrowing in confusion.

"Welcome to the final trial," Chancellor Kinsey said, spreading his arms. "The rules are simple. Find your way back to campus in an hour, and you'll have completed the trials. Fail, and you'll forfeit the competition. Are we clear?"

Noelle wasn't sure how this could be a test of intelligence, but it wasn't her job to question the shadowborn and their weird-ass rules. After this trial, they would be finished... And then what?

She'd seen the articles in the Northeastern Tribune, felt the stares in class. And, though Kitty usually managed to clean it up before Noelle could see, she knew about the weekly vandalism on their dorm door. It wasn't hard to figure out what everyone thought of the Swan sisters. So what if they completed the trials? At this point, Nell doubted the faculty and students here would change their minds so suddenly. They would just find new things to nitpick, twisting their narratives in any way needed to pain the Swans in a poor light.

The trials were a farce, at the end of the day. Because when everyone was rooting for them to fail, they would, regardless of the outcome of some silly test. Kinsey knew that, which was why he had 'allowed' them to participate: it was a lose-lose situation from the very start. The odds weren't just stacked against them—the entire game was rigged, and the Swans weren't holding any cards in the first place.

Kinsey disappeared between the trees, and the fog seemed to thicken with his departure. Noelle found it odd, but then, the weather in the Veil was always off. She hated it here, in this land without qi.

"This doesn't sound like a test of intelligence," Jax said warily, saying aloud what she had been thinking earlier.

"No," Noelle agreed. "Sounds more like a Hansel and Gretel situation to me. There has to be a magical element to this, some sort of trickery."

"Or, he left us for dead in a forest of monsters, without our weapons."

"That too."

Kitty shut her eyes, bracing herself on a tree. "Can you smell that?"

Jax's brow furrowed. "Seriously, what have you taken today, Kitty?"

"I've never seen her so...out of it," Noelle added.

"There's a smell," she insisted. "Rotten. Like someone died. It's...getting stronger."

"Ferals?"

Kitty shook her head. "No. Not quite. It's...it's familiar. I *know* this smell."

"She's babbling," Jax said worriedly.

To be honest, Noelle was concerned too. She hadn't seen much of Kitty since their argument on Halloween, if you could call it that. When she looked back, it was more of a one-sided bitch-fest on Noelle's part. Not her finest moment. She'd been working up the courage to have a real conversation with her sister, but no time felt appropriate. And now, Kitty was, what? Spiraling? Noelle had never seen her in such a bad state.

"Put her on my back," she said, crouching down. Jax obeyed, and Kitty's arms curled around her sister's neck. Noelle stood, feeling her sister's weight like a stone against her back.

"I can walk," Kitty murmured.

"Sure you can. Jax, scout ahead. We need to get the hell out of here quickly."

"Right."

They followed the path the chancellor took, though the ground was littered with stones and roots, and it was hard to tell where they came from and what trail they followed. The paths all looked the same.

There had to be a trick to this, more than just finding their way through a dense forest. But what could it be? Nell thought long and hard, but with so little context, she couldn't come up with anything.

The forest floor became a marsh, and the siblings had to watch their footing in the soft mud. The visibility worsened, too, and it was all Noelle could do not to panic. "Jax, do you sense something? Jax?"

She couldn't hear her little brother's footsteps anymore, nor did he answer when she called him. Panic seized her throat, and she looked around, her chest constricting.

"Jax," she tried again, trying not to let the fear bleed into her voice.

"It hurts," Kitty gasped, clutching her arms.

"Kitty, what's wrong?"

"My back. It burns."

"Okay, okay," Noelle said. She lowered Kitty onto a stone and crouched before her, her hands on her sister's shoulders. Kitty's skin was cold and clammy. She couldn't even hold herself upright. Noelle bent her body over her knees and peeled her shirt up her back. Maybe she accidentally scraped her back on a tree branch, or some—

"What the fuck?" Noelle exclaimed.

There, on Kitty's back, was a black tattoo. Or, what Nell assumed was a tattoo. But the skin around it was raised and inflamed, and the ink itself pulsing with magic. Not qi—but Veil magic, spreading like an infection and leaving a host of blisters and scabs in its wake. She didn't recognize the symbols carved into her sister, but she didn't have to know what they meant to understand they were pure evil.

"How did you get this?" Noelle demanded, her voice shaking. "Kitty. Answer me, right now!"

Kitty coughed and moaned. "I don't know."

"Shit." It looked like a curse of some sort. Noelle didn't

even know such magic was possible. In her classes, they only talked about the benefits of magic, not the more sinister uses. She needed to get Kitty to the infirmary, but the trial wasn't over, and Noelle had no idea where her brother was. "Look, once we return to campus, we're getting you help."

"Please," Kitty agreed, which was doubly worrisome because Kitty never asked for help. She demanded it like a queen would from a subject.

"Can you stand?"

She shook her head, closing her eyes. "No."

"Fine. Hold on, and whatever you do, don't pass out. I—"

A sharp cry sounded in the distance, and Noelle whipped her head around. "Was that Jax?"

Noelle cursed and stood. She was about to turn back to Kitty and tell her to wait there, but a shadow emerged from the fog. Human-shaped, thank goodness, which meant it wasn't a feral.

"Jax?"

Kitty's hand reached out to grip her pant leg, but Noelle pried it off.

"It's okay. It's just our brother."

"No," Kitty panted. "It's not."

The ambush was sudden and vicious. Hands—dozens of them—shot out from the shadows, clawing at Noelle's clothes and yanking at her hair. She was overwhelmed in a matter of seconds, her body dragged across the slick mud. She flailed, her fingers scrabbling at the wet earth, but it was no use. Each attempt to free herself only ensnared her further in the grasp of her unseen attackers.

Above her, a dark figure loomed. He didn't partake in the assault but watched with a cold, detached curiosity, as if observing the struggles of a trapped insect beneath a magnifying glass. "闭嘴."

Noelle's heart pounded in her chest. The implications of his Chinese were chilling, but before she could even begin to process them, a heavier thud resounded next to her. Kitty's body was unceremoniously dumped beside her, her eyes vacant and staring into nothingness. Noelle's breath hitched, fearing the worst. She wanted to crawl toward her. Her first instinct was to reach out, wipe the mud from her cheek. With her thoughts a mess, the only coherent thing coming to mind was the fact that Kitty would not like dirt of any kind on her face (unless, of course, it was a mud mask).

For a horrifying moment, Kitty appeared lifeless. Then, a torturous, wet cough wracked her body.

Noelle wanted to scream, to call out to her, but her voice was strangled by abject dread. She watched, powerless, as a man in black robes crouched beside her sister. His hand flashed, a glint of steel in the dim light, and he plunged a blade deep into Kitty's abdomen. There was no scream from Kitty, no cry of pain—only a haunting silence as she lay there. With ruthless precision, the man's hand disappeared into the wound he had created. When it re-emerged, it was clutching a small, golden sphere, larger than a marble but smaller than her palm.

Her golden core.

THE AIR FRYER had to go. George eyed his newfound enemy with contempt as it sat in the corner of the kitchen. He had purchased it second-hand online, thinking it would be more convenient for reheating food than the microwave. It was convenient, all right—*too* convenient.

Ariana, bless her heart, couldn't cook. She could use a microwave, though, and apparently, an air fryer. To the point where she didn't need him anymore.

Now that they had similar work schedules, he enjoyed pampering her. Of all the people in the world who deserved it, his wife topped the list. Alright, so he didn't know every single person in the world. But in his heart, his wife was number one. She worked hard, and life hadn't been kind to her. When they weren't in the lab doing research—or whatever that farce was that Dr. Woods had them do—George didn't want Ariana to lift a single finger. He reveled in caring for her. But with the air fryer, she could (and would) take care of herself.

"What are you looking at?" Ariana asked, walking into the kitchen.

George snorted. There was once a time when she wouldn't have dared step foot in his domain. "Nothing, dear."

"Have you heard from the kids?" She glanced at the clock. "They should have started the trial, right?"

He nodded. This was the final trial, and he had no doubt the children would succeed. And, when they returned, he would have a warm, home-cooked meal ready for them. "They should be finished soon. Why don't you set the table?"

Ariana hummed in response.

George didn't need to ask if she was nervous. He was worried about the children, too. But he knew he couldn't fight their battles for them. Not after The Incident.

When Kitty was thirteen, she brought home her first male friend, Peter. Unfortunately, George was home and awake at the time. He was also a very good judge of character, so after a mere two-minute conversation, he knew that this Peter fellow was interested in his daughter. With him being three years older, and a high schooler, George didn't feel comfortable with this arrangement.

Peter was the first boy who'd ever shown any interest in Kitty. She basked in his attention. And, when he inevitably broke her heart, George wanted to kill the sixteen-year-old. So a week later, completely by accident, George hit the boy with his car.

Not really 'hit'. He preferred the word 'tapped'. No major bones were broken, and he walked away with only a concussion. Peter and his father were convinced George had done it on purpose, and Kitty had to spend the better part of a year convincing them not to press charges. Afterward, she yelled at him for the first time.

"I can handle myself," she'd told him. It was very hard to take her seriously, given she was 5' and the cutest little thing on the planet. Still, she made a good point. And so, he resolved to let her settle her own problems. All his children needed to face adversity and grow in their own way; he could give them the tools, but he couldn't be there to fight their battles. Restraining himself from doing so, however, was not easy.

At least he could cook. That was his one skill, his advantage, and he wasn't letting the damn air fryer take that from him!

The phone rang and Ariana swooped in to answer it. "Hello? Ah, Stefan?"

She put it on speaker. Soon, Stefan shīxiōng's voice came through. "Ariana, George? Are you there?"

Ariana's face scrunched, as it often did when she spoke with their brother-in-arms. He had been a troublemaker in the sect and, as such, did not always get along with Ariana, a stickler for the rules. "We're here."

"Ah, I am so sorry! I have been trying to get ahold of you for weeks. But there were some complications..."

"...Do I hear slot machines?" Ariana asked, her tone hardening.

"Anyway!" Stefan rushed to say. "You know the cultivator I sent to help you?"

"Yes, he's fantastic," Ariana said, relieved. "A little arrogant, but he's very intelligent. He's been good, keeping an eye on the kids."

"What?"

"I can't thank you enough, Shīxiōng. This is just what we need, with all that's going on."

"Um, what?" Stefan's voice echoed through the apartment. "I just called to tell you that I received word he's dead. He died on the journey to you. I'm sorry."

Ariana went pale. George, too, felt the color drain from his face. He couldn't think. He couldn't breathe.

"No," Ariana said. "Chen Jianhao is here, living at Northeastern."

"What?" Stefan demanded, his voice rising an octave.

"He's been with us since summer," George croaked.

"He's been helping us," Ariana explained.

"Chen Jianhao is dead. I buried the boy myself."

Ariana's lips parted. "Then who is the man we've had in our house for the past three months?"

THIRTY-THREE

FAST FOOD BURGERS were surprisingly good. While Veronica was eating them, at least. After a few hours, her stomach began to hurt. Fortunately, she arrived at the SNPD facility just in time and rushed to use their restroom. After that embarrassment, she went to the front desk and asked to see Sabine.

The receptionist, a young blonde smelling distinctly of Miss Dior perfume, stared at her for a long moment. "You want to see Sabine Everleigh?"

Veronica nodded. "Yes. I know I probably need an appointment, but it's urgent. Is there some sort of form I can fill out, or—"

"She's not available," the receptionist cut her off.

"Look, I'm coming from Northeastern; it's a long drive. Can you please just tell her Veronica Halliwell is here to see her? I think she'll want to speak with me." Veronica hoped so, anyway. If she wanted answers, Sabine would have them. The problem was knowing the right questions to ask—and how to get the good doctor to spill her guts.

"I'm sorry, honey, but Sabine Everleigh has departed this facility." The woman didn't *sound* very apologetic.

"Where did she transfer to?" The case wasn't even put to trial yet.

"It wasn't. She departed, as in, she *died*. You know—kicked the bucket? Passed on Got ghosted?"

"She *what*?" Veronica sputtered.

"She died a few months ago."

"H-How?"

The woman sighed, lowering her voice. Not that it mattered—the lobby was huge, like a fancy hotel, and there was no one else around. "I don't know. One minute, she was the picture of health. Next—dead as a doornail. I kind of assumed she offed herself."

"Um, that's a horrible assumption to make about someone."

"Well, what other choice did she have? She would have been found guilty and/or been tortured, which is of course, humiliating. Better to die on your own terms."

"I can't say I agree," Veronica said, eyes wide.

The receptionist shrugged. "Look, her family was notified. If they didn't choose to share it, it's their prerogative."

She had a point—Everleigh hadn't said anything, and shadowborn news channels hadn't reported on it. How was that possible? Sabine was the number one suspect in a huge case, and when she died, no one knew except her husband?

"Is there a visitor's log that I could look at?" Veronica asked, trying desperately not to make this a wasted trip.

"Nothing much interesting in there, hon. The only people who visited Sabine Everleigh were her husband and her boss, Kinsey. He's handsome, isn't he?"

"Sure, very." For a sleazeball snake.

The receptionist didn't have much other information for her, so Veronica returned to her car, slightly defeated. Another dead end—this time, literal. What was she supposed to do now? Drive home with her tail between her legs?

Unfortunately, that was exactly what Veronica ended up doing. The untimely death of Sabine had left her grappling with more questions than answers.

With Kitty incapacitated and unable to contribute to the investigation, Veronica found herself in desperate need of a confidant. She was still hesitant to involve Ryder, hoping to unravel some threads of the mystery independently. But with no other options, he was at least a reliable listener. Perhaps he could offer insight into Sabine's death, and what her involvement might have been beyond creating the feral lures.

With a six-hour drive ahead of her, Veronica ended up staying the night at a hotel and continuing in the morning. She made it back to campus before lunch and walked straight to Ryder's dorm. She hoped she wasn't too late to catch him before he headed to class, and was surprised when a young man answered the door.

"Hey," he greeted. Veronica didn't recognize him, but he was clearly a fellow student. "Looking for Ryder?"

"Yeah. Have you seen him?"

"He went to grab breakfast. He should be back in a few." He stepped aside, allowing her in. "You're different from his usual type."

Her lips twitched. "We're just friends."

The young man shrugged. "Well, make yourself at home. I'll be out of your hair soon."

True to his word, the guy left shortly after, and Veronica took his place at the desk. She was fairly certain he wasn't

Ryder's roommate. His presence in Ryder's dorm, particularly in his absence, piqued her curiosity.

She scanned the room, taking out her phone to text Ryder. She should have done that before coming over, but everything happened so fast, she barely thought about it. She figured the slip in etiquette wouldn't bother him much.

Her attention shifted to Ryder's laptop, casually left open on his bed. Curiosity overcame her, prompting her to press the space bar. But she only saw a password screen. Disappointed yet not surprised, she wondered why she had even entertained the thought of snooping. It was unlikely she'd discover anything Ryder hadn't already chosen to share with her. As she closed the laptop, it shifted, revealing a few papers tucked underneath.

Veronica couldn't help herself. She was in detective mode now, and she wanted answers. Pulling the papers free, she realized she'd seen these before. They were articles written for the Northeastern Tribune.

"Monster in Our Midst." "Harvest Festival or Devil-Worship?" "Miss Saigon? Try Miss Swan!" There were countless articles here, all marked up with a pen. Almost as if Ryder had written them himself.

No. He couldn't have. Veronica tried to dismiss the notion, but it nagged at her. If Ryder had written these articles, it meant—

The door opened, and Ryder stepped inside. He looked startled to see her. "Veronica?"

"Were you going to show these to me?" she asked, holding up the papers.

"What? Were you snooping?" He didn't sound angry at all. In fact, he smiled. "I *knew* you were interested in me, Vee."

"What are these?"

"They're nothing." He tried to grab them from her, but she moved her arm.

"Why do you have them? If they're not yours, whose are they?" she demanded. "Don't lie to me."

He sighed, his smile vanishing. "Fine, but you're going to be mad."

"I'm *already* mad."

"Has anyone ever told you that you're really hot when you're angry?"

"Ryder."

"Alright. I drafted some of them and edited others. I'm doing some part-time work with the *Tribune* on the side, okay? It's no big deal."

"No big deal?" she repeated. "These articles are filled with hateful comments about the Swan family. About my *friends*."

"No one reads the *Tribune*."

What kind of lame excuse was that? "Are you kidding? Everyone has been eating these articles up! Even some professors have been talking about them in class, not condemning them, but *praising* them! How can you condone this?"

"You think I wanted people to react like that? It's a bunch of small-minded sheep that don't think for themselves," Ryder sneered. "It's a social experiment, Vee. Nothing more."

She couldn't believe it. "Tell me it's all just a big conspiracy. Tell me you don't actually believe what you wrote."

"*Edited*. And of course not. It's all a bunch of racist crap."

"Then why would you have the paper print it?"

"My father wants them gone. Better this way than, well..." He jerked a thumb across his throat. "Look, if you think about it, it's really the lesser of two evils. My dad doesn't care how they're gone, as long as they are."

"Gee, that's nice." So Chancellor Kinsey wanted the

Swans to leave? "Your dad is the chancellor. He's in charge of the entire school. Why can't he do anything himself?"

"Because my dad doesn't want anyone looking into anything at the school too closely. Or so he says. Look, with the things going down at Southeastern and Lady Torren, my dad's boss, coming back to the mortal realm, he's paranoid. It's not my job to question it, Vee."

"You're telling me you didn't write this stuff because you believe it?" She wasn't sure if that made the situation better or worse.

"I edited it. And of course not. I'm not racist," he insisted.

Anger flared through her. "Then what are you, Ryder?"

"What am I?"

"Yeah. You don't believe in this crap, but you 'edit' it anyway, to prepare for publishing, with the explicit purpose to get the Swan family kicked out of school. And you do this without protest because your father asked you to."

"It's more complicated than that."

"It doesn't seem like it is," Veronica spat. God, and she had kissed him! What a fucking idiot. Shame dyed her cheeks, and she looked away. "Is this why you challenged Kitty to a duel? Because you wanted to humiliate her or something?"

"Kitty's a bitch. She deserves everything she gets," he said, with such conviction it disgusted her. "Look, Vee. Let's not fight. She's not worth it. I mean, the articles have a bunch of shitty lies in them. I'll give you that. But there is some truth to it, isn't there? She and her family of mortal monsters don't belong here. I'm doing her a favor by forcing her out. Can't you see that?"

"I'm done." Veronica turned on her heel and strode out, Ryder following her.

"Come on, Vee, just wait a second," he called, rushing to keep up with her. "Veronica, slow down."

"Leave me alone!" she snapped, whirling around.

"Can't we talk about this?"

"There's nothing else to talk about. You're a scumbag, Ryder. And I'm an idiot for thinking you were any different. God, I saw the way you treated her—the way you treat *everyone* at this school, like you're better than them!—and I *still* let myself fall for it. I can't believe I was so stupid, again."

When was she going to realize that she wasn't special? Not to Blake, not to Ryder...not to anyone. Her entire life was a series of disappointments, in others and in herself.

But as she strode down the hall, with Ryder following hot on her heels, a roar sounded in the distance. Veronica barely had time to look out the windows before every single one shattered, blasting glass directly at her.

THE FIRST AND most logical place George thought to find his kids was the Veil. Not only did he know they were undertaking the trials there, but he understood it was the most perilous place they could possibly be. And naturally, where else would his children be but the most dangerous spot?

'Jianhao' was nowhere to be found, either, which could be either a good sign or a bad one. George believed in Murphy's law: what can go wrong will. Still, he struggled to comprehend the imposter's motives. All he knew for certain was that anyone who falsely assumed someone else's identity didn't have good intentions.

"You don't think he's from Qingshan?" Ariana questioned, following George downstairs.

He didn't want to think about that. Yes, it had been nearly twenty years since they fled their sect, but immortality and lengthened lifespans made the passage of time feel different. Suddenly, a decade was not very long at all, and the gods knew immortals held grudges for ages. George and his wife hadn't just burned bridges when they'd fled; the couple had razed the village. Figuratively, of course.

Alright, so they'd set one or two buildings on fire, but that was an accident.

The two raced across the campus green. The scene before them was utter chaos, with ferals attacking in droves. Ariana whirled around, her blades up, as she cut through the backs of two passing wolves on the prowl. Students fled the scene, racing toward the buildings, while others joined the fray and attempted to close all the rifts opening outside.

Ariana wiped her bloodied swords on the dead ferals' fur and kept moving, with her husband following on her heels. While he preferred working with potions, he'd learned how to use a sword well enough to defend himself. His wife, however, was the more skilled of the two. She dual-wielded—a rare fighting style, even in Qingshan.

As they approached an open rift, one of the faculty members grabbed Ariana's wrist. The man wore a torn tweed jacket and his eyes widened when he saw her, spittle flying from his mouth as he spoke. "This is *all* your fault!"

"Unhand my wife," George said calmly, though he didn't *feel* particularly calm. He felt like punching a hole through the fucker's skull.

"I'm alright," Ariana told him, shaking the man off with ease. But he could tell she was rattled.

"I should have known," the professor sneered. "It's your kind that caused this!"

George's blade would have cut through the man's neck easily, but Ariana pulled him along, ignoring the man. Their children were out there somewhere, and they could not delay in finding them.

Though the duo had been to the Veil before, George was apprehensive about going there. They could get trapped, being cultivators and therefore unable to open a rift. Still, he imagined the predicament was the same one his children currently found themselves in.

They stepped through a gaping rift, only to be nearly blinded by thick mist. The temperature was freezing, ill-suited for their thin clothes. Ariana turned, pressing her back against her husband's as they began to move. It had been ages since they hunted together, in formation like this. Normally, their senses would be razor-sharp, amplified by the flow of qi, but here in the Veil, their abilities were dulled. But they didn't need to rely solely on qi to be aware of their surroundings.

The forest was alive with the presence of lurking ferals. Yet, something about their behavior struck George as unusual. These monsters didn't strike with the random, chaotic savagery typical of their kind. If they had, then the Swans would have been attacked right away. Instead, a group of them moved in a pack. Only their silhouettes were visible, but from what George could tell, they were different types of creatures.

During the first horde incident, the ferals had struck anything in sight—even each other. But now, from what he observed here and on campus, there was a methodology to their movements, a pattern that suggested some form of intelligence and cooperation they hadn't seen before from the ferals. Almost as if they were being controlled. But how? And by whom?

Stepping lightly over the underbrush, the couple

continued their careful advance, every sense strained for any sign of their kids. The fog pressed in closer, muffling sounds and distorting shapes, making each step feel like a move in a high-stakes game of chess.

Without warning, the eerie silence of the fog-shrouded woods shattered. Gloved hands, swift and silent as the grave, shot out from the mist. The ambush was sudden and brutal—before either George or Ariana could mount a defense, they found themselves violently seized and torn apart from one another.

His wife's muffled screams were like daggers to his heart, and a burst of pure rage surged forth. George struggled madly, writhing and bucking, trying to free himself and run to her.

"*Xiaoyan!*" Her name tore from his lips as the hands forced his face to the ground, grinding his eye into the dirt.

No. No. No.

His attackers were numerous and skilled, overpowering him with a practiced ease that spoke of extensive cultivation, even in this hellhole of a realm. George writhed under their grip, his mind racing. The strength and coordination of the ambush were unlike anything typical of the rogue elements they had encountered before. This was different, calculated, and chillingly effective.

As he fought against the hands that held him down, a voice whispered directly into his ear, cold as ice, speaking in fluent Chinese. "We've been waiting for you, Cao Zhipeng."

George fought harder, but his desperation only made the men holding him down laugh. "You—"

"It is time to come home."

THIRTY-FOUR

"I DIDN'T KNOW they made literary porn mags," Melody said conversationally.

Cyrus had a litany of responses, none of which felt more appropriate than a simple, "What the fuck?"

His little sister held up a magazine from Chancellor Kinsey's drawer. They'd snuck in pretty easily, while the secretaries were on lunch break, using Wyatt's lock-picking and hacking skills. That was to say, they brought Wyatt along—anticipating they'd need him to bypass the digital lock with his father's security clearance—only to discover the door ajar.

Cyrus didn't mind Wyatt. Mostly because they both had a 'y' as the second letter of their name. And, of course, because he had the not-so-rare ability to get under Blake's skin. It was funny, how jealous he got of the guy's popularity.

Wyatt grabbed the magazine from Melody's hand and flipped through it. "Wow. You think he confiscated this from a student?"

"I hope so," Cyrus grumbled. He didn't want to think of the implications of Kinsey buying smut and having the balls to stick it in his desk drawer: Kinsey either had an ego the size of Texas, or he had a brain the size of an M&M. Neither boded well for a leader of a magic college. "Keep looking."

"I don't really have to. I get the gist; it's all breeding kink stuff."

"I meant the desk."

"*Right.*" Wyatt grinned and slid the magazine back, opening another drawer. "I bet all the juicy stuff is on the computer, anyway."

"Probably, but it's password protected. You can't just use your dad's phone to unlock it."

"No, but I can use the password he wrote on a sticky note." Wyatt held up a bright yellow slip of paper, covered in the chancellor's messy scrawl.

"Oh," said Cyrus, feeling rather stupid. He suddenly understood Blake's distaste for Wyatt. "That works, too."

"And we're in!"

The two men crowded around the computer screen while Melody continued to look through the bookshelves. Hopefully she wasn't looking for more porn.

"You find anything yet?" she asked, not looking up.

"Bills." Cyrus wrinkled his nose. "The university's spending a lot of money, apparently."

"What'd you expect? It's a school."

"I thought they'd get money from donors and tuition," Wyatt mused. "I didn't think Kinsey would *give* money to donors."

"What?"

"A million dollars to Neil Abbott. I know him; he works on the Ruby Council. If memory serves, he doesn't even live in the Northeast; his daughter attends Southeastern."

"You know her?"

Wyatt nodded. "Yeah, she's pretty famous in some circles. But as far as I know, the Abbotts are loaded. Why would Kinsey need to pay them?"

"With school funds, no less," Cyrus said. "Kinsey is a shadowborn angel—and if Abbott is on the Ruby Council, he's a demon trueblood. Something smells, here."

"More rotten than a bag of broken eggs left out for three days in the summer," Melody added. "What other payments have been made?"

"And why didn't he encrypt these files?" Wyatt asked.

"He wrote his password, which is 'password567', on a sticky note on his desk," Cyrus pointed out. "There are more payments. Donations are on his sheet, and payments are on this one. But if I filter by recipient instead of payment amount... There. Seven million, over the last three years, to Neil Abbott. The payments go directly to his own personal account, and they're coded as refunds for donations. But if you check the donations tab, it doesn't show Neil Abbott making any donations to Northeastern. So what is he getting reimbursed for?"

Melody squinted at the screen. "Who are the top donors at school?"

Cyrus sorted the spreadsheet. "Mr. Churchill is one of them, no surprise there."

Actually, it was as if all Mr. Churchill's money was just... flowing through the school and going directly to Neil. The payout dates and amounts matched. But why would they need to funnel money through the university? Why not give him the money directly?

"This isn't what we came here to look for," Mel reminded them. "But...if it's shady, maybe we should report it to the authorities?"

"It is suspicious," Wyatt said, "but the payments aren't illegal, unless he's writing them off as business expenses on his taxes or something. Dig through his files. There has to be an email or something with the list of missing students. Didn't the SNPD investigate?"

Cyrus looked through Kinsey's emails, but there was nothing incriminating in there.

"Go online, not through the email app," Melody urged. Cyrus followed his sister's directions, checking through downloads and history. "Alright, there's a frightening amount of WebMD.com searches in here."

Cyrus needed eye bleach for some of the stuff Kinsey had looked up. "This is pointless. We don't have much time left."

Wyatt stood up and stretched, cracking his knuckles. "Why don't you get an enrollment list before and after the horde attack? Look through the names and see if anyone's missing. It's not perfect, but at least we'd have a list. Just filter the spreadsheet and print it out."

"Good idea," Melody said, nudging her brother aside. She began typing away at the computer. The printer hummed quietly in the background, and soon, they had what they needed.

Wyatt glanced out the window, at the campus green. "Uh oh. Looks like Kinsey is on his way back. Let's scram."

"I'm done," Melody said, and the three of them hurried out the door, down the hall, and out of the building. They ran across the quad to the dorms, stopping only when they reached Cy's room. Inside, Blake was nowhere to be seen.

Melody held up the papers. "So, the list of missing students. Let's cross off people who we know are alive. A bunch of students transferred or dropped out."

"We know some bodies were found, too," Wyatt

remarked, grabbing a few sheets. Cyrus did the same, combing over the names. They were alphabetical, and it didn't take them long to each take a pass through the list. Finally, after coming up with the finalized list, more or less, Cyrus realized something.

"All the missing students are shadowborn. No magicians, no psychics," he commented.

"And there's the same number missing from each subspecies. Isn't that weird? Why would the same students from each group go missing, and not a single non-shadowborn?"

"Because...it's a controlled experiment," Cyrus realized. "The missing students weren't killed in a horde attack. They were taken. Their bodies were never found because they never died here. Just as Jax suspected."

"But that means we don't know where they went." Melody sighed. "We've hit a dead end. Now what do we do?"

"Maybe we start looking at the connection between Neil Abbott and Chancellor Kinsey," Wyatt suggested. "It's not a coincidence that they're connected. Kinsey must have been paying him to get the demon truebloods involved."

"In what?"

"I don't know. We have to figure that out. But now we know they're working together, and the missing students were probably kidnapped for a reason. We just have to figure out what that is."

"And why they need more," Melody said, glancing out the window.

"What?" Cyrus walked over, peering outside. Screams pierced the air, and across campus, rifts began opening and feral beasts pouring through.

"It's happening again."

THE FOG REMINDED Jax of Stephen King's movie, 'The Mist', which his sisters (namely, Kitty) had forced him to watch when he was twelve. Suffice to say, he was scared shitless. He tried not to show it, wandering around in the forest.

"Kitty?" he called. "Noelle?"

Nothing. He couldn't see his own hands in front of him, much less his sisters. He didn't know how they'd got separated. He wandered forward, unsure if he was going in the right direction. But when he heard a loud rumble behind him, he knew he was in trouble.

He began running, as well as one could over uneven, slippery mud. Shit. He had no way of getting back to the mortal realm, and no weapon. No qi, either.

The ground rumbled, forcing Jax to his knees. A low snarl emanated from somewhere behind him. He didn't even see what hit him; one moment he was upright, and the next, he was on his back. Blood seeped out of a wound in his head. He stared, dazed, at the cloudy sky.

"Jax!" A voice cut through the noise, and hands pulled him to his feet. "Are you okay?"

"Veronica?" Jax's vision hadn't cleared fully, but he saw the mop of red hair. She pressed a palm to his head.

"Shit."

"Just leave him," another voice insisted. A male, by the sound of it. Annoying, too.

Veronica wrapped an arm around Jax, supporting him. "*No.*"

"Vee—"

"Help me get him back to campus," she insisted. "You owe him that much."

"Me? Owe *him*? I don't think so," the guy spat out. "Don't be an idiot, Veronica. Let's just go back and have a conversation about this, like adults."

"We're taking him with us."

"He's a dead weight! And did you see that monster? That's a fucking wyvern. It'll kill us all!"

"Jax is a kid! He's seventeen!"

There it is, Jax thought. He might have grown over the summer; he might have towered over his sisters, but in their eyes, he was still their little brother. In their friends' eyes, too, apparently.

"I don't need anyone to take care of me," he said gruffly. It was a hard sell, considering he was leaning on Veronica for support. It hurt to breathe, and he was pretty sure whatever had hit him had broken a few ribs in the process.

"Come on. He's not worth it," the guy said. Jax's vision finally began to clear, and he recognized Ryder Kinsey, of all people.

"You said you didn't believe those articles," Veronica hissed.

"I don't. They were filled with crap, but one thing they got right? These people are not like us, Vee. They have some weird form of magic, sure, but they're monsters through and through. And they don't belong here, nor do they deserve your care. Just listen to me, for once!"

Jax had enough sense to know this wasn't about him; not really. He didn't fully understand what they were talking about, but judging by their tone, he surmised that Ryder wanted to control Veronica. And Veronica had enough of it.

She ignored him, pressing forward with Jax. But the wyvern wasn't so eager to see them leave. It roared again, appearing over the fog. Jax lifted his head to see the creature, expecting the feral to be like all the others: a zombified monstrosity. But this creature wasn't dripping black goo and rot. No, this beastblood was a magnificent palette of colors. Red and blue scales covered its serpentine body, with spikes along its spine. Two leathery wings extended on either side of its shoulder blades, and its tail ended in a black barb that shined with a rainbow of colors, like a slick oil spill. Its eyes glowed gold as it threw its head back with a roar, shaking the trees around them and clearing the surrounding fog.

Veronica and Jax hobbled away as fast as they could, but it wasn't nearly fast enough. The wyvern swooped down, knocking both of them to the ground. Jax cried out in pain.

Ryder ran toward them, shouting. "Veronica!"

The beastblood roared in response. Jax's body moved on its own. Everything else became a blur, and he only recalled what happened in flashes. He saw Ryder, frozen. The wyvern, its mouth open. Veronica, falling back. And then, his body was on fire.

He wasn't sure how he'd landed on the ground again, but it was much wetter than he remembered. Maybe the wyvern tossed him so far away, he'd landed in the ocean. But no, if he was in the ocean, he wouldn't have heard someone screaming, right? His ears rang, and he realized the scream was coming from him. He shut his mouth, trying to calm his breathing. Pain. Agonizing, terrible pain.

It took a minute for his mind to catch up, but when it did, Jax nearly passed out. He couldn't stand, but with much effort, he turned his head and saw his arm, a mess of flesh and blood. Bone poked through his muscles, torn and shredded. He couldn't feel his hand, or anything past his elbow.

His stomach churned at the sight. He tried to roll over, but the pain was so overwhelming, he really did black out for a second. Or maybe longer, because the next thing he saw was Veronica, holding his face.

"Stay with me," she urged.

"Vee, you should've listened to me," Ryder insisted.

"Shut the fuck up and help me!"

"He's dead weight, as I said. Only this time, it's more literal—"

"Help me get him back!" she shouted.

Jax wanted to tell her to run, to save herself, but all that came out was a bloody cough. Veronica and Ryder continued to argue, but their voices sounded farther and farther away, until they disappeared entirely.

THROWN OVER RYDER'S SHOULDER, Veronica kicked and screamed until he finally let her down. He wasn't gentle, either, letting her body fall to the ground once they were back on campus. The green was a bloodbath of shadowborn and beastbloods alike, hardly a place to have a civil conversation, much less a heated argument.

"What the hell?" was all she could muster, because really, what was he fucking thinking?

Jax was still in the Veil, bleeding out. And his arm—oh God. Ryder hadn't slain the wyvern or helped her carry Jax out. Instead, he stood there, watching the fight unfold, like...a coward. No, that wasn't right. He wasn't afraid. He was indifferent. Arguably, that was worse.

"Veronica," he said, reaching out.

"Don't touch me," she said, swatting his hand away. "How could you do that? How could you let him *die*?"

"He's not dead, yet," Ryder stated matter-of-factly. "Look, Vee. I couldn't have carried him out *and* guaranteed your safety. I was just trying to protect you."

"Guarantee my safety? We were both unarmed!" Veronica countered, her voice rising with frustration. In fact, she had a better chance than he did in a fight, using with her magic spells. "You didn't even try to help him!"

"You're more important to me. Can't you see that?"

She could see it, all right. At that critical moment, he had prioritized her. And wasn't that what she always wanted? Someone who put her first? Someone to make decisions for her, to take care of her and relieve her of the burden of indecision?

But at what cost?

Ryder hadn't made any real effort to save Jax at all. He could argue all he wanted about the articles he'd 'edited', but Veronica suspected that despite his protests, he harbored a belief that the Swans were—in a way—lesser than him. Or maybe it was that he believed everyone, except those he personally cared about, mattered less. While Veronica understood prioritizing friends to some extent—she would do the same—she hoped she wouldn't do so at the expense of others.

"If we had taken him, the wyvern wouldn't have left us alone. Leaving him behind was the best option," Ryder tried to justify. "He would have bled out anyway. You can't save everyone, Vee."

"I know I can't," she acknowledged. "But I'm going to do my darndest to try."

She stood up, and Ryder blocked her path.

"Get out of my way."

"If you go back, Veronica, I'm not coming to save you," Ryder warned, his voice low. "You'll regret it."

"You won't have to," she replied. "Because I can save myself."

She stepped around him and headed into the rift.

THIRTY-FIVE

IT HAD to be another Nightmare, a prolonged vision from the second trial warping time and space to make Noelle believe the worst had happened.

Her sister wasn't dead. She *couldn't* be. Kitty was injured, yes, and now lost somewhere in the Veil. But she wasn't dead, which meant there was still hope.

Or so Noelle tried to convince herself.

She needed to stay rational, a trying task in the face of abject horror: her sister, who was supposed to be immortal, was...

And, despite Noelle's host of powers she thought so special, she hadn't been able to do a goddamn thing. She'd watched as her sister was mutilated, watched as her body was dragged away and Noelle herself was lost to the fog. She didn't remember how she escaped the evil cultivators, just that she was alone in the forest, calling for her siblings and hearing no response. She didn't feel anything either—no qi, no emotions, just vast emptiness.

What am I going to tell my parents? That she had let her

sister die? After they had a fight and she hadn't even worked up the nerve to make amends?

Noelle kept moving forward, trying to remember where her siblings were last, hoping they would appear. They had to be somewhere nearby. And Kitty couldn't have just disappeared, could she? And who were those men grabbing at them? She was certain they were cultivators, but everything else was a mystery. Either way, they stole her sister's golden core and...hurt her.

Though their relationship had been strained as of late, Noelle didn't want her sister injured. And the thought of losing her outright was just too awful to think about.

Perhaps now was not the best time for self-reflection, but one did not choose when an epiphany would strike. Noelle's hit her hard.

She was not a good person. Yes, she had, through conversations with Blake, come to realize this. But now, she could accept it; embrace it, even. Despite her many flaws, her family always believed in her. She always thought they needed her to be the 'smart one', but in truth, it was the other way around: she needed them. And if they were in trouble, she would have to be willing to do anything to save them. Even if it meant breaking the rules.

While she boxed herself in as the most intelligent sibling, perhaps Kitty too thought of herself as the protector of the Swans. The sisters had more in common than they realized. But as adults, it was time for them to break free of the rigid molds they cast for themselves. It was time for Noelle to be the protector.

Certainly she would be capable of the same level of love and devotion, right? Even if it hurt...

She bit down on her arm, as hard as she could. Breaking

skin was not as easy as she thought. She gnawed on her flesh until she drew blood. Digging her fingers into the wound, she tried to ignore the pain. It was almost comforting, the sting of her nails scraping the raw gash, her blood trickling out.

This was what love felt like. What devotion felt like.

"Come on!" she yelled, though she knew the ferals around her didn't understand. They scented her blood, though, and it wasn't long before a large, muscular centipede—not exactly a creature she'd ever want to tangle with—appeared in the clearing, clicking its mandibles. It had human hands, which made her vomit a little inside her mouth. Of all the creatures to curse the Veil, the ugliest one had to answer her call? Could she redial and try again?

Worse, it was feral, black goo dripping from its eye sockets. Lovely. It dragged its body toward her, the skin on its hands muddy and rotted, with flies buzzing around its eyes. It was longer than seven train cars, or so Noelle estimated.

"Hey, big guy," she said, keeping her voice steady and calm.

It clicked its mandibles in response, the equivalent of what she could assume was a growl.

Moving toward her with its long body, it circled around her, making the ground shake. Against her better judgment, Noelle shoved her bloody hands onto one of the bulbous segments and closed her eyes. She knew ferals didn't have qi inside them, but with no way to get out of the Veil, she had limited options. And so, she searched for any sort of energy she could use inside the creature. She envisioned a ball of thread, tangled and knotted. The feral thrashed, swinging around to dig its mandibles into her shoulder. But it was no use.

Noelle found it: the tangled web of demonic energy that

held the feral together. Without hesitation, she let the energy flow inside her.

FIRE ERUPTED FROM THE TREETOPS, sending a cascade of embers into the air, accompanied by a guttural roar that vibrated through the forest floor. Clutching her ax tightly, Charity sprinted through the dense woodland. She had no particular destination in mind, driven only by a singular purpose: to eliminate every feral that crossed her path.

When the ferals broke through the rifts on campus, she already had her ax in hand. All she had to do was swing.

Her motives weren't noble, nor was she driven by bloodlust. All she knew was that moving, fighting, felt like the only way to prove she wasn't just taking up space—though her father probably thought otherwise. While her actions weren't driven by heroism, at least they contributed to something greater than herself.

Navigating swiftly, Charity ducked and weaved through the trees, alert to any sound. The forest was covered in a dense white mist, unusual but not totally impossible in the Veil. Magic made the weather unpredictable.

The rustle of underbrush ahead caught her attention, but she couldn't identify the creature lurking. She poised her ax, ready to strike, when a flash of bright red caught her eye. It was human—a woman—and turning, Charity recognized Veronica with a rush of relief.

"Charity?" Veronica exclaimed. She was unarmed, blood splattering her shirt. "What are you doing here?"

"I could ask you the same thing. You need to get back to campus and go into a safe room."

"Jax is in the woods. A wyvern injured him. I...I need to find him."

"You can't even open a rift back, and with the fog this dense, we could get separated and lost," Charity protested.

"I'm not leaving without him."

She was surprised Veronica cared so much about Jax Swan. But of all three siblings, he was the least abrasive...and the youngest. "Alright. I'll help you find him, and then you both need to get back to campus. Okay?"

Veronica's shoulders sagged in relief. "Thank you. I owe you one."

If it was anyone else, Charity wouldn't have bothered. But with Veronica, things were different. She felt like she owed her somehow, after everything that had happened with Blake.

Even without the rumbling and occasional flames, Charity sensed the beastbloods lingering in the forest around them. The girls moved quickly and quietly, deeper into the thicket of trees.

"What's the plan when we find him?" Charity whispered.

"I can carry him back, but I need you to open a rift."

"How injured is he?"

Veronica hesitated. "It's not good."

That was all she needed to say. Charity crept forward, taking lead, when a familiar screech pierced through the trees, followed by the loud thump of a body hitting the ground. Charity looked back, and Veronica's gaze was locked onto something. She followed her line of sight and froze.

A wyvern towered over the treetops, its scales a rainbow palette, its wings spread, casting a shadow that enveloped the entire forest. It roared again, its maw opening to reveal rows and rows of sharp teeth. It wasn't feral, but somehow, that was worse.

Charity reacted instinctively, swinging her ax up in a defensive stance as the creature bore down on them. From her beastblood biology courses, Charity knew its rough scales were nearly impervious to attack, like built-in armor. Veronica, standing slightly behind, channeled her magic, her hands glowing with intense heat as she prepared her spell.

As the wyvern swooped in, Charity dodged to the side, narrowly avoiding its snapping jaws. She knew it was strong enough to break her bones with a single bite. The ground shook as the creature landed, turning to face them as its barbed tail swept the forest floor.

Veronica stepped forward, thrusting her hands out as she unleashed a blast of fire toward the wyvern. The flames engulfed its face, and it reared back with a deafening scream. Charity ran forward, jumping into the air as the wyvern thrashed its head. She brought her ax down, embedding it deep into its hide. With a roar, the beastblood bucked and sent Charity flying backward, her ax still lodged in its body. Fuck. She missed its more sensitive, fleshy area on its neck.

"Charity!" Veronica cried, running toward her.

"Run!" Charity shouted, pushing herself to her feet. The wyvern froze, but her ax remained wedged into its scales. She couldn't get it out, not in time.

Its tail snapped around, sending her hurling into a tree. Pain exploded from her spine, her vision darkening as the impact knocked the wind out of her lungs.

The wyvern loomed over her, its shadow encompassing her body. She could smell its rancid breath as its mouth opened.

"Hey!" Veronica shouted, waving her arms wildly. "Over here, you dumb fuck!"

The wyvern roared, swiping its clawed foot in her direction, but she was too far away.

"Veronica," Charity said, wincing as she tried to sit up.

Veronica waved her arms, a ball of light gathering in front of her. The problem with magic was that users generally lacked control, failing to do nuanced spells seen in television and movies, like teleportation or freezing time. In a fight like this, however, all Veronica needed was power and good timing.

She released the spell, fire shooting from her and hitting the wyvern's underbelly as it reared up, exposing its less armored parts. The fire, fueled by the Veil's magic, scorched the soft skin and elicited another agonized cry from the beast. The wyvern flapped its wings desperately, trying to lift off and escape the onslaught, but its injured leg hampered its efforts.

Charity saw her chance. As the wyvern struggled to gain altitude, she sprinted beneath it, grabbing her ax from its leg and wrenching it out with all her might. The wyvern shrieked as she withdrew the blade, iridescent blood gushing from the wound. It took flight, crashing through the treetops as it disappeared from view.

Veronica stood, panting. She rushed over, kneeling next to Charity, who dry heaved on her hands and knees.

Laughter, chilling and discordant, echoed through the trees. Both girls tensed, rising to their feet with caution. The sound coiled around them like a chilling breeze.

"Did you hear that too," Charity asked slowly, "or am I totally losing it now?"

Veronica's response was a sharp glance, her vivid green eyes scanning the shadows between the trees. "I heard it."

"Who's there?" Charity called.

The fog responded, curling and twisting as if contemplating its answer, then gradually began to withdraw, unveiling the dense forest bit by bit. The trees, gnarled and towering, seemed to stand as silent witnesses, their branches swaying slightly in a non-existent breeze.

At first, the clearing appeared empty. But then, her eyes caught movement—a figure, barely discernible at first, leaning casually against a tree not far from where they stood. As the fog cleared further, the figure became clearer, and the initial relief turned into a tightening knot of dread.

"So this is the girl who they say looks like me," came a voice, breaking the quiet as the woman stepped forward into clearer view. Her blonde hair cascaded to her shoulders, catching the weak light filtering through the canopy, and her eyes—a striking, vibrant green that matched Veronica's and Charity's, the Churchill green—analyzed them with amusement. The pure white dress she wore fluttered softly around her bare feet.

She moved toward them with the ease of a predator, her footsteps silent on the forest floor.

Charity would never forget her sister's voice, much less her face. And that smile! Pure fucking evil, a grin spread unnaturally wide across her perfect face.

"How are you alive?" Charity managed.

"Does it matter? It's good to see you too, little sis. How's Blake doing? Oh, that's right. He chose Veronica over you. I wonder why," Tessa taunted. "You loved him, didn't you? Growing up, I mean. He was probably your first crush. And then he chose me."

"*Stop it.*"

She didn't. "And after I left, he chose someone who resembled me. You weren't even second best, Char. In our family, too, you never made runner-up. Sometimes, I doubt you even left the starting line. It's funny how you tried to compete with me, as if you even had a chance. Truthfully, I never saw you as a threat."

Charity tightened her grip on her ax, anger rolling like the ocean in a storm. "I don't know what kind of sick game this is, but—"

"Oh, Charity, Charity, Charity. It's okay. Shouldn't you be happy that I'm alive?" Tessa mocked. "After all, I am your sister."

"You are *not* my sister." This thing had to be a shapeshifter, or a magician using a complicated spell, or just a plain old nightmare she couldn't wake from.

"Don't worry, Char. It's me, in the flesh. You know, they say that energy can't be destroyed, only transformed. Think of my death that way. It didn't really die; I just changed. And now, as your big sister, I think I'm going to help you change, too."

With that, Tessa spread her arms wide. Her feet lifted off the ground as large, pink wings unfurled behind her, like a butterfly's.

Impossible.

Charity had seen fae with those kinds of wings, like her father, but that was because they were trueblood—

They were trueblood.

And Tessa, born shadowborn, was now just like them.

NOTHING IN BLAKE'S life could have prepared him for this; not even the first horde attack. When the ferals began their invasion, the first thing he thought to do was call Cyrus. Of course, at the worst time possible, he wasn't answering. Blake hoped that meant he was busy fighting, and not...

Blake grabbed a sword from the weapons closet nearest to him in the hall. Melody and Cyrus were together, and with Wyatt on their side, they would probably be fine. As fine as they could be, fending off zombies. But the Swans were in the Veil, and according to Noelle, Kinsey wasn't going to let them take their weapons for the third trial. Blake needed to find them, fast.

He sprinted across campus and hopped through the closest rift he could find. Plan? Who needed one of those? He had... Good looks? No, monsters didn't care about that. Charm? Not much of that, either. Good luck? Ha!

An empty head? Winner, winner! Where was his chicken dinner?

Well, he'd worry about that when he returned, and his friends were all safe.

Dense fog covered the Veil, obstructing Blake's vision. He tried his best to navigate through the thick air, but the further he moved, the more his surroundings became distorted. It was like a maze without walls.

"Noelle?" he screamed at the top of his lungs. "Kitty? Jax!"

Nobody answered. He couldn't hear anyone over the moans and groans of ferals around him. He kept running, his heart pounding in his ears, desperate to find someone—anyone.

Then, he saw them, both huddled together in a macabre tableau. He nearly tripped over their bodies. Jax was first; his eyes fluttering open yet unseeing, his complexion ghastly pale, his arm a mangled mess of flesh and bone. Next to him lay Kitty, pale as a corpse. Someone had torn open her stomach, blood drenching into her clothes.

Blake's knees buckled as he dropped beside them. "Fuck. Fuck, fuck—"

"Blake," Kitty rasped. Her eyes darted around in panic.

There was something profoundly unsettling about seeing her like this. It wasn't just that his best friend had feelings for her. Kitty seemed invincible, despite her flaws, her strength being a foundational component of who she was. Now, before him, she struggled for each breath, and he found himself wondering how she was even still alive.

If this could happen to her, what's to say it couldn't happen to anyone else?

"Kitty, what happened?" Blake choked out.

"You have to take Jax. You have to get him back to the mortal world. His arm is really bad. You have to help him."

"Kitty, you—I can't carry both of you," he stammered. He wasn't even sure how he would manage with just Jax. Thankfully the boy wasn't conscious, otherwise the jostling of that arm would cause him immense pain.

"Carry Jax right now. Don't argue with me," she demanded, her authority undiminished by her frail state. "You're going to carry Jax. You're going to bring him to the mortal realm. Get him to a doctor or a healer. I don't care what it takes. You're going to do that. Okay?"

"Kitty—"

"Please." It was a word he didn't expect to hear from her.

There was no time to argue. And Blake knew she would fight him, if he tried to take her first. The only thing he could offer was a weak promise, one he intended to attempt but seemed impossible to keep: "I'll come right back for you, okay? You...stay here."

Like she could go anywhere.

"Just save my brother."

Time was of the essence. Blake opened a rift then and there—he wasn't going to wander around the Veil to find one already open—and lifted Jax carefully, trying his best not to injure the kid further. As he stepped through, he turned back to reassure Kitty once more, regardless of how empty the words were. But she lay completely still, her eyes closed, her chest unmoving.

His body moved almost automatically, carrying Jax through the rift. But the sight of Kitty's body burned into his mind, and he was afraid the image would stay there forever. Because, love her or hate her, she was yet another woman he'd failed to save.

THIRTY-SIX

EVERYTHING BLURRED TOGETHER: sounds, visions, and memories. Jax's mind slowly clawed its way back to consciousness, each sense sluggishly piecing together the reality around him. He was in a hospital, the stark white of the walls and the sterile smell confirming it. Everything hurt—a dull, persistent ache that seemed to saturate his bones.

He blinked, trying to focus his eyes. The room was oddly quiet, save for the beep of the heart monitor that punctuated the silence. He scanned the room—it was small, with just the essentials: a bed where he lay, a narrow bedside table and a single chair that remained unoccupied.

His family weren't around. They were probably getting free food.

He had never been in a hospital as a patient before. His sister's panacea blood had always been enough to mend their wounds. The thought of Noelle brought a pang of worry. Where was she? And Kitty? He needed to check on them.

"Māma?" he asked, feeling a bit childish, calling for his mother. His voice was raspy, dry.

Reaching for the nurse call button to summon help, a sharp pain shot through his shoulder. Jax slowly looked down and realized that his arm was gone.

CYRUS THOUGHT FIGHTING a dragon last semester had been difficult. Nothing could have prepared him for the second attack. After roughly four hours, all the rifts across campus were closed, and the ferals were either slain or returned to the Veil.

Cyrus was lucky; not only had they not got caught in Kinsey's office, but his dorm's emergency weapon closet had just been redone, and all the blades inside were sharp and new. Melody, Cyrus, and Wyatt had managed to fend off around twenty ferals and escort numerous magicians and psychics to safe rooms. But it was as Cy had feared—the ferals were working together.

It was subtle; he wouldn't have noticed if it wasn't looking for it. Stranger, there were all different types of beastbloods who normally wouldn't interact. A feral dragon and a giant frog worked to kill a few teachers, herding them into a corner and crushing or burning them to death, until Wyatt intervened.

After getting checked in the medical office, Cyrus began looking for his other friends. He'd lost his phone somewhere during the fight, so he had to go around and ask for Kitty. He didn't think just her name would spark such hatred.

A woman from the admissions office glared at him from the campus green, where she sat massaging her bandaged leg. "Kitty Swan? That traitor deserves to rot in hell with the other ferals that came through! It was her fault—all the ferals escaped because of *her*."

"Do not talk about her like that," Cyrus warned.

She sneered. "Figures *you'd* be on her side."

"What does that mean?"

"It means your blood is soiled with the same filth that runs through her veins."

Cyrus had heard some offhand comments about his heritage before—the shape of his eyes, the tone of his skin—but this was different. These comments weren't said out of ignorance; they were said out of hatred.

He didn't bother with her again, instead going around asking for Blake instead. Despite being a womanizer known for cycling through women faster than tissues, he didn't inspire the same hatred Kitty did. Cy found his friend coming out of one of the makeshift medical tents, his eyes haunted and his shirt drenched in blood.

"Shit. What happened?" Cyrus exclaimed.

"It's not my blood," Blake said, his eyes vacant. "It's Jax's."

"Jax? Where is he?"

"Hospital. I...I don't know if he's going to make it." He shook his head. "It was bad, Cy. Did you see what was going on in the Veil?"

"No. Wyatt and I were too busy here." Cyrus had only stepped through two rifts, when the fight called for it. He saw fog, but not much else. "

"I should have done better," Blake said, running a hand through his hair. "If I had just done something-"

"Blake, you were trying to help everyone. You're not perfect. None of us are. Don't beat yourself up." Cyrus tried to offer some comfort, though his own heart started to race with a premonition of worse news.

"It's not that. It's..."

"What?"

"Kitty... Kitty's not..." Blake struggled. Finally, his shoulders slumped. "She didn't make it."

Cyrus blinked, uncomprehending. "Didn't make what?"

"Kitty didn't make it. She's gone," Blake choked out. "I'm sorry. I'm so sorry. She asked me to bring Jax back, and her stomach—"

The rest of his words didn't register. They *couldn't.* He continued to speak, but his words sounded like static.

Kitty was stronger than anyone Cyrus had ever met. "She's alright, though, right?"

Blake looked at him, not with pity, but with something much worse: pain. Just like how Cyrus had looked at him when Tessa died.

Cy and Tessa had been friends, but they weren't particularly close. He cried at her funeral though; how could he not, when his best friend was breaking down too?

"No, you don't get it," Blake said, gently as he could. His words failed him as he tried to explain the nasty truth of the situation. "She... You didn't *see* her. She was... She bled a lot. There was a hole in her stomach, her organs... There was so much blood. When I carried Jax back to the mortal realm, I looked back and... There's no way she survived her injuries. I'm sorry."

"You are wrong. Kitty is fine. Maybe she's at the hospital right now." His voice was rising, and Cyrus was well aware of how he sounded. It was like he was having an out-of-body experience, but he couldn't stop himself. "Kitty's not *dead.*"

God, the word felt so wrong in his mouth. Like an obscenity.

Kitty's name and 'dead' didn't belong in the same

sentence. She was invincible, unstoppable, an immovable force. She wasn't supposed to be the one who died first.

"She was alive when I left her. I know, but—"

"She's not dead. Kitty can't be dead," Cyrus repeated.

"Cy..."

"*She's not!*" Anger filled him, and a sudden urge to hit something overtook him.

Blake was lying. Kitty was fine. Cyrus would find her, and they would laugh about how Blake's sense of humor was getting worse. And then he would tell her that he loved her, and that he didn't care about the fact that she was a cultivator and he was shadowborn. He didn't care that she would outlive him, that he would age and she would stay youthful. All he cared about was her, and even if he died before her, he was positive he could promise her more happiness in his short lifespan than anyone else could promise her in centuries.

Kitty's not dead, his mind chanted. But Blake didn't laugh at his insistence. He didn't take it back.

He reached forward to touch his arm, and Cy stumbled away. "I'm going to look for her, if you won't. I'll be back."

"Cyrus, don't," Blake warned.

But he was already gone.

CHARITY WOKE ON A METAL SLAB. She couldn't move her limbs, but with much effort, she managed to pry her eyes open.

The light above nearly blinded her, so bright that her vision blurred white. The world came to her as if she were seeing it through a cloud of dust. She squinted, and her surroundings swam into focus.

Her memories came in fragments, scattered images. She had scoured the Veil with Veronica, searching for the Swan siblings, and then...

Tessa.

It shouldn't have been possible. The bitch was dead.

But we didn't bury a body, she thought.

No body, no dead bitch.

Speak of the devil. Tessa leaned over her sister, her long, blonde hair tickling Charity's chin. "She's coming to."

Charity didn't know who her sister was speaking to. She tried to open her mouth, but no sound came out. Probably better that way. She had a million questions, but the one at the top of mind was the cruelest. She'd learned from the best.

Why couldn't you have just fucking died?

Tessa leaned in closer. Her face looked more angular than Char remembered. "It'll all be alright. And, after this is over, you'll be just like me."

"Tessa." A voice cut through the room, masculine and familiar. But through the fog of her mind, Charity couldn't quite recall where she'd heard it. "We have a guest."

"I don't have time for that," Tessa said. "I need to prepare the procedure."

"It's a VIP from Southeastern," the young man replied, his voice sharp and clipped. "He's brought the timekeepers."

"I hate those things. You wouldn't think they'd be so slimy, but..." She shuddered. "Fine. But you keep my little sister company until I get back. Inject her with another dose, if you need to. I'm not going to let her ruin this."

"As you wish."

The young man stepped into Charity's field of vision. He wore a dark suit with a white button-up shirt, the collar unbuttoned and the tie hanging loose around his neck. But no matter how well his clothes were tailored, there was something about his proportions that reminded her of a lanky teen who still had yet to grow into himself.

Rory Everleigh looked down at her, his expression impassive. It seemed like there was so much he wanted to say, but he held it all back. “Let’s begin the experiment.”

1 NEW VOICEMAIL

Hey, Kitty. It's me.

I know you're not using your phone a lot these days, but...
No one can find you. I'm...worried.

...
They said...
They think you're...
Fuck.
...

I don't know why I'm calling.
I guess I wanted to hear your voice.
I needed to hear you say that it's not true. You're not...
...Call me, Kitty. When you get the chance.

NORTHEASTERN TRIBUNE

HORDE HAVOC: THE SWAN FAMILY'S STRANGE DISAPPEARANCE

In the wake of yet another harrowing horde attack on our peaceful enclave, the once-trusted but increasingly suspicious Swan family finds themselves at the center of a swirling vortex of blame and mistrust. As the dust settles and the community takes stock of the chaos unleashed, a troubling pattern emerges: most of the Swans have mysteriously disappeared.

The timing of their disappearance, coinciding with the horde's assault, raises questions that demand answers. How could a family, once considered part of our ranks, vanish at such a critical juncture? The correlation is too strong to dismiss, and the implications are unsettling. It points to a disconcerting possibility: the Swans, far from being innocent victims of circumstance, may have had a hand in orchestrating the attack.

The Supernatural Police Department (SNPD) has acted swiftly and decisively in response to this betrayal. A warrant for the immediate neutralization of any Swan family member on sight has been issued. Shoot first, ask questions later. Such measures, though drastic, are deemed necessary to safeguard the shadowborn community.

Amidst this turmoil, Jackson Swan, has been detained and is currently under heavy guard at an undisclosed hospital in New York. His incapacitation ensures that he, at least, will not be contributing to any further disturbances.

While the community reels from the Swans' betrayal, there is a glimmer of hope on the horizon. Dr. Calista Woods, a leading researcher, has reported an imminent breakthrough in her studies on the feral illness. Her work promises not only to unveil the mysteries behind this devastating condition but also to offer solutions that could prevent infection.

In these trying times, it is crucial to remember the values that unite us: trust, loyalty, and the shared responsibility to protect our community from those who would do us harm.

EPILOGUE

MARIA ROCHESTER WAS A TIME TRAVELER, though lord knew she shouldn't have been. She didn't know a thing about history, and everything she knew about time travel had been learned from *Back to the Future*... and *The Lake House* with Keanu Reeves.

Neither of those movies would help her save Kitty Swan. But Maria had to do it anyway. And *not* just because the talking tree told her to.

Okay, *mostly* because the talking tree told her to. But did you blame her? If a psychic tree told *you* that one girl was the key to saving the world, surely you'd listen. And the Wisdom Tree had been right about almost everything else. Mar was out of ideas, and—ironically—out of time.

"Be careful," her boyfriend told her. "If you don't return within fifteen minutes, I'm coming after you."

"Um, that's not a good idea." Mar had no idea if it would be safe for a non-time-traveler to enter the portal. She had enough to worry about, finding Kitty and dragging her to the future. It could have deadly, unforeseen consequences on her body. Unfortunately, Mar didn't have much choice.

Most of her plans were like this—half-cocked and panicked. Some worked out. Others failed miserably. She hoped, for her own sake as much as Kitty's, that this would be an incident where the plan went smoothly.

"I'll be back soon, I promise," she told him. They didn't kiss goodbye—he was shy, and she hated goodbyes. Instead, Maria stepped through the rift.

The Veil smelled like death and decay. Dead ferals littered the ground, along with shadowborn corpses. This must have been the right place, according to her sources.

Maria quickened her pace, searching the bodies for any sign of Kitty. She also tried very hard not to vomit at the sight of dismembered limbs and organs spilling out on the forest floor. *Yuck.*

To the average observer, Mar didn't *look* like a time traveler. Not that she even knew what a time traveler *should* look like. But she didn't appear to be special at all. Everything about her was plain and average, from her height, to her facial features, to her brown hair, which fell limply past her shoulders. The only 'supernatural' quality she outwardly possessed was her eyes, yellow as lemon rinds.

Her eyes gave her excellent night vision, but during the day—even on an overcast day like this—her distance sight was not the best. She was sensitive to light, and she had to get closer to the bodies to discern whether or not they were Kitty.

Ferals howled in the distance, startling Mar as she moved through the area. Kitty had to be there *somewhere*.

Just when Mar was about to return empty-handed, she saw something—a figure near a cave.

Kitty Swan was curled on the ground, her skin pale as

paper and her body cool to the touch. She looked...dead. Her eyes were open. Her chest didn't move, and frankly, staring this close to a corpse creeped Mar out. But a faint noise coming from Kitty's mouth gave her pause. Kitty's chest moved slightly. It could have just been a death rattle, but Mar pressed a hand to it.

Please don't be dead, she thought. She didn't like touching corpses, fresh or not.

There was a heartbeat. Slow, low, and barely detectible... but a heartbeat nonetheless.

"Time to go," Mar said, mostly to herself. She dragged the body toward the rift, pulling them both through to the future. *God*, Kitty was heavy for a skinny bitch. And while she technically wasn't dead yet—she might be in a few minutes—Mar wanted to go home and shower immediately after touching that clammy skin.

Mar and Kitty exited the rift, reaching a parking lot. With great effort, Mar set the girl down and called 911. They were going to send an ambulance immediately.

"She passed," Mar's boyfriend said, horrified.

"She can't die." Mar took a dagger out of her boot, determination blazing in her eyes.

No, Kitty couldn't die. Not now, not like this. Mar needed her, as selfish as it was.

"What are you doing, Maria?"

"Saving her." Mar took a dagger from her boot and cut into her hand. She didn't even wince at the pain anymore, she'd done it so many times.

She had no idea if her magic would work, but she had to try. Smearing her blood on Kitty's stomach, near her wound, the girls' blood mixed...and nothing happened.

"She's dead."

"No, she isn't!" Mar insisted, plucking out a hair from her own head and Kitty's. Improvising, she tied the strands together with her bloody hands. "She's going to be fine."

And, after a dozen tries and a lot of blood, by the time the ambulance arrived, Kitty Swan came back to life.

GLOSSARY

AS EXPLAINED BY NOELLE SWAN

AIYA: an exclamation of sorts. Like "oh" or "ugh". It can express surprise, pain, frustration, etc.

ARRAY: a magic circle for cultivators; a spell drawn usually drawn on a flat surface.

BEASTBLOOD: a sub-species of truebloods. Beastbloods are magical creatures from the Veil as well, but they are non-humanoid. For example: manticores, dragons, lycans, hydras, etc.

CHINESE DRAMA: a type of television show in Chinese (Mandarin, Cantonese, and other dialects). I particularly enjoy historical dramas, but my older sister usually ropes me into watching modern romances, too.

CINNABAR: red ink; often used for talismans.

CORE FORMATION: the third stage of cultivation, which my sister is currently at. Cultivators work on strengthening their golden cores and expanding them to hold more qi.

CULTIVATION: the practice of training the body to process qi more efficiently, resulting in supernatural abilities, enhance-

ment of senses, and expanding one's lifespan. The ultimate goal of cultivation is to achieve immortality.
Cultivator: someone who practices cultivation.
CULTIVATION MANUAL: an instruction guide for cultivation techniques.
DANTIAN: the area in the body where the golden core is located. There are technically three areas considered the dantian (upper, middle, and lower) but generally when we refer to the dantian, we are talking about the lower dantian, which lies below the belly button.
DARK ENERGY: the opposite of qi. Dark energy comes from the dead, but can be used in the same way as qi to cultivate. Be warned: Dark energy is not as stable as qi, thus, it often leads to qi deviation and a slow, painful death.
DEMONIC CULTIVATORS: cultivators who use dark energy and forbidden cultivation techniques to cultivate.
FERAL: beastbloods infected with an unknown disease that strips them of their sanity, turning them into mindless, aggressive beasts who attack anything and anyone on sight. What's worse, if you survive an attack, you can be infected through scratches and bites. The disease can take twenty-four hours to develop, and up to a month to kill its victims. Once it runs its course, the body rapidly decomposes, making it extremely difficult to study.
FOUNDATION ESTABLISHMENT: the second stage of cultivation, which Jax and I are currently stuck at. Like the title, the main point of this stage is to prepare our bodies for core formation and refine our control of qi. The stage ends once a cultivator forms a golden core; if they cannot, they will never be able to progress their cultivation further.
GOLDEN CORE: between the second and third stages of cultivation, cultivators form a golden core in their dantian.

This is like a storage unit for qi and helps one gain better control. Generally, if a cultivator doesn't form a golden core or theirs is destroyed, they can no longer cultivate.

HEAVENLY TRIBULATION: from the third stage of cultivation on, righteous cultivators must undergo a heavenly tribulation. In other words, after breaking through each stage, we're struck by lightning. It's believed to be a method the gods use to prevent mortals from becoming immortal.

HUMAN PANACEA: a person born with special blood which can cure most ailments, poisons, and diseases. Unfortunately, we're a rare breed, and our blood attracts monsters. We can't help the way we're born—but that doesn't stop monsters and humans alike from trying to capture us and drain our blood.

IMMORTAL RULES: the rules all righteous cultivators must follow; these rules are universal and are different from sect rules.

MAGICIAN: the child of two shadowborn parents. Due to blood dilution, a magician is generally less physically powerful than a shadowborn. However, they can wield magic and cast spells, which is pretty cool.

MANDARIN: a dialect of Chinese spoken widely across Mainland China.

Simplified Chinese: in reference to writing; simplified characters are modern and also used in Mainland China.

Traditional Chinese: in reference to writing; traditional characters are used in Taiwan, Hong Kong, Macau, and other areas. (According to Māma, the sect still used traditional characters. Thus, most of the cultivation manuals we have to use traditional characters, much to Kitty's ire.)

MERIDIANS: spiritual veins; pathways through the body which qi travels.

MORTAL REALM: where I currently live. Earth, the 'non-magical' realm, according to shadowborns. But I wouldn't be so certain....

QI: spiritual energy, life energy, chi, etc. It's energy naturally produced by all living things.

RIFT: a portal between the mortal realm and the Veil. Looks like a literal tear in the fabric of space.

SABER: a type of blade my sister uses, made for hacking and slashing. Usually curved, sabers have one sharp side and one blunt side; this makes them easier to wield, in a way, as opposed to the dual-edged sword. Thus, they're often associated with unskilled warriors. (Don't tell Kitty.)

SECT: a group of cultivators using the same cultivation techniques. They often live together in seclusion. Children born within the sect are automatically considered members.

SECT RULES: a set of rules each member of the sect must follow; these vary widely by sect. Some sects are stricter than others.

SHADOWBORN: a child with one trueblood parent and one mortal parent. Shadowborns can open and close rifts from either side—the Veil *and* the mortal realm.

TALISMAN: a spell often written on a yellow, rectangular strip of paper with red or black ink.

TAOISM: an ancient Chinese philosophical and religious tradition that emphasizes living in harmony with the Tao, an underlying natural order of the universe, and teaches principles of simplicity, naturalness, and balance. We are Taoist cultivators, so we try to follow the teachings of Taoism, but some of us (me) have better luck than others (Kitty).

TRUEBLOOD: an umbrella term for (Western) magical creatures. For example: fairies, vampires, angels, demons, banshees, werewolves, etc.

VEIL: a realm separate from the mortal world, where true-bloods originate.
WUWEI: a Taoist concept that emphasizes 'effortless action' or 'non-action', advocating for actions that are in natural alignment with the flow of life and the universe, rather than forced or contrived efforts.
XIǍO LÓNG BĀO: soup dumplings, another type of Chinese food.

TERMS OF ADDRESS

AS EXPLAINED BY JAX SWAN

CULTIVATION TERMS OF ADDRESS

In cultivation, a sect is viewed as a 'family' of sorts. Forms of address are used to show closeness, respect, etc. They do not imply blood relation.

Shīgōng: one's master's master; grandmaster
Shīfu: one's master or teacher
Shībó: martial uncle; a form of address for men of one's parents' generation
Shīgū: martial aunt; a form of address for women of one's parents' generation
Shīzhí: martial niece or nephew; a form of address for those of one's children's generation
Shīdì: martial younger/junior brother
Shīmèi: martial younger/junior sister
Shījiě: martial older sister
Shīxiōng/Shīgē: martial older brother

NICKNAME CONVENTIONS

Nicknames can be random, like pet names in the US, or they can follow these nicknaming conventions. However, they suggest a familiar relationship; you would not call a stranger by a nickname like this or someone you've just met.

Xiǎo: a prefix denoting affection or familiarity, used for someone younger than the speaker. The character itself means 'little'. This comes before the last character of one's given name. For example, Kitty's Chinese given name is Zixing, 'Zi' being the first character and 'Xing' being the second. Her nickname would be 'Xiao Xing'—roughly, Little Star.
Èr: another nicknaming convention, this time added to the last character of the given name. Again, it means 'child'. Using the above example, the name Zixing would be 'Xing'er'.
Ā: a prefix added to the last character of the given name. For example, 'A'Xing'.
Double Character: A nickname could also be simply saying the last character of the given name twice. For example, 'Xingxing'. (If you call my sister this, she'll chase you with her curling iron.)

Additionally, my full name is Jaxon, but I introduce myself as Jax. It's a nickname. Kitty would not introduce herself with any of these nicknames.

FAMILY TERMS

Māma: mom
Bāba: dad

Dàgē: eldest brother.
Gēge: older brother; 'Gē' is more common. 'Gēge' sounds either childish or it sounds like you're acting cute.
Jiě: older sister.
Mèimei: younger sister.
Dìdi: younger brother.

Particularly with Gē and Jiě, these terms don't necessarily imply blood relation. You can call someone you are close with but not related to Gē and Jiě.

AUTHOR'S NOTE

THE SHADOWBORN CHRONICLES CHRONOLOGY

The Timekeeper's Daughter and Something's Wrong with Kitty Swan can be read separately and each series stands on its own. The timeline for each series is as follows:

- ***Just in Time*** (TD #1)
- ***Hour of Need*** (TD #2)
- ***Immortal Rules*** (SW #1)
- ***Immortal Trials*** (SW #2)
- ***Down to the Minute*** (TD #3)
- ***A Matter of Seconds*** (TD #4)
- ***All at Once*** (TD#5) **and** ***Immortal Path*** (SW#3)
- ***Mortal Monster*** (SW #4)
- ***Immortal Blood*** (SW #4.5)

All at Once and *Immortal Path* take place at the same time, and there is a major crossover with shared events told from different perspectives.

ABOUT THE AUTHOR

Samantha Gao is a New Adult author with a passion for all things fantasy and paranormal romance. Her writing is fueled by her love for paranormal romance, and she enjoys creating compelling characters that readers can relate to and root for. After graduating from college with a degree in a completely different field, Sam decided to pursue her lifelong dream of becoming a writer.

When she's not busy crafting stories that will transport readers to another world, Sam enjoys watching Asian dramas (with subtitles, of course!), listening to music, and indulging in her weakness for chocolate.

Sign up for her newsletter here: subscribepage.io/SamGao

facebook.com/imberhousepublishing
instagram.com/imberhouse
amazon.com/author/samgao
bookbub.com/profile/sam-gao
goodreads.com/samgao

www.ingramcontent.com/pod-product-compliance
Lightning Source LLC
LaVergne TN
LVHW050911080826
845145LV00001B/55

* 9 7 8 1 9 6 2 0 9 9 2 4 0 *